DEFECTORS

THE KAIYO STORIES

BOOK III

The Adventures Continue!

Cliff

A NOVEL BY

CLIFF COCHRAN

ISBN 978-1-0980-4624-8 (paperback)
ISBN 978-1-0980-4625-5 (digital)

Christian Faith Publishing, Inc.
832 Park Avenue
Meadville, PA 16335
www.christianfaithpublishing.com

This story is a work of fiction. Names, characters, businesses, places, events, locales, and incidents are either the products of the author's imagination or are used in a fully fictitious manner. Any resemblance to actual persons, living or dead, or actual events is purely coincidental.

Printed in the United States of America

In the world you will find trouble.

—John 16:33, (OEB)

ACKNOWLEDGMENTS

Thank you to the many readers of *Kaiyo—The Lost Nation* and *Raphael* who loved the stories and encouraged this sequel. Please keep enjoying the adventure. To MarketWake LLC and the talented Brooke Little, I have seen your tireless efforts and skill at bringing the *Kaiyo Stories* to the reading public. Thank you. To my children—Brooke (a different Brooke but also the CEO of MarketWake), Bin, and Lily—never forget that you are the source of the inspiration that created the *Kaiyo Stories*. Brooke, long ago you thought up Kaiyo's predecessor, *Happy Bear*. Bin, your strength and courage make Dean McLeod easy to describe. And, Lily, you, in your joyful way, forced me to imagine stories that were deeper and better. To Kriss, my wife and business partner, you make my life fun to live. Your constant edits and encouragement kept our projects moving. Without you I really don't know if I ever would've been able to do any of this. To God, thank you for answering my prayers and giving me the ideas that are the *Kaiyo Stories*. I pray that these stories help us to understand not only the forgotten fullness of what mankind lost but also to better understand the amazing relationships that await us when we come home to you. People forget that part. They shouldn't.

CHARACTERS

McLeods

1. Dean Mcleod: Seventeen-year-old son of Sam and Susan McLeod
2. Grace Mcleod: Twelve-year-old daughter of Sam and Susan McLeod
3. Kaiyo McLeod: Five-year-old adopted grizzly bear son of Sam and Susan McLeod
4. Libby McLeod: Twenty-year-old daughter of Sam and Susan McLeod
5. Sam Mcleod: Rancher, husband of Susan and father of Libby, Dean, Gracie, and Kaiyo
6. Susan Mcleod: Rancher, wife of Sam and mother of Libby, Dean, Gracie, and Kaiyo

Gibbses

1. Aliyah Gibbs: Friend and neighbor to the McLeods and mother of Kate and Jack
2. Jack Gibbs: Eighteen-year-old son of Gunner and Aliyah Gibbs
3. Kate Gibbs: Sixteen-year-old daughter of Gunner and Aliyah Gibbs
4. Steve "Gunner" Gibbs: Friend and employee of the McLeods, father of Kate and Jack

Specials (Extraordinary Creatures)

1. Amorak: Alpha male dire wolf
2. Anjij: Alpha female dire wolf
3. Annag: Sobek, mother of Haydar
4. Aylmer: The aurochs (prehistoric ox), friend of the McLeods
5. Benaiah: The watcher, a.k.a. Rimmy, friend of the McLeods
6. De'AaVaa: Male leader of the wolf folk
7. Dohv/Dovie: The black bear, friend of the McLeods
8. Eanna: Wolf folk daughter
9. Eli: Kaiyo's bear father
10. Esa: Bone-crusher wolf
11. Goliath: Very big grizzly, mentor of Kaiyo
12. Gyp: Polar bear
13. Halqu: Epicyon
14. Haydar: Sobek warrior
15. Hexaka (Hex): American elk / wapiti
16. Ilya: Dog and companion to Gunther MacDonald
17. Jael: Wolf folk daughter
18. Jana: Kaiyo's bear mother
19. Kaiyo (McLeod): Five-year-old grizzly bear and adopted son of Sam and Susan McLeod
20. Kelba: Epicyon
21. Karmu: Genosqwa/watcher
22. Lavi: Mountain lion
23. Rapha: Wolf folk son
24. Roan: American elk / wapiti
25. Sepsu: Epicyon
26. Skiri: Bone-crusher wolf
27. Taalaa: Female leader of the wolf folk
28. Tamraz: Epicyon
29. Te'oma: Wolf folk son
30. Tracker: Wolf friend of the McLeods
31. Wardum: Genosqwa/watcher
32. Yeeyi: Small wolf, a messenger

Animals (Ordinary)

1. Cali: Susan's palomino quarter horse
2. Chevy: Jack's quarter horse
3. Duke: Grace's pony, buckskin welsh cob
4. Hershel: Sam's horse, a bay with a blond flax mane and tail
5. Jet: Libby's horse, black with a white patch on her face
6. Major: Mcleod's guard dog (a mix of large German shepherd and Carolina dog)
7. Moose: Mcleod's guard dog (a mix of Dogo Argentino and Anatolian shepherd)
8. Peyton: A huge shire horse, chestnut brown
9. Rosie: A young alpaca
10. Solo: Dean's horse, a slate blue dun mustang

Spirits

1. Aymoon: Archdemon over the American West
2. Meginnah: Cherub
3. Raphael: Archangel
4. Ruel: Mediator and mentor

Other Humans

1. Andy Tompkins: Sarah's brother
2. Alan Osbourne: Major, Park County Sheriff's Department
3. Bill Adams: USFS ranger
4. Cindy Rich: Veterinarian
5. Danielle Klein: Child abducted by the Sobeks
6. Davey Carter: Friend of the McLeods, airplane pilot
7. Glennon Wraight: Leader of the assassins
8. Ed Hamby: Captain, Montana State Patrol
9. Emma Garcia: Wyoming State Patrol trooper
10. Elliott Bray: FBI special agent

11. Everett Ferguson: Backup assassin
12. Griffin Molqui: Professional assassin
13. Gunther MacDonald: Sniper and assassin
14. Justin Martinez: Lieutenant, Madison County Sheriff's Department
15. Kelly Stahr: Troy Stahr's daughter
16. Kent Thomas: USFS ranger
17. Kurt and Linda Tompkins: Sarah's parents
18. Landon Haldor: Libby's fiancé and professional guide
19. Lee Tuttle: Madison County Sheriff, wife—Ellie
20. Lowe Brigham: Game warden, Montana Department of Fish, Wildlife, and Parks
21. Lylah Paulsen: Sarah Tompkins's boss
22. Pete Harred: Local criminal
23. Rachel: Sarah's sister
24. Robin and Chris Klein: Parents of Danielle Klein
25. Sarah Tompkins: Family friend, Troy Stahr's fiancé
26. Tracey: Neighbor of the McLeods
27. Troy Stahr: Sarah Tompkins's fiancé; captain, Madison County Sheriff's Department
28. Ty Vernon: Backup assassin
29. Vicki Ernst: FBI special agent
30. Zoe Stahr: Troy Stahr's daughter

INTRODUCTION

GRACE

We enjoyed several years of wonderful peace since we battled the Sobeks in their world. But peace is only a season, and seasons always change. Eventually, the evil came for us again.

The world has always been a restless place, and all of us at home were restless too. I first noticed it in the eyes of my family. We found a savagery in our natures that clashed with our culture. At first we didn't understand, but we grew into what we were made to be. We confronted the evil as it attacked us all. The wounds have healed, but there are many scars.

This is the story of my family and of my little brother, a grizzly bear named Kaiyo.

Prologue

Run—Kaiyo

I tracked the bear killer for a week. What I didn't know was that he had been tracking me even longer. Over a few weeks, he had killed two grizzlies and left their carcasses to freeze. The tracks in the mud and snow told me he had a method. Each time, he chased a panicked bear and shot it at close range. The first time, he used a dirt bike. When the first bear was killed, the killer's boot prints showed that he left the bike and walked up to the bear and then around it. The second time, he used a snowmobile. The tracks in the snow told the same story, except the second time he had a big dog with him. He wasn't a poacher killing for profit; their handiwork is easy to spot. But this shooter confused me. All he did was look at the dead bears. Then he moved on.

Autumn had been unusually warm and wet, and normally those bears would have been hibernating. The first one was killed right around Thanksgiving; the second one was killed a few weeks later. Though smaller than me, they were both large male grizzlies.

Because of the warmer weather, just after Thanksgiving dinner, I left the farm to get in a quick visit to my Eden home before Christmas. Christmas is wonderful there, and it was good to see everybody again. After a week, I began my return journey back to the farm. On the way back, the cold had broken through and the wind howled. It was then I found the first bear.

13

Seeing that poor dead bear brought out my temper. I should have controlled my temper and gone home. But I didn't. I hate poachers, so I checked it out. I had plenty of time. Within a few days, I had followed the poacher back to a small Forest Service campground that was at the end of miles of dirt road. With elk and deer seasons over, the campground was empty, and the poacher had moved on. I decided to keep looking. I wondered though what I would do if I found the poacher. I had no good answers to that question.

I decided to follow my nose and not go home just yet. A few days later, I was much farther east when I heard gunfire miles away. It was still hunting season for wolves and mountain lions, but that type of hunting was rare in the Eastern Wilderness. I headed toward the sound and found the fresh tracks of a snowmobile. I didn't want to be found, so I left the open spaces and kept to the timbered slopes close by to the north. A few miles later, the scent led me to the second bear. He was chased down before he could get into cover.

I waited in the timber. We are told to be wise as serpents, so I waited to make sure the poacher had gone. From my position in the woods, I could see the tracks left by the poacher as he rode away from his kill, to the southwest. After an hour, I came down onto the flat, snowy plain. The dead bear was cold, and only the wind kept the snow from covering him up. I recognized him. He wasn't like me; he was just a normal bear, but I had come across him many times. For a grizzly, he was always friendly and good-natured, and he was part of the wilderness.

The wind was gusting hard, and I caught no scent of the poacher, but I was upwind of where the poacher had gone. But he had been here; his tracks were everywhere. By chance, I looked up and saw a muzzle flash about a half mile away. I knew immediately what that was. The poacher had hidden himself and shot at me. Before I heard a sound, the bullet passed through me, up high where my neck met my shoulder. The bullet went too high to kill me but too low to miss me. The pain was blinding. I felt my bear rage begin to race out of control, but I knew I needed to think. I turned and broke hard for the timber behind me and ran at top speed away from the shooter. I knew what I had to do.

I saw snow and dirt kick up around me well before I heard the cracks of his rifle. I tumbled into a frozen creek bed and kept running. I hit the timbered slopes right about the same time I heard his snowmobile. I was being hunted. And I was leaving a bright-red trail of blood.

I needed separation from the shooter. The farther away I got from him, the more trees would be in his way. Tree trunks stop bullets. I ran, zigzagging through the trees, upward toward the far-off ridgeline. This was no place for a snowmobile, and I heard it bog down. Then a dog started barking. It was a deep, throaty bark, which told me the barking dog was big and made for the chase. I kept on, powering my way through the deep snow and racing for the far away tree line. It was times like this where I loved my bear strength. My lungs took in the air, and my muscles responded by propelling me forward.

With every push, the killer was left farther behind. I heard the dog, and it wasn't getting much closer either. Even if the shooter strapped on snowshoes, he could never keep up. His dog was probably getting stuck in the drifts. These slopes were long and steep, and there were frequent blow downs; we could play cat and mouse all winter before he could ever get a glimpse of me. And that was only if I was still bleeding. And if his dog caught up to me, he could be the biggest, meanest dog on the planet, and he still wouldn't get a bite in. But I would.

Dad always told me to respect guns and I always have. I knew if I got out in the open my advantage would disappear. If he tried to follow my blood trail in this forest I would eventually circle around and ambush him. And that was my plan. My nose told me that he and his dog were following my blood trail. I had plowed through the snow too so any fool could track me. But that didn't mean I could be tracked down. And the killer knew it.

Pride rarely helps, and the killer's pride didn't help him. He stopped before he went deeper into the woods. I heard him whistle his dog back in. He knew the playing field had leveled itself. Then instead of being wise, he decided to boast. "You got away today, bear, but I'll still get you!" he yelled. "You can't hide forever. We know where you live. And you can't protect that family of yours either. They're on the list too."

I heard his dog bark in anger, but it wasn't directed to me. They almost seemed to argue. Then they got back on the snowmobile and left. From my vantage point a few hundred yards below the tree line, I watched as they headed south and west across the vast snowy landscape until they rode out of view. All along, I thought I was hunting a poacher. I was completely wrong. He didn't want to kill bears; he wanted to kill me. He knew who I was, and for whatever reason, he wanted to kill me because of it. He also threatened my family. My mind was swimming.

At least the killer had shown his hand. Because he and others knew who I was, he thought he knew how to get to me. I needed to talk to Dad and Dean soon. And maybe Gunner. He's the best shot I've ever seen. Hopefully, Raphael, Meginnah, and everybody else at home would understand what we needed to do.

I waited until it was dark. Every bone in my body wanted to follow the poacher and end this. But that was the bear part of me thinking. The bear killer was a smart hunter, and he might be looking out for me to follow him. He could even have camera traps set up. His dog could sniff me out too. Dogs I could handle, but the cameras bugged me. I could walk right by them and never see them. But I could almost always smell them. When that happened and if the cameras were on our land, that always meant poachers or trespassers. I'd circle around, find the camera, and rip it to shreds. Then I'd rip out the memory card and crunch it to smithereens. Once, on our own land, I found a camera watching another camera. The owner obviously wanted to know who was tearing up his cameras. I went and got Dean, and he climbed up the tree to get one camera while I destroyed the other.

Anyway, I knew I was about thirty miles away from the farm. I decided to go north, away from my hunters, and then turn west. If I pushed hard all night, I could make it home before sunrise. All I could think about was my big brother, Dean. He could be reckless, but right now, I needed his help and his courage.

PART 1

SPECIAL FORCES

THREE WEEKS EARLIER—DEAN

Kaiyo's growth into a big bear has been impressive. This year he tipped our scales at a thousand pounds, and he's still growing. His strength is beyond measure. We still roughhouse, but it's ridiculously one-sided. Compared to him, I'm a fragile, breakable weakling. But we are still brothers. I tease him like every big brother should tease their little brother. But when he gets grouchy, which is rare, I give him his space. He's still a bear.

With him at my side and teaching me, I have learned to be wild. Not totally wild, but close. On many occasions, we have wandered out into the wilderness and enjoyed raw survival. He's good at it; I'm getting better. And I must obey the hunting laws; he doesn't. Still he shares his kills. He kills 'em; I cook 'em.

The minute he walks off the farm, he basically changes into a real bear. His senses come on full alert, and he moves differently. I have learned to run next to him for miles just to keep up. And while I do that, I have to stay aware of my surroundings too.

Dad wouldn't let us enter the Eastern Wilderness alone or together during elk or deer season, and I didn't blame him. So last weekend, I was bored. We had won our football game from the night before, so there was no Saturday practice. Harvest was over, and the snows were late. Thinking about what I could do, I decided to start taking back the Southern Forest and rid it of all that had made it evil. Evil spirits had long claimed the Southern Forest, and a clan of dangerous watchers made their homes there. Kaiyo agreed to help sometime in the future, but he wasn't as enthusiastic about it as I was.

That afternoon, Libby was home studying for some tests. She said her apartment was too noisy. She was taking a break and was at the shooting range at the northern edge of the farm. The cracks of her rifle pealed across the entire farm. The animals didn't flinch. They were used to it. She learned long ago how to shoot, but she'd made herself far better. Except for Gunner, she's probably the best shot in the county. Taking advantage of the distraction, I grabbed my shotgun and bear spray and slipped out the front door while Kaiyo was in the horse pasture with Peyton, our huge shire horse. They like to graze together, and there was still some good, lush grass by the creek and pond. I wasn't quite sure why I was doing what I was doing, but I guess I was seeing how far I could go.

I know I have a good life, but whatever I have here is not mine. It's my parents' farm, and at times, I can't stand being here. Running away or just leaving, one of the stupidest things I could do, crosses my mind all the time. The fact they've done nothing to deserve my crazy emotions makes everything worse. My father once told me that if I was lucky, I would have a few villains in my life.

"To fight for something, especially for something that's good, is an honor, and it opens your mind to appreciating what you could lose," he said. "It may well be the best thing that could happen to you. But it will test you. Your biggest fear will not be of your villain, it will be whether you'll measure up when it counts. I don't doubt that you will, but my confidence is mostly meaningless. Your fears will be yours to conquer. Except for some encouragement, no one can walk through that valley but you."

So I have been looking for villains to fight and doing crazy stuff to test my courage. Everybody says I'm brave, but I fear a lot of things. Sometimes, fear is the only thing I feel. I hate it and fight it, but it's always there. I have looked for villains in school, on the football field, and elsewhere. I was comforted by knowing that I had faced real villains before, and I didn't back down. But I had forgotten one thing. At least for me, I needed something good to fight for, and I had forgotten that. So I decided to pick a fight with some watchers. That was a bad idea.

Nearly every Native American tribe has stories and legends about watchers. A lot of those legends describe them as kidnappers and cannibals. A few tribes even describe local wars called to avenge their losses and rid their tribal lands of watchers. Occasionally, somebody goes missing in a National Park or a National Forest. I cringe when it happens because I suspect watchers are sometimes involved. They're not always involved in the disappearances, and maybe they're not involved in most of them. But they sure aren't totally innocent either. Some are man-eaters.

I jogged down the driveway about a mile to the gravel road that was cut in years ago by the oil company. I took that road and headed straight south another four or five miles, not too far from where Libby and I skirmished with watchers years before. I stood in the middle of the gravel path, surrounded by briars and forest, lifted my head and sang a song. I didn't even try to sing well. My point was to let the watchers know I was not afraid. Unfortunately, my plan didn't work out so well.

I heard crashing in the briars next to the road. In a split second, before I could bring up my shotgun, I saw the crazy eyes of an enraged cow moose. She was huge, and she came flying out of the forest and slammed into me. It happened so fast I didn't have time to square my shoulders or even brace myself for the attack. The force of her body sent me flying, and I landed hard. It was lights out. My next-to-last thought was that I was going to die being stupid. That wasn't my plan. My last thought was wondering if the strange laughter I heard was real.

When I came to, I saw my little brother straddling me, huffing and looking at the woods. He's protective of me, and somehow he figured out I left without him.

"Calm down, little brother," I whispered.

Kaiyo moved as I got to my feet and wiped blood off my face. I shook my hand, flinging thickened blood to the ground. I was bleeding a lot and had to tilt my head forward to get the blood to drip to the ground. The silliness of the situation got to me, so I started softly laughing. Kaiyo saw nothing funny in my situation. He reached over with a paw and lifted my face to get a better look. He had seen me worse but never quite so bloody.

"It was a moose. A big, angry cow moose!" I said. "I think she hated my singing voice. Her calf was probably with her."

I knew I had goofed and let my guard down. Arrogance has consequences. "She lashed out at me with her hooves, but what really happened was she slammed me hard with her shoulder as she was busy running me over. I went flying into the gravel. Headfirst. Are the cuts very big? If they are, the coach won't let me play."

Head and face wounds bleed a lot, and my wounds were no different. I desperately wanted to play in my last few football games, and if I was hurt too bad, I wouldn't be able to play. That would let my parents, my coach, my team, and my school down. I screwed up.

Kaiyo made me stand, and he gave my face a look over. Whatever he saw would add to my growing collection of scars. It was then I realized how angry Kaiyo was with me.

"Aww, c'mon, Kaiyo!" I tried to say with some conviction. "Don't be mad at me. I never saw her."

We walked home in silence, and Kaiyo ran straight into the kitchen and growled at Mom. He pointed at me the second I walked in, and she started asking questions. I gave Kaiyo a look like he had betrayed me. That was a bad idea. He walked over to me and roared right in my face and then went outside. Mom had no idea why Kaiyo was so mad, but she knew he was.

WARRIORS—SAM

I walked out of the barn just as Kaiyo was coming out of the house. From the beginning since Susan and I adopted him, I'd been a student of my son's vocalizations. From whimpers to roars, I could usually understand Kaiyo, at least in a general way. Kaiyo also had a variety of roars, and figuring them out got easier over the years. The one I just heard was one of pure frustration mixed with raw anger. We both stopped in the courtyard and joined Aylmer, who was lying there chewing his cud. Kaiyo then went on a two-minute tirade that I didn't begin to understand. But Aylmer did. He mooed a bit, and then he gave a bovine laugh. Kaiyo was not amused. I took a guess.

"It's Dean, isn't it?"

Kaiyo nodded vigorously and pointed at the house. On all fours, Kaiyo was almost five feet at his shoulder. When he held his head up, he easily looked me right in the eyes, and I'm six feet tall. Giving my son a hug no longer required me to bend. So I gave him a hug, thanked him, and told him I loved him. I didn't know what else to say.

I left them and went into the kitchen to see Susan wiping off Dean's face with a bloody towel. He was sitting on a stool with his back to me. The back of his coat was scuffed up with gray gravel dust. Susan looked past Dean and winked at me. Dean was talking a mile a minute. I walked over to get a better look. I'd seen him worse, but his clothes were extra bloody. He had one decent cut on the bridge of his nose, and he had some road rash on his forehead and on the right side of his face. More importantly, the story he was telling had me concerned. Dean was heading in a dangerous direction.

"What do you think, Susan, a couple butterflies or a stitch or two?"

Susan was putting the final touches on cleaning Dean's face. She got the last of the dirt out of his skin and said, "Oh, I think I can patch him up. These things bleed out of proportion to the size of the cut. Could have been a lot worse. It's not bleeding much anymore."

"Dean," I said, "why don't you shower up in the mudroom. We'll bring you some clothes. Brush off your coat, throw your shirt and jeans in the wash, and when you're done, let's have a talk. I'll be in my office."

Dean winced. I didn't blame him; no teenage boy looks forward to a *talk* from his father.

"Yes, sir."

Twenty minutes later Dean came talking into my office. "Okay. I know what you want to talk about. Let me tell you what happened."

So I let him. Dean talked about his plans with the watchers and today's unexpected moose attack. He minimized the danger, and he seemed to enjoy his talk. When he got through, he stood up to leave and said, "Anything else?"

It was my turn. "Plenty. Sit down, Dean."

He grimaced as he sat back down. "Dean, there is an old movie called *Rebel Without a Cause*. It starred a young man named James Dean. It was a good movie. James Dean, in real life, was a lot like his character in the movie. He ended up dying too soon in a car crash. It was his fault, of course. People always wonder what he could have been had he lived. But they'll never know."

Dean looked confused. I kept talking. "So I hear about all this stuff you're doing, and I must admit, I'm impressed. For a seventeen-year-old, you have had quite a life so far. You have Kaiyo as a little brother, there are Specials in your life, you've rescued people, you've been in combat in another world, you go out into the wilderness with Kaiyo or Goliath, and you do things that boys, even boys with your strength, shouldn't be doing. And you're hardly done. Trust me—adventure will always come your way. But you keep pushing the limits. So what are you so afraid of that causes you to do some of this crazy stuff?"

"What?" Dean said. "Do you think I'm afraid? I don't know anybody who does the things I do. What are you getting at?"

"Everybody is afraid of something. You're no different, and I bet you know it. Something is eating you. What are you so afraid of?"

"Do you mean like snakes or spiders?"

I smiled. "Dean, we all know you're scared of spiders. And no, that's not what I'm trying to get at. What is it about getting older and growing up that scares you so much?"

He slumped in his chair. Bingo. I could tell Dean understood the question, but I doubted he knew the answer.

"Dad, this is not a dig at you or Mom or about growing up. I know I need to grow up and I have to, and want to, keep on learning. But sometimes, I just want to leave and not come back. That's crazy, I have a great life. But I am so afraid of settling. It happens to people all the time, Dad. They just sort of fall into line. I just see myself going to college and getting married and taking some job where I am paid dirt, and each month means just more bills to pay. I am so afraid of losing all this. Of losing Kaiyo and the Specials. In fact, I lose sleep over it. I can't shake it, Dad. And then there's Kate, and I don't even begin to know what I'm supposed to do there."

"That's a lot of weight on those seventeen-year-old shoulders," I said. "You do know that twenty-four-year-old Dean may look at life quite differently than seventeen-year-old Dean, right?"

Dean nodded.

"But first," I said, "I think it would help if you knew what your problem is and then what your purpose is. You are here for a reason, we know that. And I am pretty sure I know what's bothering you and what your purpose is. Want to know?"

Dean looked at me. "So are you telling me you know what's going on inside me? I don't even know that."

I nodded. "Of course you don't, but I do. Hear me out."

Dean seemed unmoved. "Let's first talk about the problem. It's simple really, but it's true. You are almost eighteen. For several years, I believe you've been uncomfortable living here. Maybe not so much at first, but more now and probably more next month, right?"

I could tell Dean was holding back and getting uncomfortable. "Seriously, Dean. Follow me and hear me out. Don't you hate curfew? Think how grating it is when Mom or I tell you to clean your room or to finish your chores. How badly do you cringe when we give you the sex, drugs, and alcohol talks? Wouldn't you love to live in your own apartment or cabin somewhere else? Maybe anywhere else? Don't you just hate harvest when you are stuck here working your tail off on weekends and can't be with friends?"

Dean started nodding. A smile appeared. "Well, Dad, no disrespect, but yeah, I kinda hate those things, and sometimes I hate it here. I don't know why, but I do. Except you're wrong about the harvest, but that's only because Jack and Kate are here. And I definitely like the apartment or cabin idea."

I kept going. "In fact, Dean, I bet you are starting to dislike every bit of guidance you get from me or your mother, even when you know you need it. But all that is good news. Really good. Every bit of that discomfort you feel is because God is putting independence and adventure in your heart. It's not rebellion, at least not yet. But it is a strong set of yearnings. You cannot fight it, and you shouldn't try to stuff it. Of course, the angry or even hateful thoughts you may have are your responsibility. But God is forcing you to be uncomfortable because you need to leave us in just a few years, and if you are too comfortable, you will want to stay. It's not right to live with your parents that way. Nobody conquers much of anything if they are coddled. Your spirit longs to be free even more than you do. Do you understand?"

"Well, that explains a lot," said Dean. "Maybe it explains everything."

"So, Dean, here's your problem. Right now, being a senior in high school, you have neither the means nor the wisdom to live independently. That's frustrating, and it won't be long before having you living here will be just as frustrating to me and your mom too. But trust that these things, the means and the wisdom, will come to you and will come quickly if you open your mind and listen. I am not saying you must always do what we say, but our advice must be factored in as a part of your journey for wisdom. So if you are determined to get a better understanding of the world, let's next talk about the means. That's the money part."

Dean's mood was on the rise. "I am all ears!"

"Well, let's start with the premise that making money and having a life begins with understanding your purpose."

Dean again looked skeptical. "Dad, do you really think you know why God created me? Nobody knows that."

"Again, I actually do. A long time ago, some wise folks concluded that the chief end of man is to know God and to enjoy him forever. That's it. We complicate it, of course, and we have opposition, we will always have opposition. But that's about it. If you set your sights on that, then looking at the rest of your life kind of falls into place. Then you work on something specific to you."

"Really?" said Dean.

He still looked skeptical, so I kept going, "Life is hard enough without trying to pin down exactly what God's will is for you. While you should certainly pray and ask God to reveal his will for you, there probably won't be any magic road maps to a specific career. Unfortunately, a lot of folks are more interested in knowing God's will than knowing God. Knowing God can take a lifetime, but he made it easy enough to start. He has revealed himself, his wisdom, and his grace already. And while you start knowing God, take the time to understand the strengths, talents, and passions God put into you and then build on them. Some folks around your age develop those strengths, passions, and talents by going into the military, others by going to college or trade school, and others by seeking out knowledge and wisdom on their own. That's part of learning God's will for you and part of enjoying God.

"Dean, I always wanted to farm, and I sense God's happiness when I do it. But I know I won't farm forever. At some point, I may want to do something else. I am not trapped, and you certainly should not feel trapped at your age. Have faith to believe that if you are open to opportunities and pray for them, then God will put opportunities in front of you. As for settling, that's easy to do at any age. Most people are usually happy in their jobs and with their families. If you want something different, start dreaming and asking God to open your mind. Dream big and write your dreams down. Where do you want to go? What do you want to see? What would make you happy? What do you want to accomplish, and who do you want to serve? Because everybody serves somebody.

"Your path doesn't have to be the paths others use. It can be—I'm not the only farmer in the world, right? But it doesn't have to be. Anyway, sometime in the next few years, if you start dreaming now and focusing on your passions and strengths, you will at least have a handle on where to start."

"Dream?" said Dean. "I like that. I haven't been dreaming at all."

"You haven't because somehow you see this farm as your prison. It's not. It's your launch pad."

I let that last part sink in before moving on. "And, Dean, one more thing. Your dreams are yours. You don't need my permission or anybody's approval. You will always need wise counsel, everybody does, but your life is yours to live.

"As for today's antics, I have to admit that I am proud of you. You are a warrior, and I love it. But I think what you did today was more out of boredom than purpose or passion. And dying young from recklessness or stupidity would be a poor way to end your story here on earth. Hopefully, you will come to believe that you have more to offer the world than a few years of that stuff.

"And my advice is that you leave the watchers alone. They will never be your friend, but they don't have to be your enemy either. You might get Kaiyo killed too. A big male watcher could possibly hurt him. Two or three watchers could easily kill him. Whether you like it or not, Kaiyo's only flesh and blood, and he can get hurt. Unfortunately, both of you are a little crazy. Good crazy, but still crazy. Now, go apologize to your little brother. Kaiyo adores you, and he's probably fed up with worrying about you."

Dean was smiling. "Fair enough. And thanks, Dad, you helped."

He gave me a hug and went to find his little brother.

2

Three weeks later—Susan

I have a memory I cherish. It was February of last winter. There was Sam, looking both curious and concerned, rushing into our room after hearing me scream. We live in a rather strange world, and sometimes there are frightening things that are fully scream-worthy. But my scream wasn't out of fear; it was out of pure, perfect joy. Sarah Tompkins was on the line, and her boyfriend had just proposed. He was still there with her. Sam saw me both smiling and crying at the same time, so he figured it out.

"Did Troy pop the question?"

He had indeed. Sam chuckled and disappeared back downstairs. A few seconds later, I heard screams from Dean's girlfriend, Kate, and from Gracie. I heard the two of them racing up the back steps. Sarah heard it too and laughed. In no time, the phone was put on speaker, and the three of us spoke to Sarah. The questions came fast, but Sarah enjoyed it all. We loved her like a daughter, and Troy Stahr was one of our closest friends. So Sarah Tompkins would soon be Sarah Stahr. That would be an awesome name.

Sarah first came to us from the wilderness. Whenever you hear about somebody going to the dark side, well, that was Sarah. Years ago, she opened her body and mind to the possession of an extremely strong demon who, for whatever reason, hated us with extra vigor.

If you know Sam, sometimes he's like a bull in a china shop. He calls them like he sees them and he was not always right. More than a few decent, normal people had hated him from time to time. But we believe Sarah's old demon hated us more than he hated Christians in general because of Kaiyo and because of the other Specials. Anyway, Sarah was patrolling the Eastern Wilderness in hopes of finding, torturing, and killing Landon Haldor, who is now the fiancée of my oldest daughter, Libby. But before she could do that, Dean found her and convinced one of our friends, a watcher named Benaiah, to capture her. The rest is history, and we have loved Sarah ever since.

She's been amazing, and I think Captain Stahr fell in love with her not long after he met her that summer day two years ago. Watching her grow and deal with her demons, both literal and figurative, has been a treat. She's become one of my best friends and like a new daughter too. She and Troy asked us if they could get married here at the farm in the main barn. We are so honored and excited. We understood too. Troy and Sarah also have some close friends who just won't be able to show up in a church, or anywhere else in town for that matter. The Specials are here often, and some of them will be at the wedding. Come wedding day, Sarah's parents are in for a treat. They don't have a clue about the Specials.

Sarah's Day—Gracie

Christmas season at the farm was always great, but this year with Sarah getting married, my parents were going all out. Right after Thanksgiving Day, we got started. Not long after Captain Stahr and Sarah got engaged, Dad drew up plans to turn the barn into both a church and what Dad kept calling a rocking reception hall. Dad and the rest of us have been turning those plans into reality. Our barn was already a nice barn, but it had to be better than that; it also had to be a nice place to eat and dance and stay warm in.

On top of that, we had five days of open house just to be friendly. Our home was open to our friends and family and to their friends and family. People were coming and going all the time. We installed a gate that could be opened remotely, but on those days, we just left it open. The open houses were a combined effort with the Gibbs family. Mom's best friend was Aliyah Gibbs, and Dad and Gunner Gibbs were probably best friends. My brother, Dean, dated Kate Gibbs; and her brother, Jack, was Dean's best friend.

Dean and Jack were seniors in high school, and they had played their last season of high school football. It was exciting, and the team made it to the playoffs, but they lost a close one in the semifinals to Glacier High in Kalispell. During the season, Dean received a lot of interest from a lot of the smaller colleges and even a few big ones, but at six feet four and 245 pounds, he said he was too little to play for the big schools. I thought he was a giant. He was the strongest player on the team, and he was also fast, but he told me he wasn't fast enough.

He is also a great wrestler, and he has a state title to prove it. This year he decided not to wrestle, and his poor coach tried everything to get him to reconsider. He asked all of Dean's friends to get him to change his mind. He even called Mom and Dad. But Dean had made his mind up. He hated losing weight to qualify for the 220-pound weight class, and so did his football coach. Dean wanted to get bigger, not smaller. I think he also wanted a senior year that had more freedom and a lot less organized sports. What Dean loved most was to grab a rifle and a can of bear spray and disappear in the wilderness. Wrestling got in the way.

We met Jack and the rest of the Gibbses the same year Kaiyo came to live with us. For years, Jack was a lot shorter than Dean, but he had almost caught up to him. He was over six feet tall, and he was fast as lightning. He could catch anything that was thrown at or near him; he could swing a bat; and he was the best member of the golf team. He was that good.

The Montana Grizzlies and Montana State both recruited him, and so had a lot of other colleges around the country. Jack seemed to enjoy the attention, but I couldn't tell if he wanted to play college football. Still, he was spending a lot of weekends on official school visits. Anyway, Jack and Dean both had a great season. Jack recently turned eighteen, and Dean was still seventeen. I didn't get the feeling Dean was at all jealous of Jack. He was happy for him.

Dean, I think, wanted something different. He wanted more. I'm not quite sure what more meant for Dean, but he wanted it. And it made him restless. For the last few years, Dean would go off into the wilderness, usually with Kaiyo, a few times with a special bear named Goliath, and he always went for at least few days. Twice he came back all beat up and scratched up. One time he got badly bitten and clawed by a wild black bear he stalked. Dean quietly snuck up on the oblivious bear and then slapped it hard on the butt for the fun of it. Dean turned and ran, but the bear caught him. He had to get stitched up and have rabies shots. He refused to tell the rangers where he was because they would have shot the bear. I think Kaiyo had to rescue him then too. I never knew what happened, but in a crazy way, Dean seems to thrive off that sort of stuff.

Sometime before Thanksgiving, Dean went into the Southern Forest to hunt watchers. That was a new thing, and it was crazy dangerous. A watcher is the same as a bigfoot, and they're bad news. Five years ago, four of them tried to kill my dad and maybe eat him. They did kidnap him, and they hurt him pretty bad. He has the scars to remind us. Dean never forgot. Dad practically blew a gasket when Dean told him what he was going to do. But Dean can be exceedingly calm and persuasive, and he talked Dad through it. Dad still didn't like it, but Dean did it anyway. He ended up getting run over by a moose. That might have been the best thing to happen to him in a while. Common sense was something Dean was beginning to lose.

Some people think Dean is headed to the Marines or the Army after graduation. But Dean is crazy about Kate, and we all are curious how that will work out. Dean told me he had settled in his mind that he would wait for Kate to grow up "before getting too serious."

They seemed serious to me, but he was right; they were both young. Kate is almost seventeen, and she's a true beauty. Her mom and her grandparents are from some country in east Africa, and while her mom is pretty, Kate is even prettier. She is tall, thin, and has long brown hair. Her skin is brown, her eyes are grey-green, and her smile shows pure joy. From just after she met him, I think she has loved my brother. When she takes me to town, I watch as men and boys stare at her. Even old guys suck in their stomachs. She doesn't even notice.

I have also noticed that ever since Dean got run over by the moose, he and Kate have been closer than ever. In fact, Dean and Kaiyo seemed to be closer too. Maybe that moose did a good thing.

My big sister is Libby. About four and a half years ago, she and Dad saved Kaiyo and brought him home when he was just a cub. She's twenty now and goes to Montana State in Bozeman. She grew up a Grizzlies fan, but her boyfriend, Landon Haldor, lives near Bozeman, so she happily became a proud Bobcat. She likes it there, and she makes amazingly good grades. But no one is surprised. Libby is smart, pretty, and very determined. She and Landon are engaged to be married, and both are running an outfitting service owned by Landon's parents. She's taking every business class she can. They're not married yet, but they even finish each other sentences. Libby is supposed to come home today or tomorrow. I have missed her more than she knows. Landon's coming soon too, and he's a great guy. He's funny, and he's patient with me. Dean and Libby aren't. At only twenty-five, Landon is already a terrific guide, and he's determined to get his license to be an outfitter. Dean and Dad both say that for a human, Landon is the best wildlife tracker they have ever seen. And Dad and Dean should know; they're both excellent trackers themselves.

The Specials come and go. A few weeks ago, Tracker the wolf spent a few nights with us. The other Specials—like Benaiah the watcher, Goliath, Dovie the black bear, and Aylmer the aurochs—usually sleep in the barn, on the back porch, or around the yard somewhere. Not Tracker. After he eats at the table with us, he goes into the den and watches a little TV with Mom and Dad. He seems to prefer the news. After that, he goes outside to do his business and say good night to the other specials. Then he comes back in, barks good night to us, takes the steps up to the guest room, and curls up in his bed. Sometimes I have to wake him up in the morning. We know he's getting older, but he's still strong and fast. He just loves it here. We keep telling him that when he retires, he will always have a home with us. Every time we tell him that, his tail wags.

Our dogs, Moose and Major, adore Tracker. He's undoubtedly the alpha dog when he visits. Moose is a very big dog, and Major is big too, but they look small next to Tracker. Their job is to guard the farm, and they're great at it. They are getting older, but they haven't missed a step.

That leaves Kaiyo. First, Kaiyo has gotten huge. He's almost as big as Goliath, and he's still growing. Kaiyo is also one-hundred-percent family but being a grizzly, he sleeps where it's coolest. Usually, that's outside. Other than that, he's family. Mom homeschools him as best as she can; he has a bedroom that is his, and just like the rest of us, he is expected to show up for dinner on time. Sometimes he gets in trouble, sometimes he's grumpy, and sometimes he seems to enjoy everything in life. He even has his own chores to do, but they are bear chores. Asking Kaiyo to do standard farm chores would be silly. He can't hold a shovel or swing a hammer. But he's amazing at guarding the farm, and he spends lots of time digging out rocks in the new pastures Dad and Gunner carved out of a small part of the Southern Forest. Dad needs to get the rocks out of the ground, and nothing is quite as good at digging as a grizzly bear. From time to time, Kaiyo leaves the farm and goes back to his other home. I hate it when he goes, but I love it when he comes back.

Kaiyo is almost five years old now. We had to guess at his birthday, so we all settled on December 20. We were all looking forward to it. He left a few weeks ago, and he should have been back by now; Mom has been worrying for days. He's been gone much longer before, and Mom was fine with it then. But not this time. I have come to learn that my Mom is usually right about these things. We were all getting concerned.

3

Shot—Gracie

I have a reputation for sleeping late and admit I don't usually appreciate waking up early. But for the last few days, waking up early has been easy for me. When Mom started getting worried about Kaiyo, I did too. In fact, sleeping at all was trouble, so around four thirty in the morning I got dressed and went downstairs. Our kitchen was cold and dark, but with first things first, I made the coffee. I started drinking coffee last year, and I took it straight black, no cream. Moose and Major joined me and watched me whenever I got close to the refrigerator. I'm a sucker for my two dogs, and I pulled out some leftover steak and cut up a few pieces for them. They love it when I wake up early.

Outside, it was pitch-dark and bitterly cold, but the winds seemed to have died down. Cold is bad enough, but adding wind turns cold into pain. I threw a few pieces of wood into the stove and got started on a bit of remaining homework.

Not much later, Dad came downstairs and stopped when he saw me. "Three days in a row!" Dad said in a loud whisper. "Miracle after miracle!"

Dad could be a funny guy, but this morning wasn't one of those times. It was cold, and I wasn't in a particularly good mood. I snarled and pointed to the coffee. "You're off your game, old man. Didn't your mother tell you not to talk until you had your coffee?"

Dad laughed and poured thick, jet-black coffee into a couple mugs. We like our coffee strong. He handed me my mug; it felt good. Cupping his mug with his hands, he leaned back against the counter.

"So you worried about your little brother?"

I looked at Dad and could tell he wanted an answer. "Yes, but I don't really know why. He's been gone longer, but this time just seems too long. Like the longer it is, the worse it is. Christmas is coming, and then Sarah's wedding, and he just needs to be here. Does that make sense?"

For the first time, Dad showed his concern. "Sweetheart, I have learned that your mom is sometimes nearly spooky with her premonitions. She's got a great track record. Because she is worried about Kaiyo, and because you are so worried you are waking up early, which, again, is a miracle, there is probably a good reason for the concern. If he doesn't come home today or tomorrow, we will start looking. I've already alerted Aylmer, he's ready to start looking, and so is Dean."

"Thank you, Daddy."

I loved my father. He had his strengths and weaknesses, but he was a father first. After Mom, I knew Dad loved us kids more than anything, and he looked at Kaiyo as his own son. I loved that he did. Dad and I talked while we finished off our coffee. Dad then poured another mug full, grabbed his keys, and kissed me goodbye.

"I have meetings this morning, and then I'll be home around two o'clock. Troy and I are meeting for lunch. And Gunner should be here in an hour or so. He's worried too."

The cold knifed in as Dad stepped outside. Shortly I heard his truck rumble and come to life. After a few minutes, Dad drove away down our long driveway. Sitting there, I prayed silently again for God to bring Kaiyo back safely. Then I got up, poured my second cup, and finished my homework.

About twenty minutes later, I heard heavy footfalls on the back steps. Moose and Major went on full alert, and they stood by the door growling fiercely. Normally, that scene would have frightened me, but I heard him. Kaiyo has his own voice, and I knew it well. The dogs immediately went from killer mode to pure joy. Still, Kaiyo didn't sound right.

"Kaiyo!" I ran to the door and threw it open as Kaiyo stumbled in.

Kaiyo is huge, and when he came in, his bulk filled the doorframe. Before I could hug him, like I always do, Kaiyo dropped to the floor. The dogs scattered but returned quickly and started licking his face. I shooed them away and saw that his paws were bloody, and his back was caked with thick, dark, gooey blood. Kaiyo was a mess, and I had never seen him this way.

"Oh, little brother," I whispered, "you found trouble. Were you shot?"

Kaiyo chuckled, and that was music to my ears. It also told me he was bloodier than he was hurt, but that was just a guess. I gave Kaiyo a big, bloody hug, and I started to cry. I was also only twelve, and I loved him so much. I feared the worst, and the worst almost happened. Somebody shot Kaiyo. He groaned, but Kaiyo didn't need sympathy; he needed help. I ran over to the landline, stuffed down my emotions, and called our veterinarian, Dr. Cindy Rich. We called her Dr. Cindy. Every farmer had an emergency number for their vet, and so did we. Dr. Cindy's recording was brief, and as calmly as I could, I said, "Dr. Cindy, this is Gracie McLeod. Kaiyo was shot and wounded. He's mighty bloody. He's here with us at the farm. Please call as soon as possible."

I then heard clumsy knocking on the kitchen door. I knew immediately it was Aylmer because of his gentle mooing. Aylmer was a lot bigger than Kaiyo, and he could never come inside. But Aylmer was a Special, and he lived with us on the farm. He loved Kaiyo too. I left the door open so he could talk, but it got too cold. I shooed Aylmer back down the steps as nicely as I could. He went back into the barn and closed the doors behind him.

I went over to Kaiyo and asked if he wanted water. Kaiyo couldn't speak English in this world, but he could make a variety of sounds that meant different things. He meant to say *no*. I asked if he was hungry. The answer I got was a clear *yes*. *Of course*, I thought. He's a bear, and bears are always hungry. "I'm getting Mom and Dean."

I kissed his beautiful bear face and bolted upstairs. I entered Mom and Dad's room and padded over to Mom. She was still asleep. I spoke quietly so Mom wouldn't panic, "Mom, Kaiyo is here, and he's been shot."

That took about a second to sink in, and Mom threw back the covers. "Oh, my baby!" she hoarsely said as she leaped out of bed. I got out of her way and ran to Dean's room. Without raising my voice, I opened the door and leaned into his stinky room. "Dean, get up. Kaiyo has been shot. He's in the kitchen."

Seriously, what is it about teenage boys that makes their rooms smell so bad? Mom calls it *boy-funk*. Whatever it is, it's not good. It's about as bad as the smell of a grizzly bear on a summer afternoon. Poor Mom is always buying scented candles to keep the air in the house breathable. Anyway, I left Dean with the news as I breathed in the better air in the hall. Mom nearly ran me over to get to the stairwell.

"Sorry, Babes. Come with me. What do you know?"

"Well," I said, "He's hungry."

"That's a good sign," said Mom, "But it doesn't mean much. Bears can probably eat for another two weeks after they're dead. So where did he get hit?"

Mom is a terrific mom, but she talks when she gets nervous. She didn't really want an answer because she was already in the kitchen and moving fast. In the short time since I left to get Mom and Dean, Kaiyo got up and started pulling food out of the refrigerator.

"Get out of there!" barked Mom.

"Mom," said Dean as he was making his way into the kitchen, "let the poor bear have some breakfast!"

It was a sweet sight to see. There was Kaiyo, standing tall and nearly touching the ceiling with Dean hugging on to him, and almost a foot below Dean was Mom hugging even tighter. She was trying not to cry. Dean was smiling. Kaiyo was making bear noises and holding on to both with his dinner plate-sized paws.

I went over and pushed the three of them away from the fridge. "I got this, Mom. Take care of your baby bear, and I'll cook breakfast. Dr. Cindy will be calling shortly, and I'm not going to school today."

"Me neither," said Dean. "It's Friday, and I don't have any tests."

The three of them went into the family room while I got started on breakfast. The dogs decided to stay with me. The good thing was that cooking breakfast for my little brother was easy. For bears, quantity is far more important than quality. With Kaiyo, bacon, eggs, salads, and peanut butter sandwiches are just as appreciated as a steak and lobster. After a few moments, the phone rang. Dr. Cindy was on her way. I then called Dad and filled him in. He tried to ask a bunch of questions, but I had no real answers. He asked Dean to call him when he figured it out. That was a good idea, and I told Dad I would.

I heard Mom cleaning Kaiyo's wounds while Kaiyo and Dean were communicating. Well, they were trying to. Apparently, cleaning a bullet wound hurt, and Kaiyo roared in pain a few times. Mom just ignored him and told him she was almost done even though she wasn't. As for Dean, no one in the family was as good as he was at understanding Kaiyo. It was like the two of them could read each other's minds. Somehow they were like twins, and translating bear grunts and paw motions to English was just a quick matter of time for them. It usually worked, but as a fallback, Kaiyo has a sandpit in the barn so he can write. Mom homeschooled him for years. He can read and write, but his handwriting is awful.

I called everybody to breakfast, and Kaiyo was first. He sat up on his rear end by the island as I served up eggs, bacon, raw meat, raw cabbage, sandwiches, leftover ham, and collard greens.

Dad loves collards, but to me they smell bad. I think collards are a Georgia thing where Dad grew up. Kaiyo seemed to like them too. Mom and Dean toyed at the food, but they were more interested in their coffee.

After a few moments, Dean put on his coat and pulled on his boots. "Come on, Kaiyo. This is serious business. We can eat more in a few minutes. You need to give Aylmer a fuller explanation too. I'm sure he's concerned."

Kaiyo rolled onto all fours and kissed Mom on the cheek. Even flat-footed, he was taller than Mom, but he was super gentle with her. He was a good son. He nodded at Dean, and the two walked out into the bitter cold.

Terrors—Susan

Gracie was thinking hard. "He's still bleeding, Mom. Who would do this?"

I didn't know, but my mind was racing too. I somehow knew Kaiyo was in danger; I also wondered if it was all related. Sarah was getting married, Kaiyo was shot, and I kept thinking of Libby. I had no reason to think Libby was part of this, but I did. Libby's last finals were today, and then she was headed home. Landon had a last-minute customer who needed a back-country guide for a week or so of snowmobiling, predator-hunting, and cold-weather camping. It sounded horrible to me, but being a guide was his business. I was certain he needed the money too. Winter is a lean time for all guides; Landon was just lucky to get the call. Libby had a nose for business, so I knew she was thrilled. She was Landon's fiancée and his bookkeeper. She was also his booking agent and IT department. She created his website too. They were a great team.

In a few moments, Sam's truck rolled back into the courtyard, and I also heard Gunner's diesel a few seconds later. Gunner probably loved Kaiyo as much as Sam, and when he and Sam walked in, Gunner had one of his rifles with him. Carrying a gun out here was normal, but the rifle Gunner had was not the type he usually carried. He had a big-scoped, bolt-action, camouflaged sniper rifle chambered for a 300 Winchester magnum cartridge. That is a good round. It's good for both big game and enemy combatants. Gunner wasn't interested in big game.

Gunner poured himself some coffee and scanned the table for leftovers. He looked at me and pointed to the bacon on my plate. "Go for it, Gunner."

Gunner had no shame when it came to scavenging our breakfasts. When Kaiyo is here, he's out of luck unless he's quick. Leftovers do not exist with Kaiyo around.

"Susan," asked Gunner, "when did you start worrying about Kaiyo being late? Because he's not really late. He's been gone for longer periods in the past. As I recall, you didn't worry so much as you have recently. Can you pin it down?"

I thought about the question. "Gunner, it wasn't long after Thanksgiving, after he'd been gone for about a week, when I started feeling uneasy. But the last three or four days have been awful. Why?"

Sam was listening. Gunner rubbed the stubble on his face and looked at his coffee. "My friends in town told me a few men have been asking questions about the farm. At first, I just thought they were real estate agents or investors, but a few days ago, one of them asked an old friend if he knew anything about the bears that lived on the farm. He said other folks were asked the same questions. They seemed to have come into town about the same time you started worrying. I don't know if there's a connection, but I don't like it."

Sam started to ask a question when Dean and Kaiyo came back inside. Standing there were my two boys; they seemed so similar except one of them was on four legs. Dean was bigger and taller than any of us humans, and he looked particularly ferocious. Even Kaiyo didn't look as dangerous as Dean did at that moment.

I had seen that look before. He was ready to do something, but I doubt he knew quite what to do.

Kaiyo winced some as Sam and Gunner went over to him and hugged on him. After a few minutes, Dean cleared his throat. "We got a problem, Dad. Kaiyo got shot at by somebody who knows who Kaiyo is. The shooter also knows about us too. He probably wants to kill us all. He killed two grizzlies just to lure Kaiyo farther away from the farm and into a killing shot."

"Sniper," whispered Gunner.

I gasped and let out a cry. I didn't want to, but it just came out. I hate playing the role of the emotional female, but I was doing it now. Our fears were always of someone shooting Kaiyo by mistake or out of fear. But it seemed we had an assassin on our hands.

Dean kept talking, and Kaiyo would correct him from time to time. He would grunt and make paw motions, and somehow Dean could figure it out. Anyway, what we learned was that Kaiyo was shot by a human who also had a big dog. We also learned the shooter said we were on *the list* too. I wasn't sure what that meant, but it couldn't be good.

As usual, my first emotion was fear. Fear seems to be my go-to emotion. But at least for me, I know fear is the least trustworthy of my emotions. I've always had to deal with fear in a way Sam never has. He has his own fears, but it's rarely his first emotion. Sam's first response is usually anger. We have both learned our first responses are usually the wrong ones. Fortunately for me, I was able to morph my fear quickly into anger. I handle my own anger better than Sam handles his. Anger helps me to think. Sam has to force himself go fully analytical. That way he can figure out if his anger is justified. Today our anger was justified.

Before I could dwell on planning, Lowe Brigham, our local game warden, came speeding down the driveway. Sam had probably called him. Lowe was an excellent lawman, and he was serious about his job. Lowe, Sam, and Gunner were very close and had been for years. It didn't start out that way because when they met, Lowe enforced the law, and Gunner broke it. A lot. Because of us, Gunner has settled down and joined the law-abiding folks of Madison County. Since then, Gunner and Lowe have become close friends.

Lowe skidded to a stop, and he was up the back steps and in the kitchen in seconds. He ignored us and immediately went over to Kaiyo.

"Oh, Kaiyo, I found the other two bears. I was so afraid you or Goliath might have been the third bear to get shot, and it looks like you were. Just—damn."

"Not a poacher," said Gunner. "Sniper."

Lowe's face turned white. He knew what that meant. There are plenty of poachers who would never shoot a human. For good or for ill, snipers shoot humans for a living. "Assassin?" asked Lowe.

Sam, Gunner, Dean, and Kaiyo nodded.

Lowe looked at Gunner. "What did you bring?"

Gunner picked up his rifle.

"Perfect," said Lowe. "So what do we know?"

Dean filled him in.

"That makes sense. Here's what I know. Our district office got a report from a pilot who said there were two dead bears east of here. He gave the rough coordinates for both, and I found the second bear a few hours after dark. Kaiyo, I saw your tracks around both bears, and I was afraid you were hunting the sniper. You were; weren't you?"

Lowe was smiling when he said the last part. Lowe despised poachers. Kaiyo chuckled and nodded. Dean smiled and congratulated him. Gunner said something stupid like, "Way to go."

But Sam grimaced. I blew up.

"Kaiyo!" I blurted out. "Why were you doing that? What got in to you? You know better! What was your plan? Did you even have a plan?"

We have told Kaiyo until we were blue in the face not to get near hunters or poachers unless we were with him. Hunting grizzlies is legal in at least one state and may soon be legal here. I was so exasperated hearing how Kaiyo was playing cop I forgot he got shot. Gracie had to remind me.

She grabbed my hand and spoke slowly, "Mom. Be nice. Your son just got shot. Be mad later."

Oh, I would. But she had a point. I crossed my arms and held my tongue. I just about had it with the testosterone festival in my kitchen. I was feeling like the only grown-up in the room. Fortunately, Dr. Cindy drove into the dark courtyard. Gracie, being the impulsive one, ran out to make sure Dr. Cindy knew to come inside the house instead of the barn. Within moments, she came into the kitchen, said a few hellos, and went straight to Kaiyo. We all stepped back as she looked him over.

"Oh, Kaiyo, you poor thing. This might hurt a bit, but I have to learn how bad you got shot."

Kaiyo's bleeding had stopped, but his back was still sticky and wet. We described how far and how fast he had run to get home.

"Well," she said, "that explains the bloody paws."

Then she got to work. Breathless, we all watched as Dr. Cindy got started. She began at the back of his head. "All righty, Kaiyo, let's start with the cervical vertebrae."

Dr. Cindy was always joyful, but she was dead serious about her medical care. Her trained fingers worked the back of Kaiyo's neck. She would ask repeatedly if it hurt, and Kaiyo would grunt in a way that clearly said *no*. After a few moments, she said, "That's good, his cervical vertebrae are all intact."

She then went to Kaiyo's shoulders. She spoke to us and to Kaiyo, "A grizzly bear's scapulae, the shoulder blades, are massive and covered in muscle. Now, Kaiyo, I'm just making sure your bones and thoracic vertebrae weren't shot too. The thoracic vertebrae are the ones behind your shoulders. This is going to hurt a little, but grizzlies can absorb a massive amount of trauma without suffering like we humans would. You're doing great."

Kaiyo responded with a smile. Sam had his arm over me, holding tight. All of us were quiet; even our dogs were watching. After a few more minutes of prodding and a moan or two from

Kaiyo, Dr. Cindy turned and said, "Well, the bad news is, somebody shot Kaiyo. Gunner, by the looks of that rifle you tucked behind the kitchen island and Lowe, with you being here, I am guessing you think it was intentional. That's really bad news. Am I right?"

Sam answered, "It seems so. But we don't know much. It does appear the shooter knew who and what Kaiyo is."

Dr. Cindy's face showed her surprise. She started to talk, but she stopped. After a moment, she smiled and said, "The good news is, Kaiyo will heal nicely. The slug went high and directly through the peak of the hump on his shoulder. I'm going to treat the entry and exit wounds and stitch them up, and Kaiyo will soon be good as new. There was some minor muscle damage, but it ought to heal nicely."

She looked at Kaiyo and continued, "He lost some blood because of his journey from wherever he was. That means he will need more red meat than normal."

She winked at Kaiyo, and he winked back. "He will also need a lot of food in general. Add lots of raw milk right from your dairy cows. The more protein and fats in his diet, the better."

Kaiyo held up a paw, and Dr. Cindy high-fived him. "Also, he needs to rest for a few days. His paws are tough, but there are a few cuts so, no long walks. Finally, Kaiyo needs a bath to get out all the blood in his fur. Keep the wound dry, but the rest of him will need a lot of soap and hot water. Rinse the soap out fully too."

Gracie volunteered immediately. Dr. Cindy went to her kit and took out a syringe. Kaiyo's eyes got huge as she held up the syringe and filled it with a whitish-yellow liquid. "It's lidocaine, Kaiyo. It will hurt a bit going in, but I have to close your wounds. I promise you, you won't feel any of that part, and that part is worse. You'll be glad I gave you this stuff."

Kaiyo groaned as we watched her get to work. We needed to talk, and we needed a plan.

Gunner was first. "Kaiyo, you might want to listen in. Dr. Cindy, there are some folks in town who have been asking about the McLeod's and about bears that live on the farm. Do you know anything about that? Has anybody asked you anything?"

Lowe was paying attention. Dr. Cindy was busy sewing up Kaiyo, but she stopped for a few moments. She turned and said, "You know, a few weeks ago, a man and a dog came to the clinic and asked me if I knew of any farms that might be for sale in the future. I thought that was an odd question and told him to talk to a real estate agent. He said he would, but he was hopeful I might know a farmer or two that was interested in calling it quits. The man gave me the creeps, and so did his big dog. Only a few dogs have ever made me feel unsafe, but that one did. Anyway, he said was looking for a special farm, 'like the McLeod farm.' I told him this farm was lovely and to talk to you about it. He said goodbye, and then he and his dog left. Until he turned away, his dog never took his eyes off me."

Kaiyo barked at Dean, and the two of them did some quick Q and A.

"What did the dog look like?" asked Dean.

"He was real big for a dog, furry, gray, with a dark muzzle and face. He was heavier than Moose. He could have been a Caucasian Ovcharka."

Kaiyo started making all sorts of noises. Dean turned to us and said, "I think that guy was the shooter."

Lowe took out his notepad.

WRAIGHT—SAM

After Dr. Cindy left, Dean started the discussion. He and Gunner wanted to leave and go right into the Eastern Wilderness, find the shooter, and capture him or kill him. Kaiyo hated that idea. I had to remind them they were talking about murder. Lowe and Gunner kept quiet, but Dean got angry.

"So, Dad, are you saying somebody can shoot your son and it's okay?"

I could have shut him down, but I needed Dean to think. "You're losing your edge, son. That's not a reasoned argument, that's just accusation, and it's damned ineffective on me. Think this one through, and come at me again."

Dean was smart. He was mad, and he looked at the others; no one was coming to his rescue. He sighed. Then he looked at Kaiyo. "Fine, Dad. I know you're right. So what do we do?"

"We plan," I told them all. "There are pieces to this puzzle, and I sense something will break. As for now, Lowe has to go to town, report his findings, and do his game warden thing. I have to go into town too. Gunner, I need you to establish a perimeter. We'll have to leave a lot of it unprotected, but take advantage of Kaiyo's nose and Aylmer's ability in the forest. And, Kaiyo, can you somehow rustle up Benaiah and Tracker? Wait. It's wolf season here, so maybe that's a terrible idea. What about Dovie?"

Kaiyo looked at me and said what I interpreted to be a *no*.

Winter in Montana is a tough sell to the animals of Eden. I have no idea why they would ever leave anyway. Plus, I had no intention of sending Kaiyo back out to find an open door; they're rarely in the same place, and his paws were a little beat up. Also, the shooter could be waiting for him to go get reinforcements.

"Dean, I think we are all targets, but Kaiyo is the one the shooter apparently wants the most. If he takes out one of us humans first, the heat will be so intense he could get caught or killed. Stand guard over Kaiyo. The fields are covered by snow, so we have great visibility to the west and north. Unfortunately, the east and south would be terrific places for a sniper. Let's move Aylmer into one of the hidden pastures south of here. I doubt they know about him. He's got a good sniffer too. And, Kaiyo, no pooping in the woods unless we know they're clear. Never be out if you're upwind of the forests in the east or south."

Kaiyo groaned at the last part, but I was serious. I kissed Susan and grabbed my keys. We needed more information, but I had no desire to live the rest of my life in fear. We would, somehow, find the shooter and take him down. And if I had to kill him, I would.

As I headed to town, my mind was spinning. Gunner's and Dr. Cindy's revelations about people asking about us was bad enough, but now it looked like one of them tried to kill Kaiyo. That person also knew killing Kaiyo was murder, but not in the eyes of the law. At best, if he got caught, he might get convicted of a misdemeanor and pay a fine. If we take the shooter out, then it's a life sentence for us. We had to think this thing through. And that's precisely what wasn't happening at the farm. I trust Lowe, but Dean and even Gunner could be loose cannons.

Once I hit the blacktop, I called Sheriff Lee Tuttle and Captain Troy Stahr. They asked a slew of questions, but I had only a few answers and a potential description of the shooter. Tuttle and

Stahr were good friends of the family, and both loved my kids and Kaiyo probably the most. I told Troy we could discuss more of it at lunch. They said they would give Lowe a call too.

Troy and I have been meeting together in town for lunch about twice a month since he proposed to Sarah. Radford is the closest town to the farm, and we go there often. It's a forty-mile drive from my house, but as the crow flies, it's closer. It feels like home. My human kids have been going to school there, and we do most of our business there. Radford is part tourist trap and part small town. The Madison River flows through the valley, and Radford capitalizes on its hospitality, the beautiful views, and great trout fishing. There are even statues of fish throughout town. During the summers and fall, Radford gets busy, but after Thanksgiving most of the fishermen leave, and the elk and deer hunters have cleared out too. It's my favorite time of year. I know or recognize most of the folks who live and work there.

There are at least ten restaurants in town, and Troy and I like to mix it up. We do that because we know the restaurant owners and we want to support all of them. Today we picked a saloon that sat just off Main Street that was locally famous for good music, flowing liquor, and buffalo burgers that had no equal.

Walking in, the crowd was light. I spotted some friends and spoke with them before taking a seat at my table. Five minutes later, Troy came swaggering in, and he spent the next five minutes doing the meet and greet. Troy was popular, and everybody seemed to be asking him about Sarah. I watched and waited. While I did, a stranger seated near me to my right caught my attention. He didn't match the description of the man who was the likely shooter, but I noticed how he watched Troy's every move. I thought he must have known Troy, but when Troy came my way, Troy just nodded his way and proceeded on to our table where he sat to my left.

I try not to judge a book by its cover or people by their appearance, but it's hard not to. However, I have lived long enough to know that caution isn't judgment, and my gut was telling me that I needed to be cautious. Sure enough, when Troy sat at the table, the mystery man stood up and came to our table. He was tall and strongly built. He was well dressed, and he sported a well-groomed, short beard. He had a Hollywood look to him.

"Hello, gentlemen. May I speak with you? Briefly, I promise."

There was no warmth in his tone, but I didn't sense aggression either. His tone was flat, almost bored. It was then that Troy looked up, and I could tell he was on guard too.

"I'm sorry, please let me introduce myself. My name is Glennon Wraight."

He said his last name slowly. Presumably so we could pronounce it. Without asking, he took a seat. I didn't remember giving him permission, but he sat anyway. He had the hint of an accent, but I couldn't place it.

"Well, what can we do for you, Mr. Wraight?" asked Troy in his folksy, smiling way.

I was not smiling, but I assumed Wraight wanted to talk to Troy and not me. Still, I had my guard up; Troy was a cop, and that made him disliked by a lot of folks. The fact that policing was a dangerous job was not lost on me. I wasn't armed, but instinctively and slowly, I dropped my right hand to my side. Wraight noticed it and held back a smile.

"First," he casually said to Troy, "congratulations on your upcoming marriage to your fiancé. Her name is Sarah, correct?"

Wraight was friendly, with a pleasant, singsong voice, but there was no warmth in his eyes. Troy was no longer smiling. I still assumed Wraight knew Troy.

"And you, Mr. McLeod, I do hope you have enjoyed your odd relationship with your grizzly bear child. You call him your child, am I right?"

Just then our server came the table to ask for our order. Wraight looked at her and said, "Of course. I think I will stay at this table. I would like a small black coffee with cream on the side. And some sugar if it's not too much trouble. And could you get that for me now, please? I doubt I will be staying here very long." Wraight looked back at us.

I spoke before he did, "You called this little meeting, Mr. Wraight. Captain Stahr here asked what we could do for you, so please get to the point. What do you want?"

Wraight's mouth smiled briefly. He shifted his oddly disarming gaze from me to Troy and back. "Gentlemen, please do not let my little parlor tricks offend you. I could have learned most of that about you in the last five minutes watching the constable here do his table greets. I merely spoke to amuse. I listen to the sweet people in this lovely town talk. Some of the talk I overhear in the restaurants and bars. I never eavesdrop, mind you. Well, at least only rarely. And I admit to even paying for information from time to time, but I have not done much of that here. I haven't had to. I have, indeed, learned that you both have many friends, and many of them are quite confused. They wonder, especially about you, Constable, why you would not get married here in town or in Helena where I hear Sarah is from. Apparently, you have even offended some people, they wonder why they were not invited. As for you, Mr. McLeod, the new gates on your driveway have raised some eyebrows. Also, the stories of what comes and goes on your farm is hard to believe, but I am, perhaps, gullible. I believe those wonderful stories."

Troy was getting steamed, but I gave him a gentle kick to his shins. I wanted to hear this guy out. Troy effected a weak smile and leaned back.

Wraight kept talking, "Anyway, by profession I am an investigator, and a good one at that. I have a client who is, for whatever reason, very interested in the goings-on around here, and especially at the McLeod ranch." Wraight sat back and waited for us to respond.

"Are you done?" I asked.

Troy and Wraight both looked surprised.

"Mr. Wraight, intimidation, even when it's coming from someone as courteous and pleasant as you, is never welcome, and it's not welcome today."

I smiled, and for the first time, Wraight looked uneasy.

I kept going, "I know you will not identify your client, but I have my suspicions, and those are sufficient enough for me. Now, as for me and Captain Stahr, is there anything else you would enjoy sharing today? If not, it's time for you to go."

Wraight's demeanor changed to pure fury, and then, in a moment, he recovered his pleasant facade as he fixed the napkin in his lap. "Touché, Mr. McLeod. I heard you lacked diplomatic skills, and it seems I heard correctly."

He sighed. "It's a pity really, but you, especially, have so much to lose in this world. You have your gorgeous ranch and an exquisite family. Everyone, including my client, I'm sure, wishes for you and your family to live in quiet peace. Likewise, Constable, the same goes for you. I only seek your cooperation on a few matters. I am perfectly willing to drive away from here and leave you both alone in this attractive country forever. And I am not asking for much. And no worries, Constable, Sarah is no longer wanted back. She is merely old news in my client's eyes. And, Mr. McLeod, no one wants to harm your natural family. I hope you see the fairness of that."

For years, I have been wondering what I would do if the government figured it all out and wanted to take Kaiyo away. But Wraight represented a much more ancient and deadly sort of opposition. I needed to know more about their plan. Wraight was a talker, so I shot him a quizzical glance, and he bit on it.

"You look confused, Mr. McLeod," said Wraight. "Let me explain. My employer is unhappy with the injustice of your situation. Indeed, he is enraged about it. I agree with him, of course, none of it is fair or sporting. You certainly wouldn't know this, but for millennia there have been some unwritten rules between the two powers as their seemingly eternal contest for the universe plays itself out. One of those rules is that a man's faith must be, or at least should be, unsupported by current acts of the supernatural. Of course, we live in the dual worlds of the material and the spiritual, so there have been, and will be, a few slip-ups here and there, but our side, at least, does its best to play by the rules."

Wraight sipped on his coffee; he was enjoying himself. "To apply those rules to your situation, Mr. McLeod, your pet bear, clever as he is, is unfair. His presence here is unfair, and it could all get out of hand. In fact, everything about him is unfair. The constable here would know this. His entire force speaks about what they call *the miracle bear*, and it has made my employer's job nearly impossible wherever the mere mention of your bear he shows up. That bear has, what would you call it, unleveled the playing field?"

Wraight looked at both of us and then smiled. "Am I clear?" he asked. "Here's just one example. Your deputy, Justin Martinez, he was once close to being a more productive member of our team, if *team* is what you want to call it. Martinez, through simple, rational, free-thinking, and personal choice, and without our adding signs and wonders, but not without much time and effort of ours to educate him, was close to rejecting, outright, your god—you know, the same god who created this flawed, chaotic sewer of a world. But unfortunately, the miracle bear intervened. That, my dear friends, was and is, against the rules."

Wraight's personality made it difficult to take him seriously, but my gut told me Wraight was a dangerous man. I have been threatened before, but it was usually by tough, crusty people, and most of them were drunk. But Wraight was a different type. He was more like a pretentious, effete college professor who was a serial killer on the side. But he wore his superiority on his sleeve, and that made having a little fun with him irresistible. And I was still curious, so I spoke, "That was just one rule. Is that all of them?"

"Good man, McLeod. You are surprisingly observant," he said gleefully. "There is one other rule, the breaking of which particularly irks my client. The rule is simple. Mankind cannot peer into Eden and walk away. And your daughter's friend, Mr. Haldor, saw too much. He should be dead, and everyone knows it. Those are not our rules, those are your team's rules. There are skeletons of our friends who merely stumbled into that place, by mistake of course, who were brutally struck down. But not Haldor. So there is a price for such transgressions, and the price must be paid in full.

I am here to encourage you both to be smart. Your families are in peril, and your interference with me or my associates will be the cause of extreme heartache for all the humans you love. If you are smart, your family will be safe, with, of course, the exceptions I mentioned. You do want that, don't you?"

Wraight was a piece of work. "So," I said, "I see that your client is enforcing God's rules? I heard that right, didn't I? Anyway, you might as well go ahead and start killing us off now. You obviously know us. We will protect Kaiyo and Landon until the last of us is dead. By the way, you have good reason to fear death, Wraight, but I don't. And neither does my family."

"Ditto for me and Sarah," said Troy. "But I'm willing to go one step farther than Sam. Let's start now." Troy shifted his gaze to Wraight. "You threatened Sam and his family, and by doing so, you have threatened me. I am sure you are armed, isn't everybody here in the West? Take your shot, and let's see what you are made of. This ought to be interesting."

Wraight sat back and smiled. "Ah, the famous Captain Stahr has finally joined the conversation. I was wondering if you had decided to remain mute and let McLeod carry your water entirely. So are you the same man who nearly got one of your men killed chasing a killer grizzly bear five years ago? Remember Deputy Martinez and his horrible wounds? Those were your fault, of course. I believe you lost a few dogs on that excursion too. You have remained just as impulsive, and because of that, you do not impress me with your childish boasting. Besides, threatening, if that occurred at all in our conversation, was only about a grizzly bear. No law against that, is there?"

Troy smiled. "You have a convenient memory, sir. You threatened a friend of ours, Landon Haldor, and you did so in my presence, a fully trained, active-duty peace officer. I am thinking you ought to spend a few days enjoying the Madison County Jail."

"You have nothing on me," laughed Wraight. His laugh seemed to lack confidence. "I am careful with my words. All I said was that the price had to be paid. Tell me where I threatened Mr. Haldor with anything other than financial harm?"

"I'll be your witness, Troy," I said. "He did threaten Landon, and then he even rambled on and on about some asinine story about the Garden of Eden. That's crazy talk, right? That's just a fairy tale, but he sure seemed serious. Troy, maybe this whacko needs a seventy-two-hour psych lock up. You know, for observation purposes for psycho jobs like him. We don't need another nutcase threatening folks."

Troy stood up. "Stand up and put your hands behind your back, Wraight. You are under arrest."

Wraight's look was one of pure hatred. Slowly he stood and put his hands behind him. Troy laughed and sat back down. Wraight was furious and started to sputter. Troy then told Wraight he was going to write up a report that Wraight was acting suspiciously and had threatened Landon Haldor. The district attorney's office would get a copy in the morning. He also said he was going to inform the force to watch him lest he try to hurt somebody.

"Step outta line, Wraight, and I'll be the first to know."

Wraight gathered his composure and realized he'd been toyed with. He controlled his fury. Putting on his coat, Wraight smiled and threw down a ten-dollar bill. "Please tell our gracious server that the coffee was wonderful. Good day, gentlemen."

"One last question, Mr. Wraight."

Wraight stopped and turned to me. "Yes, Mr. McLeod?"

"Why tell us any of this? You are a man of purpose, so you obviously had some sort of a reason. Your associate has already taken the first shots, so fair play and sportsmanship isn't something you care about. Care to share it with us?"

"Of course. I was wondering if you were going to ask me."

I noticed a new cruelness in Wraight's attitude. He continued, "You see, we play by certain rules. Some of them are our rules, some are by agreement and some are imposed upon us. One of our rules is to address early the inevitable blame that is soon to come. We want you to know that if any one of your family gets hurt, or if you do, it will be your own fault and no one else's. You will be able to blame only yourself. Any guilt will be yours. Because the only way your family, or Captain Stahr here or his fiancé, could get hurt or worse, would be if any of you stupidly involve yourselves in our job of righting the wrongs that have occurred here. The futures of your families are in your hands, not in my client's."

Wraight stood there enjoying his threats. I stood and stepped toward him. I was seething, and I needed the time to get ahold of myself. I waited a few moments before talking. "But you are wrong, Wraight," I said, "and you know it. You want to kill my son and my future son-in-law. My rules require that I stop you. So I will. As for blame, it will be solely yours, of course. Your client is a serpentine liar, and a lot of that has rubbed off on you. But you are not nearly as good a liar as your client. Moreover, you have given me no choice."

Wraight fiddled with his gloves and looked bored. He expected me to be loyal, and he obviously wanted me to die. But confederacies are never perfect, and his confederate was a buffoon. He was dangerous and even capable, but he was still a buffoon.

I continued, "By the way, Wraight, your loudmouthed associate has already revealed your intention to kill all of us. I already know my family and I are, in his words, on *the list*. So your absurd morality play about giving us a chance to stay out of harm's way is a lie, and we all know it. Foolishly, we have been forewarned. Your intentions are murder."

Wraight was clearly astonished Kaiyo's shooter would have spoken so brashly. True to form, his smug character reappeared. "Well, I don't know anything about that," he said.

I decided to change the subject. "Wraight, do you ever read westerns?" I paused. "One author said that the most dangerous thing in the world is a man with a gun who thinks he's right. I think the author has a point, don't you?"

"Oh, I suppose so," said Wraight.

I leaned into Wraight and smiled. "I'm right."

"We'll see," smirked Wraight. "Oh, there's one more thing. We are leaving the supernatural out of this. It's just up to us humans. It's a bit like the school yard. We're all going to be on our own. There will be no *parents* around to protect us. So what I am trying to say here is that you won't be getting any help from your animal friends because they stay out of our wars, crimes, and disputes. You know that to be true, don't you? And that leads us to your god. You won't be getting any help from the spirits either. Despite the lies in your Bible, life shows us that we live and die without much help. Unless, of course, we help ourselves."

I had to laugh at that one. "Geez, Wraight, you've been drinking the Kool Aid for way too long. Trust me and trust God. You, this, and whatever is coming next, is under his control. Prepare to lose everything. And do you really think our kin folk in Eden are going to sit back and watch you try to slaughter one of their own? You are deluding yourself again."

Wraight paused. He tipped his hat, sighed, and said, "Well, the issue has been joined. It begins."

We watched as he left our table and walked to the front door. He paused briefly, spoke to someone outside, looked back at us, and smiled. Then he left.

I looked back at Troy. "That kind hates to be mocked or challenged. I think he's got a streak of cruelty in him too."

Troy was looking at the menu and said, "Should've put him in the pokey, but his threat about Landon wasn't clear enough. Right now, he looks like some sort of religious nut, and that's about it. But he'll show his hand. Those types always do. And then I'll get him. Let's eat quick and focus on catching the shooter. Wherever he is, he needs to go."

I wasn't hungry anymore, and it was no time to eat. I picked up the phone and called Landon several times. He didn't answer, so I called Libby. I needed her to warn Landon. I said goodbye to Troy and kept calling as I walked to the car.

GIFT HORSES—LIBBY

It was still early when I drove over to our office in Belgrade. I had finished my last exam this morning, and I was nearly brain dead. The Bozeman airport is nearby in the little town of Belgrade, and we leased office space there to be close to the airport. I was thrilled to get my exams behind me, and I still enjoyed Christmas like a ten-year-old. I loved all of it. I also knew I was going to miss Landon, even though it would only be for a week and a half. But my Christmastime good mood was strong, and I was looking forward to going home and getting in some family time, some sleep, and a lot of great food.

Landon's father has owned Haldor Valley Outfitters for over thirty years, and he intends to hand off the business to Landon soon. He's active in real estate and semiretired from being an outfitter. But he loves how Landon wants to grow his business, so he comes in frequently to help out and give us much-needed advice. After each elk season, Landon's parents leave Montana for Arizona, and they stay there through April. I sure didn't blame them. Montana's winters are tough, and the business slows down. Why stay?

It was Mr. Haldor's good idea to put the company's office near the airport. We are able to meet our customers in the airport because most of them are from out of state. Mr. Haldor started this business right out of high school, and it succeeded because he has terrific business sense. He was even a better businessman than he was a guide. Landon is a better guide than businessman, and that's where I excel. We make a good team.

Winter, especially around Christmas, is a tough time for out-fitters and guides. Hunting season for the more popular species like elk, moose, and deer is over, and this year, fishing is spotty. Because of the warmer autumn, ice fishing is not yet safe, so several cus-tomers canceled or postponed their trips. That is why we were so pleased when a customer booked us for a week and a half of cold-weather camping, fishing, snowmobiling, and predator-hunting. It was like an answer to prayer. We certainly needed the business, and the fee we were getting was big. The man who Landon was guid-ing apparently had plenty of money. We like customers like that, and Landon was going to give him his money's worth. He had a great week scheduled for him. He was even okay with the minor blizzard that was predicted for this afternoon and tonight. He told Landon, "the more snow, the better." He also said he wanted to get away from the crowds and the novice snowmobilers. I hoped the customer would be as tough as his talk; winter out here can be brutal, and it takes tough people to face it.

The only reason I drove to the office was to see Landon before he left. Because we saw each other just about every day, a week and a half was going to be an adjustment. I was missing him already. As I pulled up, I saw Landon loading his truck. I pulled into our parking lot and parked right next to his truck. It was brutally cold outside, so I waved him over to my jeep. Landon ran over, slipped, and nearly fell. His smile never left him though. I've seen that smile ten thousand times in the last two and a half years, and it never gets old.

Landon jumped in and immediately started talking. The cus-tomer was due, and he wanted to pay in cash. For a lot of reasons, cash is king to a small business. We have a no-refund policy for trips, but some folks get angry if they don't get to catch or shoot whatever it was they came here to catch or shoot. All we can do is lead them to the animals or to the fish. We can't make the fish bite, and we can't make our customers good marksmen. But we have had customers stop payment on checks or instruct their credit card company to reverse the charges. Landon's dad says it is part of the business, but I get furious when that happens.

Anyway, when Landon told me about the cash, I screamed. We both high-fived each other and then hugged. Landon asked me to wait until the customer came so I could take the cash to the bank. Because of the cold weather and because it was getting close to Christmas, Landon quoted the customer a steep fee. It was steep enough to pay our bills for the next few months and enough to put some money in our pockets too. It all seemed too good to be true, but I don't look gift horses in the mouth.

"That's him," said Landon.

I looked up and saw a late model Dodge Ram 3500 dually towing a top of the line travel trailer. "Landon, I think this guy can afford the fee."

The driver passed us and parked his rig about seventy-five feet away. "Come on," said Landon. "I want you to meet him. And get the money. Oh, and this guy is a little different. He's booked a trip that's mostly for fun-seekers. You know, like snowmobiling. But he seems all business."

I thought about that, but maybe he just needed to unwind. I mentioned that to Landon.

"Yeah, maybe," said Landon. "Anyway, make sure to get a good look at his dog. It's the weirdest and meanest-looking dog ever. And it's coming with us too. He says he never goes anywhere without his dog."

I put on my hat and gloves, grabbed my coat, and stepped out. Landon got out on the other side. Right then, the door to the pickup truck opened, and the first thing to come out was an enormous dog. It had a wide chest, and its fur was thick and wavy. It had a black muzzle and face, and the rest of its coat was gray silver, with black tones. It had a big, blocky head. And it stared at me. I'm not much afraid of dogs, but if I was, that one would be the one to fear.

Behind the dog came its owner and Landon's customer. If I thought the dog gave me the creeps, the owner was just as creepy. He was a big guy, probably about forty-five, and he just didn't look like somebody who wanted to have fun in the snow. He had broad shoulders, a broad chest, and a thick neck, but he wasn't fat; he walked with ease. He smiled a lot even though his eyes looked a little cruel. He wore a cowboy hat and a western-style duster. I couldn't help but notice how he kept licking his lips. He was almost as wolflike as his dog. I immediately didn't like him or his dog. And that was strange to me because I almost always liked dogs. But not that one.

"I told you that the dog was strange," said Landon.

"Landon, they're both strange. I don't envy you for a second."

"We're burning daylight, Landon!" yelled the customer from across the parking lot. Then he laughed.

He and his dog came straight over to me. "Hello, young lady. I'm Gunther MacDonald. You must be Landon's fiancé. What's your name?"

Landon looked at me strangely and then asked, "How did you know she was my fiancé?"

"Easy," said a smiling MacDonald. "I saw the ring when she was in her Jeep. I simply put two and two together. Am I right? You are his fiancé, correct?"

"I'm Libby McLeod. And yes, we are engaged. Who's your friend here?" I asked, pointing to his dog.

MacDonald looked surprised for a second and then asked, "You're not related to the McLeods who live over toward Radford, are you?"

This guy was giving me the creeps, and him knowing who I was didn't help. "I am one of those McLeods. How do you know about us?"

I said it as coolly as I could. I did not want to give this guy any sense I was uncomfortable. MacDonald never took his eyes off me. "You all have a lot of land, and I'm always in the market for land. I was told you have a nice place over there. Maybe someday I'll visit."

"Call first before you do. I doubt we will be interested in selling, and I wouldn't you to waste your time. Or ours."

MacDonald smiled and grunted. Eager to change the subject, I asked again about the dog.

"The dog's name is Ilya, but don't go petting him. He doesn't like to be touched. He's safe if you leave him alone. If you don't— well, I warned you."

MacDonald kept his snickering smile as he looked back at me and then to Landon. "Good learners," he said, "I like that."

I looked at Ilya, and if a dog could look hateful, that dog did. It sat and stared at me with total attention but with no emotion, almost like it was sizing me up for dinner. I had lived on a farm for years, and I have learned the hard way that animals have moods and personalities. And the dog was not in a good mood. I started worrying about Landon when MacDonald walked over and handed him a thick envelope. Landon opened it up and started counting a thick wad of hundred-dollar bills.

"Can we go now?" asked MacDonald.

"In a minute," laughed Landon.

MacDonald acted bored. Landon handed the money to me and asked to walk me to the Jeep. I watched Gunther MacDonald the whole time. He clearly didn't enjoy watching Landon hand me the money. In fact, a quick look of anger crossed his face and then disappeared just as rapidly back to his snide smile. But I knew what I saw.

The silence was slightly awkward as we stood in the cold parking lot. "Mr. MacDonald, if you and Ilya can wait in your truck, I'll say goodbye to Libby and finish loading the trailer with the snowmobiles and gear."

"Sure, I understand," said MacDonald with his snide smile. "A little privacy is always nice." Then MacDonald's smile melted, and he said, "Just don't take too long."

When we got to the car, Landon hugged me and whispered in my ear, "Go straight to the bank. Guys like this are never satisfied."

While Landon spoke into my ear, I kept my eye on Ilya. As MacDonald walked back to his truck, Ilya walked closer to my Jeep as he watched us. He cocked his head a bit. That dog gave me the creeps. "Hop in the Jeep with me," I told Landon.

Once inside, I started the engine. Landon hopped in and looked at me oddly. "Landon, honey, you know I love you, but keep an eye on that dog. He's not right. I could swear he was trying to listen. It's like he's a Special."

Landon kissed me on the cheek and smiled. "I get it," he said softly. "Gunther is definitely pushy, and his dog is scary, but that breed is not known for being pleasant. It's some sort of Russian wolf killer. Still, I'll be careful. And don't forget, I'll be back at the farm in less than ten days."

I drove back to Bozeman and straight to our bank to deposit the cash. Once inside, I handed the envelope of cash and a deposit slip to the teller. She took the cash and started counting. There was a lot, and I saw her raise an eyebrow at the size of the deposit. People don't use cash much anymore, at least not for legitimate operations.

"It's all drug money. You know how Landon is," I said.

I knew the teller, so we had a good laugh. A few minutes later, I drove back to my apartment, cleaned my place up, made some coffee, wrapped some Christmas gifts, and then packed and loaded the car. After running a few necessary errands and buying some last-minute gifts, I finally turned my Jeep onto Highway 191 and drove west in the direction of the farm. During the drive back home, I was comforted by Landon's promise that I would see him soon. For me, it would not be soon enough.

The hour-and-half drive from Bozeman to the farm passed by quickly, and I expected to arrive around lunch. My mind wandered as I tried to articulate my uneasiness with Gunther MacDonald and his stupid dog. MacDonald did pay a big fee, and he paid in cash. That was good for the business and for Landon and me. MacDonald certainly wasn't the first customer I didn't like. And fearing a dog who never barked at me or even uttered a growl seemed sillier the farther away I got from Bozeman. I soon decided I was overthinking the situation. I concluded everything would be fine. I turned up the music and thought better thoughts.

I had already made it home and was just getting my Jeep parked when Dad called. He seemed in a hurry and wanted to know where Landon was. Then Gracie ran out of the kitchen straight to me and started knocking loudly on my window. With Dad trying to pry information out of me and with Gracie now motioning for me to come inside, it was obvious something was wrong. Then I watched as Kaiyo bounded out of the kitchen and loped my way. I quickly told Dad I would call him back. I hung up over his objections. For me, there was just too much going on. And why was Kaiyo limping? My phone was ringing; it was Dad again.

Plans—Dean

I watched from the kitchen window as Libby picked up her phone. I knew it was Dad calling. I saw Libby talk to Dad for a few minutes. I saw Libby's face morph from slightly annoyed to terrified to pure anguish. Mom was right there to console her, and Libby took her up on it. Libby held on to Mom and cried. Gracie and Kaiyo tried to add whatever comfort they could. The situation was indeed grim.

Just before Libby got here, Dad called Mom and described his conversation with some stranger in Radford. Dad had tried to call Landon on his cell and at his office to warn him. The stranger threatened Landon because Landon had broken the rules, whatever those were. Landon was obviously in trouble. During all the commotion outside, they connected the dots and figured out that Landon and Libby's customer was probably the guy who shot Kaiyo. It was a total setup, and Landon was in real danger.

Libby and the rest of my family came in out of the cold. Libby was upset, but her mind was working fast. We all hugged, and she described her meeting with the customer and his creepy, scary dog. Kaiyo huffed a few times. They all moved upstairs to get Libby settled.

I turned and looked at Gunner sitting there looking at his cell phone. He was lost in thought. Jack had come over right after Dr. Cindy left. I guess he wasn't going to school today, either. Only in a senior year could we decide just not to go, and we decided not to go. He knew about Kaiyo, but the issue with Landon was new to all of us. Unperturbed, Jack reached into the refrigerator and started pulling out whatever he needed to make a sandwich. Jack and his dad, Gunner, were at home here almost as much as at their own house.

Jack was my best friend, and he was one of the best athletes I had ever known or seen. Several Division 1 colleges have been hounding him to play football for them. He stood six-foot-two and weighed 215 pounds and was still growing. As both a running back and a receiver, he shattered a number of county high school records. He's strong too. He's not as strong as me, but I'm not as fast as him. We both won our share of awards, but my football playing days were probably over. Jack still loved the game. I was tired of it. I knew I was going to miss him when he moved off somewhere to play football, but his path was not mine. My path was still unknown to me, but Jack knew what he wanted to do, at least for the next three or four years.

I cleared my throat to get Gunner's attention. He looked up at me. "Okay, you were in Special Forces, right?"

Gunner nodded, and I saw a slight smile creep up on his face. Gunner is a man of action, and he liked the way I thought. He probably thought I had a point to make, and I did. "How would you guys handle this? Just for fun, assume there is no law enforcement."

"No cops?" asked Gunner.

"No cops," I said.

Gunner rubbed his chin and thought. After a few moments, he responded, "Your assumption won't work because we in Special Forces always factor in as many variables as we are aware of. And cops are a big variable. Law enforcement keeps us from kidnapping the man your dad talked to today and employing whatever measures would be necessary to get the information we need. So I can't assume no cops. That's not the world we're living in. Do you understand?"

I nodded. "Keep going."

"So we have to either work with cops, without them or against them. In this case, we would gather all the information we could on where Landon was going. If we knew that, then we simply drive over there and get him and bring him home. If he's on the trails, we track them down. If he's deep in the backwoods, then we enlist as many of Kaiyo's friends as are willing to help and we still track them down. But we know one thing. The man who shot Kaiyo fancies himself to be some sort of sniper. He must have lain in wait for a few hours in the bitter cold, so he's dangerous. The fact he missed a target as big as Kaiyo tells me he's not as good a sniper as he thinks he is. The other factor is that he won't be fooled by our animal buddies. He knows who and what Kaiyo is, so he probably knows about Tracker and Goliath. Finally, we can't expect the kind of supernatural help we had last time with the lizards. There will be no cavalry coming in to save us. This time, it's probably an all-earth battlefield. We are a little more on our own. We will have to fight and pray like everybody else. Those bad guys think this is their best chance. They don't want Raphael coming to our rescue, so they are just going to go after us the old-fashioned way. They're going to use assassins and evil people. It's worked ten thousand times before.

"As for cops, I am glad they're in the know. We know we can trust Lowe Brigham, Captain Hamby at the State Patrol, Sheriff Tuttle, and Captain Stahr and most of their deputies. We will need every one of them."

"What's most important?" I asked.

"Speed," said Gunner. "Landon's life is already in danger. They have a big head start on us. Maybe too big. Hopefully, Libby and your dad can reach him on his cell phone so he can cancel the trip. But Landon left hours ago, and if they made it into the mountains, then it's probably too late. If that guy convinces Landon to go snowmobiling off the marked trails, then today or tomorrow will probably be when he tries to kill Landon."

"Then what do we do right now?" asked Jack.

"We?" asked both Gunner and me in unison.

I held up my hand, and Gunner let me talk, "You're not coming. You have a terrific college career ahead of you. You're still growing, and that means you have a shot at playing on Sundays. You even have a shot as a pro golfer. The chance of injury or worse is just too great. We can't let you risk it. You're going to have to sit this one out."

I spoke so Gunner didn't have to say those words. Coming from me, Jack would just get mad. Coming from Gunner, Jack would get his feelings hurt. It's just the way it is.

Jack was furious. "Who do you think you are, Dean? You sure aren't my father, and you sure aren't my boss. Where was I when Landon got rescued the first time? I was there, right by you. Where was I when we roped Aylmer? Remember? Where was I when we both charged into another dimension to rescue Kaiyo from the Sobeks? Again, I was right next to you. Weren't we on the same football team? Also, I'm as close a friend to Landon as you are."

Jack was mad, and he wasn't done with me. "Dean, at some point in your short life you have to quit thinking of me as your sidekick. Hell, I'm even older than you. You're probably the bravest kid on the planet, but you're wrong on this one. I am coming, and I really don't want to listen to any more of your garbage about football or sports. If I get hurt or even killed helping Landon, then so be it. Football and golf are games, finding Landon is life and death. I will not be a coward."

Gunner looked to me and then to Jack. "Well, said, Jack. I love a good argument, and that was a good one. Again, I'm proud to be your dad. You're in."

Jack looked triumphant. I was impressed too. "I agree. Except you still have to be my sidekick."

Jack gave me a quick "Never!" Then he asked again, "What do we do? Right now, what do we do?"

"Hopefully," said Gunner, "Landon told Libby where he was going, and if he didn't, maybe he sent the assassin an itinerary, either by e-mail or by letter. A copy of e-mails and correspondence ought to be in their saved documents or archived on a hard drive at their office. Let's figure out who this guy is while we're at it."

I called Dad. He picked up. "What do you need, Dean?"

Dad could get curt whenever his brain was working too fast. I knew he had a lot on his mind, so I just handed the phone to Gunner. Dad may be Gunner's boss, but those two are like brothers, and they respect each other a ton. At this point, Gunner would be better at talking to Dad than me. Dad probably doesn't trust my judgment when it comes to things like this. First, I'm only seventeen. Second, Dad thinks I take unnecessary risks. That's kinda true, and my little stunt with the cow moose didn't build up any credibility. I push myself hard, but I would be dead by now if I was as reckless as Dad feared.

While Dad and Gunner were speaking, Jack and I ran upstairs to Libby's room. Libby was talking to Mom. She was leaning back against Kaiyo who appeared sound asleep. She was staring into her laptop and was trying to access the company system. For whatever reason, Libby couldn't connect. This whole story was getting bad. And we had no idea who the bad guys were.

We went back downstairs. Gunner was off the phone.

"Troy contacted the Gallatin County and Park County Sheriffs to be on the lookout for Landon. They're also going to check to make sure the company's office is secure."

Just then there was a kick at the back door. I knew that kick. It was Aylmer. From time to time he gets lonely, and he wants us to come out just to be with him. He's used to getting his way. But today Aylmer didn't look lonely. He bit onto the sleeve of my shirt and pulled. In his direct, bovine way, Aylmer made it clear he needed us.

Aylmer was a high-energy, no-nonsense type of bull. Though he was much bigger, he looked and acted like the type of bull bred for Spanish bull fights. He was mostly black with a thick coat and a shock of hair that grew between his horns. He was pure muscle. When he wanted to make a point, which was rare, he was forceful. Today he was forceful. He stepped into the doorway to demand my attention. He already had my attention, and he wasn't playing around.

Jack and I threw on our coats and gloves, and we followed Aylmer to the machine shed. The machine shed is a large heated metal barn behind and to the north of our main barn. Dad had it built a year ago because we had farm equipment spread around in sheds, barns and under tarps. It wasn't a good way to work or treat our stuff. Behind the barn was the path to the shed; we kept it nicely plowed. If it moved, plowed, planted, or harvested and lived on gasoline, then it was kept there.

We followed Aylmer into the shed. He led us directly to our snowmobiles. Some people called them skis, some called them sleds. We called them sleds. We used these a lot in wintertime, and they were stashed up front. Once there, he pushed us in their direction. We figured out he wanted us on them. That was enough for me and Jack.

I got on mine, and Jack borrowed Libby's snowmobile. They were both good vehicles. We rode around the barn to the courtyard, got off, and ran inside. We had no idea what Aylmer had in mind, but we knew it mattered. Once upstairs, I gave Jack one of my bibs and a coat while we talked in low tones.

From behind us, we heard, "What are you doing with my sled?"

Libby stood there. It was obvious she had been crying. Her eyes were red, but she was still made of iron.

"I can explain," said Jack. "Aylmer wants us to go somewhere. He took us directly to the snowmobiles in the machine shed. And he was certain about it. So we are going to leave. I think it has something to do with Landon and Kaiyo."

Libby looked at us for a few moments stone-faced. "Fine. Aylmer doesn't play around. Be careful. I'll tell Mom not to worry."

Jack explained that nicely. We both armed ourselves downstairs. I would normally take my 12-gauge shotgun, but today I took my AR-15. Bears were hibernating, so I was willing to exchange the throw-weight of 12-gauge slugs for the distance and quick firing of an AR. I was afraid of snipers. Bears, moose, and elk were the least of my concerns. Jack borrowed my shotgun. We both took extra ammunition.

As we got to the kitchen, we explained to Gunner what little we knew about what we were doing. "At least you're doing something. Hurry back. Remember the storm's coming."

Just before I got to the door, we heard Kaiyo charging down the back steps. Kaiyo has a strange huffing sound that is like part of his breathing. Other bears do it too. "Uh, Kaiyo, you're not going," I said. "Dr. Cindy told you to stay put and take it easy. We'll be back soon enough."

Every once in a while, Kaiyo shows that he is a bear. Bears are incredibly strong, and sometimes they eat people. I think Kaiyo was close to being furious with me. A furious bear, even a bear who is my brother, is a dangerous thing to have around. From deep in his gut I heard him growl. I knew he was about to blow a gasket, so I needed to give him an out. He was stressing out, and that wasn't good. "But hey, it's up to you. Aylmer wants us to go somewhere on our snowmobiles. You know your paws. But please run it by Aylmer first because I have no idea where we are going."

Kaiyo seemed to calm down, if only a little. I opened the back door, and he went straight to Aylmer and started in on him. Aylmer is fearless and huge, but it wasn't but a minute or two when I noticed Aylmer backing up as Kaiyo faced him down, talking in bear language the entire time. Aylmer finally gave a cow laugh and said a few things I didn't understand. Whatever it was, Kaiyo got his way. Kaiyo turned and walked to the sleds. Jack said something about snowshoes and retrieved two pairs from the barn. In minutes, the four of us headed north. None of us felt that time was on our side.

6

Issues—Landon

Not too long after Libby left and after I got the gear stowed, MacDonald motioned me to come over to his car. I had given him three choices to pick where to go snowmobiling and camping. I offered a beautiful area not far from the town of Lolo, a series of wonderful sites in Paradise Valley or the Boulder River Valley. Of the three, Paradise Valley was my favorite. The trails were great, I had permission to hunt and camp on several pristine tracts of private property, and the valley was nice and wide. Also, it was close to Bozeman and to Libby's farm where I was headed after this job. As for the area near Lolo, it's beautiful, but it's far. It would take us about four hours to get to Lolo's camping areas.

The Boulder River Valley is only a little farther east than Paradise Valley, but it's not where I wanted to go. The valley is not nearly as wide as Paradise Valley, and there's not as much private property there. There were four church camps along the river, but they were closed. The valley ran mostly north south through some of Park County but mostly through Sweet Grass County, and it went deep into the Absaroka-Beartooth mountains. Also, because it was surrounded by designated wilderness areas, I had to be extra careful not to go into areas where snowmobiling is illegal.

I jogged to his truck and waited for him to roll down his window. From the time I met him, MacDonald carried himself with an annoying swagger. He smiled too often, and his disrespect for me and everybody else was always just under the surface. The only time I saw his facade falter was when he learned Libby was a McLeod. That interested him, and it bothered me.

I stood out in the cold while MacDonald responded to a few texts. I turned to go away when I heard the window roll down. "I think I am interested in the Boulder River area you gave as a good choice."

Of course, the least preferable of the three. "Are you just interested, or is that where you want to go?"

MacDonald looked up from his phone and smiled. "It's where I want to go. It's wild country, right? Not a bunch of people, right? I told you awhile back I don't like crowds, remember?"

I did. "Then Boulder River Valley it is. Follow me. The road is plowed up to a point. We'll get there and maybe have time to hit a few trails before the storm hits."

I wasn't totally disappointed with the destination MacDonald picked. It wouldn't be as social as Paradise Valley or Lolo, but at least it wasn't too far away. In Montana, nobody needs to drive far to find beauty, and winter made everything even prettier. I laughed at the thought of MacDonald being a fun client. Creepy? Yes. Fun? No.

But he was obviously wealthy, and whether I liked him or not, he was a customer, and I treated my customers well. I also knew many people who lived and worked in Boulder Valley. With only a few exceptions, they're some of the best folks in Montana.

I turned my truck and trailer and pulled up to the exit of our office park. I noticed two pickup trucks with out-of-state plates turn by me and then park near my office. The trucks caught my attention because they drove too fast, and our shared parking lot was mostly empty. MacDonald honked and was riding my bumper, so I forgot about the trucks and pulled out onto Airway Boulevard.

From there we headed to I-90. We were driving to the little town of Big Timber, and that was only an hour away.

MacDonald rode my bumper the entire way. It fully annoyed me, but it was in keeping with his bully-boy persona. It also put me in a bad mood. We stopped briefly to get some coffee on McLeod Street in the middle of Big Timber. Years ago, when I first met Libby, I wondered if she was related to the McLeod family who settled this part of Montana. It made sense; the name was not common. The settlers came from Oregon in the nineteenth century with a small herd of cattle. They moved into the valley and set up a ranch. MacDonald and I would soon be passing by the McLeod Post Office farther south into the valley. I remember being surprised Libby was not related to the settler. It was just coincidence.

I went into the café and ordered two coffees and two orders of bacon for Ilya. That creepy dog should appreciate me for it, but I doubted he would. I paid for the order, took the coffees, and the bag of bacon and walked out of the restaurant to MacDonald's truck. Gunther rolled down his window as I handed him his coffee.

"This is for Ilya," I said as I gave him the bag.

The dog's tail actually wagged for a moment. Everybody likes bacon.

"Mr. MacDonald, the next road is no interstate. It's a two-lane. Most of it will be snow-covered, and there will be wildlife. So keep your distance, and quit riding my bumper. I'll be braking a lot."

MacDonald rolled his toothpick in his mouth as he looked me over. He smiled slightly. "Sure, kid. Whatever. I just don't want to waste any more time. I paid a lot of money for a nice trip, and I'm eager to get started doing what I want to do. I'll be a good little driver."

Ilya's tail wagged again. Apparently, the dog liked condescending sarcasm. MacDonald smiled, but he looked me in the eye the whole time. That would be another intimidation tactic. This guy was really getting annoying. I stared back and leaned into his open window.

"Gunther? May I call you Gunther? Well, Gunther, I think we're getting off to a great start! I'm sure you do too. So listen up." I smiled, but MacDonald's smile disappeared. I continued. "The highway will start winding its way through some mighty rough country. Parts of the road may not be plowed. Like I said, don't get too close. But if you keep riding my butt, you're going to get both of us in trouble. So try to drive like a grown-up. If you can't stay on the road, I'll come back and get you. Once we get on 298, make sure your all-wheel drive or four-wheel drive is engaged. And once we slip into the valley, your cell phone coverage will be spotty, and after a few miles, there will be no coverage at all. Make your calls now. We will set up at one of the campgrounds or one of several summer camps. I like the summer camps most because they're empty. I have permission to set up on all of them. And we have another hour or so of driving. If you need me, just pull over. I'll come back to you."

Smiling, I turned quickly and walked back to my truck. My coffee was getting cold, and I was starting to believe Libby was right.

From behind me I heard, "You think we'll get to some back-country snowmobiling today? I told you that's what I wanted to do."

I turned, looked back at Gunther, and then slowly sipped my coffee. His impatience was suspicious.

"Well?" barked MacDonald.

After a few moments I said, "No way. Today we stick to the road and the marked trails. I don't even know if you can ride a bicycle, much less operate one of my powerful sleds. You're pretty big, and I don't much feel like dragging your carcass out of the wilderness because I was stupid enough to take some novice where riding is dangerous even for the best riders."

MacDonald was furious, but I was serious.

"I guarantee you, boy, I'm a better rider than you'll ever be." For the first time, he lost his cool.

"Good," I said, "I like the attitude. And fortunately, today you will have a terrific opportunity to prove it. But you will only be on the trails that I say are safe. It's your job to convince me."

I smiled and walked back to my truck.

We got moving and turned south. Within a few miles we were driving along the floor of the valley as the roadbed gave way to hard snowpack. The Boulder River meandered through the valley, and we crossed bridges several times. Other than a needed roadside saloon, there wasn't much commercial development in the valley. The road hugged the steep slopes of some low mountains before the valley narrowed and the mountains rose up on both sides. The going was slow, and MacDonald was pushing me to move faster. He had a beautiful travel trailer, and he seemed not to care much about it. Potholes and slick spots did not seem to slow him down. My goal was to get to one of the summer camps south of the McLeod Post Office.

Several times we had to pull over to let snowmobilers pass, but after an hour and a half of hard driving, we pulled into CVP Christian Camp. It was closed for the winter. I had keys to the camp, including a key to one of their newer log cabins. The cabin was located close to the entrance, and that would be my home for the next week and a half. I directed MacDonald to back in and park close to the entrance.

I told MacDonald to take some time to secure his quarters and get dressed for riding. The weather reports said hard snows would start falling by mid to late afternoon and end sometime early the next morning. I would have to be watchful of that. Whiteouts are real, and they're dangerous.

After unpacking and then dressing and prepping for riding in the bitter cold, I met MacDonald outside, near my trailer. He was already trying to unload one of my sleds from my trailer. That wouldn't do.

"That's not your gear, Gunther. Act like the customer, and let me do the hard lifting."

I tried to be nice, but MacDonald pushed back. "You were taking too long. You must have been taking a nap in there. Anyway, we're burning daylight and decent weather, and so far, I've gotten nothing for my money."

I noticed Gunther had his rifle case with his gear. Pointing to the case, I said, "We won't be needing those today. We'll be on marked trails with other riders."

Gunther smiled again and said, "I never leave home without it. And I'm the customer, right?"

He enjoyed intimidating people just by being big and pushy. "Well, yes you are. Bring it if it makes you feel safer. I don't think you need one, but I don't want you to feel insecure."

Gunther went from triumphant to seething after our little discourse. I was getting tired of him. I was certain he thought little of me. That was fine. Most bullies I have known usually had to learn about me the hard way. Discernment and wisdom were not their strong suits. I knew that before this winter excursion was over, he would know who I am.

I am part Cherokee. I was born in the reservation hospital in Cherokee, North Carolina. I have the blood of ten thousand Cherokee chieftains and warriors in me, and I am more at home in the wilderness than many of the beasts who live there. I have tracked down every animal in the forest, and most never knew they had been followed. I have climbed the tallest trees and mountains and have survived blizzards. As for MacDonald, I will let him try to prove he is the better man. Perhaps he is. But if he wishes to intimidate me, then he will be going home with nothing but disappointment. His fee though, will stay with me.

HASTE—KAIYO

I was being grouchier than normal, and Aylmer let me know it. In my defense, I got shot yesterday. But I know Dean was only looking after my best interests, and I probably shouldn't have been so crabby. Dad would be furious to even know I was going back outside. A brown bear in the snow stands out, and if there was a shooter, he could easily spot me. Since it looks like the sniper who shot me was after Landon, I was feeling less concerned. But we knew whatever was going on involved at least two people or more. That meant there would probably be more shooters. But I desperately needed to be a part of this, and we didn't have much time.

Somehow, Aylmer had arranged for a door to be opened only a few miles to the north of the farm. Where the doors appear has never made any sense to me. Sometimes a door will open around here, sometimes in China. I even got dropped off in Wyoming once. Well, to be honest, that was my fault. It's up to us to make sure the door opens where we need to be going. We never have to get out if we don't want to. Meginnah, the cherub, once told me it was none of my business where doors appear. Then he laughed. I might be a bear, but Meginnah is more than scary. I wouldn't think of giving him any trash talk. While he laughs a lot, I'm not sure he has that kind of sense of humor.

What we were doing was dangerous, and it could get Jack and Dean killed. Aylmer and I could even get banished. My plan was to go in first and ask for permission to bring them through the door. Whether anybody has ever tried to bring humans into the door's pathway is not known to me. But it's been a long time since creation, so I was certain it had been tried before. As a warning, there are skeletons of a few humans and a variety of other creatures scattered about around the entrance to Eden, but the pathway is at least a mile long. So far, it looked to me like nobody got killed until they got too close to Eden. That probably wasn't enough to give me much hope, but it did.

It wasn't long before we were off the farm and into the Eastern Wilderness and headed north. Jack and Dean were making good time, and so was Aylmer. I was lagging. It was not my paws; they were okay. Instead, my shoulders hurt like fire, and I was worn out. Aylmer ignored me and led the group up a long slope and toward thick timber. Right at the edge of the timber, the terrain started to get rough, and I was having more trouble keeping up. Fortunately, the snowmobiles couldn't keep going in the forest. Halleluiah. I caught up to the three and waited while the boys put on their snowshoes. From now on the going would be super slow. People on snowshoes are slow.

Aylmer looked at me, "I'm glad you came, Kaiyo. Just so you know, I was going to make sure you did. I also know your wounds hurt and that you are exhausted. And fortunately, the door is nearby. I admire your perseverance, old friend. We are almost home. And, Kaiyo, you do know you must obey Meginnah, yes?"

"Of course," I replied. I smiled and thought Aylmer was being sentimental. The part about Meginnah was right. Trying to get people into the door is certain to be an issue Meginnah would have something to say about.

While waiting, Dean and Jack were covering up their sleds with branches and snow. They were smart to do it too. The sleds were colorful, and their reds and royal blues can be seen by people easily. We bears can see those colorful things too. People think bears are color-blind, but we aren't. And we can see hunter orange. That especially helps us Eden bears a lot because seeing color is one thing, knowing what it means is more important.

Jack, Aylmer, and I treaded farther up slope into the timber until we were deep in the forest and fully concealed. Except for the crunching of snow beneath us, all was peaceful. The wind worked its way through the treetops while off in the distance a few crows called to one another. We were on alert, but I felt safe. All along I had been testing the winds and was sure there were no humans or anything else unusual upwind of us. Dean stayed back down the slope and hid behind a deadfall to watch our back trail. Dad, Tracker, and Goliath taught me how living in the wilderness often depended on checking back trails. It's easy to forget to do it, especially now that I weigh a thousand pounds. I have no predators after me. Until a week ago, when I saw the first poached bear, I thought I was safe from humans.

The three of us waited. Jack knelt and had his shotgun ready. Aylmer and I just stood there and enjoyed the wilderness in a way no man could. We were designed to thrive out here. Every sound, every scent was relished. Aylmer's ears were working the sounds of the forest while my nose was taking in the crisp, cold air. It was wonderful. I could tell Jack was cold and eager to move on. He had no idea where we were going or what we were doing. This was going to be interesting. Landon had told him about the path beyond the door and about Meginnah, but hearing about it and seeing it were not the same. He was in for a treat. Fortunately, in the land of the Sobeks, he had met Raphael and a few dozen talking animals, so he was mostly prepared.

After another twenty minutes, Dean was making it up the long slope to where we were relaxing. He was alert, and his eyes were scanning the slopes of the forest around us. Even though he was on snowshoes, he moved with ease as he glided through the trees like a cat. Jack might be the better athlete, but when it came to wilderness, nobody was better than Dean. Landon was close, but Dean, Benaiah, Tracker, and I were probably the only ones who knew that. Almost everybody else underestimated Landon because of his friendly personality. My hope was that his assassin underestimated him too. Everybody seemed to have forgotten how Landon followed Tacker for many miles and Tracker never knew it. That took amazing skill. As for Dean, he was not made to thrive in the wilderness or just endure it even though he could do those things. He was made to wage war in the wilderness—and win. And I needed him now.

Jack turned to look at us. In a whisper, Jack asked, "How much farther, Aylmer? Are we close?"

Even though we were hidden in the forest, voices and sounds can travel long distances, especially over the snowpack. But today we had a breeze and steady snow flurries, so we had little to worry about, but it was good to see Jack being cautious. He has learned much. Aylmer didn't answer, but he nodded. That's about all he could do. It seemed to satisfy Jack.

It wasn't long before Dean made it to us. Quietly Dean came into our group. "How you doing, little brother? Are you okay? The fact you're out here and that you are running a few quarts low on blood must be tough. I can see it in you. Plus, everything has to hurt too. I'm sorry this happened to you, Kaiyo." Dean then looked at Jack and Aylmer and said, "Where are we going anyway."

Aylmer laughed his bovine laugh, and he cut back to the west along the side of the wooded slope. That was Aylmer's way of saying, "Follow me."

For the next ten minutes, we held to a tight trail going across the mountainside, one behind the other. Aylmer led, Dean followed, and Jack followed Dean. I followed everybody. Soon, a tall cliff came into view along the trail. The trail seemed to be carved into the cliff itself. Then I saw it. A few steps later, Dean did too.

"Whoa—" whispered Dean as he stopped in the trail.

Jack didn't see anything. "What? What do you see?" asked Jack.

"Look straight ahead. There's a door."

Aylmer kept plodding ahead.

"Yeah, I see it now," said Jack. "It looks a lot like the one we rode through to rescue Kaiyo from the Sobeks. Let's follow Aylmer."

And we did. Aylmer stopped, looked back, at us briefly then he marched through the door. He was there and then he wasn't. Dean followed, then Jack, and then me.

Just as I saw the amazing colors of my Eden home radiate from the pass between the low hills, I heard Meginnah bellow in his four voices, "Who has chosen to face the will of God?"

I was hoping for something else as an introduction. Dean and Jack were probably going to be killed for being here, but at least I could talk in here.

"Turn back!" I yelled at Dean and Jack. "Now!"

Running, I passed our group and ran the mile to where Meginnah stood guard at the entrance to home. Whatever plans I had in mind to explain everything to Meginnah melted away, and I was terrified. I closed the distance quickly and stopped ten yards from the cherub. Meginnah and the other cherubim are winged animals that guard Eden from all outsiders. They tower above me, and they look like nothing else. Their bodies are huge, and they have the faces of a lion, an ox, an eagle, and a man, and somehow all seemed to be watching me approach. And the cherubs are not angels. They are, among other amazing things, efficient killers of trespassers.

I passed the old skeletons of long-ago trespassers and skidded to a stop. I was winded and breathing heavily. I glanced into Eden and looked briefly into the vast, colorful countryside. I wished I was in there. I also spotted many friends waiting near the gates. That was interesting, but I couldn't finish the thought. I looked up at Meginnah as his eyes stared down at me. He looked ferocious.

"Please let me explain—" was all I could croak out.

Meginnah paused and then spoke, "Are you going to introduce me to your brother and your friend?"

I almost threw up right then and there. With good reason, I was terrified, but somehow everything was okay. I feared that

Aylmer and I had led Dean and Jack to their deaths by bringing them here. "I thought you were going to kill them and then kill me for bringing them," I said as I choked on my words.

Meginnah's faces looked amused. "I would rather kill myself than kill a noble and great bear like you, Kaiyo. The Master loves you dearly, and therefore, so do I. You are also one of my favorites among many favorites. You do know that, yes?"

Well, actually, no, I didn't. But I smiled and thanked him.

He laughed at that and continued, "And you did not really bring them here. Aylmer was told to bring them into the path. Tell them I am coming to speak to them, and tell young Jack to fear me not. He has the heart of a fighter, but I see him clutching his weapon, and his eyes betray some fear. Also, tell your delightfully foolhardy brother to come no further than halfway. Prudence does not guide him as it does for Jack. In fact, it is your brother who should fear me because his life is in peril at this very moment. This you must know, the grace that saved Landon when he peered into Eden is not extended to your brother. Landon knew no better. If Dean comes close, I will surely slay him. So hurry and do as I have told you. Dean is already arguing with Aylmer and Jack about coming here. I have many ears, I know what is being said. His time is short if you do not stop him. Tell him I will be there momentarily."

I thanked him, turned, and ran back. Dean was already on the trail, but he stopped and waited for me. It took a few minutes, and my breathing was labored.

"So where do you think you're going?" I asked.

I loved being able to talk to my brother. "Well," he said, "I want to go see Eden and meet your amazing friend. What kind of thing is it?"

"Wrong question," I said to Dean. "But you asked. Meginnah is a cherub, and he's the guard today. There are others. He already told me he will kill you if you came more than halfway. There's enough skeletons near the entrance to convince me he's serious."

Dean's eyes got big. "Skeletons? I want to see some skeletons. Where are they?"

I was tired and wounded and frustrated with Dean again, and my voice showed it. "Don't be a problem, Dean. For once, count your blessings and realize I know what I'm doing here and that you don't. Can you just do that?"

Dean got silent. "Of course, Kaiyo. I do not want to be the fool. And I think we are here because of you and Landon, right?"

"Right," I said. "And Meginnah just told me somebody contacted Aylmer to bring us here. I don't quite know why Aylmer didn't tell me that, but he didn't. Anyway, Meginnah is coming to speak to us shortly, but he didn't tell me anything else. In the meantime, now that you can understand me, I'll tell you more about me getting shot."

Disappeared—Sam

I had made it home but was still in my truck when Troy called with news. Sheriff Tuttle asked the Belgrade police chief to send a cruiser to do a quick security check of Haldor Valley Outfitters. The first thing we wanted was make sure Landon was not dead in the office. The second thing was just to make sure the place was locked up. Once the Belgrade Police got there, they knew Landon wasn't there because the front door was wide open. When they went inside, the place was a mess. The two company laptops were destroyed, and their hard drives were missing. Drawers were rifled through, the current calendar was gone, and files were torn and tossed on the floor. But Landon was gone, and based on the look of the place, the police said they were glad he wasn't there.

Whoever had trashed the place knew what they were doing. Any recent records that could shed light on Gunther MacDonald were missing or destroyed. Whatever was done was done quickly, and so far, there were apparently no witnesses. The police did locate some surveillance cameras on nearby businesses that might be helpful. On top of that, it was clear Glennon Wraight had more soldiers than we thought.

Almost immediately after the Belgrade police found the office vandalized, they put out a missing person's report on Landon. The sheriffs of Missoula, Gallatin, Park, Sweet Grass, and Stillwater counties were all given personal calls by Sheriff Tuttle. It was obvious Landon was tricked into taking his potential assassin deep into the wilderness where there would be no witnesses, no cameras, and more than enough predators to dispose of his remains. Libby had known he was either headed to Lolo in the north, to nearby Paradise Valley, or to the Boulder River Valley. Those were the three places where he took many of his winter clients. Plus, Landon told Libby that MacDonald had decided to go to Lolo.

Susan, Gracie, and Libby were in the kitchen with Gunner when I walked in. I gave them the news. Poor Libby had been given a steady drip of terrible news today. I expected this to be the knockout blow, but it wasn't. Libby stood there and listened. Susan held her tongue, and Gunner looked at his shoes. Gracie watched everybody. Libby's back got stiff.

"Dad, I know where they are."

Gunner stood straight up, and Susan looked at me. Gracie watched everybody. Libby was clearly thinking this out.

"Think about it. MacDonald would want to get Landon out of touch and away from the world as soon as possible. He obviously knew you would be confronted by Wraight around noon. MacDonald said he wanted to go to Lolo but he also wanted to keep the other two options open. If they were going to Lolo, then Landon would have answered his cell phone because it's at least a three-hour drive up Interstate 90 and probably longer with this weather. Cell coverage on I-90 is mostly good. Paradise Valley is the same. It's really close to the office, and there's cell coverage here and there in the valley. And there's a lot more people there too. That leaves the Boulder River Valley. Most of the cabins in the valley are vacation cabins, and there really aren't many of those.

The valley is remote, and the minute Landon left Big Timber his cell coverage would get spotty at best. By lunchtime today, he would have been deep into the Absarokas and unreachable. I think he's there, Dad. I would bet everything on it."

Sweet Grass County has a small population and only a handful of deputies patrolling almost two thousand square miles. But with one primary road leading into the river valley, finding Landon or his truck shouldn't be hard. With the weather turning messy, that might be easier said than done. It was then I looked around and noticed something.

"Where's everybody else?"

"They're gone!" said Gracie. "They left about an hour ago. Aylmer took them away. Kaiyo went with them. But don't worry. They took guns."

Well, that didn't make me feel any better at all. Though I trusted both Jack and Dean, there was danger out there. I was also stunned they left. I started to get angry, and I looked at Gunner.

"Did you know about this?'

"I did," he replied, "but let me explain."

Gunner was calm, but I was getting angry. And he was using my own method of explaining my answers. I said that all the time to put people at ease. Gunner then proceeded to tell me how "Aylmer nearly kicked in the kitchen door and then he led the boys to their snowmobiles. Then Kaiyo figured out they were leaving without him, and he nearly mauled Dean because Dean tried to stop him."

Gunner tended to exaggerate but not on the core issues. The story actually made sense. Aylmer and Kaiyo took the boys someplace, and if they had to take them there, it wasn't in Montana. They were probably going to a place where they could talk to each other. Unfortunately, based on Landon's experience there, that place wasn't entirely safe either.

I was lost in thought when Libby cleared her throat. "Dad," she said calmly, "let's go get him."

Libby was right. Everybody, even Gracie, was nodding.

I looked at Gunner. "We need a plan."

KATE—SUSAN

Just then Aliyah and Kate drove into the courtyard a little too fast. Kate was driving, and she skidded to a stop. Through the window I saw Aliyah scold Kate, but Kate kept smiling. Over the past few years, Kate had trained herself into a superb equestrian, and apparently now she was a talented driver. The driveway was covered in packed snow and had parked trucks here and there, and she never lost control. Impressive.

I watched as the two of them hopped out. Immediately greeted by Moose and Major, they hurried through the brutal cold and into the kitchen. Aliyah went directly to Libby and hugged her. I think Libby didn't have a tear left in her, but apparently, she did.

Kate scanned the room. "Where's Dean?"

I think Kate loved my son, and I think she knew Dean was struggling. She also didn't trust his judgment. Dean and Sam were so alike it scared me. Sam has made some big-time blunders in his life and, he seems to get himself hurt a lot. His body is covered in scars, and he has some emotional scars too. Dean is bigger, faster, and stronger than Sam ever was, but both tend to charge into fights before thinking things through. Dean thinks nothing of walking off into the wilderness alone or of rescuing some person or animal. Boredom, or the possibility of it, scares him, and not much else does.

Except maybe Kate. Kate scares him. Dean once told me he feared falling too deeply in love with her. "Beautiful girls," he explained, "especially the smart ones, never stick with their high school honeys. And, Mom, that's all I am right now."

I tried to tell him how Kate was different, but he had a point. Most high school romances never survive graduation. It also explained some of his restlessness. He didn't want to fall for Kate, but he had. Add the strong lure Dean felt for something still unknown, and that created a young man filled with raging angst.

As for Kate's question, Gracie answered it. That caused Aliyah to raise an eyebrow, but she knew Jack had seen amazing things and had even battled vicious reptilians in another world. The fact he might be headed to Eden for whatever seemed to be acceptable to Aliyah. I loved her for it.

After a few minutes of discussion, Sam asked Gunner his thoughts. Gunner is a former Air Force Special Tactics officer, and those guys consider themselves on the same level as Navy SEALs. I don't know much about that, but Gunner is a tough man. In regular society, Gunner is friendly and self-effacing, and he acts like he's harmless. He's nothing at all like that though. He's serious, smart, and very capable. He's also a trained sniper with kills he won't talk about. He might as well be Sam's brother too. They're that close. When Officer Brigham joins them, it's the three amigos, and they practically read each other's thoughts. As for Aliyah, she is my best friend and like a sister. Whatever was next, we would all face it together.

Gunner's plan was uncomplicated and left us with little comfort. We would arm up, load our snowmobiles onto trailers, prepare for the worst, and head into the Boulder River valley. There was no way to sneak in, and only one road was passable. Anybody could see us coming. Any element of surprise would be lost if MacDonald had any associates keeping watch. Fortunately, we knew folks who had property there, so if the weather became an issue, we could stay in several cabins located up and down the river. Otherwise, our plan was to charge in and rescue Landon. Speed was critical, and we had no choice. Moreover, there was only one real way in. Stealth wasn't available.

Lowe called Sam, then Gunner was added into the call. The three of them discussed the Boulder River Valley as being the likely spot for Landon to be. When Lowe left today, all we knew was somebody tried to murder Kaiyo. The threat to kill Landon was new to him, and so was the fact that we, all of us, were on the list. Lowe was shocked. Lowe is a solid lawman, and he's analytical, professional, and courteous. But he has a streak of savage in him that comes out from time to time. I heard it.

"Then, folks, this is going to be vicious. There will be no moral impediments to their behavior. These people, whoever they are, will be nothing more than bloodthirsty monsters prowling in the forest. They have a mission, and I bet failure is not acceptable to their boss. We must be careful. So what's your plan?"

Gunner explained the plan, but Lowe didn't like it. "Well, that won't work. Your cars all have tags that show you live here in Madison County. That will be spotted by the bad guys pretty quick. Load up your stuff now and meet me in Bozeman. You're going to have to rent a big SUV with a different tag. And I bet the killers know your vehicles anyway. That goes for the Gibbses' cars too. Let's try to look like three recreational snowmobilers. The Sweet Grass County Recreation Association helps maintain the trails in the valley, and at times, there are a ton of snowmobilers there. We'll act like them. I'll get my own sled and meet you in Bozeman. And, guys, time is short."

Lowe hung up and Sam started to move. "The three of you?" I asked. I was mad. Again. "Sorry, guys, but this is a family affair. I'm going with you."

"So am I," said Aliyah.

"And I am most certainly going," said Libby. "This is not how we do things. We have always done these things together. And besides, except for maybe Gunner, I'm the best shot of the group, and you need another shooter. And let's not forget, Landon is my fiancé, and we're getting married next year. So yes, I'm going."

Then from behind us came wisdom from an unexpected source. "Sorry, ladies, you aren't going."

It was Kate. There were quick objections, but Kate kept going, "First, you aren't ready, but Dad and Mr. Sam are. There is no time to waste. Landon is not just in danger later, he's in danger right now. Second, you only have two snowmobiles left here. We have two at our house, but that's just more time wasted. The men have their go-bags and can be gone in less than five minutes. Can you beat that?"

I like to pride myself on raising strong children, but Aliyah might get an award for raising Kate as a strong, assertive young lady. The problem was, I didn't like what she said. The other problem was, Kate was right.

Libby was about to jump into an argument when Kate turned to Libby and told her to saddle up. Libby was stopped with that comment.

"Mom, Miss Susan, I don't know what you two are going to do, but Libby and I are going to Eden. Invited or not, that's where we're going, and we're going to do it as soon as we can get ready. Libby, I'll need a rifle, preferably your 243. I'm about as good with mine as you are with your 270. Seriously, I'm a better shot than Jack and better than most men. Dean and Dad trained me well. Once we get there, we are going to try to use the portal to get over to the Boulder River Valley where Landon probably is. If it works, then we'll be the only ones with the element of surprise."

Kate then quit talking. I was not happy with that plan. Gunner looked up, smiled, and said, "Now that's a plan!"

"Dang good plan!" said Libby.

They moved fast. They kissed their fathers' cheeks and then hugged the other. "See you there," said a serious Libby.

She and Kate turned and ran upstairs for more gear.

Aliyah looked at me. "What just happened?"

I had no idea.

"Aliyah," said Gunner sweetly, "you three need to stay here and stay together wherever you go. Tonight, don't go home. Stay together here. Call a neighbor to feed our animals tonight and maybe tomorrow. Sam and I will need a home base for communications. Keep your phones on and fully charged and arm yourselves. We Gibbs are probably on the list too. We will call from the road."

Sam hugged Gracie and then me. He told me everything would be okay. I knew better. Nothing about this was okay. He grabbed his gear, his 45, his AR-15 rifle, a lot of extra ammo, and then he and Gunner walked into the snow flurries outside. Aliyah and I had totally lost control. We were shelved, and it hurt. Worst of all, our roles made sense. Still, something told me no; something screamed at me that we weren't safe.

Sam loaded up the snowmobiles onto the trailer, and minutes later, he and Gunner were driving down the driveway. I watched from the front windows as Sam's truck disappeared into the blowing snow by the far western forest.

Then Lowe called again. The sound of it startled us. He was stressed.

"Susan, I can't reach Sam, but you need to know this. I called my counterpart who oversees the Absaroka and Beartooth Wilderness areas where Landon probably is. I was going to ask him to go look for Landon. He told me that every law enforcement officer in Sweet Grass County has been called to a developing disturbance in Harlowton. Two churches have been fire-bombed, and strangely enough, so was a liquor store and a bar. Molotov cocktails. So far nobody has been hurt, but somebody posted some sort of brief manifesto on the town's social media page. The manifesto threatened similar targets today and tomorrow in Bozeman, Billings, Livingston, and Virginia City. With this development, there's no way we can get law enforcement personnel down into the valley. In fact, I've been ordered to Virginia City to add to existing law enforcement assets there. It looks like we have more than a few angry, crazy people in Montana."

Harlowton is in Wheatland County and about forty-five miles due north of Big Timber. It's a nice little town, and we know some ranchers in nearby Two Dot and Melville. But the whole fire-bombing thing seemed strange. I'm all about bringing the Baptists and the bar-hoppers together for a mutual cause, but by bombing those types of buildings, it also maximized the number of terrorized people. Around here, folks go to their favorite church or their favorite bar, and a lot of them go to both, at least from time to time. That would be true of Sam and me.

Also, Molotov cocktails take no competence to make or use. "Lowe, the whole thing seems like a bunch of malarkey. Do you notice how the only cops interested in Landon's case are now either being redirected or are staying put? I'm just betting that until this whole thing blows over, we aren't getting any help for you folks. It also means Troy has been told to report to Virginia City. Does that sound like a fair analysis?"

Lowe was quiet for a few moments. "Stahr is definitely stuck here, but I'll ask Tuttle to call my chief to release me from the order. You may be right. In fact, the whole thing is perfectly timed against getting help to Landon. They already have the weather on their side. This will guarantee no cops. At least for another day or two."

I said goodbye to Lowe and told Aliyah what was happening. She chewed on a piece of celery. "That means," she said, "we won't get any patrols way out here either. We need to be ready for something too."

Before I could think about that, the girls came downstairs. The looked grim and were loaded for bear. But for the first time today, Libby didn't look helpless. And I preferred Libby heading out to find Eden than going straight to the Boulder River Valley where the danger was extreme. I also doubted she could find Eden; the doors never stay open very long. I suspected they would return after a few hours in the snow.

Hours later, it became clear to me and Aliyah that our girls were not coming home.

8

DIMENSIONS—LIBBY

I had to hand it to Kate. I always assumed she mostly lived in Dean's shadow. While I had been off to college and paying attention to my studies, to the outfitting business and to Landon, and not in that order, Kate had grown in several ways. When I left for college, she was a sweet, shy fourteen-year-old. The almost-seventeen-year-old Kate was still sweet, but she was strong, and I saw no hint of her former shyness. If I ever wondered if Dean truly loved Kate, it disappeared when I watched her talk to us. While Kate was beautiful and intelligent, I knew Dean wanted a different kind of girl, and I wondered how Kate could ever be that girl. I remember Dean once telling me how he wanted a girl who didn't walk behind him or in front of him. Instead, he wanted a girl to ride the river with.

I understood what he meant, and after spending an hour with Kate tracking Aylmer and our brothers, I knew Dean had, indeed, found a girl to ride the river with. Kate was all business, and she rode like she and Dean's horse, Solo, were one. They both anticipated each other's moves, and she worked the trail even in areas where the wind had blown drifts over the tracks. The cold was brutal, but that was just Montana in December. While she might not have been born here, Kate had become a Montanan.

Despite the snow flurries, following the tracks was possible. The storm was coming later, so we were able to keep a good pace. Kate pulled up next to me. She was dressed warmly, and all I could see were her gray-blue eyes, but they were expressive. Raising her voice above the sound of the wind in the trees, she said, "Once we see the door, we have to ride in fast. Expect it to be guarded. If it's Benaiah guarding the door, he'll try to stop us. If it's another watcher or something else, we might get attacked. Once we see it, we must react. If you see it first, just spur Jet and I'll follow. If I see it first, then follow me. And keep your voice down. You okay with that?"

Who was this girl? I nodded, and we kept moving. The wind was blowing and was covering up our sounds. Any animal guarding the door would not hear us, but it probably could catch our scents. The flurries also made seeing us a bit harder. We kept going, slowly moving uphill toward the timber. We found the concealed snowmobiles and continued following the tracks. Following the group, we weaved in and out of the trees and then along the face of the slope. We both heard a slight static-like buzz. Just then, Kate stopped abruptly and raised her fist. I was riding behind her and pulled to a quick stop. I could tell she was looking at something uphill. She bent low and put both hands on the pommel. She slowly leaned from side to side as she kept low. Whatever she saw was hidden from me by the trees around us. She turned slowly and looked at me. Pointing to our left along the slope, she mouthed, "Polar bear." Well, that was bad news, but nothing surprised me anymore. Then she pointed up hill and mouthed the word, "Door."

I looked as best I could but still saw nothing. When I looked back, Kate whispered, "Now!"

Kate spurred Solo, and I spurred Jet. Solo was a mountain pony and quicker than Jet, so I knew Kate would get a good start. Jet reacted and followed Solo. Kate and I were riding hard and fast, but Kate started pulling away. Then I heard a roar. From behind me, I saw the polar bear. I knew he was on our team, but his eyes showed pure rage. Jet didn't need any encouraging because the polar bear was in full sprint. I then saw the door just as Kate ran through. I was right behind her. Immediately, the air was warm, and the forest was gone.

Kate and I didn't let up until we heard a chorus of voices, all yelling at us to stop. Kate pulled up and immediately turned Solo around. Dang, she was a good rider. I turned hard as well and was just in time to see the polar bear come flying through the door. He was still angry, and he kept running right for me. I jumped off Jet and walked toward the charging bear. That surprised him, but it didn't slow him down. Walking, I saw he was still furious. Unfortunately, his rage seemed to have drowned out the sound of voices as he looked fully predatorial.

Years before, Landon had told me that when he passed through the door, the animals weren't allowed to kill him. The polar bear was acting like he missed the memo. Accelerating, he charged. It happened so fast I braced myself as he leaped. Ducking as he flew over me, I heard Kate pull out her rifle. I could have sworn I heard it laugh.

I opened my eyes, and Kaiyo was between the polar bear and Kate. The polar bear was now on his enormous back, laughing uncontrollably. "Aren't you supposed to be guarding the door?" asked Kaiyo.

"Nope!" laughed the polar bear as he rolled onto his feet. "The door is gone."

I turned, and he was right, the door was gone. "Miss Libby and Miss Kate, that is who you are, right?"

Kate, still on Solo and now leading Jet, came over and said that he was right. I nodded as he continued though in a more serious tone.

"We were hoping you both would come. Never before has a door been left open for so long, but Raphael told me to wait until you showed yourselves. It is an honor to meet you both, but especially you, Libby McLeod. You are the one who saved Kaiyo, and you were the first to notice his difference. We bears, and all of the other animals, mourn the Divorce, and we long for the future return to our brotherhood with mankind. So when we see your pure joy because of Kaiyo and the sacrifices made by your family and your friends, especially the Gibbses, we here in this world rejoice as fully as we can."

"May I ask you your name?" said Kate.

"Forgive me, Miss Kate. My name is Gyp. And welcome. Do not leave this area, however, or Meginnah will kill you. Though I can assure you, he would not enjoy it."

Kate didn't look surprised. "Is he the cherub?"

"One of them," responded Gyp.

Kate kept on, "First, please just call me Kate. So how did Raphael know we would be coming? In all respect, I didn't know myself until a few hours ago."

Before Gyp could answer, Meginnah flew out of a hidden valley filled with colorful light and came toward us. He was enormous and the strangest, most-fearsome-looking thing I had ever seen. Gyp had to raise his voice to get us to quit staring. He led us to the others. I gave Dean and Aylmer a quick hug as we waited. Jack never took his eyes off Meginnah. Strangely, our horses were not afraid of Gyp or of Meginnah. I learned later Eden called to them as if it were a memory of a different and better home. Maybe that's why many of the farm animals accepted Kaiyo and the Specials so readily.

"Well, Libby," said Aylmer, "it is so good talking to you again. However, I look forward to the day when Gracie is old enough to travel with me here. She is so special."

I laughed. Gracie loved Aylmer and spent countless hours with him. I missed not having that relationship. But I was focused on Landon.

"Libby," he whispered, "we are facing fearsome forces. Time is short. But Landon is far more capable than any of you humans know. If anyone can evade the evil one's soldiers, he is the one."

"Yes," I whispered back, "I know him as my fiancé, and a clumsy one at that. But he did manage to follow Tracker."

"Precisely," said Aylmer.

Our group was huddled together though Dean and Kate stood to the front. Jack seemed to have relaxed after Kaiyo spoke to him. The animals stood behind us or to our sides but only because they were so much bigger. The cherub came our way and stood on the path. If it's possible to be honored, impressed, and terrified at the same time, well, we were. Landon had told me his experience with the cherubs, and cherubs are described in the Bible, but what we saw with our own eyes was stunning.

He looked at each of us with his eyes and faces. "Greetings. I am Meginnah, the Defender. I am one of the living creatures described in scripture. Among my roles, I guard Eden and the Tree of Life from both mankind and from Satan. Evil resides in the hearts of both. So I do not distinguish one from the other when they trespass."

I didn't know where he was headed, but I wasn't feeling too comfortable. His voice was everywhere, and he spoke with all four mouths. Fortunately, he kept on, "But know this. You are our guests, and your being here is no accident. I commend the four of you for your bravery in coming here. Because I know some of your past acts, I already knew three of you are bold as lions. That is a quality of the Master. As for you, young Kate Gibbs, I have heard of your grace and strength. We are proud of you."

Kate let out a little squeal as she squeezed Dean's arm. Meginnah smiled at Kate and then looked at us. "Raphael has allowed you here to make your plan. Landon is in great peril, and so are each of you. Your adversaries despise the Master and you and your entire families. They are quite dangerous. They lie and kill. I am told by our spies that Landon has entered the valley and has set up his camp. He is with a known killer. Also, more men have moved into the valley to keep Landon from leaving.

"If you can save him, you must plan well and then move with speed. I have given you Gyp as your helper. He is brave and strong, and he will disappear in the snow. Aylmer, I will want you to go back to your new home and guard them from the trouble likely to come. Kaiyo, you will be staying here until Raphael releases you."

Kaiyo started to sputter, but Meginnah's fierce look shut him up. Kate raised her hand, and Meginnah looked her way.

"Mr. Sam said one of the bad men told him it was human against human only. Are those the rules? How much help can we get from the Specials?"

Meginnah seethed. "They do not write the rules, they misuse them and misquote them. Their very language is to lie, and they serve only the father of lies, the one who has been a murderer from the beginning. They wish to kill Kaiyo and the rest of you. More than just humans will be involved in this war. If they choose to ignore your animal allies, then you will have an advantage. But expect them to use every asset available. This is war, and they are good at waging it. They intend to wipe out each of you. And I promise, each of you will be tested."

It was Dean's turn. Meginnah smiled when Dean spoke, "Is it possible for a dog to be against us? I don't know if it's possible, but from what Kaiyo and especially Libby said, Gunther MacDonald's dog is different. Have dogs from here ever gone bad?"

"Every kind who has ever resided in this wonderful country has some of their own that have forsaken the Master. And yes, even dogs. Why?"

I jumped in, "Meginnah, have you ever known or heard of a big dog named Ilya?"

I then described what I knew of the creepy mongrel. Meginnah listened intently and rubbed his faces. As bizarre a creature as he was, it was surprisingly easy to get used to him.

"I know this dog. He was once one of our best. Three years ago, he left and never came back. I have wondered if he was one of many who departed and was lost in the world. Earth is a dangerous place, as all of you know. As of now, I rather wish that he were dead. I had missed him. Now I do not."

Meginnah paused and looked at my little brother. "Kaiyo, your bear mother, Jana, knew this dog. When she was last seen, on this very path awaiting the door to open, Ilya was among the citizens who exited with her. She never came back. He did. He came and went several times later. We know you want answers. If he is allied with the evil one, then he may have a role in why she left us to live in your world."

"Then let me go with my friends!" pleaded Kaiyo. "I must— speak to that dog."

"Kaiyo, I do not think speaking with the dog is what you intend. But Raphael has spoken. You must stay. Do not second-guess the Master's wisdom. Raphael only does what is required and expected of him by the Master. Do you understand me?"

"Yes, Meginnah."

Then Meginnah looked at the rest of us. "The door will open briefly to the place where you left your machines. Bring them in here. You will need them. The assassins desire to kill you only because of us and your love for us. Unfortunately, we cannot offer much help from our citizens. Winter is hard on all animals, and dark coats and deep snow take away all advantages. Beyond me, in our world, your friends and others have gathered to pray. Some, like Dovie the black bear, are insisting they be allowed to go. Others are more willing to obey orders."

Meginnah smiled briefly, then he got serious again. "Nevertheless, in addition to Gyp, I will allow Tracker, Goliath, and Benaiah to join your band. This is your original team, yes? They are fearsome but please use their bravery wisely. Tracker's gray coat will hide him well. Goliath's blond fur will stand out less than Dovie's black fur, but keep in mind he can still be noticed. All other bears are hibernating. If he is seen, he will be shot. As for Benaiah, even with his dark fur, he is better than most at remaining unseen. They are coming now. Before you go, I am sure you have time for prayer, yes?"

We all agreed. We saw Tracker, Benaiah, and Goliath exit Eden and run our way; they were at our sides in seconds. After a few moments of truly joyful reunions, we settled in together to pray with each of us praying out loud. Meginnah closed out the prayers. He laid out the dangers we faced and the protections we would need. Finally, he begged for confusion among the enemy. I thought of my life and how I was honored to be in the presence of creatures like the Specials and especially Meginnah. But those thoughts were crowded out with my longing to see Landon and the stark fact the assassins intended to kill Landon first and then kill the rest of us.

With Kaiyo in my life, I have become accustomed to amazing and wonderful things. But I was troubled. I have not become accustomed to this well of pure hatred bubbling up within me. I was surprised at my own emotions. I was not out of control, but I could not make my hatreds go away. I don't think Dean hated our enemy. He seemed to view this endeavor as a deadly competition. Kate probably did too. Neither seemed afraid to die. But they weren't like me. I couldn't push down the bile of my hatred. I tasted it.

"Oh, Father," I prayed silently, "I know I am to love my enemies. Help me to understand, because those people, even if I could somehow find a way to love them, they are still my enemies. Loving them will not stop their attacks to kill me and all who I love. I only want to kill them before they can kill us first. They are strong, and they hate us. Father, how do you hate without sin? I want to love them but can't. I hate with blackness in my heart, but please remember, it is them, not us, who are the lovers of violence. Save them, Father, from our wrath by putting fear in their hearts and sending them back to their holes. If not, Lord, please forgive us for what we must do."

9

SPIRITS—TRACKER

To live with those humans who I consider family is my final goal in life. It is the hope of all of us here in Eden to return to something wonderful like what was here at the beginning. I am blessed to be with these people. And soon, I intend to finish my duties here and live out my life on earth with them.

Like a younger brother, I've been waiting for Dean to go to college so I can have his room. I am not too old to be adopted like Kaiyo, and I am already part of the family. They have wanted me to stay with them for years.

To be with them here, in the pathway, is wonderful. I didn't know it was allowed. Landon did it, but I thought he was the only one. To be able to talk to my future family made it so much the better. After Meginnah's prayer, I spoke first.

"Dean, when you go off to college, can I have your room?"

Everyone stared at me. Gyp looked thoroughly confused. Meginnah seemed especially perplexed. As for most of the others, except for Dean, it seemed nobody was pleased with the question. Aylmer and Benaiah, the proper ones, seemed shocked. Apparently, they were expecting something more profound. But I was serious. Sleeping in the barn was okay, but I wanted inside. I did get a wry smile from Goliath.

"Hah!" said Dean. "If I get shot and killed today or tomorrow, do you still want it?"

"Even more so," I replied. "It would be an honor to inherit the room of a hero. Either way though, I still get your room, right?"

Dean laughed. "Tracker, it's my honor. Consider it yours."

"Really?" said Benaiah looking at me. "Why are we even talking about this? It's inappropriate."

Benaiah was serious, as usual, but I had to get the question into Dean. I really did want to spend the rest of my life on the farm, but I wanted my own room where I can keep my own stuff, whatever that would be. And besides, wolves, if lucky, only have a life span of ten to eighteen years. I'm already eight years old, so I could be a goner in two years. Since I knew I was joining the McLeods, I sure as heck didn't want to die sleeping in the barn or even in the guest room. I want to be with my loved ones on that great day. Plus, I just wanted my own room.

Satisfied with the answer, I thanked Dean and continued, "Now, to the issue at hand. Reports are that Landon and his potential assassin are just getting started riding their snowmobiles on the roads and marked trails. There are many other riders out there, so the assassin cannot make his move. We expect him to either make his move tonight, in the darkness, or sometime tomorrow morning, after the storm passes through. The assassin has many confederates, including occultic soldiers of the dark arts, an unknown number of betrayers like Ilya, and perhaps possessed humans. Aylmer, when you go back home today, go straight to the farm and convince Kaiyo's mother to call Sarah. She needs to get out of her town and make her way to the farm, her life is in danger. She is an apostate from the oppressor, and because of who she knows, her life is in danger. You also must learn what she knows about possessed people. They're particularly dangerous, and they bring terror because of their closeness with the oppressor."

Everybody was quiet. It seemed Kaiyo had come to accept that he had to stay back.

Jack looked up and asked, "Wait. What do you mean by calling the bad guys occultic? I don't understand. What does that mean for us?"

That was a good question. As always, truth is the best response.

"Jack, many of the world's leaders and some in the highest of society are this very day practitioners of the occult. It is a darkness and an ancient voodoo, and it makes victims of those innocents who do not know Jesus, the Master, like you do. The great butcher, Himmler, was an occultist. Your nation's capital has many occultists. Some, who are quite prominent, have bragged about their powers, including the killing of innocent people with spells and hexes. They are the witches, warlocks, sorcerers, and mediums. However, most are quiet and private. They are unified only in their hatred of the Master and their desire to harness powers to control both nature and the spirits. Most think of themselves as good people, but they are deceived. It is they who are used by evil."

Jack's hand was again raised. "So how do we deal with that power?"

Benaiah answered, "Jack, if the Master is with you, who can be against you? Nothing is greater than he who created everything, including knowing you long before you existed, and making you, with you in mind. Anyway, you will note that when you are present, they will have lost all or most of their occultic power. The Comforter frustrates them."

"That's true," said Goliath. "When I was in the pit, I could no longer hear the voice of my oppressor. Of course, I never thought of him as my oppressor because he fed my hatreds and my pride. When I could no longer hear him, my eyes were thankfully opened. And it was you, all of you, who had the spirit of God, the Comforter, within you. And that spirit vastly overpowered the voice. It confused me at how easily my oppressor yielded to the Master."

Benaiah continued, "Dean, do you remember how Sarah, when possessed, knew you were somewhere nearby because she felt your prayers? Her possessor was confused in its vile hatred.

When you are near them, you may be discovered. But that is the risk. Finally, keep praying. Libby, you once told me of a time when you and Dean came to the abandoned house where your father was held captive. You told me both of you could sense the oppression. Your prayers lifted that, do you remember?"

"Yes, I do remember," said Libby. "I almost forgot. Are you telling us to be sensitive to the presence of evil?"

"Of course," said Benaiah. "But not only the spiritual kind. The men you are about to encounter are evil enough on their own. Landon's assigned assassin is that way. He is not an occultist nor is he possessed, though he is a tool, nonetheless. He perversely enjoys torturing and killing things that live and he's good at it. He will not be confused. He, and several others, including the man who spoke with your father, the vile sorcerer Glennon Wraight, will not run from prayer. They are evil, and though they may serve the oppressor, they are not possessed. They will have to be confronted."

Meginnah spoke, "There is more, much more, but the time demands action. Remember who you are, and remember the grace you have received from the Master. I do not know how this will end. I, like you, will be praying. Look now, the door is open. Reclaim your machines, and return immediately. Soon you will be placed in the far-off valley. Though your army is small, it is made powerful. And, Kaiyo, I expect to see you momentarily."

Meginnah left us and took up his guard station at the entrance to Eden.

I looked at Libby. "Landon, if he survives, will be your mate. The future you have chosen is in peril. You have much to lose. Because of that, I chose you to be in command, if you wish that responsibility."

Dean spoke up, "Guys, we know Libby. We also know people in her situation could be too emotionally involved to do a good job. But she's not made that way. I fully accept her leadership."

Everyone seemed satisfied. Libby gritted her teeth and affirmed her role.

"Libby," I asked, "what are your orders?"

Enemy Territory—Dean

Kaiyo was completely devastated. I understood. We were headed to war, and grizzly bears were made for just that sort of thing. The angel Raphael was probably just protecting him from getting shot again. He said goodbye to everyone and left down the path toward Meginnah. I think he was crying. We all tried to encourage him. He really wanted to confront Ilya too and find out more about his mother. Kaiyo was so disappointed he could barely talk. I felt sorry for him, but he was the main target of the assassins.

About two years ago, I learned Kaiyo wanted to figure out who killed his bear mother and why. I didn't blame him. If it was me, I would want to know. But it hasn't been easy; even Raphael did not know. The mystery was Kaiyo's to solve. Everybody around here knows Goliath was the one who actually killed his bear mother, but somebody or something lured her out of her home in Eden and made sure her path and Goliath's paths would eventually cross. That was the same as pulling the trigger. At the time, Goliath was spoon-fed a nearly nonstop mix of lies and hatred by a powerful demon who rules over this part of the country. It made him a treacherous bear, and had my dad and sister not intervened, Kaiyo would have been killed by Goliath too.

As disappointed as Kaiyo was, Libby was on fire. Jack and I quickly went back to Montana and ran a rope from each of our horses to drag our snowmobiles back through the door. From the time we got to the door the first time, the snowfall had gone from flurries to heavy snow. The storm was building. Because it was getting late, we knew our time was limited. Not only was a storm coming in, we had to think of making or finding our own shelter if we couldn't find Landon before nightfall.

Libby gathered our crew. I held Kate's hand, and we listened as Libby rolled out her ideas. She didn't really have a definite plan of rescue because we had no idea where Landon was. Instead, Libby rolled out a plan of surveillance and discovery. She broke us into two groups of people and then two groups of animals. Aylmer was going back to the farm to protect Mom and Aliyah if need be. It seemed Aylmer was unknown to the bad guys, and as big as he was, he was at home in the forest around the farm. He could provide some well-needed security.

Tracker, Gyp, Goliath, and Benaiah were told to stay away from people if possible. Having wolves, bears, and a watcher seen together in this weather, or at any other time, would alert our enemies. Bears, wolves, and watchers are ancient enemies, and they usually steer clear of one another. If they were seen together, then all elements of surprise would be lost. But the bear's noses were probably better than any technology at finding Landon. Benaiah's strength and speed could also be critical. They were told not to get directly involved unless they had a chance to ambush either a human or a Special. For the most part, they were asked to lurk in the wilderness and watch. If they found Landon, they were told to get him away from harm as best as they could. As hard as it was for Libby to say it, she told them both she had no desire to trade one life for another. Goliath was ordered to keep his grizzly rage in check, and Benaiah was told not to get too close. The bad guys probably had thermal imagers, night vision scopes, and everything else to keep Specials from being a factor.

Gyp spoke up, "Libby, I shall team with Tracker. Wolves do not hibernate, so wolf tracks would not be too unusual. And with me being white, I can hide in plain sight. We can get closer to humans than Goliath or Benaiah."

That made sense, and Libby quickly agreed. As for us, we would need to act like we were in the valley to have some fun. We didn't look like miners or ranchers; we looked like teenagers. So we would act like we were two unrelated couples enjoying the outdoors in different ways. Before Landon was Libby's boyfriend and before Jack became a local sports phenom, Jack had a serious crush on Libby. Lots of guys have had crushes on Libby, and they, like Jack, were disappointed. But Jack has moved on, and he's become serious about life. He's also super popular in school, and he's a bit of a player. But Jack is solid, and he and Landon are close. As for me, I trusted only me to be with Kate.

Meginnah had told us the entrance to the valley was being watched. Because of that, we hoped to look like local valley residents out for some fun. The door would open us deep into the valley, so it would be assumed we got there before any bad guys got there. From there, we would fan out, depending on where we would be dropped off. After pinning down the details, we looked back to see Kaiyo slip over into the valley and into Eden. It was time to go.

Jack and I had gone through doors before but not one with a path. Except for this one here, the last door we went through was merely an abrupt opening into another world. A particularly evil world. The path here allowed us to stage our arrival. Kate and I would ride the horses while Jack and Libby would take the snowmobiles. It made sense. Jack is a good horseback rider, but the rest of us are better. But being the better athlete, Jack is amazing on a snowmobile or anything else with wheels or tracks. Libby is good on both.

The nine of us hugged one another and separated into our groups. Kate and I moved over to our horses.

Then Aylmer stepped in the middle of us and said to all of us in his beautiful deep bovine voice, "We are family. Fellow warriors let not our hearts grow faint. Instead, let us do glorious battle with evil and let God lead us to victory. Our very heartbeats belong to the Master, so give him your best. And if we fall, then we shall soon meet at the cross."

Aylmer spoke in a formal, theatrical way, but he was correct. There are things far worse than death and either way, dead or alive, we would be okay. But when I looked at Kate, I sure didn't plan on dying. It dawned on me just then that I was probably hopelessly in love with her. I laughed to myself because being honest, at least to myself, was oddly refreshing.

"Why did you laugh?"

It was Kate, and she was staring right at me. Kate was somehow both strong and innocent, and those two things don't usually go together. Looking into her eyes, I wasn't about to tell her why. "Just thinking of you and all this. When I thought of us, never did I see you fighting by my side. I promise to take care of you."

Kate leaned into me and kissed my chapped lips. "And I will take care of you," she whispered. "I'm not the reckless one, remember? You are. But tell me, how do you see me. How do you see us?"

She was looking right into my soul with that question, and all I had was fear. I really didn't want to love her so much, but I did. My fear was of Kate moving on from me after high school. And if she did, I wouldn't blame her. Almost everybody moves on from their high school romances. And Kate was amazing in so many ways. I just didn't see her satisfied with this life or with me. I wanted her to have more. I wanted more too. I just had no idea what it was. I couldn't ask Kate to be tied to me. So I answered as best I could. "Kate, we're only in high school. I can't ask you to tie your life to mine. It is not fair to you. We just have to see what comes, okay?"

Kate leaned back into me and held my hand. She laughed a little. "It's too late, Dean. I decided to tie my life to yours the day I saw you at the bus stop, and nothing has changed. In fact, everything we have done together and in this amazing life has made me more certain I was right. Don't blame me for knowing what I want. I want you. That will never change. Dean, you are the bravest person I have ever met. But it seems like the only thing you are afraid of is me. That has to end. If you want to love me, then do it, without fearing the future. I cannot imagine life without you."

Maybe for the first time in my life, I had no words. And more than anything, I wanted to ask her to marry me right then and right there. At that same moment, poor Landon was in the company of his assassin, and I had totally forgotten about him. I was lost in Kate's eyes and in what Kate just said. I probably had the silliest-looking grin ever, but I was so happy.

Kate kissed me again and said, "Now you know. And, Dean, I know you feel the same way even if you can't bring yourself to saying it. That is why I have no fear about you. I know that the only way you'll ever leave me is by getting yourself killed. Am I right?"

"Yes, Kate, you are," I whispered.

I didn't know Gyp was behind me until he cleared his throat. "Sorry to bother you two. Whatever is going on, you guys look really cute. But we need to get going. We have a war to fight and your friend to rescue."

Kate and I looked at the others. Everybody had their game face on as they fixed their gear, stamped their paws, hooves, or feet and spoke to one another in low tones. Just then, I missed Kaiyo. Only Kaiyo was like me. I was alone in this group, at least among the humans. I was the only one looking forward to the fight. Nobody else was. They were normal. Except maybe Kate. I turned to look at her.

"This is going to be awful, Kate. People and animals, either some of us or some of them or some of both, will surely die. Others will be wounded. You and I both know this is no place for a sixteen-year-old girl."

Kate smiled as she counted rounds of ammunition. "Sixteen yes but almost seventeen. And to be honest, I am only afraid I will lose heart. As for fighting or rescuing Landon, I want to get started. So maybe, Dean, I have a touch of savage in me too."

I think I just loved her even more. And it was time.

"Steady," said Libby. "Kate, mount up and follow Jack and me. Dean, when the door opens, I need you to walk out and figure out where the door has placed us. Gyp, go with him."

Libby was in charge, and it felt good.

"Come on," said Gyp as he stuck his nose in the small of my back. "Let's go see what we can see."

The door was not far. Gyp was even bigger than Kaiyo and Goliath, and having him walk with me was reassuring. Like all my bear friends, his demeanor changed the closer we got to danger.

Gyp looked at me and said, "I shall go out first. My nose will tell me if we are not alone. If we are in danger, I will return. Count to ten before exiting. Stay low and hide yourself."

I watched as Gyp slipped through the opaque fuzziness of the door. I counted to ten and stepped into Montana. I was shocked again by the cold. I wrongly thought I was ready for it. The snow was falling in big, thick flakes, making visibility hard. That was good. Gyp was next to me, nose in the air, searching. Libby had given Gyp a scarf she and Landon both used. Gyp could separate the two scents. Our door opened on a wooded slope that faced south. The openness beyond the trees not far from us told me we were probably near a trail. Gyp worked the air and then motioned for us to go back.

Once inside the door, Gyp said, "I think Landon passed by here recently. We have good cover. Let's go get the rest."

We moved fast. Gyp quickly described to our group what he saw and smelled. I told them what I saw. As a group, we left the warm safety of the path and plunged again into winter in Montana. Immediately, Goliath and Benaiah went upslope while Tracker and Gyp waited for us. I took Solo and Kate took Jet. Jack handed me a walkie-talkie. We all decided to use it sparingly because walkie-talkies aren't private. We gave ourselves code names, and we left to find the path. Libby and Jack waited in the timber. After a few dozen yards, we came across a wide, well-marked snowmobile trail. Even though the snow was falling heavily, the trail was packed down by a lot of use. It would be easy going for us. I double-clicked my walkie-talkie. In seconds, I heard the snowmobiles roar to life and head our way. Kate and I turned our horses downhill and to the right. We watched as our snowmobiles plunged out of the timber and turned left and uphill. They headed up the slope, and we lost them as they rode out of view.

I knew this area by looking at a few maps earlier today and by attending many seasons of summer camp in the valley. It had been years since I was here though. I suspected we were in the south part of the valley and that we were near Independence, an old ghost town. In the summer, this was a popular but rugged four-wheel drive and ATV trail, but it's snowmobiles only now. I had no desire to be stuck in this area after dark, especially with the weather getting worse. I instinctively patted my rifle scabbard and felt the extra magazines in my vest. Kate's eyes were trying to peer through the blowing snow. Her scarf was up over her mouth and nose, and all that was exposed were her eyes. When she looked back at me, I could tell she smiled because her eyes gave it away. I had to remind myself to focus on the task at hand.

"It is rugged from here until we pass a few miles through Independence. Expect the road to get slick. I'll keep an eye on Jet's footing. Solo is made for this. We have to be alert for snowmobile tracks up any side trails or anything that looks curious. Jack and Libby are going to the areas around Blue Lake. Then they'll come back our way. Hopefully, we will find Landon somewhere along this trail and get him away from MacDonald. Dad and Gunner should be coming in from the valley entrance. Keep your eyes peeled for them too."

We descended toward the ghost town. What we didn't know was that we would soon be hunted too. The fighting was almost at hand and much sooner than we expected. But we were made for this.

10

CLOSING IN—SARAH TOMPKINS

I was at work when I got Susan's text. All it said was "*911.*" Well, that couldn't be good. It was a slow Friday afternoon, so I threw on a coat and stepped outside in the biting wind to make the call. While Susan has a great sense of humor, joking like this wasn't her style.

Susan and I are close. She's a mix of big sister and mom to me. She's also a close friend, and we have shared some amazing life events together. Her joy is contagious. Usually, whenever she called, it was a positive experience. Not today.

She answered her phone immediately. She was not panicking, but we certainly didn't exchange pleasantries, either. She told me to be quiet and listen. So I did.

One of my old nemeses, a giant, grouchy bull named Aylmer, somehow conveyed to Susan that I needed to be at the farm because somebody wanted to kill me. Then she told me about Landon's predicament. I don't scare easy, but this one left me a little frazzled. Whatever was going on had no sense of randomness. It was planned and organized. I thought the whole firebombing thing in Harlowton seemed too weird. Susan is convinced it was done to freeze law enforcement into inaction. If so, it was working. My fiancé, Troy Stahr, was currently guarding an empty courthouse in Virginia City.

After I got off the phone, I went back in to speak to my boss, Lylah Paulsen, and asked her for the rest of the day off. Lylah owns and runs a small Helena-based construction company off Prospect Avenue east of Highway 90. Even though I still have difficulty dealing with authority, my boss is amazing, accomplished, and a terrific businessperson. I respect her.

I quickly told her that the invoices were all mailed out and that our subcontractors had already been paid. I reminded her how I was hourly and that it just wouldn't be right to ask her to keep paying me to just wait for the phone to ring.

"Yeah right!" Lylah said. "You have more energy than three of anybody else. Last time you were bored, you built us an interactive website from scratch. I have half a mind to say *no* just out of curiosity. The more bored you are, the better my company looks. But no problem." She then paused. "Wedding stuff?"

I naturally wanted to lie even though I didn't need to. I am an especially good liar. Much of my life has been lived as a liar. Some have called me a grifter, and I am, unfortunately, quite an accomplished one. I learned how a pretty young face fooled many. For several years, I made a living conning people out of anything they had that I wanted. Usually it was drugs. Sometimes it was money. But that was usually to buy drugs. So same thing, I guess.

As for the drugs, I wasn't too particular about what kind either. Sometimes I did anything to get them. I tricked people, and I stole from people, good and bad. I snuck into houses, barns, and sheds; stole tools, motorcycles, and cars; and sometimes I sold myself. It makes me shudder to think of it. I can't go there without hating myself, and hating myself is probably what got me into all that stuff at the beginning. God must have plans for me because I should've been dead a couple dozen times over. Even though I believe it fully, the whole grace thing from God is surprisingly hard to accept. My walk of repentance isn't easy either, but I'm improving.

I do better when I focus on the future. And except for some-body wanting to kill me this weekend, my future looked pretty good. And lying to Lylah wasn't in the cards.

"Well, Lylah, I'm sure we'll do some wedding stuff. But Landon Haldor, you know him, right?" She did. "Well, he's guid-ing some fool in the Absarokas, and it looks like that fool is going to kill him. Or at least try to. Landon's office in Belgrade was ran-sacked this morning. Whoever did it only stole a few files and the hard drives."

Lylah's mouth dropped, but then she clenched her jaw. Lylah was a woman in the construction industry, and she didn't get successful acting like a victim. When she runs a job, she's all business.

"Anyway," I said, "the assassin has friends who want to kill the McLeods and I have heard that I'm also near the top of their list. So if anybody comes to the office today looking for me or if they call for me, feel free to tell them I went to some farm near Radford to see friends. And, Lylah, these guys are not nice. Keep your 357 where you can get it."

Even though she was tough, Lylah just stared at me. Finally, she asked me when it would be over.

I laughed and told her, "By Monday or Tuesday. Susan McLeod tells me these folks are the devil's own. So either way, our group or theirs is going to come out of this weekend dead or alive. And just so you know, I expect to be back at work by Monday afternoon, Tuesday at the latest."

I may have boasted, but I didn't lie. "One more question," asked Lylah. "Why the McLeod's farm? Why not just get out of here for a few days and lie low?"

It was a good question. So I had to be honest. "Well, Lylah, there's only a few ways in. Hopefully, we can control the kill zones on the farm. Our hope is they stay away from us because of that. Troy will be bringing half the department. If things get dicey or if Troy gets delayed, we'll escape to the east. Most of the McLeods are trying to rescue Landon now. If he can be rescued, maybe the bad guys will back off and leave us alone."

Lylah was thoughtful. "Sarah, they won't back off, will they?"

I paused and then spoke, "No. I don't think so. But don't worry too much. I'm not the helpless type. If I live through this, I'll see you on Monday."

Lylah thought about that for a moment. "Sounds great, but I'm leaving too. People like that don't like witnesses. I'll just close the shop early on this grim Friday afternoon and forward the phones to my cell. If they call, I'll tell them where you are going."

We packed up quickly and locked the doors. At my car, Lylah hugged me and whispered in my ear, "You're packing, right? Please tell me you're packing."

I laughed, "Always."

We both drove out together.

It's odd that the road to Radford also goes right by my office. Prospect Avenue is also Highway 287, and I take that road for two hours south all the way to the McLeod's driveway. Having just one road to follow allows me to daydream as I drive. I turned up a new playlist, and after a while, I started to think about what kind of enemy we were facing. Among us, I probably knew most about the enemy because I knew their boss.

Several years ago, I was possessed by a powerful demon. It wasn't like I was some victim; I had fault because I allowed the possession. Once in though, it didn't want to leave.

The two of us even tried to hunt down Landon with real plans to torture him to death. That bit of irony tickled me. Now I am on Landon's side and have been for years. It was Dean and Benaiah who caught me, and it was Landon who cast that hideous demon out of me. It was Libby who accepted me. My gratitude for them is strong. Fighting alongside them will be an honor. I look forward to it, which is probably strange. But I do.

People tend to glorify evil and make it out to be far more exciting than it is. Being on God's team is far more exciting. First off, we win. Even my old possessor knew that. He hates God so much he just wants to destroy as much of what God loves as he can possibly destroy before God pulls the plug on time and space.

Second, Landon had told us stories of seeing the gates to Eden. I figured Eden was sort of like our first shot at a perfect place and even it, amazing as it is, will pale compared to what's next. Some people, whether they admit it to themselves or not, truly buy into the stupid notion that heaven will be boring. The harp and cloud thing sticks in their heads. That's lazy, pathetic thinking. I like to think of it more as an endless Montana with some amazing beaches and wonderful towns. There I will dance and laugh and find pure freedom with my redeemer. Best of all, I know my imagination can't compare to love that's thicker than maple syrup and more life-sustaining than pure oxygen. On top of that, I'll be in a future world that cannot be made any better.

Unfortunately, I do not have to imagine the slimy, crawly, filthy feel of pure evil. I had it live in my body for too long. That is over, and I know where I stand. I have no desire to go to hell and live with that thing as my eternal cellmate. Sam once underestimated the fullness of my conversion. He treated my turn to God as if it was some sort of half-thought decision. He learned better. And because I know the enemy, my old possessor and his boss want me out of the picture. I don't blame them. I'm not a sweet, smiling Christian who just wants to stay comfortable. God saved me for perhaps ten thousand reasons, but one of those was to play my part in the ancient war between all that is good and all that is not. I look forward to the battle too. Life is short, and I want to go out fighting.

As I drove south, I couldn't help but think of my parents. They lived in a beautiful house right on Lake Helena. I had everything as I grew up. I had great schools, new cars, new clothes, and every time I got into trouble, my dad hired smart lawyers. But I threw it all away numerous times.

My poor parents tried grace and then tough love and then counseling and more counseling. Unfortunately for all involved, counseling rarely works on people who don't want to be fixed. And

I didn't want to be fixed. I also didn't want their life or their values. I was always happy to take their stuff, but I had little love and no respect for them. They didn't deserve my treatment of them, of course. Unfortunately for them, I was truly a rotten kid and a worse twenty-something.

One of my former friends always said I would try anything. He was so wrong. I never tried anything that was good. I never tried to help anybody. I never tried to return love to my family. I never tried to excel at school. If it was true, pure, wonderful, lovely, or admirable, it wasn't in my playbook. There was a ton of stuff I never tried.

The fact that my parents welcomed me back after I was rescued by the McLeods was fully unexpected. I had been gone for years, and during that time I didn't even have the courtesy to call them more than a few times, and when I did, it was just to ask for money. I broke their hearts on multiple occasions. I have a little brother and an older sister who are just now reaching a point where they are willing to consider my departure from the darkness as sincere.

Even though it's been two years since I came back, I don't blame them for not accepting me yet. I have a history of conning them and my parents out of love and money. Repeatedly. Two years isn't a long enough time to prove that much change. So that is why I am so excited about the wedding. My family doesn't have a clue about the Specials, and they probably fear the McLeods and even Troy are just new marks for me to target. But once they meet them, they will understand how I got saved from myself and from the raw, living evil who, at least for a while, controlled me.

My mom has been so supportive of the wedding, but I have made sure she and Daddy don't pay a nickel of it. My siblings need to see a change in me, and mooching again off my parents wouldn't be right. My parents did let me live at home rent-free, and that has been a huge blessing. Fortunately, with the McLeods hosting the event and with an otherwise tiny guest list, Troy and I could pay for a nice party. But it's still not cheap. Troy and I were going top-notch with the best meats, cheeses, grains, and pies for the Specials and good food and even better booze for us humans. I just laughed out loud thinking how wonderfully amazed my family, and Troy's family, will be.

Then the phone rang. I was driving near the end of Canyon Ferry Lake when Lylah called.

"Well, darling. You were so right. I got a call from some guy asking for you. He said he stopped by the office 'to say hello to an old friend.' He wouldn't give me his name, but he said wanted to see you. I told him he was too late and that you were on your way to Madison County. He thanked me politely and said something like, 'Maybe next time then.' I thought he would ask for your number, but he didn't. He did ask when you left, but I lied. I told him you had to deliver a complete set of plans to Green Way Country Club before you left. He thanked me and quickly hung up. Hopefully, he'll head over to the west side and waste enough time to get you clear of him."

I was lucky to have her as my boss. "You're wonderful, Lylah. See you next week."

Troy called, and immediately I felt better. I learned early on that Troy might be an impulsive bull in a china shop, but he loved me dearly. The good thing was I loved him and his two little girls right back. Zoe was nine, and Kelly was seven, and they are burned into my heart.

The fact that I was marrying a cop still surprised me. Up until a few years ago, I made a practice of running away from cops. Not this one though. It took me awhile to trust myself that what I was feeling for him was real, but once I gained my confidence, I fell hard for him. Troy had already fallen for me, but during that time, he gave me all the space I needed to heal.

I filled Troy in on the call to Lylah. He had been alerted by Susan already, and he was racing north to meet me. While I was on the phone, a Broadwater county sheriff's SUV pulled up behind me. Instinctively, I slowed down. Troy told me to let him pass and then follow him and that I probably needed to speed up.

The highway was only two lanes, and it had a decent snowpack on it, but we raced south, down the middle of the highway. The deputy threw on his lights whenever we passed other vehicles. We made great time. It was pure fun to be able to drive that fast and not fear getting caught. No doubt it was dangerous too, but I loved the adrenaline rush.

We finally pulled over at a gas station just off Interstate 90, and there was Troy. Seeing him was always good, but today it was especially good. I did not want to get ambushed, and driving a car was a vulnerable place to be. If somebody wanted me dead, I wanted to be able to fight back. Having the escort ensured a fighting chance.

We thanked the deputy and watched him turn back north. Troy and I tried talking but the wind and bitter cold forced us back into thinking about the situation. We needed to get to the farm, and the sooner the better.

After another hour, we pulled off the road and onto the McLeods' ridiculously long driveway. Fifteen minutes later, we were pulling up to the house. Susan and Aliyah leaned out the kitchen door and waved us in. Troy had to return to work because of the bombing. His boss, Sheriff Tuttle, was also convinced the whole bombing thing was fishy. He thought Landon was probably dead by now. The Sheriff is a good man, and he's smart, but he didn't know Landon like I did.

Once inside, it was clear we were preparing for a war. Aliyah and Susan had rifles slung behind their backs and the kitchen table had several big boxes of ammunition. They told us what Sam and Gunner and probably Lowe Brigham were doing. They also told us about the journey the boys and then the girls took earlier today. We digested that. After twenty more minutes of Q and A, Troy and I stepped into the den. We both knew we were all in danger. We hugged for a while; letting go was not easy.

"No hero stuff, okay?" whispered Troy.

"Same for you, Troy. You talked to their ringleader today, and I'm sure he hates you. And you humiliated him and then laughed at him. Satan has his pride, and that character trait has rubbed off on his henchmen, both demonic and human. I believe that as fact. Trust me, your lunch guest has a score to settle."

Troy didn't laugh or make light of my concern. He tended to downplay the opinions of others, and I expected to hear something like that. But I didn't.

"Sarah, I know you are right. And those guys want you out of the picture as much as, or more than, they want to take me down. They're going to come for you first. Sam or Gunner aren't going to be back tonight, but I will be. The enemy will need to act fast. If anything happens, it will probably happen tonight, during the storm, or sometime tomorrow as we dig out. Keep your phone charged.

"And, Sarah, I love you more than I ever thought I could love anybody. It's hard to even think of you without my heart racing. But you worry me too. Somehow I get the feeling you are looking for payback with these guys. You aren't scared like you should be. At least not scared enough. Please lie low and don't go hunting for trouble. Law enforcement is already on this case, and more assets will be involved. Let us handle this."

"Troy, I'm getting married in a few weeks to the man who has fully swept me off my feet. Sweetheart, I love you. I intend on spending a real, actual lifetime with you. I promise, I won't do anything stupid."

That seemed to satisfy Troy. And I didn't lie. But he should have pressed me harder.

We walked back in the kitchen. Troy was in a hurry, so he gave a quick pep talk to us and promised to be back sometime tonight. He kissed me on the cheek and walked out into the snow. In moments, he was headed down the long, flat driveway toward the western forest.

I looked at my friends. Susan laughed.

"I heard Troy try to pin you down. Promising not to do something stupid isn't much of a promise. But you made him feel better."

"Yeah," I said. "Anybody can say that, and I said it. Ladies, I have no intention of being stupid. But I am not going to hide in this house and become a victim. A well-placed shooter could take all of us out. One by one. This house was made to soak in some beautiful views. But if us on the inside can look out and enjoy the views, then somebody on the outside can look in. I have every intention of going on the offensive. I hope that's all right with you."

Aliyah looked grim. After a moment, she spoke, "Sarah, Susan knows this, but when Gunner and I moved here and after we met the McLeods, we decided that we were never going to run again. I am a proud Somali Christian. My kind are rare, and in Somalia, Christians there are persecuted and always in danger of being killed for the faith. Because I converted in college and then married a Christian, Gunner and I had to run for our lives from my own family. We ran for a decade. Sometimes we had to wake up the children in the middle of the night and flee from family members who were determined to kidnap me and the kids and force a conversion or worse. They probably would've killed Gunner in the process too."

Aliyah sighed and continued, "Anyway, we finally have peace with my family, but it only happened when we decided to take a stand. Plus, they love Jack and Kate. Fortunately, we never had to get violent to defend ourselves. But I am not going to run for my faith ever again. The types we are facing are true evil. While I may be a Christian, I am one-hundred-percent Somali and proud of my ancient heritage. We believe waiting for an attack is pure foolishness and invites death. We must find our attackers, and as you said, Sarah, we need to take them out, one by one."

Susan looked at the two of us. "Yeah. You don't have to convince me. But we need a plan. A quick one too. Failure's not an option, right? Let's go over what resources we have here. Then we figure out what to do with whatever stuff we can use if we plan to fight back."

Susan threw out some legal pads and pens.

Then it dawned on me. "Where's Gracie?"

Susan grimaced. "She's probably in grave danger."

Orders—Kaiyo

I left my family and friends while they fight my war. It was their war too, but it all started with me. And because of me. I brought the trouble onto my family by choosing to live on earth. That's why I didn't want to leave. But I was ordered to. I wish I could say that I trusted Raphael to do the right thing, but I didn't. I was so disappointed and frustrated I even cried a little. Maybe more than a little. Big as I am, I'm still only five years old. And I didn't understand why I was being taken away from everybody I loved when they needed me most. I knew I shouldn't lean on my own understanding of things, but it's so hard to trust sometimes.

I passed Meginnah without speaking and trudged into Eden. I was so focused on my predicament I failed to notice my friends. I was quickly surrounded by Dovie, my bear family, and a host of warriors who fought with me in the Sobek world. Even Lavi, my old mountain lion enemy, was there. As usual, I was pounced on by my cousins, and as usual, I threw them off.

Dovie then took over. "What's wrong with you animals?" she yelled. "You know he's been shot, and here you fools are crowding him and jumping on him. Are you stupid or what? Now back up and let our hero breathe."

I couldn't help but laugh. I needed a good laugh too. I guess everybody does sometime, especially when they've been having their own pity party. Everybody came up and thanked me and wished me well for what was next. Some prayed briefly over me. I had no idea what they were talking about, and nobody would tell me. It became obvious my presence here was purposeful. I quickly started to regret my bout of self-pity. It's not becoming of a grizzly either.

Some people confuse grief with self-pity. Grief is real and honors what was lost. Self-pity honors no one. And that was what I had chosen. I could have wondered what was in store or marveled that an angel wanted to meet with me. But my plans, whatever those were, were spoiled, and that was the way I acted. Spoiled.

Except for Dovie and Lavi, the last to leave were my aunt and uncle. They gave me long-lasting hugs. Bears are good at hugs. My aunt sat and held my face with her paws.

"From the beginning," she said, "they wanted to kill you. They knew you were special, and somehow, they knew you would be a reminder to man of what was lost and what is in their futures. The evil ones hate it when people think about what's in store for them. If they knew what they could have, they would rejoice. You are a reminder of that. And that's why they will not rest until they kill you. But be glad. The maker of the universe is with you and against them."

They both hugged me again and turned to join my cousins and walk back home. The others left too. All except Dovie and Lavi.

Lavi went first, "Did you hear, young one? I have been invited to Sarah's wedding. I love the irony. She and I were once companions in murder, well, attempted murder, and now we are both saved from ourselves and our current enemies. I am more pleased than you know. Anyway, when I get there—"

Lavi talks too much, so I interrupted. He could talk for days, and I had to nip that in the bud. "Why am I here?" I asked.

"Oh, you are an impetuous cub," said Lavi. "Patience was never your strong suit. You know we couldn't tell you even if we knew. But we don't know. All we know is, you are headed to more danger than ever."

"Lavi! What is wrong with you?" yelled Dovie. "Ignore him, Kaiyo. Lavi doesn't know anything."

What Lavi said though was like music. I wanted to matter, and now I would have a chance at mattering. "Lavi, thank you. You have restored my spirits. Dovie, please give him some grace."

Dovie grumbled and said something about swatting his shoulder. Lavi still limped noticeably from our battle years before, and he wisely took a few steps away from her. Lavi looked at me for a few moments and then choked up a little.

"We have to go, Kaiyo. We love you. We will see you at the wedding."

They left me there. Hungry and tired, I wandered into an enormous field and started grazing on the amazing grass that is plentiful here in Eden. Among other things, it's perfect for everything my body needed. It doesn't exist on earth. Raphael once told me it was an ingredient in manna. I ate until I was full and lay down in the sun. In seconds, I was fast asleep.

Three hours later, I awoke to the smell of smoke and a gentle nudge to my face.

"Kaiyo. Kaiyo. It is time. You are needed at the front."

Still groggy, I looked into Raphael's eyes. Raphael's eyes never change. His form changes, but his eyes are always the same. Raphael says he appears in the way least likely to frighten. On earth, he has appeared as every racial and national type of human there is. He has appeared as different animals to citizens from here who had lost their way on earth. This time, Raphael looked like he always did in Eden. Here, he usually took a human form that was a mix of characteristics from every land. It made sense.

"You have lost your mighty bear strength," said Raphael. He was smiling. "Bears live by the power of their characters and of their bodies. You need both to be at their peak."

The smoke was drifting from a small pile of flat stones placed on a fire. None of that was there when I fell asleep.

"Arise and eat."

Raphael had baked what looked like a small loaf of bread. "It's cake," Raphael said, "and I want you to eat."

Cake? Well, yes indeed. Who doesn't like cake? But it all seemed a little odd.

Raphael kept going, "The Master once made this for the prophet, Elijah. Do you know about him?"

I did, sort of.

"Elijah still enjoys this very same cake. I made this for you because if you eat of it, you will not need to eat again for a week."

I laughed hard at that; Raphael wasn't amused. I must have looked like a skeptic.

He gently rebuked me. "No, no, do not doubt me. I have never given you a reason to doubt me. In moments, you will see. You will not feel hunger for many days. Since you remember the story of Elijah, then you will also remember the story of Daniel."

Just then, Raphael held my face and looked into my eyes. Something amazing happened. Through his fingers, like warm, fluid electricity, strength raced into my body, as if the strength belonged to me. My strength was more than restored; I was made even stronger than normal. I could feel the power in my muscles; my fatigue had changed into energy.

"Kaiyo, you are highly esteemed by the Master and by me also," Raphael said. "Be strong now, and take in the peace the Master has given you."

Raphael stood and told me to rise. I did and was amazed at the ease of the effort.

"Are you physically ready for what awaits you?" he asked gently.

"I sense that I am. And my shoulders don't hurt anymore."

"Kaiyo, that is one of the reasons why you are here. I hope it's obvious to you why I demanded that you stay. You are now stronger and faster than you have ever been. Through me, the Master has given you your strength. I now demand you to focus on something far more pressing than Ilya. That must come later."

He let that sink in. It didn't bother me as much as I thought it would.

But then he kept going, "Your mother and little sister, as well as Aliyah and Sarah, are in grave danger. Their appointed assassins are approaching the farm right now. They will be there this very night."

I was immediately focused. That did bother me. In fact, it blinded me. Rage, fear, and hate merged and welled up in my throat like thick, greasy, burning vomit. "I gotta go." That was all I could say.

"Stop it, Kaiyo. Your rage is not helping you. Neither is your fear. Your hatred, however, will only help them."

Raphael's sharp tone got my attention. He knew me well. "I know," I said. "I know I'm not supposed to hate."

"Far from it, Kaiyo. Who told you that? Because it's not remotely true."

"Wait," I said. "The Master told us not to hate."

"Really?" asked Raphael. "You can read. Where in the Great Book does it say that? Does not the Master hate injustice? Shouldn't you do the same thing? Does he not hate lies? Does he not hate cruelty? Just because he forgives your sin, do not think he doesn't hate sin, because he does. He has felt the pain of the nail, the fist, and the whip and he knows the shame of being mocked and spit upon while he bore man's sins. He, more than all others, understands the destruction caused by the daily betrayals of his own creation. A creation that he adores.

"Lucifer, the beautiful *Son of Dawn*, the *Seal of Perfection*, has angered him just as man's rebellion has likewise grieved the Master. The Master hates what Lucifer does and so many of the things that mankind does every day. But as for man, the Master knows there is always hope. Neither I, nor you, nor mankind, are to hate one another. The Master fully knows that hating what the man does or thinks is not the same as hating the man. If man is to be hated, that is for God, not for the rest of us. Only the Master is pure enough to hate his chief creation without sin."

I was confused. "But, Raphael, I may have to kill men to save my family. Isn't that exactly what hate is? It's murder, right? How can I kill without hating the one I kill?"

Raphael smiled. "Oh, Kaiyo. I do love you. We all know that with the Master, anything is possible. It's not just a cute phrase. Those words represent power. And yes, Kaiyo, you may have to kill, but if you do so to save or protect your innocent friends or family, then such a death is not murder nor is it your fault. Rather, it is simply the horrible consequence of the sin of your attacker.

"Are you not glad that Dean did not hate Sarah? He certainly did not approve of her sin. But he loved the idea of what she could be. She was doing hateful, disgusting, sinful things, but he had a heart for her. Do not be confused. As young as he was, Dean surely would have killed her if it were necessary. But by loving her instead, look at the amazing young woman she has turned out to be. At first, she hated Dean, but he returned love for hate.

"And Goliath, what a warrior for the Master he has become. Again, it was Dean who saw Goliath's value. Goliath was a despicable killer, and he surely deserved death. Many times, death approached him, but the Master had called Goliath to be his own before Goliath was even a cub. But Dean had no such knowledge of that. All the angels, including me, thought Goliath would perish at the hands of your family. Many of us also believed his pride would forever keep him from the love he now receives so fully. God still surprises us, even those of us who speak with him face to face. The Master uniquely knows how wonderfully each person and creature is made and because of that he has shown patience beyond our understanding. But in his sinless wrath, he may well hate their every thought and deed. And because he gave life to the rebellious, he may take it at any time. But he does so knowing the painful loss of a soul who he created."

That made sense. "Got it. As for me, hate what they do and even who they have chosen to be, but I cannot hate the person."

"Well said, young bear. And there's one more thing. Remember this, if you hate the people or things that are coming to attack and kill, your mission will change, and you will not even know it. Your mission now is to protect your family and to stop their attackers by whatever means at hand, including killing them if necessary. But if you hate the attackers, then your focus will subtly shift on destroying the attackers and when you do that, you run the risk of forgetting to protect your family.

"The evil one will eagerly lure you away and sacrifice ten thousand of his own simply to fulfill his death wish for you and your family. He has no love for man because he knows that men who serve him do so only to acquire powers that are his alone. Plus, he despises all of God's creation because he correctly knows man cannot be trusted to remain loyal to him. He grimaces when he thinks of the billions of defectors.

"Finally, Kaiyo, it may be true that one day, perhaps one day soon, your mission will require you to seek out and destroy the assassins. But that is not your task now."

"I understand. I do. So what can you tell me about the enemy?"

For the first time, Raphael looked uneasy. "Kaiyo, some look at the world of evil as if it were somehow exciting. In truth, there's not much of that. Everything done has a consequence, and evil offers the worst of consequences. Some imagine Lucifer's kingdom as a midnight party, others see it as an eternity of self-indulgence. But the sad reality is far from it. His kingdom is more like a dreary, lifeless, pointless, government bureaucracy run by hopeless, hate-filled, vindictive demons. Some of the fallen angels are fiercely loyal to him, others are lazy, some are even resentful because Lucifer lied and convinced them to follow him. They know the rebellion didn't work out so well.

"Some of the demons are content to haunt homes and forests, others are far more aggressive, and they relish destroying anything that is good. Most are somewhere in the middle with existences marked by suffocating boredom. They once were my friends, and they worshipped God. But withhold your sympathies, Kaiyo, none of them are good. All of them know that earth is their only shot at something remotely akin to heaven, and even that will be temporary. And, Kaiyo, you who believe and contend for the Master, earth will be your hell. All have that choice. The mockers will have their lives here, on a pain-filled earth, as their only heaven. And their stay here is likewise temporary. None will look back from eternity and value their sinful choices."

This was fascinating to me. "So what you are saying is that for the demons, and I guess a lot of people, their stay here on earth is sort of eat, drink, and be merry because tomorrow you're going to a dark, dreary lonely, tormenting hell for eternity?"

"Yes," said Raphael, "something like that. Many pagan religions have multiple gods doing all sorts of things that are petty, cruel, perverted, and selfish. The pagans didn't make up all that stuff. A lot of it really happened by the demons that confused them. The pagans, like many others, chose to worship creation and not the creator. It happens all the time. It's happening now. In fact, Lucifer doesn't even believe he is evil."

That surprised me, and it must have been obvious.

"It's true. Sometimes, the most dangerous lies are the lies we tell ourselves. Satan, unfortunately, believes his own press and the constant flattery coming from his entourage. I speak with him frequently, and trust me on this, he can still be quite charming.

"He has never given up on the Revolution, so he oddly thinks he can still recruit those of us loyal to the Master. He looks at his rebellion as a victory. He knows he came close to recruiting half of the angelic beings, and if he had, he believes he would have won the war. It's preposterous, of course. Even angels and the other angelic beings are God's creation and God, if he were alone, could destroy all of us. Satan doesn't get that.

"Even worse, he fully believes he could do a better job running the universe than God, and because of that, he has a history of creating false religions. Some religions have a false god that reflects on many aspects of Satan's character and even some of the Master's. He puts a nice spin on things though. Some false religions exist next to the truth. Like all counterfeits, they may look authentic and sound authentic, but they are worthless, and millions are deceived. Unfortunately, many are deceived willingly. There are even things written about me, both ancient and current, that aren't remotely true.

"Even after countless millennia, Satan somehow believes he would be a better god than God. Unfortunately, Satan believes the means justify the ends and he's determined to win. Most of mankind is not safe. The Master gave Lucifer enormous powers, but it's all part of the plan for man's eventual redemption. As for the fallen angelic beings, redemption is neither offered to them nor wanted by them. And you, Kaiyo, are safe from Satan and his legion, but not safe at all from his earthly soldiers. They're dangerous and that's why he has them. They use physical warfare and you live in a physical world. And their business is murder."

Raphael kept going, "There is an order among the world of demons, and the fiercely loyal are given top commands. Competence is secondary to Lucifer. He appreciates loyalty and rewards the loyal with privilege. He secretly hates all demons because he sees most intelligent beings as threats to his power. He has even quelled a few demonic rebellions against him. Brutally, of course, and with the maximum infliction of pain possible. Even Satan himself, with all of his might, cannot kill the lowliest demon. But Satan is an expert at inflicting pain, shame, and guilt and most demons shake in his presence. Most of all, he hates mankind because mankind cannot be trusted.

"Without knowing it, men and women typically default onto Satan's team. Most don't realize that. The unborn and the young innocents are claimed by the Master, but as for the others, the Master loses no one to Satan because the lost are already in Satan's grasp. Remember, one does not come to the Master without first wanting to be with him. That confirms they did not start with him. Of course, most people do not consider themselves that way, but one is either with the Master or against him. When someone comes to God, Lucifer considers them as traitors and defectors. And as you know, there are billions of them. And countless millions more will be swelling the ranks of our wonderful defectors. Every time someone choses the Master and loves the truth, Lucifer loses a soul who was once his and his alone.

"That doesn't mean some of the Master's followers are not highly influenced by Satan. Some are so deceived they are of little use to the Master. It is confusing. Some may sin greatly and still be of God while others may sin far less and be Satan's. That is why judging one's salvation is left to the Master.

"Satan looks at all who chose the Master as betrayers, and because of that, he hates them more than he hates the poor fool who hopes he or she can remain neutral. It doesn't work that way. There will be no unclaimed souls on the last day. And you, Kaiyo, in this great war of the ages, are a defector. So are all in your family."

Raphael paused then said, "Anyway, do you know the part in the book of Daniel when an angel was blocked for three weeks by the Prince of Persia until Michael came and broke the resistance?"

I remembered and nodded.

"Well, the Prince of Persia is a mighty demon and his organization was, and still is, quite effective and powerful. He's remains Persia's prince, unfortunately. Of course, things changed since the Resurrection. Nobody delays the Master's angels like that anymore. But as for this area where you live, a new ruler has been given authority. His name is Aymoon. It means *faithful* and he is certainly that. Aymoon has been ruler in the western part of North America for only a few centuries. He has a reputation for cruelty and for ambition. He serves Satan by developing new strongholds. Basically, he follows the populations of man.

"Once Aymoon creates an organization, it is given to another prince to run. He's not the worst of the angels, some of those are so terrible that they're in chains waiting to be released in the last days. They're almost mindless in their savagery. But there is nothing good about Aymoon. He is brutal, and he seems unable to exhibit the persuasive nuance of other archdemons. But he is useful to his lord. Aymoon wishes to rule the continent but as for now, he is focusing on the American West. He has been somewhat effective in hardening the hearts of people against the Master. Other areas of the country are more resistant but, for whatever reason, the American West has been more successful for him and his boss.

"It is Aymoon who wants you and your family destroyed. You are in his way."

Raphael paused to let me absorb all I heard.

"So does that help, Kaiyo?"

I truly didn't expect to be told all that, but Raphael had his reasons. I nodded. "Raphael, what is the current situation?"

"Sarah is now at the farm with Aylmer, your mother, Gracie, and Aliyah and others. Your father, Gunner Gibbs, and Lowe Brigham are at the north end of the Absarokas. Your brother, Kate, Jack, and Libby are south, deeper into the Absarokas. Gyp, Tracker, Goliath, and Benaiah are with your siblings. Landon is between them."

I nodded. "Where are the bad guys?"

"Everywhere your family is, your enemies are there too. But there is some confusion among them. In the valley to the east, they do not yet know that it is your family and friends who are there. But they are suspicious of everyone. The animals have escaped their notice. As for the farm, the attackers are not confused. And they are close. That is about all we know now."

Then Raphael dropped a bomb. "One more thing, Kaiyo. Just as God creates, Satan has wished to do the same. He makes counterfeits of everything God does. So he has created a few monsters. He doesn't create like God creates, of course. Only God can create something out of nothing. Satan simply steals life and manipulates their minds. Man does no different. People clone animals and breed animals to suit their needs. Aymoon has managed to acquire some monsters that you may have to confront.

"Treat them like men, and try not to kill them like you would an ordinary animal. These monsters are loved by the Master, though most of those poor beasts have no such love to offer in return. They do not know. And they are dangerous. Aymoon has lured citizens out of this world for his own purposes for many years. These are the tortured offspring of such creatures. Cruelty is not new to Satan or to his followers. Those creatures are born in cruelty, and they will offer that same cruelty to you if you give them a chance.

"Kaiyo, as the fight develops, you may think the Master has abandoned you. That thought is dangerous but perhaps inevitable. Even the Master cried out in Gethsemane. Remember, you are a warrior beloved by the Master. And of course, by both me and Meginnah. I cannot promise you a victory. You may even die today, and members of your family may also die. But death, when defending your loved ones, is not defeat. If death happens, then you will surely hear the best words one can hear. You will hear '*Well done, good and faithful servant,*' and the next and final stage of your eternal adventure will begin. And remember, when it's all over and the last day is upon us, we win. Whether you live or whether you die, your efforts will not be in vain. You will always be a soldier in an army that is forever victorious."

Raphael stood up, hugged me, and smiled. "Meginnah will take you close. The door will close immediately. Make your way to the farm. Darkness approaches."

Then Raphael vanished. I turned and ran out of Eden and back up to the path. Meginnah was on guard. I slowed briefly and yelled, "Get me close, Meginnah. I don't want to run far."

The path itself was only about a mile and with my newfound strength, I covered the distance quickly. Just before I got to the door, I slowed and passed through. It was dark, bitterly cold, and snow was falling heavily. I was finally in my element, and it felt good.

Setup—Sam

We had been driving almost recklessly. I-90 was a snowy mess, but it still had traffic. We grimly understood Landon might well be dead now and our attempts to save him could be in vain. Regardless, we knew we might as well start the fighting because we were *on the list*. We exited and passed through Big Timber and then turned south on Highway 298 into the valley. After a few miles, we passed the long, thin parking lot of a well-known roadside saloon. The road had been treacherous, and stopping here would normally be a great idea. But we didn't have much farther to go.

We all knew this saloon, but it had been a year since my last visit. The food here was good, the beer was cold, and the company was great. Gunner and I drove behind Lowe's truck. Though the weather was bad and getting worse, the saloon still had a crowd. There were trucks and SUVs with snowmobile trailers parked around the bar and on the road's shoulders. Most of the trailers had their snowmobiles strapped down, but there were still plenty of snowmobiles parked here and there. With the weather coming in, the smart riders were calling it a day. Some of them were apparently tossing down a drink or two before heading home.

We knew better than to go inside because all of us had been there before. We needed to look like tourists, and we couldn't afford to be recognized. Gunner and I noticed two big SUVs parked side by side near the crowded edge of the parking lot. Their drivers watched us drive by. Lowe clicked his walkie-talkie twice. He noticed too. We kept driving south because we had a cabin waiting for us at a closed rustic resort in McLeod. Gunner knew somebody who worked there, and he arranged it while we drove.

Our cabin was a rental and made for summer fly-fishing in the Boulder River. It was only a few steps to the water. Here, in winter, the scene was beautiful. I scanned the area, looking for anything unusual. I heard snowmobiles coming up from the south and a few coming from the north. It crossed my mind that anybody on a snowmobile was a suspect. Whoever was out there in this weather was either tough or they were up to no good. But this is Montana, and tough people are everywhere. Gunner and Lowe unlocked the cabin door and motioned me inside.

We threw our duffels on the bunks and hurried to get going. I pulled on my Carhartts and put on the rest of my cold-weather gear. We carefully loaded our rifles and packed extra magazines in our pockets. Our sidearms were already loaded. Each of us used chest holsters, so all we needed to do was unzip our coats for quick access. Otherwise, they were hidden. The snow was falling heavily, and we were wanting to get on the road to wherever Landon was. The three of us were determined to find him. Our fear was that we wouldn't find Landon but that we would find his body. We quickly gathered in a circle, and Gunner prayed.

"Did you hear that?" asked Lowe.

During our prayer and somewhere nearby, the three of us heard angry, scratchy screams. The screams were faint, so someone could've explained it away as the wind, but we knew better. I had heard it before. We all smiled. I knew what that was, and so did they. Still, Lowe looked a little surprised. Gunner smiled.

"The enemy just lost a few team members. Whatever spooky help the foot soldiers were receiving has vanished. But our location and our cover may have been compromised. Still, just because we are supposed to be tourists doesn't mean we can't be Christians, right? Any praying Christians would have run that thing off. So if any foot soldiers ask who we are, we keep to our story."

We then grabbed our duffels, headed outside, and got busy. We didn't know exactly where we would be spending the night, so we left nothing in the cabin. The three of us all had electric-start snowmobiles, but all the starts would be cold starts and those are tricky. Carefully adjusting the choke, I turned the ignition and let it turn. After a bit of chugging, the engine came to life. Easing off the choke, I kept the engine at 1,500 rpms and let it warm up for another three minutes. I watched people, usually young ones, rev their engines too soon. That's always a bad idea. The three of us knew machinery, and our machinery needed warm oil to bathe the cylinders. We all knew our machines could mean the difference between life or death. And today our snowmobiles were critical. In a few more moments, the snowmobiles were off the trailers. I put my rifle in the scabbard and hopped on. Looking back, I motioned toward the road and eased back on the gas.

Our intent was to simply ride south until we found Landon. We all knew it wouldn't be so easy. First, it was getting late. Second, the weather was bad and getting worse. Big, fat snowflakes were falling fast. It wouldn't be too long before the wind kicked up. Then those big, fat snowflakes would be broken into small pieces of ice that would fly sideways and sting exposed flesh. I trusted God that the bad weather was just as big a headache to the bad guys as it was for us. The fact was, we were all in danger because the bad guys wanted to kill us all.

Once on the road, we motored south. We waved at a few riders who passed us going north. They seemed normal. After a few miles, we saw no more snowmobilers, and it was obvious to me that most of the recreational riders had packed it in. Anybody else out here would be suspect. We kept our speed to twenty to twenty-five miles per hour because we needed to be able to observe anything that could be a clue. Any tire tracks and snowmobile tracks were being filled by the snow. We could still make them out, but eventually all tracks would be wiped clean.

After ten miles, we made it to Natural Bridge State Park. It seemed like every state had its own natural bridge state park. Basically, whenever the pioneers found a span of unsupported rock, they threw a nice park around it.

It was getting late in the afternoon, and we had been in shadow for hours. It was terribly cold, and sunset would be around 4:40 p.m. We stopped in the middle of the road at the park's entrance. The three of us turned into the small, looped parking lot to see if there were any hints as to Landon. A lot of people use this park as a starting place to go snowmobiling. It looked like everyone had gone for the day. We exited out of the south entrance and stopped again. Despite the snow, there were telltale signs that several vehicles had passed through here hours before. The tracks on this side of the park were those of several pickup trucks and several trailers. One of the trailers was heavy, and the pickup truck toting it was a six-wheeled dually. That was them. We could tell they went south.

Neither had come back north. We were thrilled. Landon could still be alive, and we knew it.

It was time to check our back trail. Being men, everybody volunteered to be the one to stay back. Doing so though would be dangerous.

"Guys," I said, "it has to be me. You two have Polaris snowmobiles. I have a Ski-Doo. They're all good, but mine is much quieter. If we have to follow any riders while they drive this way looking for us, then it needs to be me."

Lowe was quick to agree. He was a no-nonsense type. In general, if it made sense, he went with it. Gunner was more emotional and more protective. Even though he tried to object, he knew I was right.

I continued, "All right, here's what we'll do. Make your way to Froze to Death Creek. Just past that is Old County Road. It's a loop so you would've passed one entrance to that road already. There's a cabin, a big one, on Moose Haven Loop. It's owned by Dan Lammons. Susan and I have known the Lammons family for years. They spend their winters in Charleston and summers here, so it ought to be empty. Nobody will be there. Before you head over there, wait for me at the intersection. Look for cover. Darkness will help. Oh, there might also be a few year-rounders who live in the community down there. If anybody asks what you're doing, stick to the story and tell them you're waiting on me to arrive. If I don't show up, there's a key to the cabin under the back-door mat. Everything is winterized, so don't use the toilets. The wood stove works great though. And the cabin has a landline phone. Call every law enforcement help you can get. And get a hold of Susan and Aliyah. I will wait here for a half hour. Don't wait for me any longer than a few minutes after that."

"Forget about it," said Gunner. "If you're late, we're looking for you."

I tried to object, but Lowe cut me off, "Stop it, Sam. That's not the way we're going to do things. If you're a second late, we're coming to get you."

I laughed and agreed, "All right. Follow me, and I'll pull off the road just past the park and find a hiding place. If anybody follows you, I'll triple click and try to the follow the followers. Hopefully, the next sled you see will be mine."

But it wasn't.

I turned my snowmobile off the road and onto the right shoulder. From there, I cut back to the right and followed a path that took me to a low hill above the roadbed. I got off my sled, and using a tree branch, I tried to cover my tracks. But my efforts weren't convincing. It wouldn't fool a real tracker, but it could maybe fool somebody focused on the tracks of the other two snowmobiles. I then rode up the path to a safe place and then turned the snowmobile around with its nose pointing downhill, toward to road, so I could get back down quickly. Turning off my sled's motor, I grabbed my rifle and binoculars and walked higher up the hill until I had a good view of the road to the north. I made sure I was well hidden, and there I waited.

Watching my back trail had saved my life on several occasions. It had become second nature to me. After about ten more minutes, I got one click on the walkie-talkie. Gunner and Lowe were near the cabin. I clicked once in return. Then I listened. The wind was clearly audible, but a city person, or even a suburban one, would be surprised by the silence. No sirens, no loud cars or motorcycles. I enjoyed listening to the wilderness. I even heard a few deep, powerful howls off to the south. Oddly, the howls didn't quite sound like wolves or coyotes. I think I knew what they were, and because of it I shuddered. I listened, but I heard nothing more. Then almost imperceptibly, I heard the disappointing whine of snowmobiles. Civilization was headed my way. And violence was coming along with it.

In moments, I saw six snowmobiles in single file appear out of the snowfall, speeding south and coming my way. They stopped near the entrance of the park where we had stopped minutes earlier. My tracks in the snow were unfortunately still clear, and I had little confidence they would go without being noticed. At the most, I was thinking one, maybe two might be following us. But no. We had a full-fledged posse on our heels.

I glassed them carefully. They all had what looked like rented sleds, and most of them rode like novices. The one giving orders knew what he was doing. Unfortunately, they were all well-armed. I dearly wanted to shoot each one of them, but I wasn't sure they were bad guys. If they were, I knew they would quickly kill me if they had a chance. Glennon Wraight likely told them we would come and try to rescue Landon. Wraight wanted me just as dead as he wanted Landon, but I had no plans on giving Wraight the satisfaction of my death.

Still, I wasn't interested in committing murder, at least not yet. I had to make sure they were bad guys. So I broke radio silence. As I talked, I kept watching. For whatever reason, they were having a discussion. One of them was pointing down road and another pointing into the parking lot. None of the riders gave me the impression they were monitoring our channel. Gunner answered. I still had fifteen minutes until sunset, and I would need every bit of light left in the day. "We got six riders. They're armed. I am going to make a break for it and head south. They're probably going to chase me. If I make it close to you and only if they start firing, take out the guy in the green Artic Cat. He's giving the orders. Out."

"Copy."

I turned and hurried downhill. My Ski Doo started quickly, and I punched it. In seconds, I was hurtling off the shoulder and onto the road. I pulled into the tracks left by my friends and raced southward. I glanced back to see the riders. They were in full pursuit, and all had their firearms aimed at me. Zigzagging, I saw at least two rounds blast chunks out of the packed snow next to my sled. I should've shot first when I had the advantage. Now I was furious. I wanted to fight, but if I did, it would be my last fight. I was scared too.

In minutes, I approached Froze to Death Creek. The group behind me had fallen farther back, but the one in front was a good rider. Because I was having to zigzag, he was gaining on me. He was close enough that I could hear his gunfire over the roars of the snowmobiles. At least he had one good ride in him before he met his maker because about two seconds later, he met him.

I saw the muzzle flash of Gunner's rifle where he had hidden in some brush on the right side of the road. I didn't see what happened behind me, but Gunner told me later how the driver's head snapped back causing him to tumble off the back of his sled. His sled coasted into a shallow ditch on the right shoulder. The driver's lifeless body lay face-up onto the road.

Then I saw more flashes of Lowe's rifle and from Gunner's. Moving fast, my momentum took me past Gunner and Lowe. They burst out of their hastily made blinds and rode past me. Gunner raised his index finger and gave it a few whirls, motioning for me to turn around. I was already turning, and in seconds I was following them. I had no idea what had just happened, but it looked like Gunner and Lowe were in control.

Not fifty yards up the road were three stopped sleds. Two others were racing back north. The three riders were all alive, but their sleds were shot up. One of the drivers brought up his rifle. I hated to see it. I heard Lowe's rifle bark and watched the rider fall. He didn't have a chance. Then the other two threw down their rifles and waited, hands in the air. That saved their lives.

The last thing I needed was prisoners. In my anger, I was thinking some horrible thoughts, and my thoughts were entertaining murder.

Fortunately, Gunner had a better plan.

12

MONSTERS—DEAN

Well, Gunner was wrong about one thing. This whole little, nasty war we were having wasn't just between us humans. Whatever demon was running the vengeance campaign against us McLeods decided to empty his bench of monsters to get an advantage. And if I scared easy, it might have worked because what I was looking at was a bona fide monster.

I feel sorry for anybody who sees things like this. If they share their experience, they are, at best, laughed at, and at worse, they're accused of being liars or mentally ill. Rarely are they even believed for seeing something odd. Fortunately, we have gotten accustomed to odd things.

Just before we saw the monster, Kate and I descended the twisting cutbacks of the road and then headed north, into the ghost town of Independence. The road here was flatter, and the area was heavily forested. It would have all been so beautiful except for the fact our path was blocked by a legitimate monster. We smelled it first.

Before we saw it, Kate whispered, "Watcher?"

She had a point. Most watchers stink. Their smells range from mostly raw sewage with a hint of dead animal to mostly dead animal with a hint of raw sewage. They don't always smell though.

Benaiah doesn't because he bathes. But a watcher can smell so bad the average person is compelled to gag. Some people vomit, and that just adds to the overall aroma of having a watcher nearby. It's that bad.

But what we were smelling wasn't quite right. What we smelled was more like overwhelming dirty, wet dog mixed with corn chips. It's worse than it sounds. Tracker can smell a little like that when he's been walking the earth for a long time. I was willing to concede it could be a watcher, but then I saw it through the falling snow. First, I heard Kate gasp. At the same time our horses' ears flared forward. Solo stopped, and so did Jet. A nervous horse on packed ice and snow is a bad thing, so we both leaned down and spoke to them. It helped.

"Good Lord," whispered Kate, "it's on two legs."

I thought the Sobeks were terrifying, but the thing barring our way was worse. At least the Sobeks had a civilization of sorts. The thing thirty yards in front of us was pure viciousness, and it looked like it had only hunger and hatred in its red rimmed eyes. The creature was like a two-legged wolf, except it was huge and almost as big as a watcher. Its chest and shoulders were massive. Its snout was filled with sharp teeth, and even in this freezing weather, it was panting. It looked like it was smiling.

Some folks call these things dogmen. The Inuit called these things adlets. Others call them werewolves or the rougarou. They are usually described as aggressive and purely carnivorous. Stories about them, true or not, are always frightening.

It stood over seven feet tall, looking at us, swaying back and forth. It was covered with thick, black fur, and it stood slightly hunched over. The beast had extra-long powerful arms that tapered into hands with thick, long fingers capped with long, sharp claws. Like a watcher, the thing was built like a bodybuilder. A bodybuilder from hell. It never shifted its gaze as it stared our way.

"Well," I whispered to Kate, "this can't be good."

I knew thirty yards was not much distance when facing a wild animal. It could close the distance in seconds. I wondered if

I would even have time to pull out my rifle. I had underestimated Lavi when he charged me years before and the distance between us seemed about the same. And that time, I even had my shotgun ready. Benaiah saved me then. I wished he was here.

"Kate, I am going to pull out my rifle, and I am going to be as quick as possible. When I do, I expect that thing to make his move. The second he comes at us, turn Jet and run. When clear, get on the walkie-talkie. Find Libby and Jack. Got that?"

"I'm not leaving you."

That just made me mad. I never kept my eyes off the rougarou, but I could still talk. "No, Kate. You listen to me. I've heard about what these things do to people. They rip people apart. I can't fight back if I am defending you too. You have to do what I say."

Then we heard a growl from behind us. I never took my eyes off the one in front of me. Kate slowly looked behind us. "Uh-oh. We got company. There's another one behind us."

That was terrible news. "How far back there?"

"About the same."

I had no idea what to do but to reach for my rifle and try to get off a shot or two. Then off to the right, I heard a wolf's bark. The snowfall was thick, and the forest was thicker, but it sounded close. It sounded like Tracker's voice. He and Gyp were somewhere in that direction. They could come in handy right about now.

"Tracker?" asked Kate.

The first rougarou snapped its head to his left. It cocked its head and howled its own challenge. The other one, the one behind us, ran wide around us and joined it as they both peered into the forest. The second one kept turning its head to watch us, but something was going on.

I leaned into Kate and whispered, "They have no idea about Gyp either."

The two fearsome creatures were both focused on the forest to our right. I bent forward and slowly pulled out my rifle from its scabbard. Kate did the same. We heard each other's safeties going off. Even in the wind both rougarou heard the metallic clicks, and they turned and growled fiercely at us. But they didn't advance. It was Kate who was cooler than I expected.

"No shooting yet. Let's see how this plays out. They're not interested in us now."

The first monster howled again, and then both he and his friend turned and sprinted down the slope and off to the north. With the snow falling fast, the two disappeared quickly. I just started sweating, thinking of how close we came to disaster. I heard Kate exhale.

"Dean, that was terrifying. How do you just sit there and accept it? You weren't even scared."

Well, Kate was wrong but only sort of. "Kate, if I had been alone, I might have been terrified too. But the man who defends his family or his loved ones is far bolder. Dad has told me that sleeping in our creaky house is only creepy when he's alone. But when others are at home, which is almost always, he said he's afraid of almost nothing. I felt that way when Goliath attacked us years ago. I feel that way today."

Kate had on a big smile. It was weird, but there she was, smiling like a kid at Christmas. At first, I was confused, and I must have looked it.

"Why the smile?" I asked.

"Well," said Kate, "you know what that means? It means I'm a *loved one*. And that means you love me. Otherwise, you would have been scared to death! So go ahead and say it. Tell me you love me. You know I love you."

My mom has more wisdom in her than in a dozen books of proverbs. She's smart too. As clear as day, I remember her sitting me down and saying to me, "Never tell a girl you love her unless you're willing to marry her. That's how you know if it's love. Too many young people misuse affection, and they cheapen love. They proclaim their love to somebody, but what they really want is something for themselves. Those words are dynamite, don't be careless with them."

And just then, I was scared and not of those horrible, walking, toothy, stinky wolf things. Kate had used my words and had mined a deep truth out of them. I did love her.

Oh no. Well, here goes, I thought. And yes, I would probably only be her high school honey, but I loved her and if that dogman was a pastor, I would pop the question right now. But I didn't want to blow the moment. This would take a few minutes. "Hold that thought please."

I walked Solo up a few lengths and then turned and rode back to Kate. Our horses were side by side and facing different directions. I was next to her and only inches from her face. She had pulled down her scarf and looked at me quizzically. Snow was blowing in my face, but it was highlighting hers. Her long, brown hair cascaded from under her knit cap and fell over her shoulders. She had a smudge of dirt on her cheek. Her gray eyes were staring me. She said nothing.

"Kate, I have determined I would save those three words for the girl who was willing to look at my face every day, for as long as I live. And those words are reserved for the girl who makes my heart leap every time I see her face. Kate, your face makes my heart leap. So does your voice. So does your laugh. So does your faith. So does your courage. In fact, nearly everything about you makes my heart leap. So yes, Katherine Casho Gibbs, I love you. And I am only seventeen, but I have loved you for years. Nothing is going to change that."

Kate threw her arms around my neck and pulled up close. She kissed me gently and cried a little. "Dang, Dean, you did that good. I can't wait to see what happens when you propose. Just know, my answer will be *yes*."

Then Tracker barked. I quickly thanked God because I was not ready to keep the conversation going forward. We turned and saw an agitated Tracker looking at us as he and Gyp stood over the tracks of the two rougarou. I had truly forgotten about Landon for a few moments. We rode over, and Tracker let us have it. Of course, we had no idea what he was growling and barking about, so Kate and I just started laughing. Gyp was laughing too. I knew this though. Whether Landon lives or dies, I will remember these last five minutes for the rest of my life. And so would Kate.

This valley has more than its share of Christian summer camps. Trout-filled waters, wildlife, and stunning views made for a perfect camp setting. Also, wherever there's a patch of private property here and there, people were slapping up expensive cabins. It was getting late, and we would need shelter and a phone. The worst of the storm was not yet upon us, so I had no plans to be outside, in the storm and in the dark. We humans can't see in the dark, and we freeze to death easily. I was thinking the closest shelters were about six miles away. There are individual cabins up that way along with a big summer camp. I wasn't above breaking open a few doors, but I sensed that a Christian camp might be more willing to understand us needing to get out of the storm. A homeowner might not be so gracious. Plus, camp cabin doors are probably a lot easier to bust in. And cheaper to replace.

Tracker had cooled off, and he and Gyp were communicating when I told them we needed to find shelter. They nodded. Suddenly they turned their gaze to the south, looking back up the road. We had no patience for more monsters, so Kate and I both pulled up our rifles and pointed them southward and into the blowing snow. Tracker got Kate's attention and made it obvious he wanted the rifles to be lowered. I trusted Tracker with my life and with Kate's, so we did as told.

Moments later, I started to hear the whine of snowmobiles. Kate knelt next to Tracker and put her arms around his big fluffy neck.

"Is it Libby and Jack?" Tracker nodded, and his tail wagged too.

Gyp shifted back into the woods. He wasn't so sure. I knew the sound of my own snowmobile though. I told Gyp, and we both waited. The horses shook off the snow and seemed comforted by the sound of snowmobiles. I guess anything would be better than a few rougarou.

The two came into view, and they were coming fast. Both were excellent riders, and they looked like pros in the circuit. Gyp came back to join us. When we came close, they throttled back and coasted up to us.

Jack took off his helmet and immediately spoke, "Hi, guys! See anything?"

"Sure did," said Kate. "But first, tell us what you two saw up there."

Libby responded, "We rode all the way to Blue Lake and stopped. There were lots of snowmobile tracks, but that seemed to be as far as any snowmobilers went. We went around the lake and rode toward Haystack Peak, but there were no more tracks. So we turned back. That means Landon is north of us."

Tracker and Gyp nodded. "We need to hurry," I said. "The weather's getting bad, and it's going to be worse. Libby, can you and Jack ride ahead and get shelter? There's a summer camp with cabins and a small community of vacation cabins right about where the thick forest gives way to open landscape. It's about six miles away, as the crow flies, but conditions are awful. Jack, once you get there, you'll have to break in. Pick a cabin that has either a woodburning stove or power. The chimneys and the power lines will tell you which cabins have a stove, power, or both. Also, if you decide to go to the camp, the main office will have a phone. Figure a way to break in. We need to get a call into Sheriff Tuttle or to Captain Stahr. And then call your mom at my house. They will need filling in. We also need to know what's going on with them. And our dads, we have no clue where they are."

"Wait," said Kate. "There's a complication. Go fast and watch your back trails. You won't be alone. There are werewolves out. We saw two of them."

I was pretty sure the rougarou weren't actually shape-shifting werewolves. At least not the man-by-day, wolf-by-night kind of werewolves. I suspect the type we saw were some sort of ancient creature that had a world like the Sobeks. The Egyptians had several deities that resembled the things we saw. The Aztecs had a god with a dog's head. The Sumerians did too. It didn't surprise me the ancients modeled some of their gods after real creatures. They were frightening. I did not attempt to correct Kate. She described what we saw to Libby and Jack. Tracker and Gyp nodded as she spoke.

I watched as Jack and Libby pulled out their firearms and slung them on their shoulders for quick access. I would be doing the same. They listened to Kate intently. When Kate was finished, Jack let out a whistle. Libby looked at me and then to Tracker and Gyp. None of us countered Kate's version. It was, unfortunately, true.

I had a thought and picked up where Kate left off. "Guys, we've been wrong. This whole thing has been bothering me, and I am ashamed I didn't catch it."

Everybody was looking at me now. "We've been thinking all along that our presence here would go unnoticed, at least if we were smart. We were thinking we were on a rescue mission to save Landon. Gunther MacDonald does want to kill Landon, but Landon's the bait. I think we have been played for fools. The goal of the enemy has been to isolate the McLeods and the Gibbses and then kill us. Think about it. Mom and Aliyah and Gracie are alone at home and our fathers, and us, their children, left them stuck on a remote, hidden farm, alone. Aylmer is there, but he's not enough.

"Dad and Gunner are together, somewhere to the north of us. Officer Brigham may be with them, but he's probably on the list too. And here we are, all alone in the middle of a hundred thousand square acres of pure wilderness. Remember, we are all on the list. Tracker, I'm sure you are too. They don't know about you, Gyp, unless those rougarou somehow figured you were there."

Gyp thought about it for a second before shaking his head.

I kept going, "For your sake and for ours, Gyp, I hope you're right. As for us, we are all separated from one another, and they probably know where we are. In short, if they kill us, our bodies won't be found until spring, if at all. They have lured us here to make it easy. Unfortunately, the bad guys are two steps ahead of us."

I let that sit in. All of us looked at each other. I saw disbelief. First in Gyp, then it spread to everybody else. I thought I had laid out a pretty good case, but apparently not.

Jack went first, "They don't know about us."

"Why is that?"

"The bad guys, even the werewolves, if they're part of the bad guy group, would not expect us to be here. Maybe at the farm, but not here. Remember, there's only one way in the valley and that's thirty miles or so north of here, and they're probably watching the road up there. We took a shortcut none of them could expect. In fact, you two guys are on horses. They would have noticed a horse trailer coming into the valley today. We look just like locals out enjoying ourselves before the snows get too dicey. We still have good stories."

Jack made some solid points. Tracker nodded. Gyp did too. But Libby was thinking, and what she said changed our strategies.

"Jack's right, but being right doesn't help much, and it doesn't change anything. If Landon is the bait, then they'll kill him the minute they track down and kill our dads. If they have a clue about us, then they'll come at us to mop up. If not, then we'll be stuck here while they wipe out our family at the farm. They will look for Kaiyo, and they may try to find us on the farm or at the Gibbses, but they won't find us. I have no idea where Kaiyo is, but the enemy will count their good fortunes and vanish. Our dads may already be dead. Meginnah told us that men were watching the approaches to the valley. We have no choice but to attack, and we have to do it fast."

Even though all of us got some of the facts wrong, Libby's plan was right. It was Kate though who gave us perspective and purpose.

"Everybody has made some good points, but we have forgotten the one thing that's important. Who believes us being here is a mistake? Libby's understanding of the situation is dead-on, but her despair is all wrong. Meginnah, a cherub, brought us here, supernaturally. He answers only to God. Raphael knew all about what we were doing. Do you think Christ has no clue or that he screwed up allowing Meginnah to bring us here? Of course not. Whatever it is, we have a purpose in being here. Dean is right saying this valley is a trap. Jack is right in thinking the trap is for our dads and maybe Officer Brigham if he's with them. The bad guys don't know we are here. At least not yet. And Libby is right. The search for Landon is taking a back seat to a new mission. We need to destroy anybody or anything that comes against us. Don't forget, Landon is amazing, and as for us humans, he's better in the wilderness than anybody I know. He's even better than Dean."

Kate smiled and glanced my way. She was probably wrong, but I let it slide.

She continued, "If Landon is to be saved, God will empower him, us, our dads, or all of us to do it. And we, being here, right now, have the advantage. There are four fearsome Specials with us, and we are well armed. And best of all, we are behind them. They are looking only to the north. We will come with the storm from the south. But we cannot shelter tonight. Landon will be dead in the morning if we wait. The bad guys should be fearing us, and if they don't, then we will kill them all."

13

INVADERS—GRACIE

When they attacked, they came at us hard. We knew they would. But we were waiting for them. I knew it was going to happen because Aylmer and I saw them first. They were liars too. They said it was just between us people, but they lied. They brought monsters.

Miss Aliyah was right about being smart and being careful about decisions made in fear. That's why Mom listened to me. I knew Sarah was coming, and the time when she should be getting here. Mom and I believed she would be followed too. We already knew some guy in Helena was trying to find her. Sarah called and told us about her conversation with her boss. It made sense the bad guys would be trying to get her too. They wanted to kill everybody who knew about the Specials.

We wanted to know if anybody was following her. If we could figure that out, then we could figure out who or what planned on attacking us tonight. So about an hour before Sarah got here, I saddled Duke and walked him to the back steps. Aylmer was with me. Mom and Miss Aliyah came out, and I told them what I wanted to do. They asked a few questions then Mom kissed my cheek and told me to be careful. Seriously, do all mother's say that all the time? I told her I would. And I meant it.

We needed to blend into the landscape of the forest. I was dressed warmly in mostly white and brown colors. Those colors are winter forest colors. Aylmer was covered in black fur, but in the deep forest, he merges into the shadows. Even in the snow, he was hard to see while we were in the forest. Out in the open he stands out. Duke was a buckskin gelding and a beautiful animal. Duke is the color of brown straw, and his mane, tail, and legs are dark brown. He's almost impossible to see in the forest too.

Moose, my bigger dog, came with us. Moose is a terrific guard dog. Mom insisted he come, and I wanted him with me too. He obeys me and would die protecting me.

We left the house and rode west, along the driveway. The snow was coming hard from our left, and the wind was picking up. The cold was brutal, but we were all used to it. We made quick time of the two miles of open driveway. Then we slid into the forest. Except for the wind swirling through the trees, all was quiet. I had a choice to make. With the wind coming from the south, the three of us could watch the gates from the south or from the north. Each had their advantages. Dad once told me if I ever needed to sneak up on somebody, then do it in a way that forces them to do something they don't want to do. For instance, nobody likes to look directly at the sun. It's blinding. So it's best to attack with the sun at your back. It's easy to remember that way. The same is true of a steady wind. Facing the wind, especially when it's snowing hard, hurts. The ice pellets sting the face and force eyes to squint. Looking into a hard snow is no fun.

But if the bad guys have Specials or even an ordinary guard dog with them, we would be upwind too. Then that could be dangerous. Unless somebody really stinks, being upwind is no problem when watching only people. People's just are not good smellers. But if the people following Sarah had a dog or some other animal, our scents would quickly give us away. So I had a choice. If I watched the gates from the north, then I might wait with the freezing wind at my face for hours. If I watched from the south, my scent could betray me.

I couldn't risk the lives of my animals or Aylmer. Or me. I didn't want to die either. We would watch from the north. It would be a miserable wait in the snow, but we would do it. I explained to Aylmer what we would do and why. He nodded. I took a trail that took me north and away from our long, winding driveway. It was one of the trails Jack and Kate use to get from their house to our house and back. After a half mile, we turned and went west, climbing up through the thickets and forest. It wasn't long before we were due north of the gates. The thickets hid us from sight, but we had a decent view of the gates. I covered up everything but my eyes and waited.

The gates were installed a few years ago. Rumors of Kaiyo and Goliath had spread into town, and we started getting people coming onto the farm at all hours of the day. Usually they were teens, but we got folks from the local press and even a camera crew from a TV station in Bozeman. They were there to report on the *miracle bear*. Nobody ever saw anything, and Dad laughed at the reporter for trying to find the "mythical, miracle bear." At one time, we had a license to care for Kaiyo, but we had long ago notified the state that Kaiyo had gone back into the wilderness. Officer Brigham verified the story even though it wasn't quite true. We just didn't need anybody snooping around. The gates helped.

Dad made sure the gates were installed far enough away from the road so they weren't visible. And Dad had cameras installed to see who was there. One of the cameras was obvious, the other was hidden. Usually, the only folks that routinely came through the gate was either us, the Gibbses, or oil company employees. Mail and packages were put in a small, roofed shed Dad built next to the gate. Looking through the blowing snow, we could see past the gate and past the shed. We were about fifty yards away, a little uphill, and we were well hidden.

Dad always told me to watch my animals. That was good advice. Animals have better senses. When Duke and I go riding, I will see him throw his ears forward or watch his head snap to the right or left. He's alerted me to all sorts of things. So when Duke,

Moose, and Aylmer turned their heads to the right, I knew we had company.

A white, quad cab, shelled pickup quietly rolled into view and stopped by the gate. A man stepped out of the backside left passenger compartment. He was a thin, hatchet-faced man. He looked around the driveway and then went to the rear of the truck bed. He looked unpleasant, but he could have been anybody from town. He waited for a few minutes and then slapped the tailgate of the truck. He opened the tailgate and the shell's back window, and out came two giant dogs. They were crazy big with thick necks and big, wide heads with yellowish fur. They didn't act all happy and jumpy like Moose or Major when they got out of cars. The dogs I was watching were all business. They spread around the truck and tested the wind. Moments later, I noticed Aylmer and Moose with noses up, sniffing and searching with their noses held high. Moose whined, and Aylmer snorted and looked angry. Whatever those dogs were, Aylmer didn't like their smell. Being downwind of them was a good idea.

Then a tall man stepped out of the front passenger side. He was dressed nicely. His coat was long, and it fell almost down to his ankles. His shoulders were broad. Even in the snow, he moved easily. I never saw a full face, but the smile I saw frightened me. He walked so smoothly he seemed to glide up to the gate. I think he was the monster because I had never been so afraid. I had to pray quick to make the sense of dread go away. The second I prayed, he started looking around him. It was like he knew somebody was watching him.

Two other men also got out. I recognized one of them. His name was Pete Harred. He used to be an outfitter in town, but he was a bad one. A few years ago, he was paid to guide some bear poachers. Those people are horrible. Officer Brigham caught him and put him in jail. The whole Harred family doesn't like us. Dad told me Pete Harred is the son of a family of low life criminals. For some reason Pete blames Dad for his troubles. Dad didn't like him, either. Mr. Harred walked to the gate, and upon the nod of the tall man, he pushed the bars back and forth fast. The gate held. The tall man smiled. Just then the man in the back of the truck held a finger to his ear. He then said something, and they all moved back to their truck. Once the dogs and everybody were inside, the truck turned around and drove back to the road and turned to the south. That also meant somebody else warned him. They probably had a lot of bad guys helping them.

"Aylmer, I bet Sarah is close by."

Sure enough, within five minutes, Sarah drove down to the gate. Captain Stahr's SUV was right behind her. Sarah rolled down her window and punched in the code. The gate opened, and she and Captain Stahr headed down the driveway and to the farm. Then the gate closed.

I wanted to see what kind of tracks those four-legged things left in the snow. I told Aylmer what I wanted to do, and he was not happy. In fact, he made it clear he wouldn't let me. I'm stubborn, but I'm not stupid. Aylmer is enormous, and he has a temper. And even if he loves me, which he does, I do not want to make him angry. If he felt like I didn't trust him, he would be hurt. And I trusted him. So we waited for the bad guys to come back.

After a half hour or so, Captain Stahr's SUV came up the driveway. Still, we stayed hidden and watched as the gate opened and Captain Stahr left. Aylmer shifted his weight and shook off the snow. The wind only seemed worse, and the snow was still blowing directly in our faces. I was about frozen and was ready to go. Just when I was about ready, Aylmer turned to the right. Through a hole in the thicket, Aylmer could see up the driveway and almost up to the road. His eyes were following something.

I heard a truck tailgate open. Then the truck I saw earlier rolled down to a position near the gate. I wasn't cold anymore. Moose was silent, but he was alert. Three men stepped out and walked up to one of the power poles that ran along the drive-way. One of them was the strange man I saw earlier; one was Mr. Harred. The other pointed to the wires, and they spoke for a few minutes. Mr. Harred held a hammer and walked straight into the forest right at us. Aylmer watched intently.

Once he was in the forest, he took a few steps, turned, and made his way through the woods to the edge of the gate. He raised his hammer, and with a few violent swings, the camera that was attached to the gate was smashed to pieces. Had the moron looked, he would have learned that the package shed had a camera too. It was recording everything he did.

He stepped out onto the driveway and walked quickly to the truck. The men got back in their truck. I couldn't see the dogs in the truck. I remembered hearing a tailgate slam earlier, and that had been bothering me.

I leaned down to Aylmer and whispered in his ear, "Aylmer, their dogs weren't in the truck. Can you slip out and see if they're nearby?"

Aylmer nodded and silently turned west, uphill, and toward the road. At the same time, the truck used the turnaround by the gate and went back to the road. We were in a thicket of tall bushes and some low trees, so we were hidden well, and the wind and heavy snowfall made seeing us even harder. As big as he was, Aylmer quietly disappeared through the bushes and up the hill. The wind hid our sounds, and with the way it was blowing, catching our scents would be nearly impossible unless something was close behind us.

Aylmer came back to us and kept looking behind us. He held his head low, and it was obvious he was ready for battle. Then we heard the truck honk its horn. After a few seconds, it honked again, several times. Impatiently. We heard the tailgate slam shut. The truck left and drove south, toward town.

They were gone. Using flicks of his head, Aylmer motioned me to follow him. The snow had piled up around us in the thicket as we moved snow dumped on all of us. Moose was thrilled to move, and he shook of the snow happily. Aylmer took the lead, and he left the thicket, and we walked about fifteen yards to the west. We came up on huge dog tracks. By the looks of their large tracks, they had caught a few whiffs of us, but we weren't upwind of them, so they couldn't pinpoint us.

"Are they dangerous?" I asked.

Aylmer nodded vigorously. It was time to go back home and let everybody know.

Runner—Landon

I had taken MacDonald south all the way to Blue Lake, and then we rode back north eleven miles until we got to Hicks Park Campground. We stopped to pour ourselves a cup of coffee and take a break. As I did so, I thought about the day so far. I did come to realize that MacDonald was right about one thing. He was a skilled, smart rider. MacDonald knew or quickly learned how to handle everything I threw at him. He kept pushing me to take him off the marked trails, but I wasn't ready. There was no margin for error. We had a storm barreling toward us, and darkness wasn't that far off. I told him why, but he just snorted.

He was already agitated with the presence of other snowmobilers on the same trails as us. He knew this valley had nothing like the number of recreational snowmobilers in Paradise Valley. For whatever reason, he wanted the valley to himself. He should've known better; he picked this valley. When we started the day, he said he didn't know much about the valley, but I suspected otherwise. He was oddly comfortable here.

When I called it a day and told MacDonald it was time to head back, he cursed me and threw a few insults my way. There were a few other riders taking breaks in the same campground, and they heard Gunther's trash talk. Gunther had already made it impossible for me to like him, and now he was embarrassing himself. It seemed he was doing everything he could to make me hate him. And that made me concerned. He had to have a reason, and I was getting suspicious.

Everybody has a choice. I could either react or respond. Reacting is bad. Responding is better. Libby explained it this way, "Nobody wants to have a reaction to medicine. They would rather respond to medicine, right?"

Right. So I swallowed my pride and responded, "Gunther, you did well today. In fact, you showed me that you're an excellent rider. We have another week and a half of this. The storm will pass late tonight. We'll get out early, and I'll take you where there are no other snowmobile tracks. I don't doubt your ability to handle it. But as for the rest of the day, only a foolish guide would let his client go off trail with the weather we're having and at night too. You can cuss me until doomsday, and you can insult me until you run out of words, but I'm not changing my mind."

"Fine," Gunther growled. "We'll head back. But I'm done taking orders from you. Consider yourself off the clock. In fact, I'll bet you one day's pay I get back to camp first. Like I promised, I can outride you anytime. So far, this excursion you sold me sucks, so I want some of my money back."

This guy was the most competitive man I had ever met in my life. He was the definition of insufferable. "Really, you, beat me? It'll never happen," I said. "But there will be no racing. You would just redline my sled the fourteen miles or so back to camp. To you, my sleds are toys. To me, they're my livelihood. So for now, we'll just have to agree to disagree."

He insulted me again, but he got my message. Along with some other riders, we rode north to our campsite. Everybody seemed tired. The other riders wished us well and continued north to load up and go home. Going home sounded good.

I was beginning to despise Gunther, and I had to be careful. He had been going out of his way to pick a fight with me, and I had been too busy dealing with his rude behavior to ask myself why. There was a reason he was pushing me, and I couldn't think of a good one. We parked our sleds, and Gunther practically ran to let Ilya out of his trailer. Ilya came out of the trailer as if he were royalty. He looked at me and then back at Gunther. I think I heard him growl. Ilya stretched and immediately started sniffing the air. Gunther retrieved his rifle from his sled. He cradled it in his arms as they watched me refuel the snowmobiles and place the covers over them. I made sure I never turned my back on either of them. Both were somehow sinister. While I was stowing the rest of our gear, Gunther started in on me again.

"I hope you brought you some snacks because I cook in my trailer. Ilya and I eat alone."

"Gunther, you told me we were 'off the clock,' so I figured you weren't looking for my company. Enjoy your evening. We're both tired, and turning in sounds good to me."

"One last thing, Landon. I need to make some phone calls tonight. Any places around here where I get cell phone coverage?"

"Short of climbing way above the valley floor, cell phone signals are nonexistent. In the morning, depending on the weather, we could ride north until we get coverage, but that could be thirty miles or so."

Gunther strangely looked pleased. "That's all right, I guess. I can call tomorrow." Then he looked at Ilya and laughed. For a moment, Ilya's tail wagged. Must have been some sort of inside joke. They both went into the trailer. I headed to my cabin.

About fifteen minutes later, I left my cabin to retrieve my snowshoes, a can of soup, and the camp stove from my truck. The snowfall had gotten heavier, and the wind had picked up. It was almost dark. I was cold and starting to dread spending another week with MacDonald. I slogged through the snow, opened the truck, and got what I needed. I shut the door, and then I heard something like gunshots. First one then several close together. They weren't all that far away. The wind was picking up, so I couldn't be sure of what I heard, but shooting guns is not rare in rural Montana.

I made my way back to the cabin. I couldn't have been more down in the dumps. I missed Libby. She was a part of everything good in my life, and I knew it. I imagined how nice and comfortable she was at Sam and Susan's farm.

After an unnecessarily long ten minutes of self-pity, I had an idea. I knew the people who ran this camp, and we were all friends. As a kid, my family had come here during family camp, and I had spent a few summers here on staff. We often referred business to each other, and they always allowed me and my customers access to the river. As a camper or as a staff member, my father made sure I knew the folks who ran the Christian camps along this valley floor. There were several camps, but it was worth it. With this camp, I knew it well.

I also knew they had a landline phone in the office.

MacDonald probably assumed I didn't have keys to the other buildings, but I did. Every time I was in this valley, I checked out the camps after they closed for the season. Then I reported what I saw to the folks who run the camps. They always appreciate it. This camp has had a few bear break-ins and a burglary or two, and because of that, I had keys. For several unarticulated reasons, I had no plans on letting Gunther know where I was going. It was just something he didn't need to know. And I didn't trust him.

I turned out the lights and waited for my eyes to adjust to the darkness. It takes longer for eyes to adjust to darkness than to adjust to light. So I waited. There was still a slight glow in the western sky, but the valley was dark. I had my sidearm, my rifle, a knife, and I was bundled up. I have heard too many stories of competent people getting killed in camp by bears that were supposed to be hibernating. I go armed nearly everywhere, and tonight would be no exception. I was also bundled up. Whiteout conditions were forecasted for tonight, and people can get lost in their own yards during a whiteout and die of exposure. I didn't want to die that way.

Without making a sound, I stepped out on the cabin and slipped to my right. I needed to put the cabin between me and Gunther's trailer. The trailer was about sixty yards away, and with the thick, falling snow, I didn't think he could see me, but maybe Ilya could. After putting on my snowshoes, I quietly made my way uphill, passing behind three other empty cabins. From there I turned left and made my way north along a camp driveway. I passed a long, newer, two-story dormitory building and then descended into the center of the camp, not far from the chapel. The camp's office was just past the dining hall. The security lights around the buildings cast a beautiful glow, but they provided proof the snow wasn't close to letting up.

The office wasn't far, but the conditions turned a short walk into a long one. Once at the office, I stepped out of the shadows only long enough to unlock the door, enter, relock it, and step away from the windows. The interior was cold but familiar to me. Behind the front counter was a chair and the phone. I had been here many times before. It felt nice, and my gloomy mood was starting to ebb. I picked up the receiver and was pleasantly surprised at the welcome tone of a working phone. I dialed the McLeods, and Susan answered immediately.

"Hey, Susan. This is Landon. How you all doing?"

She gasped. "Oh good Lord! It's Landon! Okay, Landon. Listen to me, and don't say anything. First, where are you?"

She had just told me not to say anything and then asked me a question. I wisely decided not to tease her. She sounded like something was up.

"I'm at CVP Christian Camp. You know, the one in Boulder Valley. Weather's horrible, but overall, it's winter in Montana, right?"

Susan went straight to the point, "Gunther MacDonald is an assassin, and he wants to kill you tonight. Don't ask questions. Just listen. He shot Kaiyo yesterday. Kaiyo was lucky, but we know their plan. They're so cocky one of them told Sam their reasons. They hate you because you looked into Eden, and they hate Kaiyo because he's from Eden. Gunther took you into the valley to kill you and leave your body in the mountains to be eaten by scavengers. He said we are all on some sort of list of people to be killed. They ransacked your office. All your recent records of customers are gone. Sam, Gunner, and Officer Brigham are coming down the valley to rescue you. Can you get away?" She was breathless.

"Yeah, maybe. My snowmobile is fueled up and ready to go. Are you telling me the truth about everything?" She said she was. "Then let me talk to Libby."

"She's not here. We have no idea where she is, but she and Kate were hoping to be taken to the valley where you are."

"Start from the beginning, I have a few minutes."

For the next ten minutes, Susan told me about Libby guessing I went to the Boulder River Valley and then about Kate and Libby going after Dean, Jack, Kaiyo, and Aylmer. She told me about Sam and Gunner coming to this valley. The gunshots I heard earlier came to mind, but I didn't mention them to her. She told me about Sarah joining them at the farm and how they were expecting an attack. She told me Troy was coming back. Finally, she told me about Gracie's spy work. Gracie always amazed me.

Susan finished by saying, "Landon, be careful. Gracie described one of the men as a monster. They have monster dogs too. They are coming after us tonight."

She told me that she and Sam loved me, and we closed the call with a quick prayer. Alone in the dark, I thought about everything she said. It was good to hear Troy was coming back, but those ladies were dangerous. They didn't necessarily need a man; they just needed more shooters. Troy, being a cop, was a big plus. All of them were good shots. And Sarah was the most dangerous of the lot. She tried to kill me a few years back. Of course, she was demon-possessed back then, but she told me she still had some responsibility. She told me she liked the hunt. She still has a sinister side to her, and she knows it. And whoever the bad guys are, she can think like them. They should be careful.

As for the monsters, I wasn't as afraid as others might be. Men are more dangerous than monsters. Men can be just as horrific as the worst demons. Being afraid of certain people is always prudent. Besides, I have experience with monsters. The forests are not always pristine, and there are things in the forests that are different. Unfortunately, some of them like to kill. I have tracked monsters, fought off a few, made peace with a few, and killed one.

There are a lot of them, but not all are against us. Some of the flesh and blood kind just want to be left alone to live, breed, and hunt. Some are defectors. But right now, Gunther MacDonald was my monster.

I was worried about Jack, Libby, and Kate. I wasn't worried in the least about Dean. Dean had learned from Sam, me, Kaiyo, and Goliath about living in the wild. He's the only one who could possibly track me down. Whatever we were doing here, he was made for it.

I thought about what I needed to do. The darkness of my office was an ally, though it would be temporary. Once this storm let up, Ilya could sniff me out if I stayed here. And it was no warmer inside than it was outside.

I took stake of my assets. I was well armed, but I didn't have much ammunition. There's never enough of that. I was well dressed for the cold, and I had snowshoes. The deeper the snow, the better. Ilya would have a tough time getting through the drifts. MacDonald never mentioned having snowshoes, but I put them on the list for things he should bring. But since all he wanted to do was kill me and leave, I doubt he would have them. I then rifled through the desk drawers and found a few sleeves of peanuts and some beef jerky.

I was ready to go; I just didn't know which way to go. South was not an option. It led only into thicker forests and nearly impassable peaks. The slopes to the east were just too steep. The west wasn't much better. Northward along the road was the way for me. But those gunshots probably meant Sam and Gunner got ambushed. If they were alive, they would have abandoned my rescue. They might be worse off than me. Also, MacDonald would be sure to follow me. So far, he didn't have any monsters, so I could outrun him. I had enough fuel to get to Big Timber and back. Killers like MacDonald wouldn't stick around too long. If he couldn't catch me, he'd leave the valley and try later. I didn't want him to have that chance, but right now, he had the advantages.

I stepped outside and slipped into the shadows created by the security lights. I smelled smoke, and that bothered me. If I could get to my snowmobile, I could simply race north and hope to make it past MacDonald's men. At the very least, I could get away from MacDonald. I waited to make sure I was alone. Satisfied, I stayed low and walked west toward the road.

In seconds, I came to the main driveway that circled and bisected the camp. Hiding behind an ornamental boulder, I had a straight view six hundred yards to the south. From my vantage point, I could see beyond the darkened basketball court to the camp entrance. For all the wrong reasons, I could see MacDonald's SUV and well-lit trailer through the heavy snowfall. Unfortunately, the good lighting came from my cabin and my truck. They were on fire, and the flames were roiling. If it wasn't so awful for me, it would be pretty. My gear, my food, and everything I needed for the trip was fueling two spectacular fires. I was far more angry than scared.

The good news was, I was well armed, and they had no idea where I was. I had set my mind on shooting Gunther for torching my car and wanting to kill me. And his stupid dog was going to get blasted if it objected. From my view behind the boulder, I pulled my rifle forward and unzipped my coat to get access to my handgun. Silhouetted by the lights and fire, I saw MacDonald and Ilya.

At times like this, I seem to engage in running conversations with God. The conversations are one-sided because I do all the talking. God doesn't speak out loud to me like I speak to him. Maybe God talks to others like that, but so far, not to me. But I was okay with that. Right now wasn't really a burning-bush type of moment. I needed to do something, and it was either flee or go try to kill Gunther MacDonald before he killed me. I wasn't interested in running, especially in a near blizzard, and killing MacDonald seemed like a quick way to end my problems. I tried to think through the options and escape routes as I watched the fires for another few minutes. They were not dying down. And then, God spoke to me. I had asked which option to take when God answered. Sort of.

There, also silhouetted by the fires, two big watchers strolled into the picture and went straight to Ilya and Gunther. They were impossible to miss. Gunther was a big guy, and he looked small next to them. Whatever advantages I had disappeared when those things showed up.

A watcher is the very definition of a monster. They live in our imaginations and in the shadows of the forests. People have a lot of names for them, with *bigfoot* being the most common. I don't like that name because it makes people roll their eyes. The McLeods called them watchers because they didn't know what sort of creatures were frightening their livestock and putting their dogs on alert. All they knew was that for years, unknown creatures occasionally hid and watched them from the thick brush of the close by Southern Forest. It wasn't until Sam got kidnapped by cannibal watchers and was freed by Benaiah that he connected the dots. He also learned that some were Specials, but most were not. Some were pure danger. The watchers I was looking at were the dangerous kind.

I appreciated God's quick answer and started to conclude that getting away was the wise choice. But I also knew those watchers could probably catch me if I fled. It was then, in a moment of indecisiveness, when I heard a menacing growl from behind the office. It was dark, but I could make out a large, hulking shadow partially covered by the small building. It growled again.

I knew what that thing was. Those creatures are some sort of mutant, paranormal type of terrors. And I knew I was in deep trouble. I was also pretty sure I wouldn't live through the next three minutes. It was not a watcher, but it was far more aggressive. These things were real monsters. I had tracked one of those things a few years ago. I watched from my blind as it ran down a deer and killed it. It was so fast. And it was on two legs. It reminded me of a watcher with the head of a wolf. Though its back legs were dog-like, the creature had huge shoulders and muscular arms that led to hands with fingers that ended with talons. I followed it for an hour. Its tracks ended abruptly as if it crossed through an invisible door. I assumed it was a door because I was familiar with such fantastic things.

In one move, I shouldered my rifle and confirmed the safety was off. I kept it pointed to my left, where I saw the monster. It was time to go. Continuing to stay low, I backed up, which, by the way, is ridiculously hard to do in snowshoes. Turning, I heard the phone ringing in the office. There was no time to answer it, and I needed to get away. I assumed that call was important, but I knew there were other homes and camps along the way. I could call Susan back later.

Keeping low, I walked west past a line of cabins and barracks that hid me from being seen from anything or anybody near the fires. I heard no more growling, but I was not comforted. That dogman had gotten close to me, and I never heard him. I made a beeline for the river. It was just past the road, and the road wasn't far. The ice on the river wasn't thick yet, but I felt that I had a shot at making it safely across. I was confident the watchers would go through the ice, and the dogman probably would too. Granted, the water was only a few feet deep, but I was hoping that monsters hated wet, frozen feet more than they hated me.

Trudging through the blizzard, I was careful not to sweat. Sweat kills in cold weather. I didn't panic, and I smartly loosened my scarf and cap. As long as I was on the run, I would have to manage my heat. Also, I had to stay alert. My plan was not to run but to hide.

My way to the river was not blocked; it was just hard to figure out where I was. It was dark, and the snow was blowing sideways. That was to my advantage. I was downwind of the watchers and couldn't be seen. I could be tracked though. But as MacDonald and the watchers hung by the warmth of the fires, my tracks were being erased by the wind and snow.

I crossed the river, but it wasn't easy. If I had been chased, I would have broken through the ice. The river wasn't deep, but a wet leg could be fatal. I took my time, counting on my snowshoes to distribute my weight. Reaching the other side, I scrambled up the bank, and I was confident I had evaded MacDonald and his hairy posse. I waited at the base of the slope of an unnamed mountain and settled in the timber and waited. I was too far to see the flames clearly, but there was a big glow easily visible in the blowing snow. I entertained the thought of hunkering down and waiting for daylight, but I was startled by a noticeable growl upslope and to the south of me. It was close, and it was exactly like the one I heard by the camp office.

That got me on the move again. I stayed next to the bottom of the slope, and I was in a hurry. I quit being concerned about sweating. I had to get some distance between me and whatever it was that growled. I knew there were some nearby vacation homes downstream on the other side of the river, and I had no hesitation about breaking in. Many of them were huge and very nice. I needed to get to a landline and hunker down until dawn. If I could hide in comfort, well, I was okay with that.

I was making my way along the edge of the valley floor and heading north. It wasn't long before the steep slope pushed me to the riverbank. Just across the river was a nice-looking cabin. I wanted in there, but as I started to go down the bank to the river, I heard a growl on the other riverbank, not far from the cabin. It was loud enough to hear over the wind. Whatever it was, crossing the river was not a good idea. So I reversed course and climbed back up the bank. For the hour, I followed the river downstream on a path along the bank. These paths are along many waterways, and they were usually made by fishermen and hikers. This path was probably made the same way but with help from moose and bears too.

I continued to follow the river as it flowed north. It wasn't long before I was exhausted. Walking fast in deep snow, even with snowshoes, is grueling, and I was quickly running out of steam. I knew I was hidden from view of anybody on the other side of the river, but I wanted to be on the road. Roads are flat, and often the wind keeps the drifts away from the middle of the roads. But each time I got near the river to cross it, I was threatened with another growl. That turned out to be a good thing too, because the road suddenly got busy. MacDonald was either getting reinforcements or he was about to get arrested. Two groups of snowmobilers passed me, making their way south. One was a group of four, and they were later followed by a group of two. The riders were either lawmen or killers, and I seriously doubted they were lawmen.

When each group passed, I would remain motionless in the dark timber. It was easy to want to stay and take a breather, but whenever I waited too long, something growled behind me. For whatever reason, I was being herded to the north. I passed several suitable cabins on the other side of the river, but each time I started to go their way, I was discouraged by a warning growl from behind me and on the other side of the river

I was apparently being followed by at least two of those things. The terrain turned to low hills and then more low hills, but eventually I made it to a parking lot on the west side of a bridge. I knew where I was, but I waited in the trees to make sure I didn't walk into a trap. I was growled at again, and this time I yelled back. That was stupid because if anybody was listening, I just gave up my position. But I was wet and beginning to freeze to death. I knew the symptoms of hypothermia, and I was in deep trouble. My shivering had long been uncontrollable, and my natural clumsiness had morphed into a problem. Standing was getting harder to do. Another growl. I got up and started moving. I fell often, but every time I fell, the growls returned, closer every time.

Ten minutes later, I slogged past Falls Creek Campground and came up close to a small community of vacation homes. I knew the area, and there were numerous dwellings. I heard a couple of snowmobiles on the other side of the river. I had no idea who they were, but I could see their lights. They stopped at every cabin and shined their flashlights. It was there I decided to shoot it out. I was pretty sure I could take out the two riders and then hold those dogmen off long enough to break into a convenient cabin.

I was worn out and had little left in me, and I was starting to get confused. That told me I was freezing to death and didn't have much longer. Whatever fear I had vanished in the blowing snow several miles to the south.

On the right was Old County Road. Not far up the road was an inviting cabin just to the left. I took the road and started making my way to the cabin. By all appearances, there was nobody anywhere. No houses were showing lights. The house I targeted had a security lamp at the left side of the home and just above their detached garage. I took a step on the driveway when one of those dogmen stepped out from behind the garage and into the glow of the security light. He howled and barred my way to the cabin. I could feel the force of his howl in my nearly frozen chest. He stood there swaying. I had nothing left. I screamed and cursed at the monster and raised my rifle. The dogman barked, and I yelled again in return. I was just about to pull the trigger when I heard something wonderful.

"Landon? Is that you?"

The dogman vanished into the darkness. And snowmobiles were crossing the bridge and coming my way.

Offense—Libby

I didn't know if Kate had a flair for the dramatic or if she had the instincts of a true warrior. Here, in the bruising cold, with monsters about, she never complained. In fact, she seemed to be getting stronger. My bet was she had warrior blood all through her. Dean was in the stratosphere in love with her, and something obviously transpired between them while Jack and I were catching up to the group. We would discuss it later.

We made our plans. Tracker and Gyp would join us. Tracker would try to get Goliath and Benaiah to come off the slopes and be a part of the attack force. The first thing we needed to do was get a call into Mom. A few miles north of us was Jordan Creek Lutheran Camp. Jordan Creek was the first of four Christian camps in the valley. They would have power and phones, so that was step one. There were also a few huge private cabins near there, and those could be broken into if necessary. Right now, I didn't give a rip about somebody's personal property. My fiancé and my future were both about to get murdered, and stopping the assassins was all I cared about. If I had to break a few doors or windows, I didn't care. Hopefully, that wouldn't be necessary.

After a few howls, we heard Benaiah. Sometimes he sounded like a bellowing bull, but it sounded good to all of us. As they got closer, Goliath roared. That sounded even better. The two enormous beasts came into view. As dark as Benaiah was, I was surprised how he blended in with the forest. Goliath's coat was a brown blond with dark legs. His coat had enough snow on it he was practically invisible until he got close. They must have been closer than I had thought because they got here quickly. Tracker and Gyp met them and took them to the rougarous' tracks. Dogman is the common word, but Dean and I called them *rougarou*. Dad has a pal in Louisiana who claimed to have seen a few. He said he was "always on the lookout for the rougarou." So at least with us, the name stuck. It sounded better too.

The Specials seemed extremely distressed discussing the rougarou. I gave them a few minutes, and I then called them over. Never once do I get used to looking at these creatures with anything but amazement. They stood there, all but Tracker looking down at me, and waited for my orders. It was time.

"Jack and Dean, take one of the sleds and a walkie-talkie. Keep it on channel 4. If you need to talk, just know somebody else will probably be listening. Remember, one click for yes, two for no. Stick to the aliases when you're using it. You two give a call name of Carl. Kate and I will be Patti. About ten miles north of here are two guest ranches right next to each other. They're on the left side of the road, you can't miss them. Landon knows the owners well. Both places are usually open for the winter. One of the guest ranches has stables we might need, and hopefully, both should have utility snowmobiles. We need those. Dean, do your talking and persuade them that it's a good idea. Don't threaten them though. Landon thinks highly of those folks and vice versa. Leave your snowmobile there, and bring the utility snowmobiles back and meet us on the road. If they have cargo sleds or skids, bring them. Those snowmobiles are critical. We have too far to go. Specials on foot and humans riding horseback won't get the job done. We will need all the speed God can give us."

Everyone nodded.

"Benaiah, take Jet and Solo's reins, and lead them to the camp as quickly as possible. The rest of you, go with Benaiah. Kate and I are going ahead of you four to see if we can find a phone that works. Dean and Jack, meet us at Jordan Creek, but keep your walkie-talkie handy. Questions?"

"We're good," said Dean. "Jack, you're a better rider, and I'm a better shot. You drive, and I'll do the shooting."

"Whoa! Did I just hear you say I was a better rider? That's a freaking miracle!"

"You're a better athlete too. Feel better?"

"I definitely do," said Jack. "I'll be careful though. We need your hands on your rifle. Let's give the helmets to the ladies."

They did, and then they left.

"Kate, same thing. You drive, I'll ride shotgun."

We got on the snowmobile. Kate had it started before I got settled. I looked back as Benaiah waved. In a sight I never expected to see, Benaiah had Tracker draped around his neck. For a wolf, Tracker was huge, but he was definitely the little guy next to the bears and Benaiah. The snow was starting to get deep, and we needed Tracker to be as fresh as possible. He took it in stride. The Specials started loping after us. They were surprisingly fast.

Kate was an excellent operator. She was a natural on anything with hooves, wheels, or a motor. We rode fast and descended about 1,500 feet over the next three miles. Kate followed the tracks of other snowmobiles, and the ride was as good as could be expected.

Ten minutes later, we were at the Box Canyon Pullout. The pullout was the end of the Main Boulder Road, and in the summer, it was packed with cars, trucks, and trailers. Today there was nothing. From here, the road flattened out, and we made great time. The wind was at our backs, and that made the sting of snowfall a little easier on our faces.

After another mile, we made it to the summer camp. Even with darkness overtaking the day, this place was pretty. All the Christian camps in the valley were nice, but this one was especially beautiful. I prayed to see some lights on in the main building, but the camp was fully closed. We drove under a metal rope gate and went straight to the steps of the two-story building that houses the dining area, several offices, and first-floor storage. I had friends who spent their summers at this camp, and I visited it several times. Years ago, a friend and I snuck out of our cabins at another camp farther north. We borrowed some camp horses, and we rode down here in the middle of the night to see some guys we liked. It was a blast until we got caught. Over a dozen years of summer camp, Dean and I managed to get kicked out of two of the camps in this valley. I deserved it. Dean didn't. He got in a fight protecting a friend. That was Dean.

Kate turned the sled for a quick getaway while I bounded up the steps. The doors were solid, sturdy doors, and they were made to keep campers in and bears out. Breaking in without the Specials would be impossible. But this is the west, and people out here know trouble sometimes comes when the weather crashes in.

The wide deck railing had a row of rocks and pots sitting on top. I turned each one until I found a key. Right then, I loved Jordan Creek Camp. I grabbed the key and yelled out at Kate. In seconds we were inside looking for a phone.

Ten minutes later, I got off the phone with Mom and then called CVP. Landon had just been there, and I needed him to come my way. He needed to head south, not north. We were safe here. The north was infested with the enemy. He was trying to find Dad, and we had no idea where he was. I let it ring until it quit

176

ringing. Then I tried again. Frustrated beyond belief, I cried. Kate was in another office on another line talking to Aliyah and Sarah when she heard me. I was slumped into the chair when she walked in. I was as defeated as I had ever been.

She stood in front of me, looking disappointed.

"What do you need, Kate?"

Kate was cool and unemotional. "Let's go kill Gunther MacDonald."

Kate stayed there as I thought of my response. She was not smiling.

"Really, Kate? So it's just that easy? Are you ready to go to jail? Because that's what's waiting for us if we're not careful. Right now, MacDonald hasn't broken any laws. I have no idea where Landon is, but he's probably on the run, and MacDonald is probably sound asleep in his cushy travel trailer. You can't just go around killing people!"

I made some solid points, but Kate was iron.

"Yes, Libby. I'm perfectly willing to go to jail, and you should too. This is Landon we're talking about. He's more than worth the risk of jail. He's worth every second of a life sentence. And we don't have a choice. MacDonald is an assassin. He's well trained. If your intent is to capture him or convince him to leave us alone for the rest of our lives, it won't work. He's going to come back at us. His boss has an endless supply of money too. He'll never quit. For most of my life, my family was on the run because of our faith. You know the story. I'm done running. And like it or not, Libby, we're on some death list. That list is made of the names of our people and our Specials, and they intend to slaughter all of us."

She kept going. It was weird to watch her. She was a graceful, young beauty, but the stuff coming out of her mouth was scary.

"Libby," she said sweetly, "you met MacDonald this morning. Was he humble? Did he seem like the type of man who can be intimidated easily?"

I answered *no* to both questions.

"That's right. He's got a lot of money riding on this particular assassination, so once he figures out Landon is gone, he'll spread out and start searching. MacDonald needs to go away. Since he won't go away, we need to act now. And hey, maybe we don't kill him. Maybe things will happen so it's not necessary. Nothing comes to mind, but who knows, right? But this I know, if we lead your brothers and the Specials into an attack, we better not try to hold anything back. If we do, one or more of us will die because of it."

She held out her hand and pulled me up and out of the chair. She was right, of course. She seemed a little bloodthirsty about it, but she was right. She might look like she's twenty-one, but she's sort of a child, and children sometimes tend to see things in black and white. She might be right too. She also seemed to be asserting herself into the command structure. I needed a second in command, but Dean was going to have that role. Kate was going to stay with me. I needed those two separated and focused on the tasks at hand.

"I'm good. Thank you. Step outside and look for Benaiah. Take your weapon."

She smiled and stepped out. There was a map of the valley hanging on the wall. I needed to get the team in front of this map. *But first things first*, I said to myself. The horses were a liability. I needed a stable where I could put the horses. They would easily survive if I could get them sheltered from the wind and out of the snow. Jordan Creek was a hiker camp. Horses weren't their thing. My eyes went from building to building. Like all camps, there were offices, cabins, a bigger sanctuary, and an assortment of sheds here and there.

For the next ten minutes, Kate and I checked out the buildings. There were a few equipment sheds, but all were too small and drafty. I walked to one of the cabins. It used to be a boy's cabin. I know because I had been here before. On horseback. This was where I got caught years before. I walked to the door and tried the doorknob. It was locked, but that was of no concern. Benaiah was headed my way with Solo and Jet.

"Benaiah, open the door and stack the bunks together in the back of the cabin. Lead the horses in there, and I'll take off their tack. We're leaving them here."

Benaiah chuckled, and with one quick turn of the knob, the door lock crumbled into pieces, and he pushed the door open. He got to work quickly, tossing bunks into a corner, and then he led both animals inside. The horses had known Benaiah for years, and they trusted him. Still, it was odd seeing Benaiah being so tender. Benaiah is a large watcher, and watchers are fearsome creatures.

When Benaiah walked out of the cabin, Kate and I went in and removed the saddles and the wet blankets. We snapped off the reins and left everything neatly stacked. The horses seemed satisfied with the new digs. They had to be tired. I was. I didn't look forward to cleaning the place up and explaining things to Jordan Creek staff, but if I did come back, I would at least be alive.

I instructed the Specials to go inside the main office and to wait for me to get there. That surprised them, and I gave them a look. Tracker barked at them, and they turned and made their way back to the main building and upstairs. Benaiah opened the doors, and they disappeared inside. Kate and I got back on our snowmobile and followed them. We were both upstairs when we heard snowmobiles coming our way. I prayed it would be my little brother.

Soon we saw the headlamps of two snowmobiles heading south and coming our way. Kate and I scrambled down the steps and took positions where we could fire if necessary. Jordan Creek has two entrances, but Dean would know to come to the second entrance. Somebody else might not. The snowmobiles were clearly different from any of ours. We watched as the two snowmobiles came through the second entrance and turn around not fifty feet from us.

I heard Dean's voice yell out, "Hey, Patti, it's me, Carl!"

We brought everybody inside. Dean quickly described how the two guest ranches gave us their utility snowmobiles. He kept it brief, but the story made me love Landon even more. They thought of Landon so much they gave us their snowmobiles to use. One was a big new Alpina Sherpa, and the other was a heavy-duty utility Arctic Cat. The best thing was they brought back three towed utility sleds. We were in business.

Jack was told that staff at both guest ranches had seen what they described as multiple two- and three-man snow patrols. They weren't recreational, and they weren't anybody with the Sweetgrass County Sheriff either. Jack said they got there not twenty minutes after a patrol came and rode through their parking lots. We all took that in.

I asked Dean to brief everyone on the geography of the valley. He pointed to the map on the wall. The Specials were especially interested. Jack and Kate were also committing the map to memory. Dean and I knew this valley well. For the next few minutes, Dean described our location and the valley in general. He pointed out CVP as the last place where Landon was located, but he had likely fled. We had no idea where he now was.

"Commit this map to memory," said Dean. "It'll be helpful if we split up."

Dean then looked at me, and I finished the briefing. "Folks, we all know we are going to battle. I expect they will have guns and Specials who will be against us. They or their ancestors left Eden long ago, betrayed God, and they are dangerous. Tracker, can you take down Ilya?"

Tracker nodded. "Gyp, you will be coming with Kate and me. We only have bolt action rifles, so we will be needing distance and cover. When they come for us, use your ability to blend in the snow and help us. Stay away from gun fire though. Take out any Specials that come for us."

Dean and Kate immediately interrupted, "Wait a minute," said Kate, "I'm going with Dean."

Dean joined in, "Libby, you don't understand. I will be responsible for Kate. She will be safer with me than with you, no offense."

The Specials listened. Benaiah looked on with interest.

I directed my attention to Kate, "Is Dean right?"

Kate said he was.

"Then my decision is final. Kate, you remember our discussion today. I can't remember when you said anything about being kept safe. Instead, you were talking about taking risks. And do you think Dean will be focused on rescuing Landon or even on the battle in general if he's busy keeping you safe? You and I are the best shots here, but if Dean is standing over you, keeping your head down, then both of you are no good to the mission. And the shooter giving cover fire that Jack would need will be too busy protecting Jack's little sister. I would rather leave you here than take you unless you do as your told. Do we understand?"

I sounded a bit like General Patton, but I had no time for a high school romance when Landon was in danger.

Dean was not pleased, but Kate was thinking. "She's right, Dean. Take care of my big brother, and fight the good fight. I have a role that will address my strengths."

Jack was quick to jump in, "Yeah, Libby's right. If Libby wasn't your sister, you would probably see it too. Just trust me on this." Then he looked at me. "What are your orders?"

"I need somebody to walk into the camp and confront MacDonald. Which one of you will do that for me?"

Dean immediately volunteered. And his mood changed. Kate objected, but I kept going, "Sorry, Kate, but we are going to do this the right way. I am not going to shoot somebody who, unlikely as it is, might be unarmed or no danger to us."

I kept on, "Goliath, right now the plan is for you to flank Dean and stay hidden. If he needs help, rush in. Tracker go in with Dean. Ilya will want to attack Dean. Your presence will stop him. Jack, find cover, and start blasting with your 12-gauge if Gunther or his patrol do something stupid. Benaiah, you are to start out hidden, and use your judgment. Do what is necessary to protect us. And be careful of walking into our own fire."

Dean and Jack rigged the towed utility sleds behind the three snowmobiles. We would get my snowmobile that they left at the guest ranches and then go straight for CVP. It was dark, and the conditions were near blizzard, but I don't think any of us were cold. Jack was grim, Kate was quiet, and Dean seemed thrilled, of course. The Specials all seemed ready.

Dean rode the Alpina, and Kate and Tracker sat in the back. Gyp was the heaviest, so he was in the towed utility sled behind the Alpina. Goliath got in the sled behind Jack in the Arctic Cat. I took my snowmobile and towed Benaiah. He looked unhappy, but I didn't have time for him to be shy and follow me in the woods.

"If a patrol comes our way, we'll stop, and you Specials find cover," barked Dean.

We pulled out slowly and made our way north. The Alpina was powerful and could power on at twenty-five miles per hour. That was fast enough. My snowmobile was normally fast, but it was toting about 850 pounds of unhappy watcher. We decided to limit our speeds to fifteen miles per hour; we were all towing some big weights, and we couldn't afford to burn out a motor.

CVP was about only about fifteen miles away. We got started, and despite the weather, we were making good time. Following the road was somewhat difficult, but much of the way trees grew close to the roadway. That made following the road easy. We rode in single file with the powerful Alpina leading the way and packing down the snow. I followed Jack which allowed me to tow Benaiah even easier. We passed Hicks Park campground, and I noted that it was abandoned. I wasn't surprised, but I was careful to avoid anybody, good or evil, who was on the road. Having two bears was crazy, having a bigfoot was nuts. They did not need to be seen. We kept going as the road crossed the river and then over Four Mile Creek. Just before we got to the guest ranches, we stopped and let the Specials off. They would make their way through the timber and meet us north of the ranches. There were observant people at the guest ranches, and they didn't need to see who our friends were.

Kate jumped off the Alpina and got on the snowmobile the boys left there. She started it up and rode over to me.

"I'm going to ride ahead about two hundred yards. If there is a patrol, stop and let the Specials get into the forest and wait for me."

We picked up the Specials by the entrance to Hell's Canyon Campground. Officer Brigham once told me that ominous-sounding place names often had ominous origins. I had no idea why somebody gave this place a name like that, but I was glad to move on.

Kate raced ahead. I could tell Dean was concerned, but having her up front made sense. Less than a mile away was Camp Yonah. It was another Christian summer camp. It enjoyed a good reputation as a fun place to go. All of them in the valley did. The road here was hilly, and my snowmobile labored with the weight of Benaiah. Just before we got to Camp Yonah, we watched Kate turn and race back to us. She sped over the low hill in front of us, turned, and skidded to a stop.

"Three riders headed our way!"

14

DEFENSE—KAIYO

Meginnah placed the door about a mile east of my farm. For door placement, that was unusually close, and I would need to thank him. I stepped into darkness and heavy, blowing snow. It felt so nice. People think bears hibernate because we don't like cold weather, but they're wrong. We love it. The only reason we hibernate is because there's just not enough to eat in the winter. If there was, we would be playing in the snow all the time.

I stayed in the woods and came in from the east, behind the farm, but south of the pastures. While it was hard to see things in the snow, there was one thing that was missing. There were no lights on. The farm always had lights. Every building had a security light or two, and I was close enough to my house to see if the lights were on.

I wanted to rush out, but that would be dumb. Mom is a good shot, and Miss Aliyah is okay. I've seen them use guns, and they seem mighty comfortable with them. Most importantly, I needed to be careful about Sarah. I loved her, and she loved me right back, but sometimes she was scary. The same crazy riskiness that led her to accept demonic possession now led her to be a fearless fighter for the Master. She is a lot like my big brother that way. Sarah is more dangerous than everybody but Dean. I think my mom knew that about Sarah. Captain Stahr didn't know it because he's all goo-goo about her. He'll learn.

I decided to make my way to the southern side of the farm. The forest was thick on the south side, and I could get close without being seen. I could hear cows close by, and that was confusing. Walking carefully, I caught some faint but strange scents riding the fast, northbound winds. I waited carefully before bolting across the tractor path that led to our hidden southern pastures. I then continued to quietly glide through the dense forest until I was just to the south of my house. I was close, and it looked like nobody was home. I started to make my way out of the forest when I was stopped cold. I heard a metallic click just as I caught the scent. Then I heard her.

"You're one step away from being dead."

I knew that voice, and I knew her scent. Sarah! I was so happy, but I didn't want her to kill me. I also didn't want to get shot twice in twenty-four hours. I couldn't help but laugh.

"Kaiyo? Is that you?"

I nodded, and she appeared from under a snowdrift. She was in all white. That was clever. In seconds she was hugging my neck. It always amazed me how little and frail humans are. But they have so much courage. It's their courage that has allowed them to conquer the world. That and thumbs. Thumbs really help. And their smarts. Monkeys have thumbs, but they're not very smart. *Bunny trails*, I thought to myself.

Anyway, Sarah and I hugged for a few moments. She clicked her walkie-talkie a few times, and then she texted Mom. I put a claw gently to her mouth. Everybody knew that meant: *Talk to me*.

"Okay," she said quietly. "It's just us ladies and Aylmer here. The power went out about fifteen minutes ago. They're coming. We suspect they know your dad and the other men are gone looking for Landon. Also, they may have some technology with them like night vision scopes and thermal scopes. That's why we herded about five hundred cows to mill about around the house. The good news, is your father has some of those toys too. I saw you coming through the forest long before you got here. Here, look."

Sarah held up her rifle so I could see. The yard and the nearby fields were dotted with cows. Everything was in black and white, but the cows stood out. There were even a few elk over to the west. They glowed like suns in a clear night sky. The view was much like my sense of smell. We bears can almost see with smell. Still, the view was amazing. "Your mom and Aliyah have these too. They're hunkered down in the barn with Gracie. They have a plan."

Sarah got a text from Mom. "Your mom wants to see you now. Go back the way you came, and enter from the back of the barn."

I nodded, turned, and made my way through the woods and then turned quickly on the path to the back doors to the barn. Gracie opened the door and was right there to love on me. She kept her voice down.

"Oh, Kaiyo! You're here. And you're just in time."

Just then, Mom and Miss Aliyah came walking over. They looked tired and tough. They had black rifles slung over their shoulders, and both had side arms and knives strapped down to their legs. I immediately hugged Mom. She needed it, and so did I. Mom held on to me, and then Miss Aliyah and Gracie joined in. Then something else hugged us all. It was Dovie! How did she get here?

"Wait, how did you get here? You were still home when I left."

"Hah, that's what you think, you big, dumb bear!"

Mom had no clue what we were saying, but she told us to lower our voices.

Dovie whispered, "First of all, you look great. Your bullet wounds are almost healed, and you look like you've been working out for years. I bet Raphael had something to do with that. Anyway, you remember your little nap you took after you gorged on grass? Well, a few of us met with Meginnah, and we begged him to let us help you guys. Did you see those elk? They're on the team. We even had two Siberian tigers try to come. Meginnah said *no* to them because they're just too exotic, but he did give us a small pack of special wolves. Even Lavi tried to come, but Meginnah wouldn't let him. He has trouble walking, and he wouldn't be able to deal with the snow. But you gotta admire him for his courage, right?"

Lavi was a piece of work, but he always had courage. If you didn't know it, just ask him. He still struggles with humility.

Dovie kept going, "Your mom has a plan. Well, it's Sarah's plan. They have gasoline cans and stacked hay in bonfire piles down the driveway and in a big arc around the west part of the house. The assassins probably have gadgets that can see through the night. Fires with floating ashes confuse those devices. We hollowed out some pits in the snow, put roofs on them, and then strung up thick wool blankets here and there. The blankets will stay cold and give them cover while the ladies get to the pits to shoot back. And the wolves want to talk to you when you have a chance. Your mom fed us well, so now they're sleeping outside. She even fed the elk."

Dovie and I went over to the horse stalls to see Gracie. She was busy. Like the other humans, she had a rifle slung over her shoulder. She was good with her gun too. She called it a .22. She and Mom or Dad would shoot it at our rifle range. When she turned twelve, they let her shoot at the rifle range by herself. I usually went with her and slept in the sun while she shot at targets. Sometimes she spent hours there. She was growing up, not as fast as me, but she was so brave. Gracie was at work saddling the horses.

"We may need to retreat, and these horses are our best way to get away."

I helped her lift the saddles. The saddle for Peyton was especially big and too heavy for Gracie. I lifted it easily. Peyton nuzzled me. I could tell the horses knew something was wrong.

Gracie worked in and out of the stalls as she talked. "Here's what we know, Kaiyo. I saw them today sneaking around the gates. They're coming, and when they do, they'll come at us fast. They have at least two huge, weird-looking dog things with them. Talk to Aylmer about them. He doesn't like them. Just before you got here, we heard them cut down trees, so we think our driveway is probably blocked. Before they cut our power lines, the gate was still holding. I think they want to make sure Captain Stahr and others can't get in here. Sarah thinks they'll be coming out of the Southern Forest, probably on snowmobiles. We'll fight back, but if they're too strong for us, we'll retreat into the Eastern Wilderness. And they have a man with them. He's different. He's tall and looks strong. I think he's more a monster than their dogs. Sarah says he's the type of man who is so evil he didn't need to be possessed. He follows orders but is still responsible for everything he wants to do. Sarah says those types are the most dangerous. She told us she knows the man's boss. I don't know how that helps, but it's better to know than not know, I suppose. Oh, at least two of the others are locals, probably more. The truck had a Gallatin County plate. But the truck was well used and too beat up to be a rental. Somehow, the bad guys are getting local help. I guess getting people to kill for money isn't all that hard. Those folks will have no idea how poorly this will work out for them."

Then she looked at me and said, "But hey, God doesn't give us spirits of fear, right? In fact, he gives us power and love for each other. And wisdom too. Kaiyo, I'm the youngest here, and everybody looks at me as a baby, but I'll be a teenager in two months. Trust me, I'm scared, but I wouldn't want to be anywhere else. And who gets to fight for God? It's an honor."

I loved my tiny big sister. She was so brave. In the soft light of her lantern, she looked far older than an almost thirteen-year-old girl. In fact, like the rest of the women here, she had somehow become savage.

Dovie tugged on me, and we left the barn and went outside. The barn didn't look like a military headquarters. Dad had transformed it into something pretty and warm for the wedding. It was all so strange.

Leaving the front of the barn, we walked over to my house. In front of the steps to the kitchen were five large lumps in the snow. I knew they were the wolves. Even in this wind, it's hard to miss the smell of dog.

Dovie smiled and said, "Kaiyo, may I introduce you to Amarok and Anjij. They're the leaders of this pack."

Two of the lumps moved, and after a few good shakes and a cloud of snow dust, two big, muscular wolves appeared before us.

The male spoke first, "Kaiyo, your mother and her friends are wonderful. And we have eaten like kings. Your mother and little sister ate with us and shared their stories. The scary one, Sarah, told us her story, and the graceful one, Aliyah, told her story too. Anyway, thank you. We have experienced a sample of the love you get daily from your human family. You are an inspiration to all of us who mourn the loss of our once great fellowship with man. Whatever we can do, we are here to lay down our lives to protect you and your family. There aren't many families in the world like yours."

"There are others?" I asked.

Anjij looked amused. "A few," she said.

The other wolves stood and shook their snow blankets off. Anjij turned toward them. "We have all heard the stories of the bear prince who travels between the worlds. Meet Kaiyo, the prince."

Immediately, four tails started wagging, and I was mobbed by sweet, but big, powerful wolves.

"I'm Sage," said one.

"Leif here," said another.

"Washoba!"

"I'm Waya!"

They all sounded so nice, but one look at them told me they were fighters. Amarok had the scars to prove it. He spoke to all of us.

"The evil archdemon Aymoon is behind this, of course. Were he not restrained by the Master, he would personally slay all believers. But he has always been free to get men to do his bidding, and he pays them well. They will give us no quarter. You know that, don't you?"

Like the younger wolves, I found myself nodding. Just then, Mom and Miss Aliyah ordered us all into the barn. Aylmer came in from the forest. I was wondering where he was.

Once assembled, Mom spoke, "Sarah is out there waiting in the snow. She thinks they will come out of the south. I still think they'll use the driveway. There are two elk out there. Their role is to act like elk, at least at first. They will run away from the attackers. If the enemy comes from the south, then the elk will run north. If the enemy comes from the west, they'll run east toward us. We have rifles fitted with scopes that will let us see through the darkness. The enemy probably will too. Stay hidden.

"Dire wolves, listen up. They have a couple strange, huge dogs with them. Take them out if you can. If there are any watchers, harass them, but stay back and don't let them grab you. They have the advantage in the deep snow. Hopefully, one of us will see you in the darkness, and we'll try to shoot the watcher. As for the human enemy, they want to kill all of us. If they're on our property, at night, carrying weapons, they will get no warning. Wolves, try to stay away from them, they'll all be armed. Aliyah will be lighting the fires the minute the elk run. Aylmer and Dovie, my gut says that they will try to flank us from the east, behind us. Please, station yourselves in sheds or deep in the trees so you can hide. But whatever comes at us from the east, behind us, must be stopped. Kaiyo, stay with us, and take out anything that breaks through. Everybody, move fast and try to stay out of the open if you can. The roads are closed, we will not be getting any help. Questions?"

There weren't any.

"If not, let's get to our stations. Everybody, stay low."

Like any of us animals could ask her a question. Everybody knows we can't talk on this side. But Anjij whimpered and walked over to the sandpit. When Mom called them dire wolves, I wasn't surprised. They were extinct, good-sized wolves but stronger and more muscular than the ones here in Montana. Anyway, Anjij used her nose to move the sand. When she stepped back, we saw "*Pray*" sketched in the sand.

"I am so sorry," said Mom. "Yes, let's pray."

From behind us came, "May I?" It was Sarah.

I have to hand it to Sarah; that girl can pray. The prayer was brief and encouraging. Most important, we felt the presence of God. Whoever was coming to attack us might be helped by some Specials, but the demons would be facing disastrous opposition. They might try to scare us, but that's about all they can do. There are many types of warfare. We were winning the spiritual war.

Sarah finished and pointed to the wolves. "Thank you for joining us. Please know we love you, and we will fight for you too. Nobody is left out or behind."

Twenty minutes later, Sarah alerted us to a glow in the sky to the northeast. That would probably be Miss Aliyah and Gunner's house on fire.

Miss Aliyah fought back tears. She whispered in my ear, "Don't worry, Kaiyo, we'll rebuild." She was brokenhearted though. Looking up, she whispered again, a little louder, "They're going to be coming for us now."

And they did.

15

PLAYERS—SAM

I'm glad Lowe was with us. Gunner still would have shot the guy trying to kill me, but when a law man is present, all those annoying questions about who shot whom vanish. And Lowe killed one himself. Gunner and I let Lowe control the crime scene. He took pictures and drafted up a quick set of notes for his reports. Gunner took the prisoners and didn't mention it to Lowe. Lowe saw it and said nothing.

In an earlier life, Gunner was, among other amazing things, an MP in the Air Force. He knew that if Lowe took them in custody, then they would get their Miranda rights read to them, and they would shut down and attorney up. Right now we needed information, so Lowe kept busy outside while Gunner took the prisoners inside the cabin.

The word *cabin* should be used loosely. This place was lovely. We put the two prisoners in separate bedrooms. Gunner quickly forced them to take off their cold weather gear all the way to their T-shirts and shorts. The cabin was just as cold inside as outside. He turned on the ceiling fans, and in minutes each was shivering uncontrollably. Then Gunner warned them that Lowe was a killer, and they needed to talk. And they did.

The first one gave his name as Ty Vernon. As Vernon got to talking, he was rewarded with getting some of his clothes back.

"I didn't want to kill anybody. I just wanted some easy money. I wasn't raised this way."

Gunner was good at this. He was calm and frightening at the same time. "What's going on? And tell me the truth. Because I need to know why you and the other fellow were trying to kill my friend here." Gunner pointed at me.

"No, we weren't. Well, maybe, I don't know. Okay, the man in the other room is Everett Ferguson. Everett and I met at the Denver Rescue Mission. We both ended up in Denver to get work. But Denver is no place for poor people. Ever try living in Denver? Everything cost double, maybe triple. I lost my job, and I was living on the streets a month later. So I'm broke and homeless. Everett has the same story."

Gunner interjected, "Ty, I'm sorry about all that. I really am. But, Ty, I'm in a damn big hurry, and you need to get to the point. There are two dead men outside, and things are going to get worse. Why are you in Montana?"

"I'm trying to get to that. Anyway, Everett and I would hang out here and there. Well, a few days ago, we were both on Wynkoop Street, and a recruiter met with us. We've been recruited before. Mostly for little things. Like we'll be the muscle during a collection or sometimes we act as a lookout. I've been hired just to sit at an outside bar on the Mall on Sixteenth and text a code when a certain man walked out of a restaurant. I've never actually hurt anybody. Anyway, he said he'd pay us double to be part of a snowmobile patrol in Montana. He said his client needed to influence some competitors to relocate. I figured the competitors were dealers or growers. When I saw your friend's badge, I realized we'd been lied to. So it's true, we were given rifles for a reason, and I figured we would need them, but I promise, I didn't think we were after people like you."

"Well, thank you, Ty. I appreciate your honesty, I really do. Now I'm going to go into the other room. If Mr. Ferguson in the next room tells me the same story, then we'll treat you nice. If not, well, you'll need to make your peace with God."

Gunner left and went into the other bedroom. I heard the door shut and Ty gulp. I stared at him. I started out wanting to kill this guy, but I was moving away from that position. "So, Ty," I asked, "who's the recruiter?"

Ty looked a bit concerned, but then he must have thought through it. "He's a weird one. He claims to be a private investigator. I just call him Mr. Wraight. Weird name, huh?"

"He's here in town. Did you know that?"

"You know him? And he's here in Montana? No way. He never goes on jobs. He doesn't even have a phone. No office either. He pays us cash only. His client must be a big deal. He usually keeps his hands clean. I do know he spends a lot of time in Denver. I've never even seen him drive a car."

"So who are the dead guys, and who are the folks that turned and got away?"

"Didn't know them, but the two guys that got away seemed like hired help, like me and Everett. They're probably dangerous though. The two dead guys were pros. They looked like they had seen combat before. They knew each other. We were told to let them do the shooting unless it was absolutely necessary. I was fine with that."

"They got sloppy" I said that like I was some sort of Clint Eastwood character. I didn't mean to say it that way, but that's what I sounded like.

"So if I can ask, what are you, sir?" asked Ty.

"Ty, I'm a rancher with a family, and you were working for a man, or a thing, who wants to kill me and my family and some of my friends because we're Christians. It's not new, at least not for Christians. They get killed all the time for their beliefs. I am just blessed enough to live in a country where I can fight back. So, Ty, are you now in the Christian-killing business?"

Ty looked horrified. "No, sir! That's not what I signed up for. My mom went to church. I wouldn't be doing any of this if Wraight told me the truth."

"Really, Ty? Do you think that piece-of-living trash has ever told you the whole truth? We are indeed competition to his slimy client, but that's as far as it goes. Wraight and his client trade in lies and deceit. They're good at it too. But when all this goes down, it won't be Wraight who gets killed or goes to jail, it will be you. You're lucky you're not dead because if you were, you'd be spending day one, roasting in hell for eternity with Wraight's client as your jailer. You need to turn your sorry life around, young man. If it had been me shooting, I wouldn't have tried to disable your snowmobile like Gunner or the lawman. You need to come to Jesus because for some reason, you're not dead. At least not yet. But that's up to you if you squander this last chance."

My theology about hell wasn't quite correct, but I wanted to make a point. I both hated this young man and had compassion for him too. Lowe came in and asked me to step into the kitchen. I gave him a brief update. Gunner stepped out of the room where we had stashed Everett.

"His story is basically the same. He said the two dead ones were some sort of mercenaries. Let's bring them in. I don't want prisoners, and I don't want to kill 'em either."

"You thinking we ought to let them go?" asked Lowe.

Gunner smiled. "Well, I suspect you ought to get statements first. I'll write up a few Miranda waivers."

Lowe proceeded to get statements from them both. He recorded them, and they signed the waivers. Having a peace officer and an ex-MP in our little rescue group was coming in handy.

"Lowe," I asked, "did you get their rifles?"

"Way ahead of you, Sammy. They weren't fired."

"Then it's up to you two," I said. "Call your commander and anybody else, and then I'm going to call Susan."

Lowe was able to get calls out to his boss and to the Sweet Grass County Sheriff's Office. They took his information and said they would be coming to get us out as soon as weather permitted. The storm was supposed to pass an hour or so after midnight, so we could expect this place to be covered up with law enforcement just after sunup. But a lot could happen in twelve hours. Might as well wait a month. We were still on our own.

I tried repeatedly to call home, but all I got was a fast, busy signal or just dead air. That meant the lines were down at my house for whatever reason. I prayed it was the bad weather; it wouldn't be the first time. But my gut told me they were in trouble. I had to find Landon and get home.

After a few redirected calls and a few transfers, I was able to reach Troy. He was near panic. The roads were ice, and he was stuck in Virginia City. It would be another hour before he could get to Radford and then another hour to get to the farm. He said he was bringing Lieutenant Justin Martinez. Martinez and Goliath were close friends even though Goliath almost killed him when they first met. Martinez could keep a secret, and he wouldn't be quick to shoot a Special. Plus, he's a tough, strong lawman. That made me feel a little better.

I had no idea where the kids were. Kate said they were going to get some supernatural help and come to this valley. If anybody could persuade the cherub to use the door, it would be Dean and Kate. Individually, they were good talkers. Together, they were probably irresistible. If they were somewhere here in the valley, I would need to get them out too.

Gunner found and plugged in a few space heaters in a room. We didn't dare use the cabin's woodburning stove. We couldn't risk being found and trapped inside. After an hour of talking and warming up, we heard the whines of a small convoy of snowmobiles making their way to the south.

"That's them," said Everett.

Ty agreed. We turned off the light and the heaters. The cabin was close to the road, but trees hid most of it from view. The snowmobiles stopped near the area where we shot up their little posse. They all got off their sleds and inspected the area. Blowing snow had hidden our tracks and covered up the blood. That was good because there was a lot of it. Lowe had wisely dragged the dead men to the west side of the road and into in a ditch. They were covered in snow and frozen solid. We didn't want anybody tracking us down.

After a few minutes of shining flashlights and talking, four of them left and raced southward on their sleds. The four remaining riders sat on their sleds and kept talking. For whatever reason, after a few more minutes, two of the riders left and followed their pals to the south. The two remaining riders started patrolling the handful of streets in the tiny community.

Old County Road is shaped like a flattened horseshoe; it enters the Main Boulder Road at the north end of the community and exits at the south end. They started at the northern entrance, slowly driving by each home and shining them with their flashlights. Then they took the bridge on Kendan Lane. It was the only road on the other side of the river.

We all stood quietly out on the porch to listen. They would soon be coming here, and that meant either more prisoners or more deaths. The snowfall hadn't let up, but the snow around the entrance to our cabin had been trampled, and it was obvious to anyone who cared. If they missed us, it would be a miracle. Everett proceeded to tell us these men were probably the group he was part of. He didn't know of any others. He said at least six of the riders were hard-core killers. Everett looked scared.

"They were real tight with the boys you people killed. But the two others will probably try to kill you too."

Just then we heard what most people would confuse with a wolf's howl. It was in the neighborhood.

"Back inside," I whispered.

But before we turned, we heard a man yell and swear at the top of his lungs. Everett bounced down the steps and peered around the corner. He looked back at us. "It's some dude, and he's yelling at something big by the cabin across the street."

I thought I recognized Landon's voice. Gunner turned to me, "Landon?"

The men on the snowmobiles had apparently heard the howl and the yelling. They turned and rode fast back up the lane toward the bridge. It wouldn't be long before they got here.

"Everett, Ty, give me a hand. Gunner, you and Lowe cover us."

In one move, we all ran through the snow. Landon had just finished yelling at whatever he was yelling at. "Landon!" I called out. "Is that you?"

We got to him quickly. I never saw what he was yelling at, but I had an idea. Gunner and Lowe ran up the street about fifty paces and took positions on either side of the roadway. By the sound of the snowmobiles, they had crossed the bridge and would be here in moments. Landon was a little confused but clearly glad to see us. Without asking or ordering, Everett threw his shoulder under Landon's arm. I did the same. Ty picked up Landon's rifle and followed us. Ty's holding a rifle behind my back troubled me, but I was determined to get Landon inside. If Ty wanted to shoot me and Landon, here was his chance. Unfortunately, Landon was nearly dead anyway. We were almost to the cabin when the high-pitched whines of the snowmobiles ceased. At the same time, we heard two screams and some animal roars that were terrifying. Then the screams and the roars were no more.

"Good Lord, what was that?" said Everett.

"Dogs," whispered Landon.

Landon was obviously slipping fast, but I think he was almost right.

"Then those are really mean dogs," said Everett.

We opened the door, and Ty immediately got to work making a pot of coffee. That was a good idea. Then he ran into the back bedroom and turned on both space heaters and closed the door. That was smart.

"Should we risk starting a fire in the wood stove? We could warm this place up. And I don't know what kind of thing killed those riders, but it's on our side. I think we're good for a while at least."

Our side? Or did we just get lucky? I thought about that while Everett was pulling off Landon's gloves and jacket. "Good point, young man. Get it ready, but don't start it until Gunner and Lowe get here. They'll be able to tell us if other riders are out and about."

Landon was regaining his senses but still shivering uncontrollably. Everett and I helped him to the room, and the warmth inside was wonderful and welcome. Landon bathed his hands in the warm air of the heaters. He said nothing for five minutes. Ty came in and handed him a mug of hot coffee. He sipped the coffee and cupped the mug with both hands, taking in the warmth. Gunner and Lowe rode up on the sleds that the riders had before something jumped them. They bounced up the steps and came into Landon's heated room. It was a bit crowded, but I was fine with that. We were all breathing out one-hundred-degree air, so the more the of us, the warmer the room.

"How you doing, Landon?" asked Lowe.

"Coffee good," mumbled Landon.

Then he laughed to himself. He was looking better too. We all stood around him. "You'll never guess," said Ty, "but a few hours ago, Everett and I was helping some bad hombres who were trying to kill Sam, Officer Brigham, and Gunner here. Crazy, huh?"

Landon looked from Ty to Everett and back to us. "Yeah," said Landon, "but you haven't seen crazy yet. And since you so recently wanted to kill us, could I have my rifle back?"

"Of course," said Ty as he handed the rifle to Landon. "But I didn't want to kill nobody. Neither did Everett. We were just playing backup."

"Not much of a difference there, right?" said Landon. "But I truly thank you for the coffee. You're forgiven, at least by me. Good to meet you guys. And thank you both for warming me up. I think I was close to passing out. How did you know what to do?"

Gunner was smiling. It was good to see the life coming back into Landon.

Everett spoke up, "We mastered being homeless in Denver winters. Ty and I have probably saved more near-dead frozen people than Denver Health. That's the hospital where us poor people go. You were easy because you were sober. Wasted people are harder to thaw out. So how you feeling?"

For the next twenty minutes, Landon warmed up, talked little, and enjoyed the coffee. Everett found a laundry rack and dried Landon's socks, gloves, and shirt over one of the space heaters. Landon seemed to bounce back to one-hundred-percent.

Gunner and Lowe told us about the riders.

Gunner started, "They had just ridden over the little bridge when a few wolves pulled them off their sleds and ripped out their throats. One of them was partially eaten, at least I think so. Half his face was missing. Lowe found the second guy. He had been dragged back up the street while he was still alive. Then he got killed too. It must have happened fast. When Lowe and I got there, the wolves must have gotten scared off. I suspect they came back after we left."

Landon looked at Gunner and then to Lowe. "You didn't scare them, they just allowed you to see their handiwork. Tell me, did you happen to see any front paw tracks?"

It was a weird question, but I knew where his question was headed. Gunner didn't remember seeing any front paw prints, but Lowe did. "Yep, I saw some front paw tracks, if that's what you want to call them. It dragged the man while it was on all fours, but then it seemed to drag him while just on his back legs. Landon, you must know what these things are because the front paw tracks looked more like hands than paws. There were some long claw marks showing too. What are those things."

Landon laughed a bit. Everett and Ty looked terrified. Then Landon told us the story of Gunther MacDonald burning his truck and cabin and being on the run from MacDonald and his reinforcements. The strangest part was how the dogmen pushed Landon to us, here at this cabin.

Landon continued, "Ty, I heard you say those things are *on our side*. You might be right. In fact, you probably are. They could've killed me anytime they wanted. But we have no idea who they serve. Until we know that, we need to give those things a lot of distance. I have no idea why they killed the riders and not me. So that reminds me, Everett and Ty, whose team are you on? And tell me why."

That was a question I wanted to get to as well. I pitched in before they could answer, "Gentlemen, you have some options. We're long on snowmobiles. They're six of us, and we happen to have nine snowmobiles at our disposal. Three sleds are shot up, so they're no good. Two or three others are a little bloody, but they'll run fine. If you want to leave, we are okay with that. This isn't your fight. You have to give us your word you won't rejoin your old buddies, but that's about it. Lowe will mention you in the report but in the best light possible. You are free to go back to Colorado and live on the streets or whatever it is you guys want to do. Or you can become part of our small fire team. This is a bad option because you might get killed. In fact, all of us might get killed. And that leads me to the one condition if you want to join us. Today, like in five minutes, you guys need to give your lives over to Christ, or you can't join us. I have no desire to lead men into danger if I know they would be going straight to hell if they get killed. Seriously, I really don't want to be enjoying heaven while you two are roasting on the spit or whatever else it is that happens to people in hell. And yes, you guys are probably liars, crooks, thieves, or worse. Don't worry about that. To a degree, all of us in here are too. So what is it? Repent and be a child of God, or hop on a snowmobile and get out of here? As for living on earth, you have a better chance if you guys take your snowmobiles and run from the fight. You two go in the other room and talk it out. Whatever either one of you wants is fine with us. You have five minutes."

We watched them as they left our room. Then Landon turned to me. "Where's Libby?"

Our initial plan was to find Landon and hustle him out of the valley and go home. Dealing with Wraight and MacDonald and their seemingly endless supply of Wraight's super villain-style henchmen would come later. But having my kids in the valley changed everything.

"Well, Landon, if the kids got their way, then they talked the cherub into delivering them into the valley. You met the cherub. Could the kids get him to do that?"

"Hah. You doubt your son?"

I didn't. "Then they're here. Let's go get 'em."

Landon stood and pulled on his now dry clothes. For some reason, I always forget how powerfully built Landon is. He has an attractive goofiness about him that causes others to not feel threatened. He does it on purpose. Right then though, my concern was for his health. When we found him, he was approaching moderate hypothermia, but I think we got him in time. His shivering had stopped, and he said he felt comfortable again. God bless space heaters, dry clothes, and coffee. I watched as Landon checked his clothes and pockets. He seemed good to go. Just then, Ty called out from the other room.

"Mr. Gibbs, can you come tell us a little bit about our options again? We're thinking about things."

That was fine. Gunner spent years as a petty criminal. He could relate. He left to speak with them as the three of us checked our firearms. Just then, we heard what I thought was thunder in the distance. But that made no sense. We stepped out onto the deck, and from the south came the sounds of gunfire. The noise was bouncing off the slopes, but there was no question we were hearing a battle. My kids were down there, probably at CVP.

Gunner stepped out. "What is that?"

"Our kids, I suspect. What's the story with Ty and Everett? They in or they out? We need to ride."

Before Gunner could answer, Everett and Ty asked me to step inside. "Sam, no disrespect here. You treated us real good, and we're thankful for that. Very thankful. But you gave us three options, and we want to take the third one."

I had no memory of a third option. "I don't remember a third option."

"Oh, it was there," said Ty, "it was implied."

"Implied?" I was surprised he knew what that word meant.

"We want what you guys got. You know, the Jesus thing. And we want it now. But we can't be riding with you fellas. A few of those guys down there are our friends. And me and Everett don't want to be part of killing friends. Guys, please believe us, they're not losers. They're just lost, like we were. But be careful, they're still dangerous. Everett and I are going to find our way back to Denver. Come see us."

"Gentlemen," Lowe said, "the four of us understand. Promise me you guys will find a way to grow in your new faith. Trust us on this. If you do, this next stage of your life will be twice the adventure."

Everett stepped forward and hugged each of us. He whispered in my ear, "I promise."

Gunner looked at me and Lowe. "I will be giving them their guns, ammo, and snowmobile keys if that's okay."

It was. Gunner pulled out a water bottle and baptized the two men in less than three seconds. I doubt history has seen faster baptisms. In the midst of the moment, I told them to stay on the road and don't get off the road until they got to Big Timber.

While we were getting our gear together, Landon spoke, "Gentlemen, there's an older hotel on the Big Timber Loop. Ride straight there, and tell the proprietor you know me. Give him your weapons, and stash your snowmobiles around back. You don't want to be spending the next day explaining things to men who don't smile, be they wearing a badge or not. Figure out a way to get to Billings, and take the next bus to Denver. Do you need money?"

"Nope, they gave us cash enough to get home and then some."

We all left the cabin and hurried to our sleds. Everett and Ty rode north; we turned south. The distant sounds of shooting hadn't stopped.

Prisoners—Dean

Kate alerted us to the riders coming our way. The Specials rolled off their sleds and took positions in the timber. Tracker went to the top of the low hill and watched. Then he ducked back into the forest. I drove my sled just below the crest of the low hill and waited. The riders quickly closed with us. There were three of them, and they were armed. They came to a quick stop and shined their flashlights at each of us. What they saw were three rifles and a shotgun pointed their way.

"Let's lower those flashlights please," I said in as flat a voice as possible.

"What are you kids doing out tonight?" asked one of them.

"If you don't lower that flashlight, I will shoot you now." That was Libby.

They lowered their flashlights, and fortunately, our combined snowmobile headlights illuminated the area nicely. I could see the riders easily. I thought Libby's bluntness wasn't helping, so I took over.

"Maybe we got off to a bad start. Is there something we can do for you gentlemen? When you answer, please keep your rifles in their scabbards. If you make a move, you'll be shot full of holes. But I see no reason for us to start fussing with each other. Tell us why you are armed and why you think you have the right to force us to come to a stop. Please keep your hands on your handlebars. And if you are law enforcement, tell us now and show us your ID, but be real deliberate about it."

I never lowered my rifle. The one in the back seemed to be giving the orders, and he didn't like looking down the barrel of a rifle. I knew they weren't law enforcement, but I wanted them to wonder if I had a problem with cops.

"No, we aren't police or anything else like that. We are looking for a guy who stole from us. We're renting a cabin in McLeod, and one of our snowmobiles was stolen."

Our group seemed content to let me keep talking, so I asked a question to keep him talking, "McLeod is pretty far from here. A thief would likely go north. South is the end of the road. So why are you way down here?"

"Simple," he said. "We watched him leave, and he went south. We've been tracking him since then. Now, can I ask you young folks what you're doing out here?"

"No, you can't. It's none of your business, and you are in no position to ask questions. But I'll volunteer it. We plan on liberating as much unneeded firewood as we can find. We will start at Falls Creek Campground and at the cabins just to the north of there, and then we'll work our way back home. That's why we have this beast of a snowmobile and the sleds. And if you guys keep our secret, I'll tell you something that ought to interest you."

I watched as they all looked at me. None of them were scared. The talker was cool, and all were confident.

"About three miles back, we saw somebody on a snowmobile head south. Could have been a girl, could have been a guy, don't know. We passed him or her before the rider turned onto the road. Last we saw, the rider was on the bridge at Four Mile Creek."

The talker looked toward the rest of us. "Is that so?" he laughed. "Sounds like malarkey to me. There's nothing down that way. Nice try. We aren't interested in the rider anymore. We made that story up. But we are looking for a thief. He's on foot, and he torched a pickup truck and a cabin about seven miles north of here. You guys aren't him, so you're free to go back home. We'll come with you."

"Mister, I've been free to go since before you stopped us. I also knew you were lying. We saw you guys patrolling the road this afternoon. I gave you that story to flush you out, and you did. So you three just turn around and ride away. We got work ahead of us, and we don't want your company."

"Well," he said, "that won't do. I know you think you have the jump on me, but I doubt you would kill me. You seem like nice kids. We don't want to start shooting. All three of us here are trained, and even if you get a shot off, we'll get off a few at you. You want to get these girls shot? I don't, but it's up to you. As for now, just go back to your cabin. If you're too cold, then snuggle. But the road is closed for tonight. I want all of you to hop on that big snowmobile, and you're going to leave the others here. We will escort you to make sure you get home safely tonight. I can't have you disobeying me. I hope you understand I am only concerned about your safety. We have a thief to catch, and I really don't need you on the road. And last thing, you are going to give us your weapons, and you're going to do it now. I'll give them back to you once we get in your cabin."

Kate spoke up, "Sir, why did you say you would be in our cabin? That makes me extremely uncomfortable. And guess what? I'm on *the list*. We all are."

Well, there it was, all out in the open. The talker snapped his attention to Kate. If he didn't know before, he did now. The other two did the same.

Kate wasn't finished, "Yeah, I thought so. And by the way, we're proudly on the list. So don't look too surprised, you know what I'm talking about. Consider our little charade to be over. Do you remotely think I'm about to let you disarm me and then herd me and Libby into a cabin in the middle of nowhere? After you have killed Dean and Jack? Because they're on the list too.

"So know this. Being in the same county with you is unappealing, but being alone with you in a cabin is repulsive, and I don't like thinking about it. Now, all three of you, get off your sleds and spread-eagle in the snow, and you might live."

I had no idea what Kate was up to. I knew we had passed some sort of line when they demanded our weapons, but she thought the situation all the way through. We were dealing with vile, pure evil.

We should expect them to do vile, purely evil things. The talker seemed to know about the list, so he probably knew who we were. They were close to being dead men too. They just didn't know it yet.

The talker slowly lowered his hands. "It doesn't work that way, sweetie."

He was bold, but he was also an arrogant fool. He must have lived a life of successful and constant intimidation. But anybody who lives that way ultimately runs into somebody who pushes back. This time, it wasn't somebody who pushed back; it was some things.

Behind them, silently stalking, came Goliath, Gyp, and Benaiah out of the snowy darkness. The talker and his two henchmen smiled as we all lowered our weapons, but we only did it to let the Specials know they were safe. It was Jack's turn.

"Gentlemen, why in the world would we lower our weapons? We had you dead to rights. We outnumber you, and we had the drop on you. You know that's true."

Benaiah growled. Gyp and Goliath huffed. Jack kept going. "I bet you are all wondering what's behind you. Right now, be real careful about where you put your hands. Remember, we could have killed you, but we didn't, and you thought it was because we were weak or afraid or both. Go ahead and look. And again, I'm warning you not to try the quick draw. You have no reflexes like what's behind you."

The fact was, the wind and the sounds of seven idling snowmobiles allowed them to be complacent. Before the talker could turn around, Benaiah grabbed him and pulled him up and off his sled. The other two riders saw it happen just as the bears swatted them off their snowmobiles. They crashed into the snow as the bears stepped on their chests. Benaiah threw down the talker viciously. Benaiah had heard enough from their threats. He was furious.

They begged for their lives, of course. I didn't blame them either. Kate and Jack moved to disarm each rider. To a man, they said they had no more weapons.

"Goliath, Gyp, check them out for weapons," ordered Jack.

Of course, they all had more weapons. Those guys were probably professional soldiers. When Goliath sniffed out the first gun strapped to one of the rider's legs, Goliath savagely bit him and shook the rider like a rag doll, dragging him screaming and bleeding through the snow. The others quickly gave up two more handguns and some knives.

The snow had let up some, but it was still swirling around us. We debated what to do with them. While we debated, Tracker joined the group and sniffed each one, causing them to cringe. Tracker spent his time on the talker. We couldn't afford to let them leave, nor could we let them get to a phone. We had surprised them, and that meant MacDonald knew nothing about us. It was Libby who had the best idea. The entrance to Camp Yonah was nearby. Libby ordered Benaiah, Gyp, and Jack to take them and lock them up in the camp. I didn't ask any questions; Jack knew what to do. Before Jack could get them moving, Kate took one of the rider's rifles. She expertly and noisily clicked the thumb safety to the fire position. Everybody looked at her.

"Not so fast," she said. She had her finger on the trigger, and she was almost shaking. "Gentlemen," said Kate, "stack your helmets, gloves, bibs, and boots. And hurry. We don't have time."

The talker protested, "We'll freeze without those things."

"You don't get it, do you?" Kate was seething mad. "I don't care. I know what you had in mind for us, especially for me and Libby. So I don't care if you freeze to death or if you bleed out right here. You are a brutal coward, and so are your buddies. I don't have time to debate. If you are still alive in the morning, you will be rescued."

The talker went one step too far. "If you're on the famous list, then that means you all are Christians, right? Good Christians would never slaughter an unarmed, defenseless prisoner. In fact, to hell with all of you. Whatever prison you try to create for me and my men, I promise you, I will get free, and you can be assured, you will never be safe."

Then the fool laughed. I'm not as fast a runner as Jack, but I'm very quick. Kate was standing in front of the talker. I was next to Kate, and I knew what Kate was going to do. In less than a second, I saved the talker's life. Not that I cared for his life, because I didn't, but I couldn't let Kate become a killer. It's one thing to kill in defense; it's another thing to kill in anger. The part about Kate that I loved may well have died forever. Killing makes recovery hard.

I was just as angry as Kate though. The talker was a big guy, maybe a little over six feet, and he was thickly built and strong. He just wasn't as strong as me. Few people are. In a flash, I delivered a savage left uppercut to his jaw. The blow lifted him up and nearly off his feet. His head snapped back and then snapped forward. When it did, I landed a near killing blow to his face. I held back, but I still knocked him out. He lost several teeth, and the rest were probably loose. I could have easily killed him. His comrades watched as their leader twitched in the snow.

"Damn, Dean," said Jack, "I keep forgetting how you're a complete freak of nature."

As their boss twitched, I offered the other two men some needed wisdom. "We are Christians, but we never said we were *good* Christians. We don't even pretend to be good Christians. Christ didn't need to sacrifice himself for good people, he did it for people who need the grace. I know if I had sinned and killed your boss, I would still be a Christian, I would still be loved and still be forgiven by God Almighty. If you ever get a next time, you might want to think twice about picking on a Christian. Kate was a split second from putting a bullet in your boss's brain. Jack was maybe one second away. Libby was probably wondering how to torture him to get information."

Libby caught on, "You know me too well, little brother."

I finished, "If you think you and your satanic bosses have an edge in savagery, you will lose that game. And by the way, my non-human friends are not afraid to eat you, and I couldn't stop them if I tried. Now, do as you're told. Take off your bibs, gloves, and shoes and take off your boss's. Pick him up and go where Jack tells you to go. And don't say a damn thing."

"Yes, sir, yes, sir!"

After they stripped themselves of their boots, helmets, and cold-weather gear, the two still standing were shivering. Jack ordered them to pick up their boss and carry him. Then Jack, Gyp, and Benaiah took them away. They would have an awful night. I didn't want to, but I prayed for their safety. Kate came up to me and buried her face into my chest.

"I almost murdered a defenseless man, Dean. That's not good. You did that for me, didn't you?"

I held on to her. "Yeah, I did. Kate, you may need to kill tonight, but the circumstances will be different. If you kill to save yourself or to save Tracker, Gyp, or Goliath or any of us, it will not make you a killer. Shooting the talker for flapping his gums would have. I couldn't let you do that to yourself, or to me, because you would never quite be the same. And law enforcement would have to ask some mighty hard questions."

"I love you," she said.

"I love you too. And fortunately, now we don't have to experience a prison romance. But if it happened, I would never leave you."

Kate kissed my cheek. "I know."

Just then Libby spoke, "Well, we're all happy for you both. I was wondering when you two would be honest with each other. But we need to get back to business."

Libby ordered us to disable the three snowmobiles left by our prisoners. They wouldn't be needing them. Kate opened each gas tank while Goliath pushed the sleds off the road and onto the shoulder. Each of the sleds had Colorado registration decals, so they weren't rented, at least not locally. I didn't want to destroy a local's property. They might be a friend. I cut the fuel lines and lit the vapors in each tank, and in moments, the three sleds were fully engulfed in flames. The environmentalists wouldn't appreciate it, and normally I wouldn't either, but we couldn't afford to have attackers on our flanks.

We didn't have to wait long for Jack and the two Specials to return. Kate and I were draping the burning sleds with three sets of gloves, bibs, and boots. They melted and burned nicely. We threw the helmets in the fire too. Libby smiled at Jack and said, "We will want to hear your story later."

"Yep," said Jack. "I told them to snuggle. I took their wallets, cell phones, and walkie-talkie. And somebody will need to reimburse the camp for reconnecting the phone lines into the camp office. Somehow the lines got pulled down. It looks like a bear or something did it."

Goliath huffed, and Jack laughed as he started his sled. The Specials got on their cargo sleds, and Tracker jumped up on my big sled. In seconds, we left the burning snowmobiles behind us, and we fell into line and raced north. We quickly passed another, bigger summer camp. I had been to this one as a little kid. I liked it too.

We made good time, and the miles passed quickly. The farther we rode, the more convinced I was the valley had been abandoned. There are a lot of cabins, homes, and small mansions out here, but I saw no lights or cars. That was good. We didn't want any collateral damage. Instinctively, I reached down and patted Tracker like he was one of my dogs. His tail wagged, and we locked eyes for a moment. I loved that wolf. He loved me too. And I feared for him. I also feared for Kate and all the others. It wasn't lost on me that we were willing to sacrifice all our lives to rescue just one of us. It wouldn't make sense to some, but sacrifice was understood by all who loved God. It didn't mean that we couldn't falter or run. Even I was scared, and that probably meant the rest were frightened too. Except maybe Libby. She was consumed with hatred right now. There was no room for fear in her heart.

We passed Chippy Park Campground, and there, below us a mile down the road, we saw the unmistakable glow of fires burning high. Instinctively, we all turned off our headlights. We pulled up to the crest of a slight rise just past the campground. Writhing like a demonic monster, fires were burning in several places.

"Form up!" said Libby.

We all gathered in a tight circle.

"Libby," I said, "I have an idea. It looks like CVP is on fire, or at least parts of it are. That's too bad, it's a wonderful place. MacDonald has either torched it on his way out, or he's still there, protected by hired muscle. If he's still there, Landon's probably still alive. Because we don't know, we approach it the same way."

Nobody had any questions, so I kept going, "We ride just south of Aspen Campground. We ought to be able to get there without being seen. The snow is falling steady, and it's still windy, so they may not hear us either. Nobody's tried to contact the patrol, at least not on the walkie-talkie, so they are not concerned about any hostiles from the south. We have one chance on this. Jack, me, and Tracker will be the fire team. We will approach the camp from the fires and go into the camp to find Landon or deal with MacDonald. With the fires between us, we will be harder to see as we approach. Libby, Kate, and Gyp, you guys are to make your way up the road and provide cover for us on their western flank. Goliath and Benaiah, make your way to the east. Stay on the slopes. Stay clear of the camp because you will get caught in the crossfire. Kate and Libby will be firing from the west. If you see any specials in camp, stay disciplined and stay put. Bullets don't know the difference between friend or foe. MacDonald may have some watchers, so just beware."

Libby interjected, "Good plan. Let's tweak it a little. Benaiah, can you and Goliath cross the river to the west of camp?"

Benaiah and Goliath nodded.

"Then make your way through the timber, and recross the river up by the Big Beaver Campground. If you see anybody snow-mobiling out of there, away from us, then let them go. But if they start taking new positions, take them out if you can do it without drawing fire. And, guys, we have no idea where our dads are or if they're even alive. If anybody comes to join the fight from the north, can you tell if it's Dad's snowmobile? It's a Ski-Doo, and it's red and black, of course."

"Go dogs," laughed Benaiah.

Benaiah could speak two words of English, and he learned them from my dad years ago. I'm pretty sure Benaiah didn't quite know what college football was about, but he was mighty smart, so maybe he did. Goliath seemed to enjoy the plan too.

Libby finished, "Gunner and Officer Brigham both ride white Polaris snowmobiles. And all three of them know people in the valley. They may have enlisted some help. It will be confusing. Are you two okay with that?"

They nodded. I needed to clear up a few things. "Libby, you and Kate need to keep your distance. You two are our snipers. You're also the best shots of the group, so it makes sense. Your rifles are bolt action so shooting will be slow. The dark will make finding targets even slower. Take two of the automatic rifles we liberated from our prisoners, and take their magazines. If anybody with a gun gets close, drop your bolt-action rifles and swing these up. Except for the automatic fire feature, you have both trained on these, so you ought to be fine. Gyp, if they get approached by specials or anybody without a gun aimed at them, do your stuff."

I paused. "Last thing. Ilya is down there, and he's bad news. If he threatens any of us, and if you have a chance, go ahead and kill him. He's not a normal dog. He's evil."

"Any questions?" asked Libby.

There were none. I gave Jack the last automatic rifle we took from our prisoners, and I strapped on one of their sidearms and gave the other two to Libby and Kate. Technically, none of us were allowed to have a handgun, and none of us are allowed to possess automatic weapons, but we would risk jail if it meant we might need them to live. In fact, our whole expedition had broken several laws. Kate squeezed my hand and looked away. She said nothing.

None of us were chatty. The Specials gathered and spoke to one another in growls and other guttural utterances. They were making plans that were important too.

Just then, the walkie-talkie we lifted from the prisoners chirped. "Team 2, report now. We need you back, ASAP. Copy?"

Libby whispered, "That's MacDonald's voice. He seems to be in a hurry."

Jack whispered back, "Now we know MacDonald is still in the valley. Dean, I think you're right, that probably means Landon's alive. I also bet MacDonald's at CVP. We know he's not south of us and our dads and Officer Brigham are to our north, hopefully. I think the fires have something to do with Landon. He may have even started them. The way they sent out that patrol proves they're looking for him."

"Team 2, check in."

Team 2 wasn't listening anymore. But we were.

We were a mile from CVP, armed to the teeth, and we had two giant bears, a bigfoot, and a tremendous wolf here. And we were in a minor blizzard that wasn't stopping us. We had no need to whisper. I thought it was funny.

"All right, guys," I said a little too loud for everybody's comfort. "I will lead with the Alpina. It's big and will flatten your path. Benaiah, ride in my sled. Tracker, ride up front with me. Ladies, one of you bring Goliath and come together. Keep your M-4s handy, your hunting rifles won't do much good in the dark. I'll be waiting at the campground. When you get close, you'll see my cell phone flashlight directing you in. Jack and Gyp, wait three minutes and then follow them. No headlights if possible, but if you need some light, turn them on."

The Battle of CVP Christian Camp began.

FAIR PLAY—TRACKER

From the time we were delivered into this valley, we had been upwind. The bears and I hated it. Bears brag all the time about how good their noses are, but mine is good too. Benaiah's nose is better than a human, but he's not close to me or the bears. Being constantly upwind crippled our advantage. Ilya would know we were coming, and that would mean they were ready for us.

Dean had an uncanny ability to understand us. For the last few years, he made a practice of being a student of us. He sensed our concern.

Dean had just jumped on the big snowmobile. He reached down and patted my head. I liked it when he did that.

"Tracker, I know the wind has been blowing at our backsides, and that has to bug you guys. I see you and the bears testing the wind all the time. Let's hope the smoke and snow masks our arrival."

That was some hopeful thinking there. Ilya would know we were there well before we could advance. Dean started the big snowmobile, and we pulled out. I looked back at Benaiah. He waved at me and smiled. He's an amazing creature.

The ride was smooth, and we made it to Aspen Campground in minutes. Benaiah rolled off the sled and ran into the little campsite's timbered area. For a creature as powerful and ferocious as Benaiah, he's mighty shy. But his shyness works because nobody has taken shots at him while I've had to duck more than a few bullets in my life.

Dean parked the snowmobile, and we waited for everybody else. I admit to being worried, especially about Dean. He's smart, but he's impulsive and sometimes too flippant about the dangers.

Dean knelt in the snow. "Tracker, my plan is to give them a chance to give up. I don't want to murder anybody. I can't shoot somebody just because they're in the wrong place. I hope you understand that. Nobody else but Libby does. It was her idea, and she's right."

He was wrong about understanding. None of our humans were murderers. He knew the danger, and we both knew he was probably going to get killed. I put my head on his knee. Dean patted my head.

"Thank you, Tracker. I love you more than you know."

But I did know. I loved him just as much as he loved me. I knew my role was to protect him. And I knew if he got killed, I would probably get killed too. There are worse things than dying for my friends.

Dean dug his cell phone out of his pockets as we walked to the road. Using the flashlight, Dean guided Kate and Libby straight to us. Goliath rolled off his sled and waited with us while Dean brought in Jack and Gyp. The bears enjoyed each other, and even as tense as things were, they pawed at each other. Everybody was extra quiet, but the sound of our snowmobiles probably gave up our position. We were very close to the enemy. We could see the fires through the trees.

Benaiah and Goliath were hugged by the humans as they got ready to leave. Human affection still seems to embarrass Benaiah, but Goliath loves it. He likes his life, and he loves his freedom, but one day I think he will choose to move onto the farm. I intend to get there before he does. I watched as the two enormous beasts silently left us and crossed the river.

We crept up to the northern edge of the little Forest Service campground. There, concealed by the brush and timber, Jack led the six of us and prayed. People wonder why we pray, but we don't wonder. We pray to change outcomes. If it didn't help, we wouldn't do it. And we needed God's help. We also needed God to deprive the assassins of whatever demonic assets they had.

I don't fight unless I have to, and I sure don't like to fight if my enemy has supernatural advantages. I wanted that advantage for us. Fortunately, our enemies were evil. This was not one of those unfortunate human situations where two opposing sides were both praying to God for victory. Those guys burning CVP, if they prayed at all, prayed to something hideous. And we were fighting for survival. Those people wanted to exterminate us and were determined to do it. We couldn't negotiate with them.

Libby lifted her head. "Everybody check your gear one last time. Dean, Tracker, Jack, the south end of the camp has a wire fence that runs from the road straight and uphill to the east. Crossing the fence might be tricky. You might want to go into the camp by the entrance. Make sure that area is clear. Kate, Gyp, and I will go past the entrance and cross the split-rail fence north of the entrance. We'll cross where we can access some cover, maybe by the cabins near the road. We won't go past the basketball court. Dean, if possible, wait for us to get in position before you start something. We all want to get Landon and go home, but we have people here who want to track us down and kill us, one by one. Tonight we will not be caught alone. Our chance to take them out will never be better. God is on our side. And if the worst comes, we will be taken to our forever home. Be cautious everybody. Questions?"

I guess there weren't any. Everybody checked their weapons again. Aspen Campground was due south of CVP. The road ran just to its east before curving to the west over the top of the camp-ground, and then it turned back north. Libby, Gyp, and Kate fol-lowed us as we crept the eight hundred or so yards until we came even with the camp's south entrance. I moved forward into the camp while Dean and Jack took positions. On Dean's signal, Kate, then Libby and then Gyp glided past us as they headed up the road, in single file.

We were quiet. Snow was still falling, and we were hidden in the darkness. I tested the air, and the swirling winds brought a multitude of scents. Smoke, humans, watchers, and a few types of ancient monster dogs were nearby. I looked back at Dean and Jack. They both smiled. My tail wagged involuntarily. Jack and Dean came and knelt next to me.

"Do you smell Landon?" asked Jack.

I responded so they knew the answer was a *no*.

"Well," said Dean, "that means his body isn't here either. Let's go have a chat."

No, that's not what it meant. The winds were tricky. Landon could be standing twenty yards to my left and I might miss him. If his body was frozen and covered in snow, I could easily miss him.

I growled and then moved into the camp. We had a good view of the area. To the northeast, a larger building was burning, flames were pouring furiously out of the eaves and windows. It was about five hundred feet away, but the flames illuminated the entire area. We could see people on snowmobiles and some other creatures between us and the burning building.

"Dang it. There goes the old chapel," whispered Dean.

Near us, not far from the camp entrance, was MacDonald's truck and trailer. Jack and Dean stayed low and moved to the truck. It was empty. We made our way silently down the side of the trailer. They boys stayed low even though the trailer hid us from the view of anything near the burning chapel building. The lights were on in the trailer. When we got to the door, Jack crouched and held the doorknob. Motioning with his fingers, he counted down from three to one. He opened it quickly, and Dean rushed in. I was impressed. Jack followed while I waited. Moments later, Dean and Jack came out.

Dean whispered to Jack and me, "Nobody home, but it's loaded with ammo. Turnabout's fair play, right?"

Jack seemed to agree. "Tracker," he said, "let us know if anybody or anything starts coming our way."

That worked. I made my way to the other side of the trailer and watched. I was careful not to illuminate myself by the low flames of Landon's burning truck, so I stayed low and close to the trailer. From there, I had a good view. I see better in the dark than humans too. What I saw was a gathering of more people than before and a few more creatures standing between us and the burning chapel. They were downwind, but there was so much smoke swirling around I wasn't concerned I could be located. But they sensed we were here. Several of the creatures swayed as they listened. Those would be watchers. They're dangerous. Then I saw three epicyons wandering about. We called them *epies*. Those things are like enormous dingoes mixed with equally enormous pit bulls. They're even bigger than me.

During history, there have been many types of animals. The epies in Eden are numerous, but God knew what he was doing when he terminated them here. Like all dogs, they're loyal. But they can be ruthless and dangerous. Evil Specials are the worst. I knew to be careful around them. This fight would be determined by humans, guns, and us animals, so I knew I would have a part in whatever was next.

Several times I heard Dean or Jack pass behind me and go behind the trailer to Landon's truck. I had no idea what they were up to, but they needed something. I trusted them to do the right thing. I saw Dean and Jack return carrying gasoline containers. Being close to the trailer, the next thing I heard was the muffled sounds of them stomping around inside the trailer and opening windows. I could smell gasoline and propane. Then they came out and called me back to the other side of the trailer.

"We drenched his truck and his trailer and threw in a few propane canisters. We have a plan, Tracker, so hear me out. Like we said, you and I are going to confront them. Jack will wait and follow us from twenty yards back and provide cover. He will have an automatic M-4 so if things get dicey, we'll drop, and he'll start spraying the bad guys. Then we will make our way back to him and decide what to do next. Hopefully, Libby and Kate will be able to give us cover fire."

He looked at me. I said nothing.

He smiled. "Like I said, let's go chat with the bad guys!"

I don't know why he smiled; his whole plan seemed dumb. They'd probably shoot us on sight or order their epies to attack us. But I had to trust Dean. Dean's bravery will one day get him killed, but I hoped that tonight wasn't that time. I nodded. Dean had a sense of right and wrong not shared by our enemies or by me. We could just start shooting and probably get most of them. But that wasn't Dean's style, and I loved him for it. I thought of Sarah back at the farm with the other females. She understood evil, and I doubt she would be trying any foolish attempts at fair play. I was glad she was there protecting everyone at the farm.

We moved away from the trailer and crouched behind MacDonald's truck. Dean pulled out the walkie-talkie he lifted from the patrol and handed it to Jack.

"Jack," he said, "there's no reason to keep radio silence forever. I'm going to call out to MacDonald. His group used channel 2. Dad, if he's alive, is likely on channel 4. Tell him to meet up with the girls. And warn him about Gyp. We don't want Gyp to get any friendly fire. Hopefully, Goliath and Benaiah will be with them. All right, Jack. When we get halfway there, fire 'em up. We'll stay low until the fire gets going."

"On it. I'll follow you guys and stay low. Be careful of those huge dogs and the watchers."

Dean and I carefully made our way up the snow-covered driveway about seventy yards before stopping and kneeling in the deep snow. Nobody noticed us even though we got close to the gathering of evil forces. I could smell the watchers. The epies caught my scent too, but there was just too much smoke and other things to give them anything helpful. Then Dean looked at me.

"I love you, Tracker. Thank you for fighting with me. If things go wrong, I'll see you on the other side."

I loved this big, brave human. His destiny and mine were now the same. We waited for Jack to throw the match.

CVP CHRISTIAN CAMP

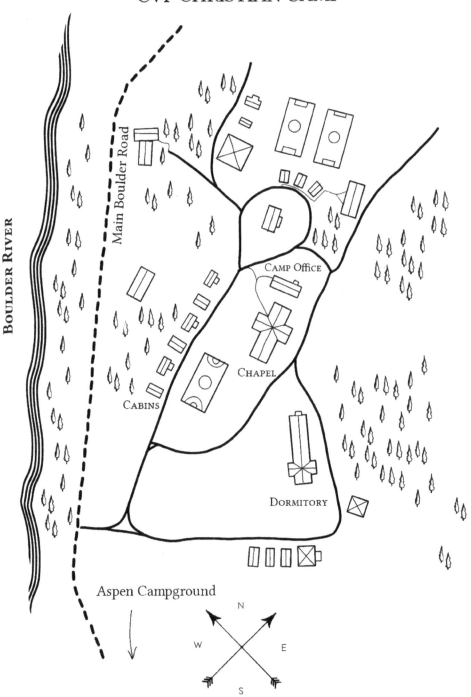

SHOTS FIRED—LIBBY

I wondered what would happen to us tomorrow when the weather cleared and the dead had to be explained. There would be some dead people. Dad often told us that when it came to dealing with legal problems, if you're explaining, you're losing. We knew if we won this little war, explaining what happened and why it happened would be next to impossible. Victory for us probably would be followed up with us being arrested and serving time in prison. But defeat for us meant torture and certain death. Better to be judged by twelve than murdered by MacDonald. It was that simple.

After Dean's group disappeared through the camp's entrance, we followed the left shoulder of the road north about 150 yards. Gyp stayed in front, always testing the air. The three of us crossed the road, pushed through the split-rail fence, and started to make our way to one of the camper cabins about thirty yards away. The cabins here were made of real logs. Not only could they conceal us, logs stop bullets. Most of the camper's cabins at CVP were along a long, looped driveway. The east edge of the loop was where a new dormitory and activity center sat. The burning chapel was up the road but less than a hundred feet from the far end of the looped driveway. I had many great memories from that place, and burning such an inoffensive place fueled my anger. At least it provided some much-needed light.

We had almost made it to the back of a cabin when we heard the *whump* of quick flame. To the south and our right, MacDonald's trailer and truck were exploding in the flash fire. That would be Dean and Jack. From our position, we could see the gathering of evil on the other side of the basketball court. They were stunned. The watchers swayed and pointed. There were some enormous dogs watching. I counted six armed men staring at the flames. Standing next to MacDonald was Ilya, and he looked tiny next to those things. In the world of being killed, we all have our preferred ways of being taken out. Personally, I would prefer a bullet to being mauled to death by a predator. That meant that even if somebody was shooting at me, my first shots would be at those horrific dogs. They were as big as lions.

The three of us watched MacDonald scream his displeasure at seeing his stuff burn up. Then like some sort of ghosts, we saw the silhouettes of Dean and Tracker as they rose from the snow and start walking toward MacDonald's group. The dogs started in with deep, roaring barks. Ilya and the six men kept quiet. They were paying attention though. The watchers stepped back and started looking from side to side. One of them might have seen us. We were crouched on the south side of a cabin. He was suspicious, and he broke from the group and started running the seventy yards toward the north side of the small cabin that was hiding us. Gyp huffed, pulled back, and went to the rear of the cabin. The watcher had no clue what waited for him.

We watched it all happen. Well, we heard it first. Kate was observant. "Gyp's gone. I'll watch our backside."

Kate left while I stayed watching Dean. Other than the curious watcher, MacDonald's group seemed to have no clue about us. The watcher must have suspected something because he closed the distance. I saw him disappear on the other side of the cabin. Right about then, I heard the sound of two massive bodies crashing into one another. Then the roars. The watcher had been caught unaware. The roars were Gyp's. The screams were the watcher's. From the sound of it, Gyp was hurting him. After a minute or so, Kate crept back up to me.

"I think Gyp bit off part of that squatch's hand. The watcher tried to leave, but Gyp caught it and killed it. Neck bite. He's making sure it's dead. He's in a full state of rage now. I'd steer clear."

The noise of the fight had distracted our targets. I was hoping to see Landon, but wherever he was, he was not with this group. Then we heard Dean. He walked up to twenty yards away from the group and then stopped. He waited for everyone to realize their watcher was never coming back. His rifle was lazily cradled in his arms. He looked confident. Ilya barked and bared his teeth along with the other dogs. I had not seen Ilya scared, and he looked scared. The three bigger dogs seemed more predacious than scared.

The other watcher was nervous and started looking from side to side. Kate and I remained motionless. We were both crouched by the cabin wall to our left, and we were hidden well. The watcher didn't see us, and nobody in MacDonald's group seemed to see Jack in the snow fifteen yards behind and to the left of Dean. Kate pointed him out to me. He stayed as low as the snow. He was good.

MacDonald looked thrilled, and I knew why. Landon had probably slipped away, and here was Dean McLeod, standing alone. Dean was no doubt high on the list, and MacDonald had to believe Dean had just served himself up for slaughter.

Dean is practically fearless, and that has gotten him in trouble more than a few times. Today would be one of those times. Dean is also a talker, and he's mighty good at it. When he wants to, he's one of the most persuasive people I have ever known. But most of all, Dean is moved by a compelling sense of justice. It wasn't in him to shoot first and ask questions later. He was giving MacDonald and his group a chance to surrender. They wouldn't just give up, of course, but Dean probably knew that. And he would be prepared. Kate will forever have a problem with Dean's willingness to sacrifice everything for his values, but it's what makes him amazing and wonderful.

"Good Lord, what is he doing?" whispered Kate.

"Giving them a chance to end this peacefully."

"He didn't have to get so close. He knows better."

"Yeah, he does. Now pick a target and wait. I've got one of those big dogs. Pick a human."

Dean spoke loud enough for us to hear, "Where is my friend?"

Even Ilya was taken aback by Dean's boldness. MacDonald said nothing. MacDonald's men observed, but they didn't seem scared like Ilya.

Dean kept going, "By the looks of things, Landon is gone, and you turned to arson. And you just lost a squatch. I like squatches, so that's sad to me. Sort of. As for your arson, you are pathetic.

Personally, I did not enjoy torching your stuff, but I needed you to stay put and rob you of any more resources. Anyway, I never understood vandals like you, but maybe you're one of those weirdos who likes to watch nice things burn."

MacDonald snorted but said nothing.

"Yeah, I thought so. I know who you are, Gunther MacDonald. You have a fetish for cruelty and murder and not much else. And, Ilya, you know who I am, don't you? And by the way, I've been thinking about you a lot lately. You might understand my little story. I spoke to Meginnah today."

Dean let it sit in. The three dog monsters seemed unimpressed, but Ilya's tail dropped.

"Don't doubt me on this, Ilya. He is so not happy with you. You probably ought to be watching your back side. At least for another few years, right? You dogs don't live very long anyway. Seriously, Ilya. I don't get it. Do you really want to spend forever, burning but never burning up, in a cramped little kennel in hell? Your sick jealously and pride made you start teaming up with the accuser. If you die tonight, which is likely, you're going straight there. Well, after judgment. Judgment's first. That ought to be especially fun for you.

"Ilya, your master standing next to you is too stupid to admit it to himself, prideful fool that he is, but you know I'm right, don't you? But hey, that's your call. Oh, one more thing. If you somehow manage to live through the night, Kaiyo will track you down and destroy you. You killed his mother and he knows it. I strongly suggest you either repent and defect to our side to accept the grace of Jesus Christ or run away. Far away. At the least, you really ought to stay away from MacDonald. He's an idiot."

Dean was so good at this sort of thing. He had them back on their heels. Ilya looked up at MacDonald and then back to Dean. The surviving watcher seemed to be backing up. Ilya's confused rage was building, but he was still scared. What Dean said seemed to sow confusion. The six men and the monster dogs did nothing but look at Gunther, Ilya, and Dean. They looked ready but amazed at this high schooler dishing it out to MacDonald. MacDonald had probably intimidated each of them and here was a teen taking none of it from him.

"Big talk from a kid!" said MacDonald. "You've had your fun. Put down your gun, and we'll talk. But your friend is nowhere to be found. I hired him to be my guide, and he quit on me. He took my money and left me out here. He's a thief is what he is. I think he set these fires too. You don't think we did all this damage, do you?"

MacDonald had returned to his swagger. He outweighed Dean by twenty pounds, but he was probably nowhere near as strong as Dean. Dean also knew to never engage Satan in a conversation, and MacDonald was just a miniature Satan. Eve was almost a perfect human and brilliant by all standards, but she foolishly engaged Satan, and look what happened.

Dean ignored him. "I am Dean McLeod of Madison County. I was taken to this lovely valley to rescue Landon and to kick your butt if I had a chance. Looks like Landon has escaped, and now you're panicking. So here's your chance. You shot my little brother yesterday. Fight me, you piece of scum. Let's see what you are made of. You're a bully boy. But hey, maybe you have what it takes. Tell your little army here to stay out of it, drop your weapon and I'll drop mine."

Gunther realized he'd been called out, and Dean didn't let up, "I'm just a high school kid. I'm not even old enough to vote! Don't just stand there and prove to your team that you got no guts."

MacDonald was stunned. I watched him go from looking like a predator to looking totally confused again. He had been called out.

Dean had to add, "While you ponder my generous offer, I do hope you've been having a great time today. Just FYI, the locals haven't been pleased with your patrols, so I took care of *team 2*. They're not coming back. Ever. Now, every one of you, put down your weapons."

The next twenty seconds was filled with awkward silence. The only sounds were the wind in the trees, the crackle of burning vehicles and buildings, and the soft grunting of the surviving watcher.

MacDonald made a slight motion with his left hand. One of the men snapped his rifle to his shoulder and started shooting at Dean. Dean was turned violently and fell to his knees. At almost the same moment, Jack fired into the man who shot Dean. His head snapped backward and he fell dead onto the hood of a snowmobile. Jack's good shooting probably saved Dean's life. Until Jack fired, they never knew Jack was there.

At the same time that Jack fired, Kate and I started firing. My first shot went through the skull of a dog monster. Kate fired into the group of men and winged one of them. To their credit, the five men were lightning fast, even the one Kate hit. They were clearly pros. In one fluid motion, they had found their rifles and were firing toward Kate and me and at Jack's last position. Jack had already moved. With fire coming from two directions, the assassins began to work their way to cover behind the north end of the dormitory. They grabbed MacDonald by his coat collar and dragged him as they tried to protect him. As the moved, two of the men covered their retreating team by keeping steady fire at us and toward Dean and Jack.

The moment the gunfire erupted, Ilya turned and ran away, toward the burning chapel while the surviving watcher ran behind the dormitory. When Dean was shot, another dog raced past his dead friend to get to Dean. But before he got there, Tracker leaped out of the snow and grabbed the enormous beast by the neck and pulled him down. Tracker was big, but the big dog outweighed him by a hundred pounds. As the two regained their footing and savagely bit at one another, Dean rose out of the snow and tackled the big dog. The dog was surprised, and he crashed into the snow under Dean's weight. He fought back and attacked, biting Dean around his head. Dean worked quickly. He stuffed the barrel his pistol into the dog's ribs and emptied his magazine. With a cry and violent death throws, Dean killed the big dog. Without pausing, Dean raised his rifle and started firing toward the retreating enemy. Dean was hurt though.

Kate's M-4 was set to three-round bursts, and she was working over the north side of the dorm. Jack had joined Dean, and they both fired toward the dorm. I was firing at Gunther as he was being spirited away by his team of mercenaries. I think I hit MacDonald, but his men were good, and they got him to safety behind the big dorm. Defending MacDonald, the last of the monster dogs finally ducked for safety behind the dorm.

My mind was reeling. "Kate, I'm going to the next cabin up. I need a better angle at MacDonald and his pals."

"What are Dean and Jack doing?" asked Kate.

She was near panicked. Off to our right, Dean, Jack, and Tracker were charging the long west side of the dorm. I think Dean got hit again because he tumbled forward. But by advancing and firing, they were preventing the mercenaries from flanking us. At least they were trying. Dean knew that unless we pressed the attack and kept them on their heels, we would be overwhelmed by their superior numbers and superior fighting skills. Those guys were professionals, and they were reorganizing as we spoke. Our element of surprise was lost.

This could still go bad. I walked to the back of our cabin, and I saw Gyp waiting. He seemed to have collected himself since fighting and killing that watcher.

Pointing to Kate, I told Gyp, "Watch her back, Gyp. Dean and her brother may get killed, and she's watching all of it."

I stuffed the horror of watching my little brother become KIA. Good Lord, he was a fighter. Between the two cabins, I saw the dead watcher. He was enormous and lying facedown in the snow. The amount of blood in the snow was gagging. The smell of the dead watcher was worse.

I powered through the snow to the next cabin. Once there, I had a good view to the east and the north side of the dorm. There were a few trees in the way, but I had eighty-five yards of a slight uphill field of fire. A few of the gunmen were shooting at Dean and Jack, so I let loose with a burst. They dove for cover and scrambled out of the way. They controlled the long east side of the dorm; we controlled the west and the north.

Dean and Jack made it to the west side wall of the dorm. They were underneath the second-floor walkway. I watched as one of the mercenaries stepped out and shot through the floorboards at Dean and Jack. Kate threw up her scoped rifle and shot out a big window next to him. It was a good-enough shot, but she didn't mean to shoot out the window. He tried to scramble back inside, but Dean fired and cut him down. He crumpled onto the balcony floor.

We had some sort of a standoff, but it was temporary. They had more shooters and were simply better at fighting than we were. We had more Specials, but I had sent Goliath and Benaiah off to look for Dad. Just then, there was hope. My walkie-talkie clicked twice. Then I heard my father's voice.

"Esperas, hija. Tres minutos."

I was thrilled to hear from him. We needed more firepower, and I was also afraid something had happened to him. As for the Spanish, for whatever reason, my dad thinks speaking in Spanish makes him some sort of Navajo Code Talker. I'm sure anybody monitoring channel 4 could figure out Dad had just told me to wait for three minutes.

I responded, "Dad, no Spanish. We're in a full-on firefight. We need you to come now. I'm at cabin 3 just west of the basketball court."

Dad knew this place well. His three human kids had attended years of camp here. And he didn't get to us in three minutes; he got here in two. He led three other snowmobiles, and they came in fast. Each of them braked hard on the road behind my cabin. The riders were good, and they were off and jogging fast, rifles up, and headed my way. Using my cell phone light, I led them to me. Kate had just shot a burst, and Dean and Jack where close to the dorm firing at somebody. Dad was astonished. Gunner threw off his helmet and ran toward Kate.

"If you see a polar bear, he's with us. He killed the watcher next to the cabin, so don't spook him. He's still grouchy."

"Got it," said Gunner as he ran to be by his daughter's side. "And Goliath and Benaiah are on the way."

Dad took his helmet off and looked around. "Lowe, could you check on Dean and Jack? We don't need them taking any more fire. We need to get everybody out of here."

"Dad, you're wrong!" I was furious. "We are not letting those assassins go."

Officer Brigham stayed. I kept talking, "They're killers, and they won't ever quit until we're all dead. And don't forget why we're here. We still have no idea where Landon is."

From the fourth rider behind us I heard, "It's okay, Libby!"

I knew that voice! Over the booms of rifle fire, I knew that voice. Landon stood in front of me and pulled off his helmet. He threw it on the ground as I raced into his arms. I didn't want to cry, but I did. Landon hugged me tight, his rifle pushing into my back. I think I was doing the same, but neither of us were letting go of our guns.

Landon whispered into my ear, "I'm all right, Libby. And I can't wait until we share stories, but I agree, we need to finish this."

It was so hard to let go. Neither of us wanted to. I turned. "Dad," I said, "Dean, Jack, and Tracker are too close to the new dorm. Get them back here. Dean's been shot. Maybe twice. And he fought and killed a monster dog. He probably took some bites too."

Dad and Lowe moved quickly to where Gunner and Kate last fired. With Landon and the men here, my strategy needed changing. We now had much more firepower plus one of us was a lawman. We were now able to wait it out until morning or to outflank them. We had options now, but before the men got here, our options were few.

Seconds later, we heard the labored breathing of Goliath running down the road from the north. Benaiah was right there with him, though he was not nearly so winded. They came right to us and went straight to Landon. The three of them had been friends ever since we rescued Landon two and a half years ago. Once again, I had the opportunity to watch males and their odd rituals. They slapped each other around like Landon had just scored a touchdown, but like me, they were overjoyed to see Landon.

I heard Dad whistle. Dad can produce the most annoying loud, high-pitched whistle ever. It was more than loud, but more importantly, Dean would know it was Dad. Landon and I ran past the cabin behind us and crossed the driveway. From there, we took cover behind a berm at the basketball court. We could see most of the dorm's north and west side by the light of the chapel's flames. The flames of the burning cabins and MacDonald's burning trailer illuminated the dorm's south side. One of the monster dogs bounded briefly into view as it raced to the south, away from the dorm and out of the camp property. Somebody shot at it, but it quickly disappeared behind the flames of the burning cabins and trailer.

We then saw one of the men slip out from behind the dorm to fire at Kate's cabin. He didn't have a chance to get his rifle aimed before I shot two bursts. His rifle flew up in the air as the shooter slipped and fell backward. He rapidly crawled to safety back behind the building. I don't think I hit him, but he was probably mighty surprised we had flanked him.

"Where did you get that? Is that an M-4?" asked Landon. "Those things are highly illegal."

"Long story, but it sure comes in handy. I'll tell you later. By the way, everything we've been doing is illegal."

A shooter on the dorm's second floor tried to hit Kate's last position, but all he got was return fire from Kate, Dad, Lowe, and Gunner. If he got hit, I wouldn't be surprised. He cursed. They could count, and they probably knew we had more strength than they did. They had at least two killed and one or two wounded.

They were still dangerous, but they had lost the advantage. Fortunately, the second-floor sniping stopped.

Five minutes later, from the south side end of the camp, I heard Jack call out of the darkness to tell us they were coming in. Gunner gave an acknowledgment. Landon and I wanted to find out more, and we were both worried about Dean, but we needed to keep watch.

Then I heard a muffled scream from Kate.

WOUNDS—SAM

Head wounds never look good even if the wounds themselves are not so bad. But what I saw coming out of the darkness broke my heart. And Kate's.

The southern half of CVP was illuminated from the fires. With all the light, Dean, Tracker, and Jack had ducked south, into the darkness, beyond CVP property and behind MacDonald's burning truck and trailer. From there, they made their way to the road behind us. Jack called out, and the three of them approached us. Dean was fully covered in blood. Jack looked grim. Tracker was bloody. He had been bitten too, but he looked a lot better than Dean.

Dean spoke first, of course, "Officer Brigham and Gunner, relieve Kate. I want to see her. And keep low. Some of those guys can shoot."

Dean spoke with a speech impediment. His words were hard to understand.

"I got shot right through the mouth. Could've been worse. The bullet blew out some molars. My mouth is full of blood and little pieces of teeth. I have a hole in my cheek. Some of my tongue got shot off too, I think. And that big dog bit me bad on my head. Check out my scalp."

Dean didn't mention a grazing shot to his forehead, another wound to his leg, or that his tongue was swollen. We had to be careful of that. He could choke to death if it got worse.

"Mr. Sam," said Jack, "your son's a freaking hero! He was spouting blood and spitting out teeth, and he kept fighting. He even wanted to sneak through the dorm and go after them. Can you believe that? He wasn't stopping. I'm glad you whistled when you did."

"Thank you, Jack," I said, "and you're no less a hero. Your dad and I are mighty proud of both of you fighters."

Kate had joined us and seemed to be more in shock than anybody. "Damn it, Dean. Why did you walk up to them? You didn't have to get that close to talk to them. They didn't deserve any mercy or some stupid chance at walking the straight and narrow. They're killers."

She was checking him out. She wasn't actually mad at him either. She was just frustrated with the situation. Susan has said similar things to me when I got hurt doing crazy things. Kate motioned to us.

"Come on, guys. Let's get some light on him."

Gunner left Lowe and rejoined us. He looked over Dean as Kate started working on him. Gunner winced and turned. He is more emotional than me except that his temper isn't quite as testy as mine. Gunner went over to Jack and hugged him.

"Proud of you, son. You too, Dean. I'm so sorry you got hit. In fact, I'm proud of Kate and Libby. Tracker, you too. We'll be checking those bites out in a minute." Gyp was next to us. "And you, Mr. Polar Bear, that squatch was coming to kill our daughters, and you stopped him. That was quite a feat. We all thank you."

Gyp seemed to smile. "Dad, Mr. Sam, this is Gyp," said Kate as she was busy looking over Dean's wounds. "He's an amazing bear."

"Wait," said Dean. "You killed it? I heard you guys fighting, but I always thought watchers were too strong to be taken down. Where is it?"

Dean was running on a double dose of adrenaline. His swollen tongue made him sound almost silly. Gyp motioned Dean and Jack on over. Kate started to object, but Dean gave her a look. He intended to see the dead watcher.

"Okay, but don't shine any lights," said Kate. They have at least one sniper, and Gunther MacDonald is a sniper too. Make it quick because your father and I are worried sick."

Then Kate gently pulled Dean by the arm. Standing close to him, I heard her say, "Don't worry, Dean. I know you worry about us. You always have. So stop. For me, okay? Yeah, you're going to have some scars, but nothing has changed, and nothing will change. You're Braveheart. And Braveheart won the heart of his love."

Dean smiled, and when he did, more than a little blood squirted onto Kate's jacket and then onto the snow. As to what she said, I had no exact idea what they were talking about. But I did understand the reference to Braveheart. Few men deserve such a compliment, and fewer men hear it. It meant far more than romance. It meant raw, selfless courage, and Kate saw it in him. I was so proud of my son.

As for Kate and Dean, I knew they were sweet on each other, but it appeared they had upped their commitments to each other a notch or two. Or twenty. Stress forces issues upfront. They obviously had issues about each other. The good kind of issues.

Dean and Jack left with Gyp. Kate turned to look at me. She was all business. "You're going to be my father-in-law someday. Maybe someday soon. Let's make sure we save your son. He's hurt bad."

I murmured something like, "Okay, good point."

I stood trying to process what she said as she went over to our snowmobiles. I was trying to figure out if she was joking but quickly concluded she wasn't. I knew she had strength in her; I saw it this morning. I suspected that if she wanted something, she would get it. And Dean was it. I admired her even more.

In seconds, Kate came back with two small first aid kits and another flashlight. Dean made it back to us. We stood him against the back of the cabin and started working on him. Poor thing. But it could have been worse. But it wasn't good either. The first bullet grazed his forehead, leaving a bloody crease. It was a bleeder. The second bullet clipped his lips on his right, punched through upper and lower molars on both sides, and exited out near the back of his left cheek. It left a hole big enough to see broken teeth when his mouth was shut. His tongue was creased, but nearly all of it was still there. His head had several bites and gashes in the back that were still dripping thick, sticky blood. He also got shot in the thigh, under the surface, just above his knee. By the way he was walking, the wound probably looked worse than it was.

Libby came and tapped me on the shoulder. "Go join Landon. Kate and I will patch him up."

I crept over to Landon's position and watched. After a few minutes, Gyp and Goliath joined us. Benaiah went back up the road to watch for anything. Tracker stayed with Dean. After a few minutes, Jack came over and briefed us. He told us about Meginnah and getting into the valley. Then he mentioned Dean and Kate seeing two monsters, and then he told us about borrowing the snowmobiles from the two guest ranches and Dean viciously slugging the patrol leader. He told us where our horses were and where the patrol was. We had a lot of loose ends to tie up. Then he brought us up to date on how they arrived at CVP. He told us how Libby commanded the operation from start to finish and how Dean had thoroughly intimidated MacDonald and challenged him to hand-to-hand combat. I was amazed at our kids.

But now my thoughts shifted to Susan and Gracie. They were in extreme danger, and I was not going to get there in time. Gunner had to be worried too.

We held our positions and waited for the expected breakout and counterattack. The shooting had stopped, but we knew they couldn't wait us out. They would be forced to at least try to take us out before dawn. In the morning, this area would be crawling with county, state, and federal law enforcement. That wouldn't work for the bad guys. Time was not on their side. Lowe had already put in one report after the shootings up near the Natural Bridge, and he would likely call his superiors tonight again. MacDonald needed us dead. Not only were we on the list, we were witnesses. Plus, we blocked his way out.

So we waited. I heard Dean laughing, and that was good. Everybody but Kate and Dean took turns keeping watch. Kate had bandaged Dean up and other than looking a little like a zombie, he was willing to get back into the fight. As for MacDonald and his mercenaries, they must have been planning something because they had quit the fight, at least temporarily. We weren't about to expose ourselves to their snipers, but we were more relaxed and taking it easy.

I was sharing our story with Gyp when Benaiah ran back down the road. He went to the back of the cabin that had become our de facto headquarters and infirmary. He was agitated. The bears ran over to him. Gyp and Goliath purposefully stepped on the body of the dead watcher. There was no love lost there, but I still felt for the poor beast. The two monster dingo dogs also died violent deaths, and the fact they were Specials and loved by God bothered me. Choices matter, and they had made some bad ones, but it was still sad.

Benaiah was pointing to the northeast and to the south. He was talking to the other Specials, and they all looked interested. Dean, beat up as he was, tried to decipher what was going on. I had my suspicions. This was no counterattack by MacDonald and his team. Instead, they were attempting to escape.

And then we heard shooting. All of us instinctively sought cover or found a shadow to crouch in. But the sound of the shootings was different. It was farther away and not aimed at us.

Based on the sounds of the gunfire, our adversaries had escaped and slipped away to the thicker timber on the slopes to the northeast, well beyond camp property. I didn't see that coming. They were probably headed to some of the nearby cabins to the north of CVP.

With the danger seemingly moved off, the humans on watch joined the rest of us.

Landon looked at me. "I think I know what they're shooting at."

I knew what he was thinking. It was a possibility, but then, when Jack ran back to us, it was almost certain.

"We got movement, folks. As best I can tell, some of those rougarou creatures that Dean and Kate saw just ran between us and the dorm. They came up from the south and slowed down to sniff the whole battle area. They looked our way but seemed uninterested. Then they ran up past the dorm and the burning chapel and ran toward the sound of shooting. They're lightning-fast too."

We offered our speculations until we heard howls. The howls were a lot like Tracker's, but deeper and with more lung power. For the next five minutes, the group of escapees tried to fight. There was a pattern to the attacks. First, we would hear a lone gunshot or two followed by horrific screams. Then the pattern repeated itself five times. Those things had managed to separate the men from each other. They didn't have a chance. The last few times there was no rifle fire, just screams. Finally, we heard the roars of a watcher. The watcher's angry roar turned to panicked screaming. Then to terror. Then silence.

Whatever those dog things were, they had been waiting. We had flushed the bad guys, and those things tracked them down in the blackness of the forest and killed each one of them. Even the watcher had no chance against the pack.

Everybody knew what those things were too.

Libby looked at Benaiah and asked him a question. "Benaiah, are those things on our side, or are they still dangerous?"

It was a good question. The four Specials spoke to one another. Goliath seemed the most animated. After each animal had grunted, growled, or whined, Benaiah looked at us, drew a finger across his neck, and made a facial expression like he was dying. We all interpreted that to mean the dogmen were dangerous. They sure looked it. Reports about them from around the country indicated they were killers. However, I remembered Ty and Everett's impression that those things were on our side.

"I have an opinion," I said. "Libby, you don't know this, but two or three of those things herded Landon over three miles to the cabin that Gunner, Lowe, and I were in."

Libby's mouth dropped.

"It's true," said Landon. "They could've killed me a dozen times over. But they didn't. In fact, they kept me away from getting caught. I did wonder what they were doing. Then they killed two armed riders who were hunting us. I'm not sure they're on our side, but they sure don't like the other guys. Oh, one more thing. I think they fed on one of the riders they killed. Part of his face was missing. Lowe tried to find it, but it was gone."

After a few seconds of letting that sink in, we heard what would be expected.

"Gross."

"Well, that's disgusting."

"Ewwwww."

Dean was more like Spock, "Fascinating."

For us humans, getting eaten is a primal fear. But not so for the Specials. Eating humans wasn't quite as repugnant to them as it was to us.

We didn't really know what to make of our situation. MacDonald was dead, but our way out might be barred by monsters. It was time for us to leave, but this place was one enormous crime scene. Leaving would bring new troubles for us. Lowe and Landon and then Libby volunteered to stay. We decided to send our specials back to the south end of the valley. At least there, if no door showed up, they could vanish into the wilderness until a door opened.

We had prisoners at Camp Yonah, and our horses were left farther down the valley at Jordan Creek. We also had some snowmobiles stashed in the Forest Service campground that didn't belong to us. It would all have to wait. We were determined, somehow, to get home.

Then not far to our south, a wolf called out. It wasn't a dogman; it was clearly a wolf. Out here, wolves were not so common. There are more to the south, closer to Yellowstone, but this far north there weren't as many. And this one got Tracker's attention. Tracker howled a response. The bears and Benaiah were at full attention. The four of them left us and went to the road. Jack and I followed, they didn't seem to mind. Near the entrance to the camp, a small lone wolf came trotting up the road, out of the darkness. She went straight to Tracker. She looked at Jack and me briefly, and then she started animal talking to the group. Heads nodded. Tracker listened and turned to us. The bears hugged me and Jack, and they followed the strange wolf and Tracker off to the south. Benaiah turned to us and pointed back up the road.

"Go dogs." Then he walked us back to the others.

The look of confusion was on everybody's faces. Dean watched and then blurted out, "I am going with you. You and the rest of the Specials are headed back to the farm, aren't you? That's my mom and little sister!"

Benaiah shook his head and motioned for Dean to stay. Dean started to object, but Benaiah growled from deep inside. He wasn't putting up with Dean, and that was unusual. Dean backed down.

"Benaiah," asked Lowe, "before you leave, I need your help. Can you wait for just a moment?"

Benaiah's temper seemed to cool down, and he nodded. Lowe reached into his backpack, and he pulled out two big baggies. "Dean, scalp the watcher. You don't need all of it. Jack, can you make it to a huge dead dingo dog and cut off an ear, some scalp, and some muscle?"

I must have looked confused, but Lowe just smiled and said, "I'll explain later, but it's our insurance. Benaiah, when you get back, bury the two baggies deep in the snow, cover them with some big rocks, and then pack the snow back on. Then leave them there. We may need it later."

Benaiah agreed. Dean and Jack hurried off. In minutes, both returned with baggies full of wet, bloody, hairy monster flesh. Dean then apologized to Benaiah. Benaiah responded with a fist bump. Benaiah pointed to the cabin and indicated he wanted all of us in it. That was odd, but we complied. He held up a hand, and Dean quickly figured out everybody had to stay in there for ten minutes. Landon had keys, so he opened the camp door up, and we made it inside. The cabin had taken a lot of gunfire. The door and the log walls took a few hits. This cabin and a few others, plus the dorm, would need some patching up.

Benaiah quietly said, "Go dogs," turned, and ran off to the south.

Not far off, we heard something like smooth static. Gunner and Lowe looked confused, but we had all heard that sound before.

"Door," said Jack. "It's a door. They're either being called back to Eden, or they're getting a lift to the farm."

Then we heard the howls and cackles. Those dogmen were running through the camp, and they were excited. We shut the door and locked it. Based on the noise alone, there were more than I had thought. They seemed to run right at our cabin, stop, howl, and move on. Some slapped the cabin walls and the boarded-up windows. At least twice the doorknob was rattled.

I was proud of our group. No one appeared scared. Everybody was well armed, and if one of those things opened the door, it would have been cut in two. I got the feeling they were teasing us. Then they ran on to the south.

It wasn't long before we heard what sounded like a vicious brawl. Well, it was more like lions and hyenas mouthing off at one another during a standoff.

"What is that about?" asked Gunner.

Lowe answered him, "That, old friend, is the sound of ancient hatreds. And they gotta work it out."

Then silence. We all looked at each other and waited. We knew it was over. Landon had been rescued, and our part in the war, at least for now, was complete. We had won a small battle in the seemingly eternal war. It felt good.

Tomorrow would be interesting. But now, Dean needed a doctor. And something told me Kate would be going with him.

And what was happening to Susan and Gracie?

PART 2

RULES OF ENGAGEMENT

16

JANISSARIES—TRACKER

We ran back to the little Forest Service campsite just south of CVP. The door was there, and that meant we were being called. The wolf who took us to the door never slowed down. She ran right to the door and leaped into space. We stopped and waited for Benaiah.

It had finally stopped snowing, and all that was left was the wind. It was cold. We milled about until Benaiah got there. Then we all jumped through the door. Inside it smelled good, and it was warm. Midway between us and the entrance to Eden, about half a mile away, stood a man. He looked young, just a little older than Landon.

"Come, my friends," he said loudly. "Join me."

We didn't question him. If he was here and Meginnah hadn't killed him yet, then he had to be all right. We waved at Meginnah, who was standing guard at the far end of the path. He waved back. We were about to step forward to join the stranger when we smelled it. From behind us was the stench of blood, sweat, guts, and nasty wet dog. For a second there, I thought it was me.

We turned. Standing just inside the doorway was one of those two-legged dogmen. Another one stuck its head in the door. Almost in unison, the four of us charged the vile creatures. They would find killing us a lot harder than five men and a lone watcher. They had no place in this holy part of the Master's kingdom. We were soldiers of the first line. And even if they got past us, they would soon be destroyed by Meginnah.

The two dogmen looked shocked, and they quickly ducked back outside. We didn't slow down, and when we charged through the door, we crashed into the entire pack of dogmen. They dispersed into a semicircle. I knew these loathsome creatures. They were a part of Satan's forces. The four of us faced them and vice versa. Those things were big, almost as big as Benaiah. I was glad Gyp and Goliath were with me because I was the little one. I sort of felt like a terrier at the dog park.

Staring back at me were the dogmen. Their huge jaws were filled with sharp, white teeth. They were leaning forward and displaying their claws with palms outstretched. I barked while Benaiah and the bears roared. They roared in return. The noise was deafening. They were telling us they had earned the right to come in, and we were yelling that they would have to kill us first. It was loud. Then we heard him. He wasn't loud, but we all heard him.

"Stop it, each of you. Now come inside and join me."

It was the man from the path. Half his body was sticking out of the door. He went back in. The four of us looked at each other. Benaiah shrugged. The dogmen seemed to sneer, but orders were orders. We went back through the door and saw the man walking back to his original spot. We all walked together the half mile to where the man waited. It was awkward.

"That's right. Over here, all of you. Tracker, Benaiah, Gyp, Goliath, please sit to my right. De'Aavaa and Taalaa, if you could bring yourselves and your sweet pups to my left.

Sweet pups? Yeah right. Those things were pups straight from hell. And they were huge. And how did this person know us by name? I looked at my friends, and we were as fascinated as we were confused. As each of us came and sat, he called us by name. De'Aavaa, the big male dogman, came and knelt. He motioned his entire family to do so. The man was quick to protest. "Oh no. We will have none of that. Once you know my story, you will understand. But no more kneeling for me, okay? I don't like it."

"Apologies, sir," said the one named Taalaa. "We thought you were someone else."

She was the female. Then the man greeted each of the pups warmly and by name. Their tails wagged. Like mine. Interesting. The man sat down with us. He looked like no man on earth. His eyes were bright, and his skin was so smooth. He also looked strong. Sam would look like a scarred-up wreck next to this man. He wore jeans, cowboy boots, and a long-sleeved wool shirt. He could be anybody. An extremely healthy anybody, but he seemed normal.

Just then, all of us heard a whiny bark. Standing inside but still close to the door was one of the epies. He would have been the one who survived. That enormous dingo dog was serving MacDonald before the dog people killed him. The epie was evil, and somehow we had left the door open. I stood and bared my teeth. De'Aavaa did too. We both shouted for him to get out and started taking steps toward him.

"Friends!" said the man. "We have room. In fact, more room than you can imagine." He chuckled at that one. It must have been an inside joke because I heard nothing funny. I looked at the big dogman standing next to me. He shrugged and went back to his mate.

"Come on over here, Kelba. That is your full name. You go by Kel, correct?"

Kel was halfway to us, but we heard him say, "I do."

"Excellent. And yes, you were invited. Hah! Technically, you were invited from the beginning of time, but the invitation that compelled your heart was issued today. Sit across from me, between De'Aavaa and Tracker."

Kel came and sat in front of the man. He looked frightened. The man spoke. "None of you know me, a least not by name. But I know you. I also know that each of you have been called to be soldiers. Not forever perhaps, but at least for today and tomorrow since tomorrow is almost upon us. The Rabbi, the great one, my lord, and your lord, in fact, sent me here."

He said that part as he looked at the monsters sitting across from me. They responded with delight. They looked at one another and laughed. A few cried. All tails but mine were wagging. Not an hour before, these guys were ripping people apart and making snacks of a few. How were they allowed to be here? As for Kel, he sat but remained at attention. The great beast's gaze was fixed on the man. I saw a tear well up and tumble down his muzzle. Gyp saw it too. The man smiled at Kel and kept going.

"Again, I know each of you." The stranger pointed to the dog-men. "I even know more about who you are than you do. You were once an ancient race. The Greeks called you the cynocephali. I will simply call you *wolf folk*. Your race existed openly, well past the Ressurection, and some of them even became followers of the Way. A few were even famous because of it. But your race was nearly destroyed by Satan and his human followers. He enslaved the children and taught them to hate the believers.

"Throughout history, unbelievers have done the same to the children of the human believers. They kidnapped children and trained them to be fearsome fighters. Those kidnapped humans, like your race, were taught to hate their noble and beautiful heritage. Your ancestors were forced to live in the depths of the world's forests and were fed nothing but hatred for man and for every wonderful thing that your species once was. You were used purely for terror. But pay attention. Like all the Rabbi's amazing creatures, you were made for great things.

"As for you, young Kelba, you are an epicyon. Your parents were lured out of Eden. I don't know how that happened, but I do know that Aymoon, the horrid servant of Satan overseeing this region, stole you and your siblings as pups to do much the same thing. You were taught to hate what your parents loved, and you have served Satan from the day you were born. But you, Kel, have a conscience. Don't you?"

Kel looked to the ground and nodded. His ears dropped, and he looked as if he were to be condemned. The man continued. "If not for Tracker, your parents would have been killed by Aymoon's agents. But he found them, and at great danger to himself, he brought them home. He's good at doing things like that." The man smiled and looked back to me. "Don't look surprised, Tracker. Your heroic deeds are well-known to the Rabbi."

Benaiah slapped me on my shoulder and smiled. The wolf folk *ooohed* and *aaaahhed*. I was in a slight state of shock. Good shock though.

Then the man went back to talking to Kel. "Kel, your parents, they still live—and they mourn for you and your siblings. Also today you lost two of your litter mates, but three others still survive. You may see them shortly, if you wish to do so."

He let that sink in. The poor epie looked so confused. "Kel, I know you feel unworthy, and you surely are, but do not leave me yet. Hear me out."

I remembered finding Kel's parents and bringing them home. She cried for her lost children, and she came home with a broken heart. The father was consumed with guilt for leaving Eden in the first place. As for their litter, I just assumed they got killed or eaten by predators. I surprised myself that I didn't figure out the relationship. Kel looked just like his parents.

The man then focused back on all of us. "My name, the one I like to hear, is Ruel. Who do you think I am?"

"Are you one of the apostles?" asked Taalaa. "You are Hebrew, aren't you? You called him *the Rabbi*. That's unusual. How old are you?"

Gyp asked if he was a prophet. One of the pups asked if he was David or Solomon. There was a bit more speculation, but none had the answer. I was distracted by the apparent fact the wolf folk had knowledge of the Book. Yet I wasn't overly impressed. Even the demons know a lot about the Master, the Book, and the events of history.

"I know who you are," said Kel. "You look like you have never walked the earth, but I believe you have."

"And why is that?" asked a smiling Ruel.

"You have been crucified," said Kel.

Well, that was shocking. Everybody gasped.

"You are both right and observant," said Ruel.

Ruel unbuttoned his sleeves and showed us the holes that remained in his wrists. "Well done, Kel. In receiving my glorified body, I was allowed to keep these reminders. As for who I am, I represent the great Gospel in its most elemental form. I was the thief on the cross. And I have a story to tell you."

We were all fixated on this man. All of us had heard of the thief before, and we wondered who he was. We have met very few who have moved on to eternity.

He continued, "I have been called a thief, but I was so much worse. The Romans withheld their cruelest punishments for the worst of humanity. Common thieves did not get crucified. Beaten, clubbed, imprisoned maybe. But not crucified. Only those who were convicted of a capital crime or treason were crucified. The excuse for killing the Rabbi was that he was guilty of treason. What a travesty.

"I certainly never committed treason in the classic sense. I was never a patriot, and I didn't much care for Rome or for Judea or for anything or anybody. But I was guilty of murder and even worse things. In truth, I never really did a good thing in my life. In fact, while on the cross, I had nothing but contempt for the Rabbi. At least at first. But by his grace I saw the injustice, and my eyes were opened. I knew he was the redeemer of scripture. Of course, I didn't have much of a theology, and I sure never earned my way into heaven, if that were possible. Instead, I was given mercy despite my heavy load of sin. And the Father gave me one last chance. That, too, was an act of overwhelming grace. Many receive no such chances."

Ruel looked at us. "So, my new friends who sit to my right, you believe the wolf folk do not have God's acceptance even though they helped save the lives of you and your human family. And to you, wolf folk, you mistakenly believe you can earn God's approval. It can't happen, but if it could, and it can't, here's a hint. Killing, mutilating, and eating people who are running away probably wouldn't be a good way to earn his approval, if that were possible. Which it isn't."

He let that sink in. "Next, none of you believe Kel should be here because just a few hours ago, he was serving Satan. But that is my story. I served Satan even after being nailed to the cross. And yet, I received a full measure of grace once I recognized the Rabbi's authority and asked him to remember me. Had I been let down from the cross, I would have repented from my sin and changed my life. Not to win God's approval but because he demands our walk toward righteousness. Unfortunately, I could not offer repentance but only remorse. I was in the presence of pure holiness, and I saw the depravity of my sin. My prideful friend hanging on the other cross refused to acknowledge his guilt. I have not seen him since that day and do not expect to ever do so.

"So here we are. Kel, are you ready? If not, you are free to leave. Nobody who is invited or born here gets killed in the path and certainly not in Eden. Your siblings are in battle at the farm, and I am sure they would like to see you. But you will be fighting your new friends here. I do not know which side will win this battle. I do know who wins the war for the souls of man. That is public record. Either way, you may die today, but that is not your concern, for you will surely die eventually. Kel, hear my words. Because you remain a citizen of Eden, you will have eternal life. But know this, eternal life is either a curse or a blessing. It is up to you to determine who you wish to call your king."

Ruel then looked at the wolf folk. "You wolf folk, you are claimed by Christ, and because of your choices and his grace, you are his adopted children. But your understanding needs work. Your walk with the Rabbi will be one of grace. If you try to earn his approval, you will open yourselves up to the perpetual attacks of

Satan. Lean on Goliath and Gyp. They are experts on this subject. Lean on Benaiah for all other aspects. He is known as a scholar.

"Finally, each of you are to love one another. Got that?"

We nodded, and then we all looked at Kel. "I'm ready," he whispered softly. But we heard him.

"Excellent," said Ruel. "As for the rest of you, Kaiyo will be here soon. Prepare yourselves, the situation has changed, and you are desperately needed, if you still wish to fight."

We all said we did. "Good. Kel may follow you soon. He may also choose to stay here and see his parents. The door will soon open. Fight as the soldiers of God that you are. If I see you soon because you fell, then it will be a great day. If I see you later, then that will also be a great day. Finally, I do not speak for the Rabbi, but I know he loves each of you. Now bow your heads. *El Shaddai, you are the protector, the redeemer, and the almighty. We ask that you go before your soldiers. Thank you for these wonderful souls with me now. Amen.*"

Ruel looked at each of us. "Finally, remember the new commandment the Master gave to the eleven. You are like them, for you know great adversity. To each of you, love one another." He smiled and looked at each of us. "More will be coming through the door. Wait for Meginnah, it won't be long. Now I must leave you."

He smiled, and then he and Kel vanished.

On the way to the door, we apologized to the wolf folk. They were gracious. None of us knew what was happening on the farm, but De'Aavaa reminded us that Ruel had said Kel's siblings were on the farm. We all agreed; that was a bad thing.

"Mr. Wolf," asked one of the young wolf folk, "my name is Te'oma. Tell us about your human family. I am glad we could help rescue Landon, and we look forward to fighting again, but who are they?"

That was a good question. Benaiah answered, "Do you recall coming through the camp and noticing that the humans were in a cabin?"

"Yes," said De'Aavaa, "They were hiding from us. They didn't know we wished them no harm."

Benaiah laughed. "You do not understand. I put them in there to protect you, not them. They are lions. As for now, we must make sure your pack does not underestimate the women who are at the farm. Susan is Kaiyo's mother. She and Aliyah, and their human allies, have bravery rarely seen in humans. If we are not careful, they will assume you are siding with Aymoon, then kill you and ask questions later. If some of you run, the one named Sarah will come after you. She spent two years walking the dark forests with Satan, and she survived quite nicely. She is now God's child, but she is dangerous all the same."

Benaiah winked at me. The big pups looked side to side. Taalaa was shocked. "Really? What sort of people are they?"

Benaiah responded, "Ma'am, I did not exaggerate. But they do not need to be frightened or confused by your entry on the scene. They are dangerous, that's true, but they are good and wonderful people who, once they know you, will embrace you and encourage you where you need it most. They are good at that. Right now, they need friends and reinforcements. This is the time for grave seriousness, and we do not know what awaits us. If I die tonight, I don't want my death to come from friendly fire because we were not careful."

"Well said," replied De'Aavaa. "Lead the way."

"Wait for me!" It was Kell. He ran to us. "I need to be with you. And when I return, perhaps my brothers and sister will join me."

A Time to Flee—Kaiyo

My mom was right about a lot of things. She was worried we might have to run, and she was right again. When they came for us, they came to kill. Sarah was convinced they would come from the south, so she and Aylmer left and took the oil company road and disappeared into the Southern Forest. It wasn't long after that when we heard gunfire.

The Southern Forest has been haunted for years, and each year we have claimed more and more of it and pushed back the angry, evil spirits that are there. Except for Dean's foolishness, the watchers that lived there were left alone and not forced out. Dad was a live-and-let-live type. When I was a cub, some of those watchers nearly killed him, but they've been quiet since then. For whatever reason, Dad chose not to hunt them down.

When we heard the gunfire, Miss Aliyah ignited the hay fires, and she and Mom took positions in the front yard, hidden in the snow. Gracie stayed in the barn, and I ran down the driveway. Almost halfway to the oil company road, I veered off the driveway and ducked into a snow-filled ditch. If Sarah needed help, I would be able to help her. I had a great view, and it wasn't long before I saw Sarah riding Aylmer running fast out of the gravel road of the Southern Forest up and onto the main driveway. They turned right at full speed and started coming our way. The elk were running along with her. That meant they saw an attack from the west. So Sarah was only partly right.

I heard the crack of rifle fire and saw an elk tumble. It got back up again and followed the others down the driveway toward us. Just then, both Mom and Miss Aliyah fired at the muzzle flash of the shooter. Then I saw something big was trying to chase down Sarah, Aylmer, and the two elk, and it was getting close. If Sarah wasn't riding Aylmer, then Aylmer could defend himself. But his job was to protect Sarah. So was mine.

I knew Mom couldn't get a shot in because the thing was right behind them. I stayed low and hid in the deep snow piled up by the edge of the driveway. When Sarah, Aylmer, and the two elk ran by me, I rose out of the snow and charged into the murky beast. As I suspected, it was a watcher running on all fours. It did not see me coming until I crashed into it. The sound of the crash was loud.

The watcher fell back and rolled. In a split second, it rose on its feet. I wasn't intimidated, and I charged into it. I heard ribs break, and it screamed as I bit deeply into its left shoulder. I shook the beast and pulled him down. His left arm was hanging limp.

As the watcher tried to rise, I reared up and smashed my right paw into its head. My claws raked deep furrows into its face, and a cloud of blood erupted above its head. The watcher fell again, but watchers are rugged. He shook his bloody head and tried to roar, but he was done. He turned and raced back to the west, holding on to his useless left arm.

Suddenly, I became a target. I saw the muzzle flashes. I plunged down into the nearby Southern Forest, and that probably saved my life. I heard bullets whiz into the trees, but they were too high and too late. I was already crashing east through the woods and back to my house.

When they shot at me, Mom and Miss Aliyah shot back at their muzzle flashes. The return fire was coming from the west and the north. They were down wind, so that was why I didn't know they were there. Once I got south of the house, I came up out of the forest, protected from the fire of our enemies. I took a position near the front of the house; I could see muzzle flashes from more than a dozen rifles. They were advancing too.

I heard Sarah yell at the wounded elk to go see Gracie and get his wounds looked at. Sarah ran around the back of the house to see who was shooting from the north. The house was taking a lot of incoming fire. Every window that faced the front yard and the north was shot out. The walls were made of logs, so I was safe, but Mom and Miss Aliyah were not. They were hidden in the snow. Every time they shot, they invited return fire. They used the fires to their advantage, and they moved from place to place. I was proud of them, but I didn't think two guns against a dozen or more were going to work.

This went on for at least five minutes. It was obvious to me we were going to get overrun. I bellowed to get their attention. Just then, Sarah started shooting from the north side of the house, and it wasn't ten seconds before every gun was returning fire on her last position. But they were late. Sarah joined me just as Mom and Miss Aliyah scrambled back to us. We were shielded by the logs of the house but those two were lucky to have made it alive.

"We gotta go," said Mom. "I might have hit one of the shooters, but maybe not. There was also a man standing on the driveway, past the oil well road, who seemed to be giving instructions, but his people are spread out. We never saw them coming."

Miss Aliyah was reloading. "And what's with those huge dogs? I saw a few watchers too. And, Kaiyo, just dang. You tore that watcher up. He never saw you coming either. After you left, I watched it try to run back down the driveway. You hurt him. Then your mom sighted him and winged him. That shot was almost eight hundred yards away. He spun around and ran off into the Western Forest. Proud of you, Kaiyo."

"I was lucky," Mom said. "But, Kaiyo, you were amazing. Lavi got it better from you than that watcher did, and you nearly killed Lavi."

Just then, as if on cue, every beast allied with the enemy howled or screamed. It was even creepy for me. Our Specials showed great discipline and said nothing, but Moose and Major barked and howled in return. Right then, one of the young wolves, the one named Sage, came up to us.

"My father says we need to get out of here. He thinks we have a better chance just about anywhere else. Your big sister, Gracie, she has the horses ready and is waiting. The barn is getting shot up too."

Mom may not have understood anything Sage said, but she was quick to figure it out. "Tell the others we're coming," said Mom.

Sage ran off, and I motioned Mom and Sarah to follow me. She understood. Miss Aliyah stayed back. The three of us ran past the house through the courtyard and past the long south side of the barn. Waiting for us was Gracie with the horses. The dogs were already there. Mom held court. At the house, Miss Aliyah's rifle barked out defiance at the attackers. She was holding them off. Sarah went straight to Amarok. She was thinking of something.

"All right, everybody," said Mom, "We have to string these people out. We will head southeast, through Aylmer's hidden pasture, and then into the Southern Forest. From there we turn east. We will make our way through the forest until we get to the Hiker Road. We may have to fight to get there."

I knew that road. Goliath and I walked it when I was a cub. We took that road to rescue Dad from cannibal watchers. That was a good plan, but the end of the road was nearly twelve miles away.

Then Mom asked, "How is the elk?"

That was a good question, and it was just like Mom to be concerned. I totally forgot about him. "He's hurt," said Gracie. "The bullet creased his hip and then hit a few ribs. They're broken. But he can get around. He's tough."

The wounded elk dropped his huge head loaded with sharp antlers and nodded. He was proud. "Kaiyo," he said to me, "my name is Hexaka. Call me Hex. My brother is Roan. He will fight, and so will I. I don't know how fast I can run, but I can keep up with you and the others."

Amorak and Anjij spoke to him gently while Roan encouraged him. Dovie had joined us and she was grim. Her talkative style was gone.

Mom kept going, "Sarah and I are going to go get Aliyah. We're going to make some noise too. When we come back, we'll be running. Everybody get ready."

When they left, it was just us Specials and Gracie. It wasn't long before the three of them were back in the fight. Mom was in the house firing out of a window. They made it appear like they intended to fight it out. I heard somebody out in the fields scream in painful surprise. Mom was a good shooter. I also heard the howls of the monsters the enemy brought with them.

Ten minutes later, the three ladies came running back. Mom was quick with the orders.

"Dovie, you know where to go, take the lead. Kaiyo, you're last. Roan and Hex, fall in, but if you need to slow down, wait until we get into the forest and then go north, downwind. They'll miss you that way. Wolves, stay with us and stay aware." Then Mom stopped. "Wait, who's that?"

Mom pointed to a wolf I hadn't met. She had walked among us, and none of us had noticed. She was smaller than the others. She looked like a smaller than normal wolf. She must have approached us from the north. We depended too much on our noses. Amorak and Anjij went over to her. Their tails started wagging.

She turned to me. "You are Kaiyo, the grizzly prince, yes?"

That whole *prince* thing was always odd to me. In Eden, there is no royalty. We are all equals. But time was short, so I went with it. "Yes. I am Kaiyo."

"I am Yeeyi. I have orders from Raphael and Meginnah. You and your sister, Gracie, are to follow me. You are to be supplied with powerful reinforcements to aid in your fight. But now, your family must flee, and we must go now. Hex, you are to join us."

"I heard all that," said Dovie. "We got this. Go."

Gracie was on her horse, and she watched everything. All the animals looked at her. Gracie and I have been siblings for over five years, and we were great at communicating to one another. Dean was better, but Gracie was good. I waved for her to follow me. She turned Duke my way. Mom figured it out. I expected her to try to stop us, but all she said was, "Take care of her, Kaiyo."

"We must hurry," said Yeeyi

Dovie growled and took the lead of Mom's group. Dovie is a powerful bear, and I was glad she was taking the lead. I watched as the ladies fired several more shots to the west just to make noise. Then my mom, Major, Sarah, Miss Aliyah, Aylmer, the dire wolves, and Roan left the farm to the enemy. The enemy had won this part of the battle. The farm was theirs.

"Follow me," said the little wolf. "We must get into the forest, and we must stay hidden. Your family is going to the Southeast, we will go northeast. The forest is thinner in that direction."

Yeeyi was right. A strip of forest, between a mile to three miles, separates our farm from the Eastern Wilderness. The normal way to get there would probably be watched. Yeeyi was being smart. Yeeyi led with Gracie following. Hex followed her, and I followed everybody. Moose stayed close to Gracie. The darkness in the forest soon became like ink; even I had trouble. The trail Yeeyi was following was used by moose, elk, and deer, but it was tight. At one point, I heard Gracie say, "Don't worry, little brother, Duke is following the pretty wolf. I am safe."

I huffed a response. Gracie was amazing.

We had been moving for less than an hour, and by the smell of the wind, I knew we were getting close to the open plain that made most of the Eastern Wilderness. We heard gunfire miles to the south. I wanted to go there, but I knew better. The worst part of the storm had passed, and the snowfall was light. It was still breezy, and I was afraid Gracie would freeze to death. Through the broken clouds a bright full moon shone through, only to disappear again. While that helped us to see, I was worried. Humans are tough, but they were not designed for the extremes. And the weather was extreme. The cold found our exposed skin and made itself known. We had full coats of fur, but Gracie had only her clothes. Clothes are not nearly as good as your own fur. I loved my tiny big sister, and I was worried.

On we went. The snow was deep, and Yeeyi was struggling. I took the lead to plow through it and clear a path. Occasionally, we heard gunfire in the distance. That was good; they were still fighting at least. Our path intersected with a trail made by a herd of bison. They were going in the same direction, and that allowed us to pick up our speed. We made quick time, and Yeeyi took the lead again. After another hour, Yeeyi stopped.

"We are close now. Prepare yourself, Kaiyo, and walk along with your sister. I am afraid her fear will overcome her. Once you are in the door and as soon as you can, tell her to fear not."

Yeeyi was a nice little wolf, but she didn't know Gracie. I had no idea what we were getting ourselves into, but Gracie would not be overcome by fear. I was concerned about her horse though. Duke is comfortable around us Specials, but Duke is an ordinary horse, and ordinary horses can get skittish in new situations.

At some point the sky cleared, and the moon illuminated a white wilderness. Even Gracie gasped at the frozen beauty of it all. But this was no cartoon, and out here, cold weather killed humans. Then I heard the static buzz of the door. That was wonderful news to me. I slipped back to Gracie. We were close. She was cold, and her lips were blue, but her eyes were clear and open. She was fully alert. "Kaiyo," she said, "I know I am here for a reason. Are we going to where you come from?"

I held my paw and moved it to say, "Sort of."

She smiled. "Is it where Landon got stuck?"

I nodded. She looked thrilled.

"Hex, take the lead," said Yeeyi. "You are our injured warrior."

Hex looked impressive. Elk are big creatures, and Hex's antlers were beautiful weapons of war. He held his head high, but he was clearly getting weak. He had lost a lot of blood, and his broken ribs were taking a toll. Breathing had to hurt.

"Thank you, Yeeyi. I will also act as your herald. I understand your concern for the precious young human. Wait twenty seconds."

That seemed like a plan. We had been traveling for at least two hours. I was glad to be close. The door was much farther east than where it was placed today. I can never understand the placement, but Meginnah has his reasons. We walked up a slope and into some timber. I poked Gracie and pointed at Hex. He was walking in front of us then he disappeared into a shadow. Gracie's eyes were wide.

"We're here, aren't we?"

I nodded. Yeeyi counted to twenty, and she slipped in. Then Gracie and Moose. Then me.

Well, I was as surprised as I thought Gracie would be. Even though I entered the door only a few moments after Gracie, she had already jumped off Duke and was racing to see Goliath, Benaiah, and Tracker. A pack of wolf people, a polar bear, and the biggest dog ever standing nearby didn't seem to faze her. Yeeyi and Hex looked on in wonder. Benaiah hugged her and then held her high.

"My wonderful young Gracie, this is, indeed, our greatest gift. Thanks to Meginnah for inviting you here!"

The three of them took a minute to love on Gracie. The polar bear even jumped into the mix and greeted Gracie. I found out his name was Gyp. He was a very big bear, and with his beautiful white coat, we would need him.

Meginnah took those moments to fly toward us. His wings rattled with power. I knew why he terrified Landon; Meginnah still scares me a little. But not Gracie. She kept an arm around Goliath's huge neck and watched Meginnah fly the mile to where we were. The wolf people looked fearful and huddled together; the big dog cowered alone. Gracie saw the dog, left us, and walked over to him. I had no idea what was going on, so I started to intervene, but a quick look from Tracker told me to stand down. Benaiah held on to Moose's collar. Moose wasn't the first earthly animal to make it in the door. Birds sometimes fly in, but they get chased back out. They're not allowed in Eden.

Gracie stood in front of the tremendous dog and gently grabbed him by each side of his head. The dog was no ordinary dog; he was big as a lion. His head was massive, and his jaws were made to snap bones. He looked scared and confused. His eyes went back from Gracie to us and then to Meginnah. The bravery shown by Gracie had the dog temporarily stunned.

"You are a huge, beautiful dog, but you have nothing to fear. He is the cherub who guards Eden. And I guess I'm a little scared too. I am the only human here. You must be new here, right? So how about you and me go meet him together?"

Kel was astonished by Gracie. He was told to avoid people and to kill them if told to do so. Love is always breathtaking to those who have been fed nothing but hatred. His tail wagged a few thumps as he sat in front of her. "I'm Kel," he softly said to her.

"I'm Gracie. Why are you so scared?"

"The thief told me I belonged. I don't know. I am terrified of the cherub. He is the angel of death. I have seen him in my dreams."

"Really?" said Gracie. "I don't see him that way. And he's not an angel. He's an angelic animal. But I understand you, he's scary. Hey, can I show you something?"

Kel didn't have a chance to respond. "See that big grizzly over there? His name is Goliath. He tried to kill me. Twice! He tried to kill Kaiyo and the rest of my family too. He even killed Kaiyo's bear mom. It was so sad. Then my big brother, Dean, shot him in the head. It just grazed him, fortunately. It's a long story, but now he is family to us. You can be just like him if you want to. Do you?"

Gracie had a way of talking that was to the point. Kel looked shocked. "But they told us our enemies would never accept us and would kill us on sight. But Goliath was just like me."

"Well, you probably heard a lot of lies," said Gracie. "Goliath is with us now."

Goliath waved. "He is welcome over there in Eden anytime and at my house anytime. We hope he eventually stays to live with us. We have had adventures together, with all of them, except the polar bear and the dog people, I don't know any of them yet. Anyway, don't be afraid of Meginnah. The time to be scared is over for you."

Well, Kel just bowed his head and cried like a pup. He couldn't stop. Everybody but Meginnah came over to him and awkwardly patted him on the back or tried to say something reassuring. Kel was all tooth and pure muscle, but his heart was breaking. Gracie, once again, showed what the Master's rule really meant. Kel went from believing to experiencing. It can shake up the fiercest of souls. Goliath was proof.

Moose joined Gracie and met Kel. They were both dogs, so they checked each other out the way dogs do. I think it's disgusting, but I'm not a dog. I assumed Kel would be different because he's a Special, but nope. I guess it makes sense. I'm a special bear, and I still do bear things. Kel is still a dog. As for Moose, Kel was the leader of his pack of two.

Gracie then went to the wolf people. Kel and Moose followed her. Feeling protective, I joined her. I didn't know much about those bizarre wolf people. Tracker gave me a look, but I ignored him. I didn't look at Meginnah on purpose.

"Kaiyo and Gracie, I am De'Aavaa. This is my mate, Taalaa."

We returned greetings. "My pups are Te'oma, Eanna, Rapha, and Jael. I am proud of each and every one."

These beasts were fearsome in every way. They were tall, muscular, long-clawed, and long-toothed. The pups were just as big as their parents, yet they greeted us with dropped ears and wagging tails. I laughed. Gracie was thrilled. Canines seem to enjoy humans more than any other animal.

"Kaiyo, we have heard the rumors of your story from the time you were a cub. It has given us hope for a future. Long ago, Taalaa and I came to believe we were being lied to. We left and hid in the forests. But they found us. When Taalaa gave birth to our children, they tried to steal them from us. They kidnap children of Eden, you know."

"Wait," I said, "I don't know. Who tried to take your children?"

"For us, it was an evil two-faced dog. He has abandoned God. He is the true thief. He kidnaps the children of both monsters and children of Eden. He serves the evil one, but he answers to Aymoon. They train the children to hate everything that is good about their own parents and about the Master. They teach them to be killers."

That was what Raphael told me.

De'Aavaa kept going, "The evil dog is helped by monsters like Benaiah and by men. We thought he was our friend, but he hated us when we felt the call of God. But he never let it show. Once the children were born, I left to hunt and bring back meat. I had not gone far when I heard Taalaa howl."

We were all listening. Even Meginnah stood with us.

Taalaa interjected, "I saw Ilya along with genosqwas, two creatures like Benaiah, come our way. Benaiah's race and ours have always been enemies. Even worse, they brought a man with a rifle. That's when I howled. De'Aavaa heard me, circled back, and took out the gunman from behind. Then we scooped up our babies and ran. Even the genosqwas cannot run as fast as us. We escaped and have been on the run for years as our pups grew. But now we fight, and we look for Ilya. We must stop him. Gracie, we see your family as fighters. We watched your human brother face us and later as he mocked Ilya. He is so brave, but I think his girlfriend is as much. They reminded us of us."

"Wait!" said Gracie, "You saw my brother? How is he and everybody else?"

Meginnah decided to step into the conversation. "Gracie, I will speak to that in a moment. First, I must speak to Kelba."

While he spoke, Meginnah smiled at the wolf folk. They noticed, and their happiness was obvious. Their wagging tails always give them away. Then Meginnah motioned for Kel to step forward. Once again frightened, Kel did as he was told and stepped forward. Gracie stepped up with him, and she put her arm over his shoulder.

Meginnah looked at Kel and spoke, "My young Kelba, do not be afraid. Your days of fear are over. But know this, your dreams of being tormented by something like me were all too real. You saw Lucifer as he truly is."

I was fascinated. Kel looked stunned. I always thought Satan was an angel and a beautiful one too. Meginnah leaned over and gently lifted Kel's muzzle as he smiled. Kel relaxed as Meginnah stood back up.

He continued, "I am a cherub and one of the hosts of cherubim. We guard Eden, and we stand with, and next to, Almighty God. We are his guards, and we are very good at what we do.

"But the cherub you saw in your dreams was Satan himself. He is not an angel, and he never was. Though he often masquerades as an angel of light or as other things, like a serpent, Satan is a cherub, like me. He looks like me in form, and he is like me in substance. He was my powerful brother and the prince of the cherubim. His role was to guard God and God's creation. Instead, he betrayed my Father and sought to subdue him and then kill him—if that were possible. He assumed that we, his brethren, would join the petty rebellion out of our loyalty to him. He was wrong, none of us followed that prideful beast." Meginnah paused and rubbed his chins. "Why he haunted your dreams though is not for me to know."

Smiling again, Meginnah said, "Perhaps you will one day find out. Perhaps not. Just remember this, you are now beyond his reach, and you are free to resist him and cast him away from you. Fear him no more."

Kel took it all in. Dogs can't really smile, but he tried. A few wolf folk patted his back as Kel thanked Meginnah for sharing what was unknown to all of us. Meginnah reminded us that most of what he said was in the Book, and he told Kel that he would love getting to know it.

Gracie listened patiently. She raised her had. "Mr. Meginnah, if it's okay, may I ask about my family?"

Meginnah then spoke to her, "I bring you some good news, though this is war not over. There were several fierce battles. Your brother was shot, many times, but he is still strong, and he will live to fight again. He fights like one of David's own.

"Landon escaped and was rescued, and your father and all the others are safe. They won their battles. The allies of Beelzebub tried to escape to fight another day, but De'Aavaa, Taalaa, and the children caught them and destroyed them. Ilya escaped.

"Now, it is time for your friends, old and new, to come to the aid of your mother, young Sarah Tompkins and Aliyah Gibbs. And you may stay with me."

Gracie stood in front of Meginnah. She was already tiny; she looked even more so because Meginnah is enormous. "Mr. Meginnah, I would prefer to go with them. My family is fighting for their lives. I need to be there."

Everybody disagreed. Benaiah was the most articulate, but everybody else also begged Meginnah to keep her here for at least a day. Kel and De'Aavaa pleaded with her to stay. I kept my mouth shut. I knew Gracie. Even Meginnah had fallen in love with Gracie and implored her to stay.

But Gracie smiled and politely said, "Time is not on our side. I will not sit this one out."

Taalaa spoke for everybody when she asked Meginnah to forbid it. Meginnah shook his head. "I have no authority to deny her wishes, and neither does Raphael. And the Master forces no one. Young Gracie has free will. The Master has total sovereignty. The two work together. I cannot keep her here, but I would surely like to do so."

Meginnah then leaned down to Gracie and said, "Grace, your name is also your heart. From this day forward, you shall be known as Grace because grace is what you offer to others. You are, indeed, rare and wonderful. But, Grace, I offer you a warning about your choice. I do not know how this battle will end. You may die. If so, it will be a good death. If you live, it will also be just as good. I only ask that you be wise and listen to Kaiyo and to the others. And remember, tomorrow night, you will be safe, whether you are with the Master or on earth with your family. And while you are special among twelve-year-old girls, fear not. You are loved deeply by the creator of all that is and ever was. He knows you by name and by deed. And he is most pleased."

Then Meginnah looked at all of us. "Kel, when you accepted him, the angels rejoiced. You need to believe me. Destroy your doubts, and be the creature God made you to be. De'Aavaa, Taalaa, Te'oma, Jael, Rapha, and Eanna, you are his and fully loved. You accepted his pursuit of your hearts, and he rejoices because of it. But remember, his love for you is from his grace. Cease trying to earn his approval, you already have it. Now, to all of you, ready yourselves for battle. I will deliver you close. Use your resources wisely. And remember, the evil one learns from his defeats. Your successes of today may not work again. Now pray with me."

We did. You really haven't lived until you get prayed over by a cherub. His prayer was so compelling, and his accent only made it better. Instead of some boring platitudes and a bunch of blah, blah, blah, Meginnah prepared our hearts for battle; he reminded us that we were all warriors, and as warriors, we fight for God. He implored us to courage and to hold fast to the fact of eternity. He told us our temporary pain will translate to eternal life. Meginnah then grinned, all four faces, and finished by saying, "Trust me on this, eternity will be beyond wonderful. I know more, but I cannot tell you everything I know. So know this, your bravery will be rewarded. And look for wisdom, even in the moment."

Meginnah quit talking for a few moments. Then he continued, "Now, who is in command? Libby McLeod led the last group, and quite masterfully. So who will it be? This you must first establish. You are mere moments away from earth. So who is it?"

It was me.

SNIPER—SARAH

I hid at the end of a pasture behind a jumble of logs and branches that Sam had long ago pushed into the forest. The big male wolf, Amorak, and two of his children, Waya and Washoba, stayed with me and patrolled the dark forest behind me. Earlier, they had scratched their names in the sandbox at the farm. I was glad they were here with me. Aylmer was with me too. He was waiting for us farther down the trail.

I didn't think it would be a long wait, and it wasn't. Our group was fleeing into the forest, and our tracks would be easy to follow.

From the farm, this pasture is hidden from view. It was made for Aylmer and the other Specials who wanted to be close to the McLeods but needed to stay out of sight from people coming and going to and from the farm. Farms are busy places.

My view was slightly uphill. The distance was about six hundred yards. Through my IR scope, I started seeing the highlighted figures of enemy soldiers, most were on snowmobiles. Some figures were small, some were big. My concern was for the small ones. They had guns and snowmobiles. Some probably had scopes like mine, but I was well hidden.

Amorak came up to me. I let him look through the scope. He growled something to the others. I picked a target. It was easy because the target was riding a snowmobile well in front of the others. When he got to 150 yards of my position, I pulled the trigger. He fell, and his sled came to a stop. Apparently, no one saw my muzzle flash because no one returned fire. All the people dived off their sleds and into the snow. Some of the big creatures ran back to the entrance of the pasture. I waited. Snipers have been doing things like this ever since the rifle was created. Sewing confusion and fear was all I was trying to do. I needed to buy time for my friends to escape. So I waited.

Fifteen minutes later, the freezing ground and heavy snow took its toll. The men started to rise. They were careful. Behind them, a watcher started to make his way through them. Poor thing.

He was easy to see. He was also being misused by his leader to take a bullet. Once he got as far as his fallen comrade, he would. That would be close enough.

The worst part of the storm had passed, and the wind was starting to shift from the southeast to a west-northwest wind. Their creatures had no idea where we were. But my wolves were catching their scents. I watched as the big beast kept low and carefully made his way to the dead rider. He stayed on all fours as he sniffed and looked at his fallen comrade. After a few minutes, he regained his confidence and rose up on two feet. He turned to wave back to his leader. His fellow soldiers started to rise. Then he turned toward the east, where I was, and roared in defiance. I suppose it was meant to scare me, but it didn't. He didn't know I was there. I squeezed the trigger and stopped the roar. I meant to shoot him in the head, but my round went low and through his throat. He stood for a split second and grabbed his neck with both hands. A moment or two later, he tumbled forward and fell face-first into the snow.

Again, all the others dove back into the snow. I could do this all night. We waited. After another fifteen minutes, Amorak nuzzled me and indicated we were being flanked from the south. It was time to go.

I picked up my two shell casings and ran down the trail. Aylmer waited. He lowered his head and let me use his horns as an elevator onto his back. Escorted by the dire wolves, we raced eastward through the wooded darkness. When the landscape permitted, I would again set up for an ambush. Susan and Aliyah needed more time. What we really needed was daylight and more people.

I thought of Troy. If he had come down the McLeod's driveway, then he would have rolled right into the bad guys and he would already be dead. I banished the thought. I needed to think clearly, and that thought only served as terror. Unnecessary terror. I focused on the attackers, and my hatred for them returned. Hatred was more useful to what I needed to do.

Running—Susan

Dovie led the way. She was a large black bear, but she was tireless. In the darkness, she was nearly impossible to see. Fortunately, the sky was quickly clearing, and the moon came in and out of the cloud cover. We moved deep into the Southern Forest. Dovie knew we needed to go southeast but frequent deadfalls and rocky outcrops caused us to stop and find our way. Our pursuers wouldn't be so delayed. All they had to do was follow our tracks. The elk and the wolves did a good job at creating false trails, and they were continually running off together to create different paths in the snow.

Sarah fired off a few shots some time ago. We trusted her and did not wait. Dovie used the game trails to find her way. It was cold, and with the skies clearing, it was even colder. After a few hours, we came into a meadow created long ago by beavers. The beavers were gone, but the meadow was flat and dotted with dead trees. In the center flowed a large, meandering creek. It was frozen over. It wasn't frozen solid, just frozen over. Dovie indicated we needed to cross. Aliyah and I dismounted.

"This is as good a spot as any," she said. "Let's get everybody across and be careful."

Dovie went first. She caused the ice to crack, but it didn't break. The much-lighter wolves and Major followed. Then I led Cali, my horse. Cali broke through several times near the banks, but I stayed dry. Aliyah, riding Hershel, did the same. Our enormous horse Peyton broke through, but Peyton was tough. The elk wandered upstream and crossed.

The forest here was set back around a hundred yards from each creek bank. We moved out of the flat meadow and climbed uphill. Once in the forest, Aliyah set up behind a deadfall with a clear view of the creek and the open meadow. "I'm going to wait for Sarah."

I knew not to order her to keep going. Aliyah had thought this one out. "Be careful," I whispered. "Anjij and Leif will stay with you. I'll take Sage with me and set up a mile down the trail and wait for you. Don't wait too long for Sarah. We have no idea what her situation is."

Saying that last part was hard. I loved Sarah like a child and friend. She was also completely unpredictable. She could be dead, she could still be stalking the enemy, or she could be on the run. Aliyah and Sarah were close friends too. Time would tell.

I left Aliyah and moved on into the darkness. I started to think about Aliyah. Aliyah was a good shot, but she wasn't as good as either Sarah or me. She should be the one moving on, and I should be the one waiting for Sarah. I called out to Dovie, told her and Sage what I was doing, and turned back. Sage wagged her tail, but Dovie was not happy. We were only a few miles away from the Hiker Road, and Dovie knew it. Once there, we could move fast. Travel in the forest was slower. A lot slower.

Sage ran ahead. I rode back, tied off the horses, and walked back to Aliyah. She was surprised.

"What are you doing? I got this."

I set up next to her. "You aren't really the best shot among the three of us. And the goal of running is to save the three of us. Why keep going if you two aren't with me? Being alone is a bad idea anyway. There have always been bad things in this forest. The addition of the assassins makes it worse. Sarah is suited for the forest, but we aren't. You're going to be my spotter."

"That works," laughed Aliyah.

I looked at my watch. Daylight was still eight hours away. The moon was full, and the snow reflected its light. Everything was illuminated. We heard a few shots. They were not very far off. Sarah was still alive.

"Anjij, Sage, can you call up Amorak?" asked Aliyah. "We need them to come here. This is a good field of fire."

"Listen to you," I whispered, "sounding all soldier-like."

We laughed while I sighted my scope. The three dire wolves howled. The call was returned from at least a mile away. The wolves called back. Five minutes later, Amorak responded; he was close.

Through the scope, I saw Amorak burst through the forest; behind him was Sarah riding Aylmer. Waya and Washoba followed. Sage howled. They ran our way. Aylmer got to the bank and waited. The younger wolves raced across as Amorak escorted Sarah across the ice. Aylmer stayed on the other side of the creek. Once Sarah had climbed up the low creek bank, Aylmer went into the creek. I had no idea what he was thinking, but he had an idea.

Aylmer is heavy, at least four thousand pounds. Quickly he broke up the ice upstream and downstream. It broke apart in slabs, and the ice flowed downstream. Sarah made it to us. We hugged her hard.

"Ice jam. I think he wants to make an ice jam," she said.

That made sense. Aylmer hauled himself up the bank and came our way. He mooed lowly. Dovie and he talked briefly. The two of them slipped into the forest behind us. It wasn't ten minutes later that a big creature, running on all fours, broke into the clearing on the other side. Through my scope I could see that he was a dog. He was huge too. He sensed a trap.

A first, he charged out into the open, but before I could get in a shot, he turned and retreated into the forest. His heat signature was clear, and I could easily see him between the trees. I knew he had been running hard to catch Sarah and the wolves. It was another ten minutes before other figures started appearing in the forest across the meadow.

"I need everybody to head up this low hill and get to the other side of the ridge. Sarah, take the horses and set up just on the other side of the ridge. We need to be hidden from any IR scopes."

Dovie, the elk, and Aylmer were thinking my thoughts. They had moved deeper into the forest and quickly crossed over the ridge. The wolves followed.

"Sarah, we're going to be running right at you, so keep that in mind if you have to cover our retreat."

But she didn't have to.

Aliyah and I stayed hidden by the deadfall. After another twenty minutes, it looked like a convention was gathering on the other side of the meadow. Sarah's sniping had taken a toll in fear. That's what snipers do. None of our pursuers wanted to go out into the open. Instinctively, I knew time was on our side. A big dog came out and took a few tentative steps into the open. Aliyah was watching through binoculars. The full moon made seeing much easier.

"Target. Big dog at one o'clock."

"Check. I'm going to wait until it tries to cross the creek. If I miss, blast away."

The huge dog walked down the slope and into the meadow. He was followed by two men. Smart. They were escorting him. They had rifles to their shoulders, and they scanned the forest edge from side to side. It wasn't but a few minutes when it became apparent that they were walking in water.

"The ice jam. It's working," whispered Aliyah.

The dog and the men were walking through ankle-deep water. "When it gets knee-deep, let me know," I said.

I figured if I missed, they would dive for cover, and the cold water might take them out of action, at least for a little while. The trio kept coming. The three didn't see us, and with the wind now coming from the northwest, we were downwind. They got to the creek bank and never saw the creek. The creek bank was only a few feet high, but it was enough for the two men to topple into the bitterly cold, fast-moving creek. The big dog backed up. The men screamed and thrashed to get out. To their credit, they kept their rifles. But they were in danger. They both managed to get out, and immediately they started back. The wind was steady, and the temperatures were well below zero. Both cried out for help, but no one in the forest budged. Each man started to splash through the flooded meadow. But they didn't get far. Their clothes froze stiff, and it slowed them down. Then the clothes froze solid onto their bodies. They fell a few times, and getting back up looked to be harder than each attempt before it. They were screaming profanities at their comrades who waited in the forest. Both men made it out of the meadow, but when they got to the short slope leading to the forest, they fell and didn't get up. After a few minutes, they were dragged back into the forest. They probably died. I doubt anyone brought a change of clothes.

We stayed silent. I could hear a deep, throaty voice ordering the dog to go farther, but he refused. We didn't blame him. Even animals can freeze to death. Aliyah tapped me on the shoulder. "It was more than knee-deep. I'm a little late on telling you, but let's go. They're going to have to find a way through or around this meadow. Now is our chance to get away."

That sounded nice. I never thought we could get away. I thought we could inflict some damage and maybe discourage them, but getting away sounded too good to be possible. But now, maybe it could be possible. Keeping the deadfall between us and the enemy, we slipped up and over the low hill. Sarah was there with our horses. "I saw it all and told everybody," she said. "Now's our chance. Aylmer's plan worked."

We mounted and rode on. An hour later, Dovie walked out of the forest and onto the broad shoulder and parking area at the head of the Hiker Road. The Hiker Road was a gravel road that went from the Eastern Wilderness all the way to Radford. Hunters, hikers, and other outdoor types used it. We were tired, but we all turned south in the direction of the town. We were used to running, and this direction made sense. But not to Sarah.

Sitting high atop Peyton, she had a commanding presence. "Hey, can we have a team meeting? I need everybody."

We all gathered.

"Okay, the assassins will get here in an hour or so. Once they figure out a way around the meadow, they will follow our tracks and double their speed. They either have to kill us or give up. Come daylight, cops will be all over the place. But we all know they aren't quitting. All they need to do is chase us down, and they know it. We won't be able to pin them down in the forest or flood any more meadows. Radford is at least twenty miles from here, maybe more.

They will be able to catch up and overrun us. Their watchers can stay hidden in the forest, so even daylight won't stop them. And our horses are only going to get weaker. They can't slog through the heavy snow and make it to town. Maybe Peyton can, but yours can't. It's too far for all of us."

Those were good points. Dovie growled, and the wolves whined to each other. Major looked happy to be with us. Aylmer listened.

"You've been thinking about this, haven't you?" I asked.

"Yep. Our hope is with Kaiyo. We don't have a clue where he is, but he's it. The door has always been in the Eastern Wilderness, and that's to our north, and not too far. In the meantime, we set up on a hill to the north and figure out how we can defend it."

"I'm all in," said Aliyah. "I'm tired of running." She looked at the rest. "Anybody want to try to make it to town?"

It was unanimous. No one wanted to keep running. We would all rather die fighting than die running.

We turned and went north, leaving the end of the road and the parking area behind us. Even though the snow was deep, the road was flat and solid. The road would end shortly, and we would soon miss it. But everybody, even the horses, sensed we were going to find a place to stop. I didn't know how much our collective exhaustion had taken its toll. It wasn't just me.

The terrain gave way to the miles of open space and random patches of timber that made up a part of this amazing wilderness. Sarah was right; this was where we belonged.

The moonlight reflected off the snow. I knew of a perfect hill about a mile northeast of us. Its slopes were marked with boulders of various sizes and cedar trees dotted the approaches to the top. We circled wide and came back to the hill from the north and we got there quickly. The perfect part of the hill was that the top was flat and somewhat sunken in. Most of us could move around without being seen.

Once up top, we all got to work. Aylmer and the elk used their horns to move the deep snow to the edges of the slopes. The wolves got busy searching the area. The three of us set up firing pits. We took the saddlebags off the horses and spread the ammunition among us. Then Sage and Waya took the horses' reins in their mouths and led the horses down the back of the hill and to a collection of boulders fifty yards away to the northeast. The boulders would hide the horses and act as a windbreak. The horses would be safer and a little warmer.

And we waited. It was the wolves who first heard something. They started whining. When wolves whine, it doesn't mean they're scared. It's just communication. The elk caught the sound too. Dovie and Aylmer went to the edge of our flat hilltop and trained their eyes to the south. The three of us waited. Then we heard snowmobiles.

That was bad. Nobody good was sledding at one thirty in the morning. "Mr. Elk, how many?"

The elk craned his tubular ears this way and that. He stomped his right front hoof twice. "All right, Aliyah, you be the spotter, and Sarah and I will be the shooters. I guarantee you they're going to follow our tracks. They won't be hard to find."

We could still see the forest a few miles to the south. The snowmobiles were easy to see. Their headlights were on, and they were riding in our tracks.

"I have eyes on them," said Aliyah. "The elk is right. Just two. Both seem to be men. That's all. The glare of the headlight is covering up everything else. One of you do an IR. Anything behind them?

I was already checking. "Don't see anything, but the distance may be hiding things."

Aliyah kept looking. She spoke to Sarah. "Sarah, the guy you shot in the snowmobile, was he towing a cargo sled?"

Sarah laughed. "Definitely not. Why?"

Aliyah never stopped looking through the binoculars as she talked. "Because these guys are. Both of them. Seems odd they would think ahead to bring supplies. Be ready. I'll tell you when they're in range."

Everybody watched as the snowmobiles closed the distance. They were careful and weren't going very fast. They followed our tracks and stopped occasionally. After another twenty minutes, they were close. When they got to within two hundred yards, Aliyah alerted us.

"Two hundred yards. Wait until they are very close. Their rifles seem to be in their cases."

They were coming from the south, and the wind had shifted to the northwest. Even Dovie was no help. Fortunately, our tracks did not lead right up this hill. We had been careful, and we purposefully went well past the hill before we had turned east and circled back. We waited as they came even with us. They never saw us. They continued, following our tracks to the north. Moments later, Aylmer and Dovie went nuts. The two had caught their scent. Dovie ran to Sarah and nearly knocked her over. Dovie grabbed the barrel of Sarah's rifle in her mouth and growled fiercely.

"Okay, okay, Dovie. I won't shoot. Do you know those riders?"

Dovie nodded in exaggerated strokes. Aylmer mooed in approval.

"Are they friends?"

Again, Dovie nodded.

Then she pointed to Sarah, "Wait, do I know the rider?"

And again, Dovie nodded.

Our mood had gone from grim to nearly ecstatic. Even the wolves were wagging their tails. We needed friends. Dovie then huffed and growled an order to the elk. He bolted off our hilltop shelter after the riders. Aliyah watched as the elk caught up to them.

"They stopped. They're looking back over here. The elk is nodding a lot. They're turning our way."

We watched as they came close. Dovie had a great nose, but I still had my rifle on them. So did Sarah. They gunned their sleds and came right up to the flattened top of our pathetic fortress. The first rider got off. He was tall.

Taking his helmet off, he spoke, "Sarah?"

Sarah let out a muffled scream. I knew the voice too. It was Troy. Sarah raced right into him. The other rider was Lieutenant Justin Martinez. Justin had been a friend of the family for years. He and Goliath were probably best friends. Aliyah ran over and hugged Justin. Troy took Sarah by the hand and did what he had always done. Troy never ignored the Specials.

"Well, Dovie, Sarah just said you saved my life? Can I have a hug?"

For the first time tonight, Dovie seemed happy. They communicated briefly. Justin waved. "Hi, Dovie." She waved back.

Troy took some time with Dovie and thanked her for helping to protect us. Turning to the wolves, Troy asked, "Well, who do we have here?"

Sarah introduced each one by name. Pointing to the elk, Sarah said that his friend got shot and he left with Kaiyo, but both elk were there with us from the beginning. Troy thanked him too. Then he wandered over to Aylmer and greeted him. Justin also met everybody.

Justin looked around. "Where's Gracie?"

He noticed. That was one of the reasons we loved him.

Sarah took over. For the next fifteen minutes, she told the two what had happened. We answered their questions. Troy was especially interested in the watcher Sarah killed. I thought he would be more concerned about the man Sarah shot or about the two men who probably froze to death, but he wasn't. She covered everything, including Gracie leaving with Kaiyo and how we got here.

"So what's in the sleds?" asked Aliyah.

"Well," said Troy, "a lot more ammunition. Two more rifles, blankets, gloves, things like that."

That made sense. It was disappointing for some reason. "And food," said Troy.

Everybody looked up except Aylmer and the elk. They knew there would be none for them. "We used our time in Radford to stock up. Dispatch got several 911 calls that Aliyah's barn had burned down. I called that number back. It was one of your neighbors, a neighbor named Tracey. She said your driveway and front yard had a lot of trucks in it. They all had trailers for snowmobiles. She spotted people moving through the house."

Aliyah threw a fist into the air. "My house is okay?"

"As far as we know. Tracey also said your horses were safe. They're in her barn. That's got to be a story too."

I knew Tracey. She was a close friend. She also knew Kaiyo since he was a cub. She lived about a mile from Aliyah's. She's tough, and I wasn't surprised to hear that she rode up to Aliyah's to see what was going on. I would need to call her.

Justin took over, "We knew your gates were closed because Tracey said they were. She also said somebody had been on your land cutting down trees. Troy and I just swaged a guess and figured out the only way to find you was the Hiker Road. Since the Hiker Road leads to Radford, we didn't have to wait for the paved roads to be plowed. We were able to ride our sleds directly from the office. By the way, Sheriff Tuttle is in on this. We have SAT phones. Anyway, when we got to that parking lot, we saw your tracks and kept going. Your house is only another fifteen or so miles to the west, so either here or there, we were coming. And I need to call the sheriff. He's pushing us for some good news."

Justin excused himself and called in to the sheriff. Cell phones were no good here, but SAT phones worked great. Justin gave a very abridged version of what had happened. Oddly, he and the sheriff spent more time talking about the dead watcher. Justin mentioned something about helicopters at sunup.

"Okay," said Troy. "The bad guys, whoever they are, are going to be here soon. Let's get some hot coffee in you ladies. And, Dovie and you wolves, I have enough meat to feed you guys. In addition to Dovie, I thought I'd be feeding Kaiyo. You can have Kaiyo's portion, which, by the way, is huge. If you can wait after the attack that's coming, probably soon, it would be better. And to you two herbivores, you didn't think we forgot you, did you? We brought oats from the sheriff's stables. Again, let's wait until after the attack."

Aylmer and the elk looked like they were going to cry. To be remembered is always good. Troy finished with, "Justin, do you want to tell Aliyah and Susan the good news?"

Good news? I needed some good news.

Pouring hot coffee in Styrofoam cups, Justin started, "We may not live through the night, but the rest of your families, Kate, Jack, Gunner, Dean, Libby, and Sam, they're all alive. They won their battle. And they rescued Landon. He's safe too."

Aliyah sank to her knees and wept. So did I. Ten thousand tons of worry were lifted from both of us. Sarah, the killer sniper, squealed like a little girl. In their own way, the Specials rejoiced too. My tears froze solid on my scarf. I don't know why I asked the next question, but it came to me.

"How's Dean?"

I didn't know why I asked. I loved Dean no more than I loved Libby or Gracie. But I knew Dean. He is drawn to danger. He was protective too. I saw Justin wince. He looked back at Troy.

"Susan, I don't know much. He's on his way to the trauma center at Billings Clinic. Sam said he'll live and recover. Kate and Sam went with him. That is all I know. Everybody else is fine though."

"Can I use your SAT phone? And more coffee. I spilled mine."

Ten minutes later I got off the phone. I first spoke with Kate. She answered Sam's phone. Dean, she said, was a hero. I believed her. He was getting sewed up and would eventually be okay. I then spoke to Sam, but only briefly. Dean had gotten shot up and badly bitten by one of those giant dogs. If we lived, he would have some amazing stories. He asked a dozen questions about our situation and where we were. I told him we were getting ready for an attack. He gulped, and I could tell he was crying. I told him I loved him and said goodbye.

"I got movement."

It was Aliyah. Everybody's mood changed. Troy and Justin recovered their rifles. Aliyah saw headlights on the Hiker Road two miles away. We all checked and rechecked our weapons.

Batteries for our thermal scopes were pulled out of our coats where we kept them warm.

"Seven sleds, maybe a few more," she called out.

"All right, guys, they don't know about Troy and Justin. They will definitely be confused about the tracks of their sleds though. They'll probably send their huge dogs first. Then their watchers. Then they'll try to overrun us. Mr. Elk, can you head north and try to find Kaiyo?"

The elk nodded. He came over and looked at me. That's all he did. We just looked into each other's eyes. It wasn't long, but it seemed long. Then he huffed and trotted off the hill. That was wonderful. He was a brave elk. I hoped to know him by name someday.

"They're still waiting," said Aliyah. "But they're all pointed in our direction. It won't be long."

I tried to use my IR scope, but the distance was too far to see much. "Aylmer, Dovie and you beautiful dire wolves, I cannot ask you to stay, but if you do, here are your orders. We may get overrun. I expect them to surround us and then try to pick us off. Then they'll try to overrun us. Aylmer, I love you, but you are too big to be at the top of this hill. They will be able to see you from a mile away. Literally. Those rocks where the horses are might be a good place to wait until a snowmobile or one of those big dogs tries to flank us. Charge them and trample them if possible. Dovie, you can hide up here. If a watcher or one of those dogs comes here, they're yours until we can shoot them. Wolves, the open snowfields may suit you better. Try to flank them as they get near. Keep your distance. Don't go after people if they are armed."

"They're coming," said Aliyah.

Their headlights were visible, and they were making no attempt to conceal themselves. They didn't know where we were yet, and they came slowly. I was starting to see clear heat signatures coming our way too. They were laboring through the snow.

"All right, folks, find your shooting positions. And try to hide your heat signatures."

My mind was racing; we had no options left. I was starting to sense some real despair. I prayed and willed myself to think better thoughts. And I was so cold. My frustration with the situation was getting the best of me.

From just behind us, I heard a howl. It startled all of us. The dire wolves went on full alert, but only for a moment. The howl was higher pitched for a wolf's howl. Then the howl was answered. I knew that howl. I had heard it for years. Tracker! And he was close.

I hurried to the north side of the hill. There, at the base of our hill, was the little wolf I saw at the farm. She was the first one to howl. She looked up at me, and her tail wagged.

Vengeance—Kaiyo

"Grace, ride up front, but just behind me. Wolf folk, stay in your pack, you are more dangerous that way. Fall in behind Grace. Kel, to my right. Gyp and Benaiah, I trust your instincts. We are going to find our family and go straight there. If either of you think going to the right or left provides an advantage, just let me know where you are going. Goliath, take Grace's left. Tracker take the lead."

I was sure Goliath was going to be with Grace whether I said to or not. He loved her more than he loved life. I just cut to the chase. As for the others, we weren't human, so taking orders from a nonhuman wasn't something any of us animals liked to do. So I basically placed everybody where they were going to go anyway. Except Kel. I needed his confidence bolstered, and having him with me was a sign I trusted him.

"Remember what Benaiah said, the ladies are dangerous. We don't need to surprise them."

I stepped out of the door first. It had gotten even colder. Everyone except Gyp seemed to shudder at the cold. A few of the wolf folk laughed nervously. We moved out quickly. Grace was dressed well. She had to urge her horse to move into the cold. I could tell Duke liked where we were. I guess we all did, but that was not our lot. We knew only to go south to the Hiker Road.

After ten minutes of trudging through the snow, Kel moved next to me. "Kaiyo, I never really knew my parents. But I know what happened now because of what Ruel told us. Ruel didn't mention it, and maybe he didn't know it, but I was raised by Ilya. He was like my father. A bad father, but a father. My memories as a puppy are not good. Sometimes he treated us warmly, sometimes he hated us.

"Ilya worked for two men. One of those was Gunther MacDonald. The wolf folk killed him tonight. He got shot, but he would have lived if De'AaVaa hadn't caught him. As the six of us puppies grew up, we lived in forests and even in houses and warehouses. We were taught to fight. As a pup, we were big, and we got thrown in pits with fighting dogs. They weren't like us, they were just plain dogs, but they were savage. People came from all around. I remember my sister, the one who is out here somewhere, she didn't like to fight. She hated it. But an evil man named Wraight beat her and threatened her. He did the same to a brother. He is with her today. My other living brother learned quickly. He seemed to enjoy killing dogs. I had to learn quickly too."

"Kaiyo, did your bear mother know Ilya? He befriended my parents. Maybe he befriended your mother. If I am talking out of place, I apologize."

The thought had come to mind. I was sure my bear mother knew him. Meginnah thought she did too. It made sense. A grizzly bear as a soldier would be a good tool. They couldn't control Goliath. He was on their side, but they had long given up on him. He couldn't control his own grizzly bear rage. "Thank you. And yes, Kel. Maybe. Today is not the day, but someday I will find Ilya. I promise. I am convinced he is responsible for killing my mother."

"I would like for you to do that," said Kel.

Not too far away, I heard Yeeyi howl. She had gone from us earlier. I saw her leave, but she was a mysterious creature. I was surprised I didn't know her before today. Tracker heard her howl too. He answered quickly. Tracker turned to us.

"She found them, they are close."

We all had questions, but there's only so much information in a howl. Basically, a howl is just a howl. Tracker ignored us and broke into a loping run. I knew that run; wolves can go that way for hours. But the snow was deep, and Tracker started having a tough go of it. Gyp ran to the front and took the lead.

"Come on, Kaiyo," said Gyp. "Let's punch through the snow. Tracker tell us which way to go."

Just then Roan, the other elk, showed up. He told us to follow him, and we did. Together we pushed through the snow. Our strength drove us through the drifts and moved enough snow for the others to travel quickly. The moon was bright. I loved this part of the world, and it was made even more beautiful by the snow and the moonlight. I wondered how my mom and the others ended up in the Eastern Wilderness. It sure made finding them easier. That was probably their reasoning too. Another howl from Yeeyi. The howl came from a low hill directly to the south. Again, Meginnah placed the door perfectly.

We got to the hill, and I knew by scent Mom was there. Captain Stahr and Justin were there too. That the men were there was a mystery, but I was glad they were. Grace rushed to the front of us, and Duke took her up the slope. We were right behind her.

"Mom! We brought friends."

My mom was so happy to see Grace. Sure, it was a dangerous place, but Mom knew Grace was part of the team. Goliath ran over to Justin, and the two roughhoused. Benaiah hugged my mom while Mom hugged Grace. I liked seeing it.

Grace then stepped back and asked everybody to hurry to her. Miss Aliyah kept watching to the south. She was last to come. "They're still far off. What's up?"

Miss Aliyah didn't see what the others were staring at.

Before them stood the family of wolf folk, a powerful dog as big as a lion, and an enormous polar bear. Dovie watched, but the dire wolves reacted with growling and hunched backs. Aylmer raced up behind us and started to act all aggressive. Aylmer has a temper problem, and tonight was the wrong time. Benaiah scolded Aylmer. Tracker ran to Amorak and Anjij. A few moments later, tails were lowered. They weren't wagging, but the aggressiveness was gone.

"Okay, everybody," said Grace. "First, Meginnah, the cherub, said my name is to be Grace from now on. I'm not Gracie anymore. I like my new name, so please try to remember that. You don't want to make him mad. And more important, please meet my new friends."

From then on, she was known as Grace, and Grace had a way of talking that disarmed all of them. Being a friend of Grace meant enough. I even saw some dire wolf tails wag. That caused a few wolf folks' tails to wag. That was good, but we needed the meet and greet over with. Grace seemed to know we had to hurry.

She started with the most obvious, "This is De'AaVaa and Taalaa. They're wolf folk, and they helped defeat the group who wanted to kill Landon. And, Mom, if you don't know about Dean, he got shot up, but he'll be okay."

"I know, sweetie, I talked to your dad. Keep going. And thank you all."

Grace kept going, "These are their children."

She walked over to them and held each of their hideously long-clawed hands as she introduced them. Each time a tail wagged. "This is Eanna. This is Te'oma. And Jael. And this is Rapha. They're wolf folk. They're on our side. The elk with you is Roan. His brother, Hex, is the one who got shot. He'll be okay."

Roan nodded and seemed happy.

"The polar bear is Gyp. He spent all day with Libby, Kate, Jack, and Dean. He killed a watcher who tried to kill Libby and Kate."

Gyp walked up and accepted quick hugs and heartfelt thanks from Miss Aliyah and Mom.

Grace finished, "And this is Kel. He was like Goliath and Sarah. He was lost and was helping the bad people. But now he's found."

Sarah stepped over to Kel and hugged him. "Okay, Kel, we have some stories to share someday if we live through the night. Just know this, they loved me, so they'll love you too. I'm Sarah."

Kel had no idea what Sarah was talking about, but he liked what he heard.

Grace finished by saying, "Kel lost a sister and a brother in the first battle. Libby shot one, and Tracker and Dean killed the other. Kel still has two brothers and a sister with the enemy right now. He wants to save them. Taalaa and De'AaVaa want to help Kel."

Miss Aliyah held up her binoculars. "Still coming, still taking their time. The sniping must have them spooked."

Mom was quick. She looked at Kel and at the wolf folk. She laughed and muttered something about them being so big. "We need those big dogs of theirs out of the fight. They're using them as shock troops to draw our fire. Kel, do you think they'll listen?"

Taalaa held up two fingers and whined. Mom figured out two of them might listen. "All right, Kel, be careful. If I have to shoot one of your family, I'm really sorry. We'll be praying for your success and for the safety of all of you. De'AaVaa, Taalaa, and family, Godspeed."

"Wait," said Sarah. She took a dark scarf and tied it around Kel's neck. "Don't want to shoot you, Kel." She then looked at Taalaa and said, "Could Te'oma and Jael stay with me and with the dire wolves?"

Taalaa agreed. Te'oma's tail wagged like a puppy. Jael was doing the same. Those two were fearsome creatures, and the whole thing looked so strange. Kel gave Sarah a disgusting lick to her face. His tongue covered her face. Sarah laughed. Then Kel and the wolf folk ran down the back of the hill and then off to the northwest. They were on a mission to intercept.

Mom wasn't done. She asked Benaiah and Gyp to come over. They did.

"Sarah killed a watcher, but they have others. Maybe one, maybe two. Can you circle around and persuade them to stay out of the fight? If you can turn them to us, give it a shot. Watchers are prideful things, so that's unlikely. Kel has a better shot at turning his siblings than you do. But hey, with God, all things are possible, right?"

And there, on than crowded little hilltop, we prayed. Benaiah finished in a language none of the humans understood but it was good stuff.

They said their goodbyes and left, heading southwest. Mom kept acting as the commander, and nobody questioned her.

"Goliath and Aylmer, you two will need to watch our flanks. Aylmer, take Duke back to the rocks and come back. We don't know much about these people or what they brought to help them. Tracker and Dovie, stay with us, but go to the back side of the hill and lay low. If they send the monsters, we will need your help. Gracie, stay with either your little brother, Tracker, or Dovie."

"It's Grace, not Gracie."

Mom laughed. "It will take some getting used to, but I'm all in. I'll just need a little grace. Get it?"

"Got it, Mom. Go save our lives now."

I went to Miss Aliyah to see what the situation was. I could see the snowmobiles by their headlights. There were ten of them.

Miss Aliyah leaned down and whispered, "Kaiyo, we knew to come to you. Sarah was the one who convinced us to run to you instead of town. Your friends are amazing."

I nodded and stayed with her for a few minutes. I turned and went to the back of the hill. Aylmer had already taken Duke to join the other horses. Sarah joined me. Goliath had followed Aylmer and Duke to the bottom of the hill.

She spoke to all of us, "Keep your eyes peeled, and don't be surprised if these people have a few tricks up their sleeves. The wind is out of the northwest. Let's try to keep an eye downwind to the southeast and be vigilant."

She turned and walked back to join the others. We followed her. The humans were fanned out on the hilltop. The females were braced by the two lawmen. All had the same black rifles. They looked grim. The dire wolves plus Jael and Te'oma stayed together.

I watched as Sarah and Captain Stahr stepped away. They whispered briefly, and when they were done, she kissed him on the cheek. Quickly she turned to face her new pack. She smiled, but her face had changed into something sinister. I knew that look. Sarah was in her comfort zone. A killing zone. They happily followed her down the back of the hill, and then they were gone.

While I was watching, I heard Miss Aliyah ask the others, "Ready?"

Mom, Captain Stahr, and Justin said, "Yes."

Miss Aliyah waited a few minutes so Sarah could get away from the hill. Then she pointed an odd, fat-looking pistol in the air and shot a flare high over our hill. The snowmobiles stopped and turned. The flare went high and then drifted off to the southeast. Darkness returned. Their monsters roared. Ours stayed quiet.

Grace whispered to me, Tracker, and Dovie, "Their attention will be on us, not on Sarah, Kel, Gyp, or anyone else. That's a good idea."

Miss Aliyah was watching everything. So were the lawmen. They had special binoculars to see in the night too. For a moment there was no movement. Then at nearly five hundred yards away, two giant dogs appeared. They waited. A watcher followed and stood with them. All but two snowmobiles motored to the north behind them. We waited, and so did they. After a few more minutes, one of the snowmobiles came at us. It was not going fast, but it came steadily on. One of the dogs came with it. Grace was quiet. I told Dovie to go warn Aylmer and Goliath. I wanted Goliath with me.

"Tell Aylmer to watch downwind. A big dog and a watcher are missing from their group. We need to find them."

Dovie growled, but she did it. In moments, she returned with Goliath. They were keeping low.

"I am sure it's a trap," Goliath said to me. "We need to watch our back side. You got this side, Kaiyo."

Goliath punched Justin in the ankle and motioned him to follow him. They went to the southeastern side of the hill, the back side, and took positions there. Justin figured it out and he was soon scanning the land behind us, to the east and south.

The advancing snowmobile crossed the white expanse. The snow was new, so the machine was throwing up a lot of snow. The area looked like a sea of white, but the ground underneath the snow was rocky and broken up by arroyos, hills, and ridges. We knew this area. Goliath knew it better than everybody but me. The snowmobile came to a stop fifty-five yards away at the bottom of our hill's slope. The rider and his passenger stood up. Both were carrying rifles. One of those big dogs stood next to the snowmobile.

The first man yelled up to us, "Susan! It's Pete Harred. Meet me in the middle. I have a message. Nobody needs to get hurt."

It was tense. Moose and Major barked furiously until Tracker growled. Troy told Mom not to meet the men, but Mom thought differently.

Mom came over to me. "Kaiyo, Dovie, come with me."

Miss Aliyah and Troy were aiming at the men and the dog. Grace stayed back with Tracker. Goliath knew what was going on, but he and Lieutenant Martinez stayed focused on the expanse behind us. They were suspicious of something.

We came over the top of the hill, and I saw the big dog's eyes get even bigger. Dovie is a big black bear, and I am four hundred pounds heavier. I've been in a few fights, and my scarred face added to the fearsome persona. We flanked Mom. We made our way to the halfway spot. The two men and the big dog climbed the hill to us. I touched Mom with my muzzle. I wanted to speak directly to the dog. Mom told Harred to wait until I was done. Looking at the dog, I detected some confusion. My aggressive body language didn't match my words. On purpose.

"Did I do something to you? What did I do to you to make you want to kill us? I want to know right now because somehow, I must have made you mad. When did I ever do such a thing?"

I waited. She did not respond, so I kept going, "I am Kaiyo, the bear who your master, and you, apparently, wish to kill. You are here to kill me, right? Yeah, it's right. You are here to kill Dovie, and you want to even kill my mother. That's disgusting. Before you talk, I just want you to know that Ilya is on the run, MacDonald is dead, and your brother, Kel, is with us. On our side."

The dog bared her teeth and growled. "That's right. Ilya and his pals threw you into the pit with savage dogs, and you learned to hate. Boo-hoo. But for some reason, you don't hate him. Instead, you hate us. Seems like you hate the only people who are willing to give you a second chance. Ironic, isn't it? So what do you say, dog?"

What looked to the humans as savage barking and growling were only words. "Who told you that? Nobody knows that about me. Are you a witch?"

I had to laugh at that one. "Hardly. But Dovie and I are bears from a wonderful and powerful place. You are still a citizen there. We can take you there tonight. Kel will join you."

"Not interested. You lie," she said.

The dog pushed Harred. She was done. Harred looked nervous. He was involved in wholesale murder, and such things are dangerous.

My mom spoke first, "What is your message, Pete? Get on with it, or I'll shoot you myself."

Way to go, Mom, I thought.

The dog bared her teeth. That wasn't acceptable. Again I spoke, "Make so much as a move at my mom, and I will smash you. My brother Dean killed one of your litter mates. My sister killed another. Adding you to the list is just fine with me."

Harred paused and then started talking, "Give us Kaiyo, and we will gladly leave. We have thirteen men plus the monsters. You are outnumbered, Susan. If you don't do what you're told, you will be overrun within the hour, and all of you will be killed. Either way, we get Kaiyo. Give us Kaiyo, drop your weapons, and you're free to go home."

Dovie broke in, "Hear that you big, dumb, dingo dog? He called you a monster. You know what our humans call us? They call us family. And they treat us like family. You gotta be the dumbest, biggest dog on the planet to stick with these losers."

Dovie shook her head. The dog clearly didn't like Harred. Of course, Mom didn't know what was being said, but she figured some of it out.

"Pete, what's the name of this dog? She's beautiful. Do you know?"

"No, Susan, I don't. It's irrelevant to our discussion."

"Not really," said Mom. She pointed to the other man. "You there, what's your name?"

He spoke. "None of your business. I don't like to get friendly with my potential future targets. But what I can tell you is that Pete's right. If we don't go back with the bear's carcass right now, every one of you will be quickly killed, and I'll soon be headed to the airport to another job. Do what he told you to do. If not, we're leaving. But we'll be right back."

In a flash, Mom had drawn her handgun and pointed it right at the talking man. "Pete, shut up and get on your knees. Now you, sir, you are obviously a wicked killer. I don't like you. Drop your weapons now. You can walk back."

Just then, we heard Justin shoot from the back of the hill. Farther away, we heard the pained, angry roar of a watcher. Goliath and Justin were right. The assassins were trying to get an advantage during the parlay. Everybody noticed. Pete looked disappointed. The other man seemed bored. Just then there was growling from behind them and from all sides of us. Sarah appeared out of the darkness holding her handgun. Where had she been hiding? The big dog growled.

Sarah kept her eye on the other man but spoke to the big dog, "Take one step, dog and you will die right here. All right, Mr. Hired Killer, time to go. Your little back door trick seemed to fail, and I don't appreciate you trying it. You violated the rules."

"Hah! I'll be back. Trust me," he sneered.

He put down his rifle and two handguns. He walked down toward their snowmobile. "No, sir!" said Sarah. "Leave your sled here. You got a few hundred yards of walking to do, so do it."

The man started walking back. He got about twenty yards when Sarah called out. "Hey. Do you really intend to kill us?"

He turned. "I look forward to it, lady, especially you."

Sarah growled. "Wrong answer. Amorak. Te'oma. Now!"

"Sarah! No!" urged Mom.

But it was too late. We watched as a dire wolf and a wolf folk rocket out from behind some boulders and then chase the man. His eyes got wide, but he managed to run to his snowmobile and start it. But he didn't get anywhere. They were on him. Before I turned away, Amorak and Te'oma had nearly decapitated him. When they finished, they howled in defiance. That caused all the hidden dire wolves to howl too.

Mom was not pleased, but she kept quiet.

Sarah smiled and stood in Pete's face. "One down, twelve to go, right Pete? Now march your traitorous butt up the hill. You are our prisoner. That means it's only eleven men to go."

Pete was reduced to pure terror. He thought killing us was a numbers game.

Sarah called to Te'oma, "Search him, and bring me his wallet and anything interesting."

Dovie and I stayed with the dog. Mom turned back to us before going uphill and looked at me. "Did she threaten us?"

I shook my head.

Mom looked back at the dog. "You're a beautiful dog. You look like Kel. Kaiyo, it's up to you if you let her go or if she stays a prisoner."

Mom went back up the hill. The dog was in shock at how bad it went for her side.

I spoke again, "First, what is your name?"

"I am Tamraz," she said. "Please thank your mother for me. She was kind. So what is to become of me?'

"Well, you didn't threaten to kill us like they did, so no one here wants to kill you. At least not until you come charging right at back at us. Or you could join us. Or you could just sit this one out and wait to talk to your brother."

She thought for only a few seconds. "I will take that option. I have two brothers fighting against you. I cannot hurt them."

"Then go north, at least a mile. Wait for your brother there. And one more thing. Your real mother and father are alive and will want to see you. If that interests you, you will need to dramatically change your worldview. Right now, you can't get to where they are."

"What? Can Kel? Has he seen them?"

"Yes. Kel can. He had a chance to see them both and live out his life in peace. But he wanted to try to get the rest of the litter to go with him. He must love you a lot."

Tamraz looked at the ground for a few moments. "That sounds like Kel. He will have trouble convincing one of my brothers. He's gone all in with those people. Good luck to you folks. Their leader is a sorcerer. He is powerful and very dangerous. All right, any special place up north?"

"Wait," I said. "Do you smell that?"

I smelled the wolf folk and Kel. The wind was to the northwest. It took a few moments for Tamraz to catch the scent. "Wow," she said, "bears really do have better noses. I thought it was a lie. It's Kel, isn't it?"

We didn't have to wait long. Out of the moonlit darkness came the ghostly shapes of the wolf folk and Kel. The wolf folk greeted us and ran to Te'oma and Jael while Kel and Tamraz collided together in pure joy. They started talking a mile a minute, so Dovie and I went up the hill. The two dogs followed us.

Justin called out, "Gyp and Benaiah coming in."

There on the top of our flattened little hill, we were all together. Three women, a preteen, two lawmen, one prisoner, eight wolves, six wolf folk, four bears, two normal dogs, an aurochs, and an elk. And then Kel and Tamraz joined us.

It was crowded, but we were waiting for orders. Sarah and Captain Stahr were whispering. Mom and Miss Aliyah were watching to the west. Goliath and Justin were still manning a lookout to the east. Grace was being warmed by Dovie and Tracker. Pete Harred was handcuffed and standing by himself at the northern edge of the hill. He looked miserable.

Sarah broke away from Captain Stahr and walked over to Harred. "Okay, Pete. Yeah, I know my fiancé gave you your rights, but you need to talk. What do they have? Who are they? You know, stuff like that is the stuff we need to know."

Harred was afraid of her, but he still spoke up, "We came in peace to meet with Susan. You had no right to take me prisoner. You had no right to kill Griff. There are rules. Let me go."

"Yeah, yeah, did you forget your little trickery with the watchers? Please, it was you who broke the rules. And now? Well, I guess there aren't any rules."

Sarah chuckled at the thought of that and started going through Griff's wallet and looking at cards. "Poor, Griffin Molqi? Is that his name? He seems to have a few aliases here. Silk, Solonik, Kuklinski. Interesting. Do you recognize those names, Pete? Of course not. Have you even read a book? Just one? Ever? They're the names of random assassins. Famous ones. I used to study them. I once considered it as a possible career path. Fortunately, I decided not to be pathetic and evil, like you are, Pete. So tell me about your pals over there. And hurry."

"I'm not telling you anything."

"Well," said Sarah, "just darn. You beat me, Pete. I tried. But you are just too tough to break. You are like a rock. Give me your hands."

Sarah took his handcuffs and removed them. "Jael, can you come protect me now that this killer has been freed? He's part of a team of assassins, and they scare me."

Jael, like her siblings and parents, was over seven feet tall and weighed at least seven hundred pounds. She bounded over and stood over Sarah. Jael's teeth reflected the bright moonlight. She stared at Harred.

"Wait," he said, "what are you doing?"

"You're free to leave, Pete. But you need to understand, we all know you want to kill us and will kill us if you have a chance. Your pal Griffie sure did, right? I assume you do too. So I suggest you try to leave. There's a bloody sled down at the bottom of the hill with your name on it. It's risky, but you might make it. Jael will wait ten seconds. You can do it, Pete. Jael is just a girl."

That poor man looked side to side. He didn't move. "All right, Pete. We seem to have a failure to communicate here. You can stay and tell me everything, and I mean everything, or you can make a break for it. You have five seconds."

Sarah didn't have to wait. At the three-second mark, Pete started talking. Jael looked disappointed. Mom and Miss Aliyah listened. Captain Stahr kept his distance and watched to the west. Pete told us what we sort of knew. They had two more of the giant dogs and four to five watchers. He also said they had two genosqwas. Genosqwas are a slightly bigger, more aggressive race of watcher. Bullets still kill them, but they're extremely dangerous. That was news; we didn't know about them. Of the eleven remaining men, seven were paid killers like Griff. The four others were from Bozeman and Billings. Pete recruited them because he met them from his time in prison.

Sarah then dragged a crying Pete Harred down the back of our hill to a lodgepole pine thirty yards away. Jael went with her.

STRATEGY—SARAH

I have two cards of fantasy style art I keep with me. Both show fully armored Christian knights in some sort of battle. They are victorious, and they inspire me. God is a warrior. And I am his warrior. He has trained my hands for war and my fingers for battle. There are seasons for war, and that season was upon us. Susan and Aliyah grimly, but bravely, accept this war. They do not find their meaning in conflict. I understand because I know they were made for beautiful things. But I was made for this, and I only fear the subtle, creeping subjugation of the world's false peace.

I dream of a more radical, aggressive Christianity. A Christianity that fights back. We have been assaulted for too long. If people understood God's coming wrath, they would treasure and understand the grace they receive, and they would be far more active in defending their brethren. But the people know little of God's wrath; it's not taught. The popular pastors play to their audience's day-to-day hopes, not to their fears. But I know something of divine wrath. It is the only thing that brought terror to the demons, and they dread its coming. I was once terrified by it too. Most Christians choose to deny the inevitability of the day of wrath, or they simply choose not to think about it. They are being fools, and they're often useless to the cause.

I'm tired of people mocking Christ and his followers. I'm tired of Christendom watching our genocide throughout the world and doing little or nothing. I'm tired of academia and Hollywood, the journalists and the mocking unbelievers who try to destroy us. And now I am tired of wandering on a frozen hill, waiting for the enemy to attack. I would wait no longer.

Pete was a petty man. He was frightened as I stood close to him and stared. He probably thought he was needed by his evil teammates. He was wrong about nearly everything.

I spoke to him, "You're expendable, Pete. You are expendable to your evil team, you're probably even more expendable to your family. In fact, why aren't you with them now, Pete? You should be. You're a crummy father, that's for sure. And you are totally expendable to us. So as we get down to the business of killing your friends, try not to freeze to death. I'll be back when this is over."

I couldn't stand his type.

I went back to the hilltop. Troy was on the SAT phone. He motioned all of us to get together. He disconnected and smiled.

"Good news, everybody. With the skies clear and the winds slowing down, Sheriff Tuttle is sending up a helicopter. It's just a helicopter, it's not a gunship. The goal is to distract the killers while we escape or take more aggressive measures. The chopper is going to follow the Hiker Road and will be using its searchlight as it moves past the parking lot. We got about twenty more minutes. The roads are still closed, but we got four deputies on sleds who are going to be waiting to intercept bad guys running away and heading down the Hiker Road. So until the bad guys do something, we will plan our next moves."

But the assassins did do something. Earlier, their snowmobiles had spread out. They were positioned to our south and west. That made sense; the farm was to the west, and the Hiker Road was to our south. There were mountains off to the north and nothing but a frozen expanse to the east. I guess they felt we were boxed in. Then they made their move. On cue, several sleds pulled out of formation, rode past our little stronghold, and sprayed us with automatic rifle fire. For no good reason, we all watched. None of us took cover, even though it was available. Bullets kicked around the rocks, and the sound of ricochets screamed around us. We hit the ground as the bigger animals hurried down the other side of the hill. Waya got hit by a white-hot ricochet and cried out in pain and fear. She instinctively bit at her right hip. Grace was immediately at her side, calming her down.

"It bounced off, Waya. I saw it. Let me check."

Grace used her cell phone light. "A little blood and a big welt. It's going to hurt, but you're going to fight again."

Anjij crawled over and loved on her daughter. The gunfire was still coming at us, and we kept our heads down as bullets hit rocks, dirt, and ice and sent shrapnel overhead. Their fire was not well aimed.

"Susan," I said, "I'm heading out. Let me pick a team."

"Go for it."

I went to Te'oma and Jael and then to Sage, Leif, and Amorak. They joined happily, and I had my team. I told Troy I loved him, but he wasn't on my team. Law enforcement has rules. I had few of those. My Special teammates had even less. We said a quick goodbye to the others and descended the back of the hill. There we huddled as I told my team where we were going and what we were doing. They were happy to be on the offense.

"Wait up!"

It was Justin. He was leading a team of the rest of the dire wolves and wolf people. They joined us at the base of our hill.

"Sarah, I'll take my team to the south side. You go more west than south, and I will try to go mostly south and a little west. Don't shoot our way unless you must. Keep your walkie-talkie on channel four. Aliyah, Troy, and Susan are going to give us cover. Godspeed."

Just past the north side base of the hill was a snow-filled arroyo that would hide us as we got closer to the enemy. We waded through it as it meandered to the southwest. We could hear shooting. Troy was firing a bigger-caliber bullet than our rifles had. Aliyah was firing single shots. She was a decent shot. Susan was a better shot than all of us, but she was managing her troops.

We managed to get almost two hundred yards out without being spotted. One of the sleds came close. It was occupied by a rider and a passenger. The passenger was shooting up toward the hill. I hushed my team.

"Quiet. They don't know about the arroyo. When their sled dips into it, take them out. Spread out and cover yourselves with snow. Look away from them too. Your eyes reflect like streetlights."

They behaved beautifully and quickly. The snowmobile raced toward us. Just before they got to the arroyo, they slowed and coaxed their machine over the edge. It would've been a good plan if they were alone. But they weren't.

The sled nosed down to the shallow bottom. Just when the driver was about to give it gas to go up the shallow bank, the rider saw me standing only twenty feet to his right. He stopped. I suppose a smiling twenty-something female in a dry, frozen creek bed in the middle of a shooting war was interesting. But stopping was a terrible idea. The snow around them exploded with wolves and wolf people. Both driver and shooter were dead seconds later. They tried to fight, but they didn't have a chance. It practically rained blood. Just like that, two more were down.

I was proud of my team. I enjoyed turning tables on the assassins. To the southeast, I watched a sled catch on fire. Its rider was gunned down, and its passenger was chased by wolves and wolf folk from behind. Like the bloody riders crumpled nearby, he died violently seconds later. Justin and his team were hard at work. Then I heard the helicopter.

Off to the south, about three miles away, we could see its running lights. The helicopter came racing north, following the Hiker Road. Its searchlight was like a sun. It closed the distance and then bathed the first sled in bright, white light. The assassins fired at the helicopter, and the helicopter banked sharply to the west. It came around again. Then I saw two snowmobiles come from behind our hill. One came my way, the other went toward Justin's group. That would be Troy. The sled coming my way was operated by Aliyah. She saw me, waved, but kept going. I told my team to lie low. The assassins were down to seven men and six sleds. Nobody needed to get hurt doing something stupid because it became obvious to me that we were going to win this one. I jumped on the bloody sled the dead assassins left, powered it out of the arroyo, and followed her.

The rider of the snowmobile Aliyah was closing in on was fully distracted by the returning helicopter. Aliyah raced to it, and before its rider knew what had happened, Aliyah cut him down with a burst of Griff Molqi's automatic AK-47. Possessing an automatic weapon is illegal, but bad guys don't care about such things. Using their own weapons against them was sweet irony.

I passed Aliyah going fast. The next assassin's sled was forty yards away to the south. He turned to fire at me, but Aliyah fired a burst at him. She didn't hit him, but she made him duck; and when he did, I got my shots in. He slumped forward and fell into the snow. I put two more rounds into him just to make sure. I didn't want to get shot in the back.

By this time, another sled not far from us came into view. It ran from us, and we gave chase. Another sled, farther away, had gotten away from us by turning back to the Hiker Road. It had disappeared racing off to the south. Aliyah and I both wanted to get the guy we were chasing before he could escape too.

I glanced to the east. Troy had knocked out one sled and shot its rider and passenger. Another sled fled, following the other one that had escaped. When it made it safely to the Hiker Road, Troy then turned his attention to the sled that we were chasing so he could cut it off. The helicopter flew directly overhead and put its spotlight right on the sled. He was bathed in bright light. He was trapped, and he had to know he was about to get shot. Suddenly he threw his hands high into the air. His sled slowed as the three of us surrounded him.

We had captured filthy Glennon Wraight, and there were no other assassins left. We had won the field, but the battle wasn't quite over.

STRAGGLERS—GRACE

Just after Sarah and Justin left, Mom got me out of there.

"Benaiah, take Grace. Take her to Duke and go north, at least a mile. Bullets are flying, and, Grace, sweetie, you are not a combatant. Gyp, can you join them? There are things out there that want us dead. And take Moose and Major. Hurry."

I didn't complain, but she should have spoken to me. I am not Benaiah's thing to be hauled off. I wasn't a problem either. I was a part of the team. I knew I was too young to fight, but I'm almost a teenager. I can think. Even though Mom was right, I would be bringing this up later.

I left Kaiyo, Dovie, Goliath, and Tracker with Mom, Miss Aliyah, and Captain Stahr. Aylmer stayed with them too. Roan and the two huge dogs came with us. Benaiah carried me to the makeshift boulder corral where the horses were. I slipped onto the frozen saddle and coaxed Duke into walking back into the snow for me. From there, we rode north to nowhere in particular. There I would wait for victory or to get a head start in case I needed to run from the victors.

Benaiah is a conservative beast, so we went farther than a mile away. I refused to go farther. I turned Duke, sat in my saddle, and from our high vista, we saw the battle go down. The helicopter came in handy for our side. We saw flashes of gunfire from the hilltop and from other places. We watched two snowmobiles leave our hill, and we watched another two burn.

At some point, the gunfire stopped. We heard the dire wolves, and the wolf folk howl so deep and so long we felt the vibrations. It was over.

"Benaiah, it's over. Let's go back to Mom and Kaiyo."

I didn't wait for an answer, but I moved Duke out slowly. The Specials and my two normal dogs fell into line. I was cold, but my excitement let me ignore it. We had won, and winning is good. When winning meant keeping my life, well, there's just nothing like it.

We had made it about halfway back when every Special except Roan started growling. The dogs broke into crazy barking. There, in front of us, ten yards away, were two of the biggest, meanest-looking watchers I had ever seen. We had heard about them. They're called genosqwas. They were accompanied by two of the huge dogs. We had, unfortunately, intercepted their escape attempt. Two more watchers ran behind them heading east, and they kept going. But the genosqwas saw me and smiled. They still served Satan, and I guess they thought killing me would salvage a small victory out of the total whipping their side just took. But I wasn't alone.

Benaiah stepped forward. That surprised them. When Gyp morphed out of the white, snowy darkness, they realized killing me would come at a cost. I unslung and shouldered my .22 rifle. It wasn't near-enough gun, but it was still a gun. Throats, mouths, and eyes make good targets, and they were close. The two big dogs decided to join the fight until Kel and his sister stepped forward. They immediately started barking furiously at one another. Moose and Major joined in, but they had no idea what the huge dogs were saying to each other.

Then I saw what the others didn't. At least they didn't at first. Light. It started near the genosqwas, but it grew around us. The barking and growling came to a stop. Then a voice. We all heard it.

"Ahh, Gracie, your tiny rifle will only cause them to become angry. You don't want that, I assure you. What none of you know is that reinforcements are coming our way. Defeat is certain for you and your family."

Then I saw him. Except for the glow, he looked like a normal human. A really good-looking human, but still a human. He raised his hand, and Benaiah was thrown back. Then Gyp. The dogs were pushed back too. I was left alone with Duke. The big dogs, Benaiah, and Gyp, tried to come back to me, but they had no power against this thing.

"My name is Aymoon. I have been shepherding lost people from the beginning of the beginning. I love them all, of course. We only want what is good for all of us who were left here, struggling for life and dignity, abandoned on this miserable earth. It is cruel, you know, that we were put on this inhospitable world, but that is our lot. I share the same struggles with you. We have much in common, Gracie. Hopefully, we can work together to improve our lots."

I knew better to argue with him or to even engage in conversation. The thing in front of me was genius-smart but totally vile. I prayed. I kept my eyes on him though. At first, he looked annoyed, but it wasn't long before he reacted like he was receiving blows to the gut.

"Stop it!" he yelled. "Don't you dare. Not in my presence. Arrghh! You are dead!"

Turning to one of the genosqwas, he pointed to me. "Karmu, bring her to me and rip her apart while you do it. Hurry!"

The beast took a step toward me and smiled again. That was enough. I lifted my rifle and started pumping rounds into the monster's face. I surprised him. The high head shots glanced off or got buried in scalp, but I adjusted and worked his face. In a split second I blinded him. I kept shooting until I nearly shot his face off. Blood spray splattered on Aymoon and on the snow. He tried to roar, but I shot at his throat and mouth. Karmu fell to his knees, screaming and grasping his tattered, bloody face and throat. He died there on the spot. He shook, but he was dead. I watched, put another full magazine in my rifle, and kept praying. Aymoon writhed in pain. He pointed to the other genosqwa.

"Wardum, you fool, get her."

The beast looked my way and shook his head. He took a step backward. I was aiming at his face but did not pull the trigger.

"Sepsu, Halqu, kill that despicable little girl, or you will feel pain like you have never felt!"

The one named Sepsu charged. My shots went high. Dad told me long ago that going forward confuses attackers. Attackers expect their victims to pull back and away. Instead, I kicked Duke, and he lunged straight into the charging dog. It all happened fast. Duke was bigger than the huge dog, and Duke's shoulder caught the dog and threw him back. Then something happened. I could feel it. Gyp was somehow released from Aymoon's control. He was on the big dog in an instant. Gyp was so much bigger. It was over in a second. Gyp didn't kill him, but he made it clear he could.

From behind me I heard, "Grace, you are much loved."

I knew who said that. I turned. "Raphael!"

In seconds I was off my horse, and I threw myself into Raphael. He hugged me, and I knew I was safe.

"Grace, you were tested, and you fought for righteousness. You did not turn, nor did you deny your Father in heaven. I was there, seconds ago, with him. He is so proud of you. He held me back. He wants you to know that you are made with strength for even greater things."

I guess it was all a lot for me to handle. My hatred toward Aymoon and my fear of the creatures melted away. I started crying in big sobs. I wanted to stop, but I couldn't. Raphael was patient. He held me tight and patted my back and shoulder. And he waited. Then in between sobs, I asked, "What happened?"

I looked over and watched Aymoon. He was not free to leave. When he saw me looking, he screamed as if his skin was on fire. "Release me, Raphael. You know the rules! Let me go!"

Raphael laughed. "Rules, Aymoon? Really? Your very presence here is a breach of the rules. But you, the one who gave Narcissus his name, felt you could convince this young one to follow you. You came in person and used your powers to take away her defenders. You have been warned about this sort of thing before, haven't you? But you just found out how powerful the Father's children can be."

"Release me, Raphael, you stupid, lazy fool. You know you cannot torture me before the appointed time!"

"It is not me who holds you in pain. It is Grace McLeod. Ask her nicely."

"Release me, horrid child!"

Raphael laughed again. "Aymoon, that wasn't very nice. You caused so many of your followers to die terrible deaths. They are now lost and with no more chances at redemption. So sad. Even your sorcerer has lost his powers. You led him astray too, didn't you?

"Aymoon, you have sown murder these past few days. By what authority do you now curse Grace McLeod? Ask nicely to be released and say you're sorry."

I knew I didn't have the authority or power to kill Aymoon, and I was not as comfortable with his torture as Raphael was. So I reminded myself of how Aymoon ordered people to murder us and that MacDonald shot Kaiyo and a killer shot Dean. Aymoon's soldiers also suffered and lay dead on several battlefields because of him. Anger welled back up in me, and I could stand my discomfort with his pain a little longer.

Aymoon changed from the handsome human he started as into something that looked reptilian and horrible. He spoke, "Gracie, I promise you that torment will be mine in the future, at the appointed time. And it will be eternal. Please content yourself with the thought of my future agonies. Release me, and I will leave you and your family alone, forever.

"Aymoon," I said, "you lie as you talk, but you are released."

He vanished. Raphael gave me one more hug. "Grace, I do surely look forward to spending eternity with you and your family. And with all of you, the great beasts of Eden. Gyp, Benaiah, Kel, you are needed to stay with us for the next few days. Come home before dawn. Grace, please tell Kaiyo, Goliath, Dovie, Tracker, and Aylmer that they need to come home too. That goes for all of you except for the lost ones. As for you, if you want to be found and serve the righteous one, follow them to the door and beyond. If not, you are free to go. Tamraz, Sepsu, Halqu, and Wardum, you have choices to make. Be thankful you are still alive to make them."

Raphael held my hand and looked at me. Without looking up, he said loudly, "Susan, feel no guilt for sending Grace here. What happened was supposed to happen. Be proud of her."

Then Raphael disappeared. I turned quickly and saw Mom and the others off to my right running my way. "I saw it all, Gracie."

"It's Grace, Mom, that's how I first knew Aymoon was evil. He didn't know my real name."

When Mom hugged me, I cried again. Kaiyo hugged me too. In fact, I was covered with fur from lots of animals who were trying to make me feel better. They surrounded me until I stopped crying. It took awhile. At least I wasn't so cold anymore.

Sometimes, great battles end with a whimper. This one did, and it was time to go. Kel and Tamraz were talking to their brothers. Gyp and Benaiah were talking to Wardum. It was dark, but I heard helicopters in the distance. This wilderness was coming under man's control.

The wolf folk and the dire wolves joined us. Everyone came to say goodbye to me and Mom. Roan looked deeply at me before turning. The big dogs acted like dogs and licked my face. The four of them were together. They were so excited. Benaiah and Wardum came to us. I told Wardum we all forgave him. Mom told him he could visit the farm when the investigations ended.

Lastly, Goliath said goodbye to me in bear language. I think he was crying. We love each other more than we can even express. Words don't work. Mom hugged Kaiyo and told him to come back home as soon as it was safe. Then she gave him *lectures 1 through 42*. That's code for be careful of just about everything.

After our friends and my brother left us, Mom walked over to the big dead genosqwa. She stood over it. "You poor, lost beast, but the choices you made were yours alone."

Mom thought for a few moments. "And very good shooting, Grace."

Mom cut off his ears and scalped him and put the bloody mess in a plastic bag. "We might need this."

We turned and walked back to our little hillside fortress. It was time to go home.

PART 3

REDEMPTIONS

18

The Montana Inquisitions—Sam

Six federal agents came to the Billings Clinic Hospital to meet with me, Kate, and Dean. Like most federal agents, they had no humor and less warmth, at least at first. I didn't blame them. My son had been shot, and the entire Boulder River Valley was talking about invading monsters and the *War in the Absarokas*. Libby called and said at least four big, twin-rotor helicopters and a few smaller ones landed near CVP, and at first light, soldiers closed off the valley from Natural Bridge all the way to Independence. At least fifteen homeowners were forced to evacuate, and others were told to stay inside. The FBI cut the phone lines running into the valley. Residents were interviewed as to what they saw or heard.

Some TV crews got wind of it, but they were forced to wait at the roadside saloon north of McLeod. It soon became a drunken rumor mill. The stories were recognizable to crazy. I suspect the Feds added to the rumor mill.

No one was allowed in or out of the valley. I watched the coverage of some government spokesperson saying that several experimental military drones had collided and crashed during a nighttime training exercise and that a total area-wide quarantine had been imposed to collect top secret drone parts, electronics, and metals. It seemed plausible. At that point, I knew we were probably not going to jail.

Hospital staff ushered Dean, Kate, and me into a conference room. Dean's wounds to his cheek, forehead, and thigh had been expertly stitched up. His dog-bite wounds were cleaned and stitched as well, but they were messier wounds. Hopefully, Dean will keep his hair for a long time. The scars will probably be with him as long as he lives.

We waited while Dean was dealing with brutal mouth pain. A local dental surgeon had been called to remove his damaged teeth and stitch the torn gums. The hospital notified us he had arrived and was waiting in the emergency room. The longer we waited, the madder Dean got. Kate was furious. I stepped outside. An agent was guarding the door.

"Mr. McLeod, you folks aren't free to leave."

Dean followed me and took over, "Am I under arrest? Because if I'm not, I have an appointment with a surgeon in ER. I got shot in the face and worse, and everything hurts. I have stitches everywhere, and I'm not done with getting more. I'm leaving. You're free to come with me, but if you try to stop me, I will be forced to resist the unlawful false imprisonment."

The agent smiled and wisely followed us back down to the emergency room. The oral surgeon was there, and once Dean got on the table, the surgeon immediately started administering local anesthetic. The relief in Dean's eyes was near instantaneous. Kate held his hand. Dean's agony was coming to a close, and it showed.

After a few minutes, the flimsy privacy curtain was thrown back, and five other agents joined us in the cramped examination space. Dean was not impressed.

"Folks, the three of us are going to tell you a true story. In about ten minutes, I'm going to be carted off and then more sedated. Feel free to ask anything you want, but you better hurry. After that, I won't be talking."

An agent identified herself. She seemed to be in charge. Looking at me, she said, "Mr. McLeod, I am Special Agent Vicki Ernst. Can we speak privately?"

I agreed. She told one agent to get the surgeon to sign a confidentiality agreement. The hospital staff was told to get Dean out of the emergency room and into a private room, even if it meant kicking somebody out of theirs. The FBI had no authority to give that order, but it probably was a good idea.

We walked back to the conference room with several agents following us. Kate and I sat down. Agent Ernst then proceeded to introduce the other agents. They were law enforcement agents from several alphabet groups. The ATF, BLM, USFS, and FBI were all represented. She was professional, but not friendly.

"Mr. McLeod and Ms. Gibbs, we have had quite a few days of excitement here. With fire bombings and the so-called *War in the Absarokas*, we have been quite busy. Washington is calling me about every half hour. Care to tell us what's going on?"

I motioned Kate to wait. She was probably too angry to be helpful. The agents were just doing their job.

"Agent Ernst, do you know Bill Adams or Kent Thomas? They're rangers with the Forest Service in Wyoming. If not, go ahead and give them a call first."

She looked at me a little quizzically. "What do they know?"

"Me and a small part of my story."

She ordered the young agent with the USFS to make the calls.

"Then please feel also free to call Madison County Sheriff Tuttle or State Patrol Captain Ed Hamby. They know us too."

Agent Ernst was not impressed with local law enforcement vouching for our characters. Like many federal agents, she didn't trust or respect local law enforcement. Kate and I gave the group our licenses, names and addresses, occupations, and other basic information. Everybody seemed to be taking notes. The USFS agent came back after a few minutes.

"Agent Ernst, Ranger Thomas said he would only talk to you. He refused to talk to me. I called Bill Adams, the other ranger, and he said the same thing. Thomas is back on the phone now."

Ernst looked annoyed, but she stepped out of the room. Kate and I exchanged small talk with the other agents. Again, we waited. Coffee and juice were brought to us. Fifteen minutes later, Agent Ernst came back in. She looked a little pale.

"All right, let's switch gears a little bit. The Bureau has dispatched assets to a Madison County law enforcement operation. Do you know anything about that?"

"Yep," I responded.

Kate and I had already spoken to our respective families. We knew some, but not most, of what happened. I was impressed with what they did. Grace was amazing too. She even saw Raphael again.

I looked at Agent Ernst and said, "As for the roles Kate and I played in the Boulder River Valley, we are willing to tell you the entire story. We also had law enforcement present during both actions. You know that, don't you?"

"We do," she said. "But we also have a lot of dead people and destroyed property, and you two were a part of that. In fact, the list of potential violations is nearly endless. Let's talk about the weapons in your car. Did you use them?"

Kate spoke, "Ma'am, we sure did. They saved our lives. So maybe you don't get it. We were in a war to rescue our friend. Fifty miles away, my mother fought in a war against Satanic assassins. There are at least four dead monsters at CVP and probably one or two in the Eastern Wilderness in Madison County. There are also the dead assassins to prove our story. We defended ourselves from people who wanted, and tried desperately, to kill us. All of us. No exceptions. So before you start flinging around a bunch of your ridiculous thoughts about violations, you might want to talk to your field personnel. They're going to find a few huge extinct dogs who are missing body parts and several monsters who have been mysteriously scalped. You're also going to learn that most

314

of the dead humans were killed by monsters. And, ma'am, those monsters are more fearsome than anything from your nightmares. So I think you ought to recognize us as the innocent, fighting citizens that we are."

Kate took a breath, but she wasn't done. "Mr. McLeod and I also know that some people, including federal authorities, prefer dead victims to victims who fight back. Hopefully, you're not one of those idiots. But if you are, ready yourselves for disappointment."

Kate paused and finished with, "So are you ready to hear our stories?"

"Ready," Agent Ernst quietly said. Turning to the other agents, she said, "Gentlemen, while I was out, I also received a call from the director. Please turn off your phones, and put them and any notebooks and recorders in the middle of the table. We are about to hear some stories that can never leave this room. And I will be the only one taking notes. Agreed?"

AGENTS—SUSAN

We decided to take the prisoners back to our farm. We couldn't leave them in the wilderness. Troy read Harred and Wraight their Miranda rights, and Justin recorded it on his cell phone. Both lawmen joined us because none of us knew if there might be other assassins waiting for us there. Two more rifles are always better. It took awhile for us the get our horses and return home. We made Pete Harred and Glennon Wraight ride Peyton together.

Around dawn, we made it to the farm. When we got to the barn, we saw how the killing crew had shot some of my cows and alpacas, apparently for fun. I was enraged. The killers had also ransacked my house.

The first thing we did was start the two diesel generators that powered the house and the barn. Lights flooded the house and barn. Then we took the horses back to their stalls. We took off their tack and fed them. They had to be exhausted. I loved those horses. Grace was fighting back tears when she got near the dead alpacas. They were peaceful beasts, and shooting them was just pure cruelty. Harred and Wraight sat on the floor of the barn and watched us come and go. Pete looked terrified; Wraight looked smug. Aliyah stood guard, and her anger was rising again. So was Sarah's. Sarah went outside. I heard snowmobiles leave.

Sarah returned. "I encouraged Troy and Justin to take their sleds and go up the driveway the six miles to the gate near the main road. It's your property, and we need to make sure there was no damage and that the bad guys are all gone."

She turned to Aliyah. "Aliyah, could you please take Pete into the house and help him to feel more comfortable? He's freezing to death. Maybe some coffee. Keep your sidearm on him though. He's tricky. If he tries something, aim for his gut. It's painful and fatal. He deserves it."

I decided to let Sarah run with it. I would stand by just in case she had murder on her mind. Wraight had started all this, so I felt no love for him, but I couldn't allow a captive to be killed either.

"Grace, could you give Aliyah a hand?"

Grace smiled and went to the house. That left the three of us. Wraight remained seated on the floor. His hands were cuffed behind him. He remained cool.

"Ahh, the lionesses have their quarry. This is so exciting. Are you now coming to pounce on your kill? But first, may I venture a few guesses? You probably want information, but you will receive nothing from me, of course. Pathetic Pete will talk, but he knows so little. So let the torture begin. Beat me if you want. You can even cut me or shoot me. In fact, I rather wish you would get on with it!"

Sarah was standing to his side, leaning on a support column. She discreetly pointed her cell phone. She was recording everything.

"Mr. Wraight," I said, "we will do no such thing. That's not our style. You started all this, remember? Once you get out of prison, like in fifty years, maybe you can get a job. You'll need one.

But until then, three hots and a cot will be your life. You committed crimes in Montana and on federal property. Under either state or federal law, arson and attempted murder is still against the law. Anyway, we heard from your boss. In fact, my daughter spoke directly with him. Your powers are gone, they will never return."

Wraight was unimpressed with everything I said until I got to the last part. "My dear Susan McLeod, I have no *boss*. I don't even know what you are saying."

"You do. Aymoon made an appearance. He even promised to leave us alone forever. I saw it all."

Wraight looked furious. I must have hit a nerve. "You lie, Susan! Aymoon would never say such a thing. He will never leave you alone. Not forever, not for a season, and not even for a moment. You were warned, and you refused to obey. Your so-called *Special* animals are all going to die, and he will simply assemble more forces to get you and your absurd family. Know this, you will never know the peace of this farm because even if I am locked away, there will always be the threat of a man or something else in the forest waiting to take you out, one by one. Every one of you, Susan!"

"Nope. It can't happen, Mr. Wraight. Aymoon depended on you to pull all this together. You recruited men from Denver, Helena, Billings, and beyond to pull off this attempt at killing us. And you will now rot in jail. Aymoon's little enterprise has been decapitated. But I do respect and even admire your skills at pulling this together. Did you think you could really win? We had God on our side. You didn't have a chance."

"That's where you are wrong, Susan. You people are fools, of course. My efforts here were not thwarted by God. Far from it! My efforts were thwarted by a helicopter. I hadn't planned for that. It won't happen again. Admit it, Susan, had I ten more minutes, you and your friends and your child would all be dead. And don't think for a moment I will have no reach from whatever prison I may find as my residence. My *boss* is quite welcome in those places, and he comes when I call. I promise you, I can, and will, come again.

And there is nothing you can do but worry about me for the rest of your short life."

I looked at Sarah. She had recorded it all. Stoke a man's pride and he will fall. "Mr. Wraight, I will not live in fear of you or anyone else. We live differently than your other victims. We fight back."

"No, Susan, you are the fool. You are hardly the first to fight back. And don't fool yourselves. This is not over."

Then we heard a line of helicopters. They sounded military. We took Wraight and cuffed him to a pole. Aliyah brought out Pete and took him straight to the machine shed and cuffed him to a piece of farm equipment. We didn't want those two talking.

I had one more thing to do. We stepped out, and I pulled Sarah aside. "Sarah, I don't trust those people in the helicopters. Go inside to my office. Download Wraight's confession on my laptop, and send it to me, to Troy, to Captain Hamby, Sheriff Tuttle, Emma Garcia, and our attorney, Mike Williams, in Helena. Then save it to at least three USB drives. Keep one, give one to me, and hide the other in the snow behind the barn. Hurry. The choppers are headed to the battlefield in the Eastern wilderness, but one of them will be here when the on-site deputies tell them we're gone. Finally, the watcher you shot while we were running through the Southern Forest, can you get Justin and Troy to drag it back here? We have a cargo tub in the machine shed. Get them to bring it back here. Like I said, I don't trust the people who are coming our way. Don't do it yourself, it's a crime scene, and the dead man that you shot is next to him. Only law enforcement like Troy and Justin can go back into a crime scene. They'll just be doing their job. It's on my property, so the sheriff has full jurisdiction here."

The three of us walked into the house. We fed the dogs and made some more coffee. Our rifles never left our sides. Sarah walked to the front door and called Troy. Troy's SAT phone worked great. Minutes later, he and Justin came motoring back. They hitched the cargo tub and took off, through the hidden pasture. Sarah got to work in my office downloading the confession.

A lot of my widows were shot out or damaged, so Aliyah and I cut out cardboard panes and we duct-taped them in place. It wasn't pretty, but it helped to keep the warm air inside. We exhaled. Grace joined us and then Sarah. As if on cue, we laughed. We had one more hurdle with the Feds, but we were all alive. For the next half hour, we cleaned the house and talked. Everyone shared their different views of the same nightmarish story. Each of us had lived more life than a thousand others combined. Grace led a prayer of gratitude that we had somehow lived. We prayed for Dean's recovery and for our next battles, whatever they were. Then the helicopters came back.

The first to land confused us. It hovered near our front lawn, and Sheriff Tuttle and two deputies jumped out. The two deputies were wearing white camouflage fatigues and were heavily armed. Lee wore a cowboy hat and a fleece-lined buck-skin coat. He rarely wore his regulation uniform, and today was no different. He wore jeans and scuffed cowboy boots. He might have been raised in Georgia, but he is one-hundred-percent Montana cowboy.

Lee and his deputies bounded through the snow and came inside. His helicopter rose and then turned south. After brief introductions, we took them back into the kitchen and poured coffee.

"Ladies, my helicopter has a dead bigfoot in it, and it is flying to an undisclosed location. Troy and Justin are coming back. More importantly, Sam and his team had an easy go of it with the investigators. But we may not be so lucky. The FBI special agent for this district in Montana is Elliott Bray. I've known him for a few years. He's young, pushy, and ambitious. He wants to be known, and this district is the wrong place for that. Other than bank robberies, credit card fraud, or commercial poaching, this area is mighty quiet. He is always looking for recognition. He's already challenging my jurisdiction in directing the defense against more bombings in the county. I'm here because I love you folks and because you live in Madison County. Madison County is my county, it's not his. He's circling now."

Sure enough, a military-style Black Hawk helicopter with Bray and three armed soldiers landed seventy-five yards north of the house. Bray hopped out and sank in the snow. He motioned to his men, and they spread out and advanced on our house as if we were criminals. Their rifles were even raised.

"Oh no," whispered Sarah. She quickly grabbed Moose and Major by their collars and took them upstairs and put them in my room. I heard the door close. They were barking loudly, but Sarah was smart enough not to give the FBI a reason to kill our dogs. The FBI has a bad history of shooting dogs who meant them no harm, and my dogs would mean them much harm. In seconds, Sarah was back at my side.

"Thank you," I whispered.

I handed Lee a USB drive with Wraight's rambling confession. I briefly told him what it was. Lee smiled. "You done good, Susan."

Lee pocketed the drive and then stepped outside. "Come on in, Rambo," Lee yelled, "and quit acting like you're advancing on the enemy. You're looking damned silly."

I noticed the soldiers pointed their weapons at Lee as he spoke. Lee's deputies were furious. I spoke to the ladies, but loud enough everybody could hear me.

"Sarah, Aliyah, spread out. Stand near the soldiers, stand behind them if possible, don't bunch together. Keep your straps on your shoulder, but have your hands on your rifles in a ready position."

Bray directed one soldier to come around to the back of the house in our kitchen while he and the other two came to the front door. Sarah and Aliyah went to the kitchen. The soldier walked in without knocking. When his eyes adjusted to the darker room, he saw two women bracing him, both with black rifles pointed at him.

"All righty, young man," said Aliyah, "you just broke the law. Drop your weapon. You are under arrest for breaking and entering, unless you have a warrant. Do you?"

From the front of the house, we heard Bray speak, "Not so fast, ladies. The sheriff told us to 'come on in.' You drop your weapons."

I was standing midway between the front door and the kitchen. "No, sir," I said. "We have been attacked, our livestock shot, and we were forced to run for our lives. We fought a battle against professional assassins, and we won using these weapons. So no thank you. Your permission to come onto my property and to enter my house is revoked. It is my right. Now either leave or listen. If you choose to stay, you will also have to submit to the sheriff's jurisdiction. This is his crime scene."

Saying all that was hard. I was exhausted, and I have always respected law enforcement. But Bray seemed the type to enjoy power more than he should. Everyone was quiet. His soldiers faced three women, a girl, and two grim deputies. And all of us were armed. Bray motioned for his men to lower their weapons. We responded in kind.

"Ladies," Bray said, "for our safety, please put your weapons on the table. Then we can talk."

Lee spoke up, "Well, Special Agent Bray, Susan McLeod is right. This is my crime scene, and I make those decisions, and as the law enforcement officer in charge of this particular crime scene, I do not believe these armed citizens pose the remotest danger to me or my men or to you or yours. So just for a while, stow your ego, and do your job. The ladies will be armed, but your soldiers here will not. I have the authority. If they refuse, my deputies here will disarm them." Lee turned to us. "Ladies, I hereby deputize each of you—except you, Gracie."

"It's Grace now. Not Gracie, Sheriff Tuttle."

Lee smiled. "Grace, huh? I like it. Grace it is."

Bray watched everything and realized he had been checked. Like most people who abused their power, he had forgotten how to do things the right way. Bullies become accustomed to being bullies. He had been pushed back.

I spoke, "Grace, can you get Agent Bray and his men some coffee? Gentlemen, I have a big kitchen table. You are going to hear some stories. The stories are true. Your common sense will tell you we are either lying or crazy, but your investigation will confirm every word we say. And we have prisoners too. So fair enough?"

Bray's eyes went wide. "Prisoners?"

"They're in the barns. Sarah, take one of these men to confirm that."

As Sarah and a soldier left, Troy and Justin motored up to the courtyard. It was a natural break, so Aliyah went up to bring the dogs down. Bray's men seemed to be enjoying themselves. Upon proper introductions, the dogs accepted their company.

Troy and Justin walked in the kitchen and saw us standing at the kitchen table. "Nice seeing you, Agent Bray," said Troy. "And of course, the rest of you gentlemen."

There was still some tension, and those two could feel it. We still had our rifles at the ready positions. We had been through too much for some ambitious fool to fly in and take us under custody or disarm us.

Lee spoke up, "While we are waiting for Sarah to return, Agent Bray has some work to do. I spoke with Washington no less than twenty minutes ago. Your director wants to speak with you. He told me he couldn't get you to respond to his calls. The landline here has been cut, so take my SAT phone and go outside. Everything is confidential."

Lee tossed him the phone, and Bray went back outside.

Sarah and the other soldier returned. He and the two others introduced themselves. It turned out they weren't real soldiers; they just looked like soldiers. They were young, new agents called in to assist Bray's investigation.

We exchanged small talk. After a few more minutes, Agent Bray returned. His mood had gone from arrogant to fascinated. "It seems I was mistaken. The director had kind words for the McLeod family. I don't pretend to know why he trusts you, but I trust him. Sheriff Tuttle, the director asked if you would be willing to cede jurisdiction on this matter."

Lee responded, "Hell no."

"He said you would say that too. I will consider it still on the table though. Folks, as my men and I flew over this house early on, the tracks in the snow told me the aggressors came in from the southwest and from the west. You folks were forced to flee to the southeast and into the forest and eventually you made it to the Hiker Road. From there you headed north to make a stand on federal property well to the east of here. It also appears from the tracks in the snow you had reinforcements who arrived out of the north. Along the way I saw at least nine dead men. We personally inspected each casualty. Some of the men were killed by gunfire, a few others were killed by wild animals of some sort. We found snowmobiles tossed around, and even a dead monster who had been mysteriously scalped and had its ears removed. All this is very strange. The director also told me there was another dead monster that the good sheriff has taken for *safekeeping*. Finally, after securing the area, I simply followed your tracks back here. Hopefully, you ladies, and you too, Grace, can fill us in with details?"

Bray looked at his men. "Gentlemen, nothing leaves this room. Please give me your cell phones, notebooks, recorders, and take off your communication headsets. Toss those things on the kitchen island. And, Ms. McLeod, if I could help myself to your coffee, I intend to sit back and listen."

There is a rule when talking to the Feds. If you don't want to talk, then don't. They usually can't make you talk. But if you do talk, it better be one-hundred-percent truth. And that's what we gave him and Lee. It took an hour. Bray called the chief of police in Belgrade to verify the break-in of Landon and Libby's office.

"Sorry," he said. "Just doing my job. I have to verify what is easy to verify. I am assuming the hard-to-believe elements of the story are unverifiable?"

That was not fully true. The dead, both human and monstrous animals, were easy to verify too.

At the end of our interview, Lee pulled out the USB drive and twirled it on the table. "It seems to me these poor people were the victim of some kind of half-insane religious fanatic. Somehow he got money to hire some thugs. A few were probably ex-FBI, no offense, and he and his crew attacked these perfectly law-abiding families for no reason. It was totally random. Here's a recording of his confession. He believes in some devil he calls Aymoon. Susan went along with it to get him to talk. And he talked. Just so you know, this was taken after he was given his rights and when Captain Stahr and Lieutenant Martinez were miles away, checking the driveway."

Then Grace spoke, "We also have surveillance footage from the gate. It shows Mr. Harred and Mr. Wraight breaking the camera. We have two cameras. They only saw one."

Bray smiled and listened. He left to make a few more calls. When he came back, he told us, "I have been told Sheriff Tuttle's version of the story is true, and the Bureau accepts it. I, on the other hand, have difficulty with all of it. What I do believe is that you ladies have done nothing wrong. We law enforcement types will have one heck of a cleanup job, and we will be dealing with the casualties. The sheriff's departments of multiple counties are coordinating with the Bureau to secure the sites and gather the corpses. All of them. Human and not human. Please, accept my apologies at my disbelief. It's all too strange to grasp in a morning."

We looked at one another in awkward silence.

Then Troy spoke, "Agent Bray, to help you with your disbelief, would you and your men be willing to act as security for a wedding? Sarah and I are getting married in two weeks, and we will need the help. We will be getting married in the barn here at this farm for a reason. Some of the guests will be—unconventional. And you can meet every one of them if you wish."

Bray smiled. For the first time, he looked pleased. He looked at his men and then at Lee. "Give me the SAT phone."

Ten minutes later, Bray stepped back inside. "Gentlemen, the director approved. Are you up for another secret mission?"

They almost cheered. And except for some small talk and some goodbyes, that was the end of the investigation into us. Bray got the recognition and attention he longed for, and because of what he had seen, he joined a tiny fraternity of trusted federal agents who knew secrets withheld from the rest of the country. His career and that of Agent Ernst would always have that as a tremendous bonus.

Sam brought Dean home later that day. Just seeing him made me cry. As he described it, "Mom, I'm all shot up, and I got bit on by a huge, extinct dog."

And he looked it. He was still covered in dried blood, and his face would show the scars for the rest of his life. Kate was by his side, and I could tell something had changed between them. It appeared to me Dean had become far more than Kate's high school honey. Hopefully, Dean could figure that out.

Sam could only stay long enough to shower and change. He hooked up the horse trailer, tossed in blankets, and feed and started his truck. I met him in the courtyard. I gave him a thermos of coffee and kissed him goodbye. He looked exhausted, but he said he was good to go. Jet and Solo needed to come home.

Meanwhile, Dean and Kate both talked a mile a minute and shared their stories with us. Lee listened for a while, and he praised their bravery. He then told them they had jobs waiting for them in the sheriff's department when they grew up. Shortly thereafter, Lee left, and we continued to tell each other our stories.

Over the next few days, we still had to deal with the sheriff's investigators and the FBI as they came to take pictures and measurements and to pull almost two hundred bullets out the walls of my house and barns. Arson investigators came to the Gibbs place to confirm the barn was burned on purpose. And during that time, we got back to life. Sarah went back to work in Helena, and Libby and Landon came here to stay during the break.

All of us worked on running the farm and getting the house and barn ready for the wedding. Details of the source of the bombings and the firefight here at the farm eventually made it to the press. The press had some fun with the case of the crazy, religious nuts. As directed, we refused to respond to the calls from the press, and the driveway gates barred their attempts to come onto the property. For a few days, the press camped out by the gates. Several times, our friend Davey Carter flew in and took us to town and to Bozeman. Like all stories, it lived for a few weeks and was forgotten. No victims were killed, and because we fought back using guns, the press wasn't overly interested.

Eventually, Pete Harred accepted a plea deal and turned state's evidence. He testified that Wraight was some sort of Rasputin who led a handful of zealots to randomly kill us for bizarre religious reasons.

As for the *War in the Absarokas*, the three men who were forced to disrobe and huddle together in a cabin at Camp Yonah survived, though barely. Their loudmouthed squad leader had tried to escape, as he promised, but all he got was a right foot that froze solid. It, and parts of his nose and a few fingers, were amputated. Also, he was wanted on two out-of-state warrants, and a request for extradition was lodged by some country in Southwest Asia. Apparently, he was a hired killer, and at some time in the past, he killed the wrong man. He was destined to rot in some hellhole in the Middle East. His two comrades were treated for minor cases of frostbite and then hustled off to some prison. They were charged with many property crimes and with making terroristic threats, and they pled guilty to all of them. They weren't guilty of all that, of course, but they were guilty of worse things.

Everett Ferguson and Ty Vernon were not followed by the FBI. All the other assassins in Boulder Valley were killed by man or beast. The assassins that escaped down the Hiker Road were shot and killed by deputies waiting for them. I don't know if they tried to surrender or not. I don't really care.

All that made things easier for the Feds. The bodies were whisked away, and the story about the fiery crash of some secret military drones was generally believed. The government paid CVP's damages for the burned-down buildings. They were careful to remove shell casings all over the fields and bullets from the log walls of the cabins and CVP's other buildings. Sam and I paid for the minor damage to Jordan Creek Camp, and we hired a few local boys to clean out the cabin that served as our horse's stall. The Sweet Grass sheriff issued a report that Dean was impaled by tree branches during a snowmobile accident. It wasn't true, but it was more than believable. Things like that happened all the time.

Our fight was over, and things returned to a season of peace. But we were all, each of us, changed people. Wars change people. Nietzsche once said that what doesn't kill you makes you stronger. A lot of people like to quote him. But it's not always true. People can become bitter or broken just as often as others become stronger or better. We became better. And our strength was revealed to those who knew us or knew about us. And that was good.

19

Big Day—Dean

I admit I was interested in how weddings worked for the first time in my life. I was only seventeen, but I could see a future with Kate. In fact, I couldn't see a future without her. But I also knew we both needed to know if our love for each other was strong enough for the changes of life. Learning that answer takes time. I don't know how much time but probably more time than I can dwell on. I do know Kate may well choose not to walk with me where I go. She may fall in love with a career, another man, a faraway place, or a life I cannot offer. And I must honor those desires. But I dread that day and pray it never comes. In the meantime, we will be wise.

And yet, I still wanted to know more about how weddings worked. So as my healing permitted, I helped get the barn ready and clean. I also kept up with how Sarah was doing. According to Mom, Sarah is part velociraptor and part Disney Princess. If you knew her, it would make sense. She is both a contemplative and bloody killer and a grace-filled beauty. Despite her faults and need for growth, she's one of my heroes.

We were still living with the cold Montana winter, so Gunner and I would plow the airstrip, the driveways, walkways, and parts of pastures after every snow, sometimes twice a day. After the police and FBI investigations, Kaiyo, Aylmer, and Tracker returned. So did our electricity.

We had a private birthday party for Kaiyo on the twentieth, and five days later, we celebrated Christmas. This year, since we all nearly got killed, our Christmas was far more thoughtful. We had Christmas in the barn because Aylmer was too big to come inside. The Gibbses joined us. This Christmas, we focused on the gift of Christ. Every Christmas we said we wanted to do that, but we didn't. Christ got a nod or two from somebody appointed to say grace, but that was about it. This time, we read to each other, we talked about our miracles, we gave thanks for each other, and we thanked God for seeing us through it all. It was an amazing Christmas.

After Christmas, we focused on the wedding. For several reasons, Sarah and Troy had selected December 30 as the date. We all had our roles because we couldn't bring in outsiders to cook, cater, or tend bar. We had to do it all. The list of humans they invited was small. Long ago, Sarah had worn out her welcome with most of her friends and relatives. Her brother, Andy, and her sister, Rachel, were coming. Their spouses remained at their homes to watch their respective kids. Also, Rachel's husband and Andy's wife didn't trust Sarah.

Andy and Rachel were also bringing their parents, Kurt and Linda Tompkins. Mr. and Mrs. Tompkins are saints for giving Sarah chance after chance. Sarah's redemption has been pure joy for them. According to Sarah, the siblings were still withholding judgment. Couldn't say I blamed them. But I knew Sarah a lot better than they did. They would be pleased.

The out-of-town guests were lodged at the Gibbses, at the Brighams, and a few other homes. Troy's mom, Loretta Stahr, was still alive, and she lived in town. Troy's sister and her husband were staying there. The Tompkinses, all of them, were staying with us. For obvious reasons, children were specifically not invited, except for Troy's girls. It caused some guests to complain, but they would understand.

Our main barn is big. It's so big I once tried to shoot Goliath in the barn, but he was far enough away that I missed. And we had made everything look perfect. Hanging lights suspended on cords were strung from rafter to rafter, and beautiful chairs were placed in rows before the altar with a bigger-than-normal center aisle. Throughout the barn, long wooden tables were set up, ready to feed man and beast. The barn was heated, but the guests were all told to bring coats, gloves, and warm shoes.

December 30 turned out to be a beautiful day. The Tompkinses got here the day before, and they had fallen in love with our family. We all enjoyed each other. Several times, either Andy or Rachel would step outside and call their spouses to say how nice things were going. They all had noticed my scars and stitches and our refusal to tell them what happened only added to the mystique of the event. We told them it would have to wait until after the wedding.

Kate came over early along with Jack. Miss Aliyah and Gunner had gotten here even earlier. It was like the Gibbses lived here. I loved it. But Kate and I are careful to behave in ways that don't alarm her parents or mine. We don't want to ruin a good thing. Anyway, Kate, Libby, and Grace were racing upstairs and downstairs laughing and having fun. Ms. Tompkins fit right in. Andy and Mr. Tompkins wanted a tour of the barn, but Dad said the barn was off-limits. He said they would thank him later. In truth, we just didn't want them to see Kaiyo, Aylmer, or Tracker. Those three were mooching off the goodies and basically getting in the way. They were told to clear out by noon.

The wedding was to start at three o'clock, but the guests were told to come early for a pre-reception. The invitations were clear that the front gates would be locked by 2:30 p.m. At one o'clock, Special Agent Elliott Bray and his three agents drove up to the house. They arrived nicely dressed and heavily armed. They came in and met our family and others already there. The Tompkinses were surprised at the firepower, but they seemed to accept it.

Dad told the agents to man the front gate and check the occupants of all vehicles against the guest list. I gave them the keys to my dad's club cab pickup truck so they could park their government special here. They could use the truck to stay warm and to drive to the house and back for coffee and goodies. As they turned to go back outside, Sarah yelled from upstairs for them to wait. In seconds, she flew down the front stairway, holding up the hem of her wedding dress. Except for her hair being in big curlers, she looked beautiful. I wondered what she would have to say.

"Gentlemen, she said, "thank you so much for coming. You understand a lot about our recent past. Please keep that to yourselves. Having you here is a true honor to both me and Troy. Again, thank you for coming and for helping us out. It means a lot to us."

The agents seemed pleased. At first.

But Sarah kept going, "But a warning to the four of you. If, for any reason, you shoot any animal without permission from me, Troy, any McLeod, or any Gibbs, I will shoot you down this very day. If you flee, I will find you and slit your throat as you sleep. Then I will drag your body into the wilderness to be eaten by the wolves. And if any of you try to stop me, I'll kill you too. Don't test me."

She smiled the entire time. They smiled in confusion until they realized Sarah was serious. Then before they could talk back, Sarah smiled, thanked them again, and grabbing her dress, she ran back upstairs. Andy and Mr. Tompkins heard it all, and their mouths were wide open. Threatening people and especially threatening law enforcement with death is wrong on so many levels. But Sarah was as passionate as she was serious. She considered the Specials to be as precious as human children, and I had to agree on that part. In the future though, Sarah would need to tone it down if she wanted to get through life. Watching Sarah leave, Dad just sighed and told the agents to call him first if they saw something weird. Agent Bray nodded and seemed relieved.

Then Dad told them if they got delayed at the gates, he would hold up the wedding until they got there.

Agent Bray turned and smiled. "Really? Why?"

My father paused before speaking. "Agent Bray, you're here because you, and maybe your men, need something. I know what it is, and I'm going to help y'all find it. We start today. So yes. We will wait."

The agents left and drove back west down the long driveway and through the forest to the gates. It wasn't long before guests started arriving. As the agents let vehicles come through the gates, Jack and I waited in the front yard. As each guest made it down the driveway, we directed their vehicle to a snow-covered field in front of our house. We owned around thirty-five thousand acres, so finding room to park less than a hundred trucks, cars, and SUVs was easy. As the guests exited their vehicles, we directed them away from the house and to the barn. When they got in, they would be treated to music, soft drinks, and appetizers. The hard stuff was visible, but that was for later. One of the invited deputies moonlighted as a DJ. The music was surprisingly good and appropriate.

Most of the guests were law enforcement friends of Troy's or ours. Even Wyoming state trooper Emma Garcia and Wyoming USFS rangers Bill Adams and Kent Thomas showed up. They parked, and Trooper Garcia jumped out and gave me a big hug. She ignored me when I told her to go to the barn. The rangers laughed and followed my directions. But not Trooper Garcia. She walked past me and went right into the house. I heard Mom and my sisters scream when they saw her. The two rangers and Trooper Garcia helped us rescue Kaiyo a few years ago. They are some of the best people we know.

Right behind them were Robin and Chris Klein, along with their daughter, Danielle. She came running up to us while her parents stood outside the car. Danielle had grown so much, and she was smiling from ear to ear.

"I have to know," she said. "Will my parents see more? They are believers now, but it would be great if they saw more."

Jack was quick with an answer, "We aren't allowed to say anything about the guest list or who's on it. But I can say that you will like all the guests. And that's all we can say."

Danielle smiled again. "Good enough!" She turned and proceeded to take her parents to the barn.

Sarah's guests were her coworkers; her boss, Lylah Paulsen, and her husband; a handful of favorites, and still loyal, cousins; some close friends, some of whom once walked the same walk she had; and her immediate family. As usual, her family knew the least about Sarah. She had changed, and they would learn how much today.

Since Sarah would be coming from the house, she would be crossing the courtyard and entering through the single door next to the two big, sliding barn doors at the front of the barn. Because of the blistering cold, the big barn doors were going to be closed to regular people. Dad had hung curtains just inside the barn to conceal the bride, her attendants, and the families. It was just too cold to wait outside. The altar and accompanying low platform that Dad built was toward the back of the barn. It must have seemed odd for such a huge barn to have only eighty chairs. Each side had only five rows of eight. And it was a very long walk from the front of the barn to the chairs. It looked slightly odd-positioned that far back, but nobody cared.

Since everyone had already enjoyed themselves with good food and good music, they were in an equally good mood. Jack and I removed the ribbon surrounding the chairs, and we ushered friends and family to their seats. It was an honor. Then it was time.

The music changed to wedding music. I ushered Mrs. Tompkins to the front, and then Jack ushered Mrs. Stahr. Troy's little girls followed them. They were loving all of it. Ushering and seating the guests went quickly. Sadly, there were no grandparents. I noticed the FBI agents slipping in and taking their reserved seats in the back row after the last of the guests had been seated.

Then the wedding parties arrived. Troy and his groomsmen came in behind the altar from a door at the back of the barn.

Sheriff Tuttle, by virtue of being sheriff, was authorized to officiate. Troy followed him, and Dad followed Troy. Dad was Troy's best man. Farther back came Justin Martinez. They took their positions. It was obvious a space for somebody was left open on purpose. People thought it was for Gunner or Officer Brigham, or even me, but they were wrong.

From the front, Mom and Miss Aliyah walked down the aisle and took their place as Matrons of Honor. Libby followed them, and Kate followed Libby. My heart stopped a few times. She was so pretty she was hard to look at.

Jack whispered in my ear, "Don't you be looking at my sister like that."

Then he laughed. I barely saw him or heard him. Kate looked like she was twenty-five. I oddly felt like I was losing her right there. Negative thoughts flooded my brain. I had no idea why she would love me, and I doubted if her love could last. I wondered how I could ever compete against older guys with more money and no disfiguring scars. I caught her eye, and she gave me a wave and a big, goofy grin. I needed that smile. It dawned on me how dangerous my own fears were. I smiled back. To this very day, I still tell myself way too many lies.

I directed my attention to Grace. Grace was the last in line of the bride's wedding party. She was no longer a little kid. I knew it, but seeing her all dressed up still took me by surprise. She was changed by war too. Somehow though, she lost none of her joy. She just seemed to have become confident and wise. She followed Kate, and she held a long, thin, black book.

Then we heard the prelude to their bridal song. On cue, everyone stood and turned back to the front of the barn. After a few moments, Sarah stepped out from behind the curtains. She held on tightly to her father's arm.

Sarah had a long walk to the altar, and she did it with style. Troy and Mr. Tompkins were both crying like toddlers. As she got closer, we heard the gasps from those who knew her from years ago. She looked like a runway model. I knew her back then, and I can attest she had changed. When I first met her, she looked like a skinny, mean, snarling, meth addict. Not now. The years had been good to Sarah. She could rival a royal in the grace she showed while walking down our tricked-out horse barn. I got a little emotional too. We all did.

When she made it to the altar, she stood next to her crying father. Sheriff Tuttle asked who gave her away. Mr. Tompkins gave her away, but barely; he was having a tough time speaking. Sarah took her position directly across from Troy.

After a moment or two, in a surprise move, Sarah and Troy turned and addressed the guests.

She spoke, "Thank you all for coming here and participating with us in our wedding celebration. You matter to me and to Troy. But all our guests are not here yet. They're coming and will be here shortly. Some of you know that, most of you do not. If you are here because of me, then I truly thank you. My life has given you very few reasons for you to drive all the way to this farm to be here. Troy and I appreciate you so much. But you should know more about me. Not everything, of course, some secrets are mine. But this I can tell you. I was once lost, fully and completely, but I have been found. The McLeod's and the Gibbses were part of that."

Then she pointed to me. "Dean McLeod, I thank God for you every day. Seriously, I do, and you know why I do. Folks, this very brave young man and someone named Benaiah believed I was worth the trouble. And I was trouble. In fact, more trouble to them than you will ever know. Then Libby McLeod stepped in. She accepted me. And all the members of these two families continue in my recovery. Even today, I have learned from them.

"Now, back to our other guests, the ones who are about to enter. First, this barn is a place of wonder and a place of love. It is not a place of fear. Remember that. I ask each of you to lay open your minds and hearts like you have never, ever done before. These guests are as important to me and Troy as you are. I ask for you to welcome them into your hearts. In just a few hours, this wedding and reception will be over. But I promise you this, you will never be the same, and your relationship with God will be as real as the guests who are coming. Please, everyone, take out your cell phones and turn them off. Also, please put your cameras and phones in your laps. Dean McLeod and Jack Gibbs will come and collect your gear."

As the crowd let Sarah's words sink in, Jack and I retrieved little burlap bags with the guests' names stamped on them. They looked good. We collected the phones and cameras quickly and locked them up. I expected blowback from the FBI agents, but they complied nicely. When we were done, I gave Sarah a nod.

She then warned the guests, "If you still have a phone or a camera, you are facing true danger. You have one more chance."

Surprisingly, two women held up their phones. Sarah was smart. I retrieved the phones.

Grace then stepped up to the platform just in front of Sarah and Troy. She held the tall, thin book, looked at the crowd, and carefully opened it to the first page. She wasn't the least bit nervous.

"My name is Grace McLeod. And I am going to tell you a story. But it is a true story."

A few people nervously chuckled. The cell phone thing probably made them nervous.

Grace started, "There once was a place where we had all the desires of our hearts. We walked with God and had perfect communion with him and with all the creatures he made. There, the animals weren't our pets, they were our friends. We loved them, and they loved us. But we brought on the plagues of sin and death, and everything changed. Eden fell away and was hidden from view. But Eden never left, it has been with us from the beginning. In fact, a door to Eden is nearby, and it is open."

Grace paused. Some people looked amused; others were confused.

"Five years ago, my sister and my father rescued a small grizzly bear cub. He was once a dweller of Eden, and he was in danger. He came to live with us, and my mother and father adopted him as their son. Please meet my little brother, Kaiyo McLeod."

She pointed, and everyone turned around. From the front of the barn, Kaiyo came ambling up toward the aisle. Kaiyo is a very big grizzly, and he wasn't hard to miss. With his scarred faced from fighting Lavi years before, Kaiyo looked fearsome. Both Kaiyo and I have obvious facial scars. It made both of us look dangerous. I watched Agent Bray hold down an agent's gun. Bray smiled big, and after the shock subsided, so did the rest of the agents. I heard more than a few muffled screams. When Kaiyo got halfway up the aisle, Sarah and Troy left the altar, ran to him, and hugged him. They embraced, and both Troy and Sarah whispered in his ears and laughed quietly. The three of them walked back to the altar where Kaiyo took his place between Dad and Justin. Justin and Kaiyo high-fived each other.

The small crowd was stunned. They couldn't take their eyes off Kaiyo. A few men placed themselves in front of their wives. I learned later that most of them thought Kaiyo was just a tame bear. They had no idea what was in store for them. Grace cleared her throat, and everyone looked her way.

"Next are five brave creatures who have joined our families as if we were shared blood."

While everyone was fixated on Kaiyo, Jack and I had slipped back to the front of the barn. On Grace's command, we opened the big barn doors. With a blast of frigid air, in came Benaiah, Dovie, Goliath, and Aylmer with Tracker leading them. They stopped, and each one came up the aisle as Grace introduced them by name. As they walked, she said something wonderful about each of them. The crowd was now mesmerized. Their world had just been changed forever. Justin jogged to the group to shoulder-bump Goliath. Grace waved to Goliath furiously. Dad came down and shook Benaiah's huge hand, and then Libby hugged him. Aylmer and Dovie got mobbed by Sarah, Miss Aliyah, and Mom.

Tracker came and sat right in front of the altar. Nearly everyone from the altar went to show their love for him. The other

Specials, being so big, took their place to the sides. Grace smiled. She was getting comfortable.

"Are you ready for more?" she asked the gathering.

Nearly everyone said *yes*. Even the FBI agents spoke out. Grace looked at Kaiyo and then back to the crowd. Everyone went quiet.

"Sometimes our best friends were once our enemies. That's one of the reasons Jesus tells us to pray for them and to even love them." She pointed to Goliath as she said, "Goliath was once an enemy, but we just love him so much now."

Goliath waved, and the crowd was well on their way to understanding that the animals were different.

Grace again spoke, "Lavi, the mountain lion, was one of our fiercest of enemies. Lavi, please join us."

From behind the curtain came Lavi. He looked good, but he still walked with a noticeable limp. Sarah ran down the aisle to meet him first. They took their time, and we let them. Sarah knelt and hugged his neck. Lavi purred like a motor. They were once the closest of friends. They were on the wrong side of history, and both were evil back then, but they were on the wrong side together.

Then Libby and Kate came. Then Dad and Tracker. A few years ago, they fought against Lavi. Dad even shot off part of Lavi's tail. After a few moments, the big cat pushed through the group and made his way up the aisle and limped to a spot directly in front of Kaiyo. Everyone was focused on what he was doing. Then Lavi bowed to Kaiyo. Kaiyo looked embarrassed. They once hated each other. It was Kaiyo who had almost killed him, but it was Kaiyo who helped him to heal. Kaiyo was the one who first took him back to Eden.

The guests realized they were watching something truly special.

Grace continued, "Some of Eden's creatures get lost. Just like Sarah was lost for a while. Some of them hear the call of God. Against great odds, they have found their way home. Some have crossed worlds to get home, others are coming out of the shadows. And they are here."

Speaking loudly, Grace called out, "Haydar, please escort your mother, Annag, and take her here, to the seats of honor reserved for you both in the front row."

The crowd had barely gotten used to our furry friends, and they jumped back at the sight of the reptilian Sobeks. Haydar gently escorted his mother up the wide aisle. Haydar was dressed in long, colorful robes, and Annag was in simpler, warmer robes. Their clawed hands and reptilian features though were there for all to see. Annag walked slowly, but her smile was beautiful. I heard Danielle Klein scream as she pushed her way to the aisle. She turned and ran into Annag and buried her face in Annag's robes. As Danielle cried big, joyful tears, her parents made their way down the aisle and embraced Annag and Haydar. They thanked the two Sobeks repeatedly.

Kaiyo came and greeted Haydar. Grace put her book down and ran to Annag. The two girls and Annag embraced. They all laughed together as Libby joined them.

The whole entourage came up the aisle together. Haydar took Annag and seated her next to Mrs. Stahr and Troy's girls, Zoe and Kelly. They loved it. Danielle joined them.

By this time, the crowd had recovered, and they were fully enjoying the spectacle. One by one, Grace announced others. The two elk—Roan and Hex—made their way up the aisle, turned, and went to stand to the side with Aylmer. Yeeyi, the beautiful little wolf, came and sat at the top of the aisle with Tracker. Then Grace called in Amorak and Anjij, the dire wolves. Each of their big, fierce, happy pups were right behind them. Grace introduced each pup. Sarah, Mom, and Miss Aliyah waded into them and greeted each one. For some reason, my dogs did not bark or growl the entire night. They did run to the dire wolves to submit and play. The dogs and the wolves stayed up front.

Absolutely nobody was checking their watches. Every face was filled with wonder. Grace then introduced Gyp. Libby and

Kate screamed and ran off the altar and practically flew into him. Gyp was a true friend, and he had saved their lives. When he stood, he was over eleven feet tall. He held on to the girls and enjoyed the moment.

Behind Gyp came Kel and Tamraz the giant dogs. No one had ever seen four-hundred-pound dogs before. But their tails were wagging fast, and their playfulness and joy was obvious. Mom, Dovie, and Kaiyo greeted them. The dogs took their places with the other canines. It was truly one funny-looking pack of happy dogs.

Grace finished by reading again. "Maybe now you know that Eden was a real place, and it is still a real place. I, along with Libby and Dean, Landon, Jack, and Kate, have come close to seeing into it. We can't look into it without dying though. We left this world for a reason. I can't tell you why we did it or how we did it, but we did it.

"My brother, Kaiyo, explained Eden to me. He said it's an enormous continent, filled with every living kind of every creature that has ever walked, slithered, swum, or flown across earth. It's so big because Eden was not built for our failure, it was built for our success. God builds things for success."

Mom or Dad must have written Grace's reading material. It was good stuff and too grown-up for a twelve-year-old. But it was obvious she had practiced her material. I was proud of her. She finished with, "Our last guests heard God's calling just like Annag and Haydar. They learned about God wherever they could. It was hard and very dangerous. But they knew that the oppression of their beliefs and culture was not right."

Grace paused then said, "De'AaVaa and Taalaa, please join us and bring your children, Jael, Eanna, Te'oma, and Rapha. These amazing wolf folks are our friends, and they, along with the rest of these amazing creatures, have been by our side when we desperately needed their help."

De'AaVaa and Taalaa walked proud. Though terrifying, they looked intelligent and somewhat civilized. The truth was, they were plenty smart, but they sure weren't civilized. As they walked up, Te'oma looked right at the FBI agents and pointed. I thought that was interesting. They must have bathed recently too. They didn't smell bad at all.

When they got closer, Sarah waded into the group. So did Justin, Mom, Benaiah, and Tracker. They just hugged and thanked each other. Then the wolf folk fell to all fours and filled the aisle. The large pack of canines lying between the chairs got even stranger.

Sarah finished addressing the guests, "Thank you to both you humans and you animals, for honoring Troy and me with your presence. Now, to you humans, when you leave here, be careful not to throw your pearls before swine. What you have seen here tonight is to be one of your secret treasures. Those outside these doors, your spouse, your friends, or even your children, they will never be able to believe you. They may try, but they cannot. And who could blame them? If you need to talk and to share, then call or visit someone else who is in this room tonight.

"Finally, to those of you who knew me in years past, you remember how I rebelled at all authority, all the time. Who would have guessed I would fall in love with a cop and with his entire department? You would also remember how I always ran with the *wrong crowd*. Hopefully, you now know, as you see these amazing creatures, that I am, at long last, with the right one."

Some of the guests laughed. They understood. But her parents just cried. Rachel and Andy did too. Sarah had given them a lot of pain in the past. They understood the depth of her change more than any of us.

Sheriff Tuttle then took over. Within thirty minutes, vows were exchanged, rings were placed on fingers, and then two of the best people I know got married. When Sheriff Tuttle declared Sarah and Troy as husband and wife, the place went wild. All the dogs, wolves, and wolf folk howled, the bears roared, Roan and Hex bugled, Benaiah bellowed, Aylmer bawled, and the people clapped and cheered. Sarah and Troy stepped down, took Zoe and

Kelly by their hands, and the four of them waded through the canines and made their way down the aisle. The girls were loving it. Then they turned to the crazy-looking crowd.

Troy spoke for the first time, "Thank you for loving us. Thank you for giving both of us more chances than we deserved. Some of you have even been willing to lay down your life for us. To the McLeods and the Gibbs family, your friendships and grace have saved more lives than you know. I wish we all still had Eden as our home. But we don't. But tonight, we can get a taste of what was lost and what our futures have in store. To the rest of you, meet each other, embrace one another, and eat, dance, and drink with us."

Well, the crowd went wild again. Even the FBI agents. For the next three hours, we danced, we sang, we had fun, and we broke bread with each other. It was a sight to see tired people hugging tired and strange creatures as all were leaving. There was laughter and tears and a lot of both. Everyone could finally understand the incredible fellowship that once existed between man and creation. It was a fairy tale. The next day, the fairy tale would be over for most of our human guests. But not for us. We lived it every day.

PART 4

AFTERMATH

20

Ilya—Kaiyo

It was February, and I was walking out of the south pasture after patrolling parts of the Southern Forest. I wasn't looking for anything in particular, but I did find the time to dig out some marmots and snack on them. They're delicious, and the digging was worth it. I patrol the forest because when I do it, watchers stay away. Anyway, Dad saw me and called me over to him. Dad seemed serious, so I hustled on over. When I got there, Dad seemed more confused than serious.

"Kaiyo, Elliott Bray, the FBI agent, called me. He wants to visit in an hour, and he wants to talk to you. Do you know anything about it?"

While I can't talk English to Dad in this world, Dad and I communicate great. I thought for a moment and then shook my head. I couldn't think of a reason.

"All right, but I want to be with you when he talks. I'm not happy. I don't trust him."

Dad didn't trust many people, so that wasn't news. Having an FBI agent here though, well, that was news. Dad was always scared the government would come and try to take me away. He would shoot anybody who tried to do such a thing, so I was concerned about Bray's visit too. I didn't want to get hauled off to some laboratory, and I sure didn't want to see Dad go to jail or worse. We agreed that I would stay hidden in the forest just in case he came with a truck and guys with guns.

One hour later, Agent Bray buzzed from the gate. Fifteen minutes later, he pulled up in a small, plain government car. I strolled out of the forest to where Dad was standing. Agent Bray waved like he was glad to see us. I relaxed, being pretty sure he wasn't going to kidnap me and stuff my body in his little car while Dad was shooting him. Even Dad seemed to relax.

Agent Bray stepped out. He was in a tan coat, a ball cap, and he wore cowboy boots and jeans. He looked like he was comfortable in his skin. Mom came out and invited him inside. He seemed different. They exchanged some small talk when he got down to business.

"Susan, Sam, and you too, Kaiyo, I owe your family an apology. That day we met, I came in here to solve two crazy crime scenes and advance my career. I didn't care about any of you like I should. Just so you know, I saw my job as dependent on an endless supply of victims. The more they were cheated, the more abused, the more injured, the deader, the better my case. And the better the case, the more attention I would get. You know, it's great for my career. Yeah, it sounds as bad as it is. I'm not alone in feeling that way either. I'm sure my men felt that way too.

"But your case was a problem. Not only were you folks a group of armed citizens who refused to be victimized, you had checkmated me and the Bureau when you folks took the bigfoot's body and scalped the others. That stunt of yours went all the way up the chain. Trust me, there are things the FBI wants to keep quiet. For a lot of reasons, some good, some bad, the existence of bigfoot and other monsters is one of them."

We had figured the FBI would not like what we did. But it was a smart thing to do.

Bray kept going, "Since I had an amazing case but with no chance of finding live, credible suspects to advance my career, I even thought of figuring out a way to bring charges against any or all of you. But you folks held all the cards. What I admire so much today, I resented then."

I was really beginning to wonder why I needed to be here listening to the agent. I wasn't even here at the farm then. And if he was as bad as he said he was, it was a good thing I was gone. I started twiddling my claws and clacking them on our hardwood floor. Dad cleared his throat to get me to pay attention, but I was getting so bored. The agent kept talking.

"That all changed at the wedding. You were right, Sam. You said I needed something. I did, and so did my men. We watched in utter amazement. We weren't the only ones who were amazed, but we were probably the only agnostics or atheists there. Thank you both for allowing us to come. We even heard Sarah's full story. She told us and didn't hold back. She told us about Goliath too. Your family is really special. And speaking of Sarah, remember when she threatened to shoot us if we shot any sort of animal? Well, you implied that she meant it. While we were checking the guests in, we saw the wolf folk shadowing our squad. It terrified us. But the four of us big, strong, fully armed agents were more scared of Sarah than the monsters in the woods. There's something about Sarah that is both disturbing and good at the same time. During the wedding, when your daughter announced the wolf folk, Te'oma, one of the young ones, pointed at us. If you saw it, that's why. At least I think that's why."

Mom and Dad listened. Even I was getting interested.

"As for Sarah's story, she told me about your son, Dean. He's more than impressive. If he ever wants to join the Bureau, I will vouch for him. He's a brave young man. He is practically a superhero if you talk to Sarah. I suspect all your kids, including you, Kaiyo, are just as heroic.

"I got sidetracked. Back to the reception. The other agents and I mixed it up, and we met both man and beasts. After the wedding, our squad talked. The four of us drove straight to a truck stop, and we talked until sunup. We were shaken up pretty good, but we weren't tired. I remember calling my wife. We live in Bozeman. I told her to meet me at a church near the house because I was driving there or someplace else to get baptized. She asked me if I was drunk. So to make a long story short, she picked one out, and she met me there. I went in and spoke to a youth pastor who happened to be there. He walked me through my confession, and right there, before my wife and my little boys, I became a Christian. My wife wasn't so sure of it, but she is now. She got baptized last week at that same church. Now it's our church."

Well, that really was big news. Mom and Dad cheered and jumped up and hugged him. I did the same thing. They were talking fast, but Agent Bray slowed them down.

"The agents all did the same thing. Two of their wives were ecstatic. But one of the agents got baptized alone. His wife was furious and said she would walk out if he did it. He did it anyway, and she left him. His heart is broken, but he's praying hard for her to return. So thank you. More than you know, thank you."

The agent wiped tears away from his eyes, and he took a breath to regain his composure. Then he kept talking, "I was offered a position in Washington. I had been maneuvering myself for a slot in Washington for years. But I turned it down. Somehow, in my transition from atheist to Christ follower, I remembered how much I loved my family and my life here in Montana. There's no doubt in my mind my family will be better off here than there. And so will I."

Agent Bray then looked at me. "Kaiyo, I have something to report. It could be nothing, but you need to know this. As Agent Ernst and I put together a timeline for this case and what all occurred, we had a lot of questions. A big question was how your brother and sister, and their friends, plus a few of those wedding guests, made it to the southern end of the Boulder River Valley. We know they didn't walk, ride their snowmobiles, or ride their horses to get there. It was like they fell from the sky or something. I suspect I'll learn that answer someday. More importantly, we still have questions about MacDonald. It appears his name was an alias. We are still trying to figure out who he was. But a bigger question, at least for me, was the dog. Do you remember hearing about MacDonald's dog?"

I was up immediately. That would be Ilya. The agent kept talking, "Everybody reported that MacDonald always had a big dog with him. But when we found MacDonald's body, there was no dog or even dog tracks around his body. There were tracks of the wolf folk, but none of the dog. There were plenty dog tracks in the area of the that first firefight, but there was no dog to be found anywhere. We assumed he was killed by either a bullet or by the wolf folk."

He looked at my parents. "Is it possible the dog is like Kaiyo and the wedding guests?"

Mom talked, "Good question. Whether they're good or bad, we call all of them *Specials*. And yes, there are bad ones out there. The dog is Ilya, and he is a Special. Kaiyo said he was with MacDonald when MacDonald shot Kaiyo. Why?"

"Yesterday I had meetings in Salt Lake City that lasted until late in the evening. I stayed the night and left well before dawn this morning. Instead of going straight home, I took 287 to meet with Sheriff Tuttle in Virginia City on another matter. He still calls me Rambo." Agent Bray laughed at that one. "Anyway, as I was leaving Virginia City around noon and before I got to Radford, a pack of large wolves crossed the highway going west to east. They were traveling with a big dog. Strangely enough, the dog was leading them, and they were moving fast. I had never seen a dog welcomed by wolves. Dogs get killed by wolves. But he seemed to be the alpha, and by his description, it was probably Ilya."

Bray paused for a moment. "That dog is bad news, and I think he is not done with you poor folks. And, Kaiyo, fighting seven very big wolves and that big dog is too much, even for you. Plus, you can't climb now that you're big. I don't want you to get hurt."

Have you ever been mad and there's just nothing to do about it? That was me. But I appreciated the news. I was wondering what had happened to that awful dog.

Dad spoke up, "We think Ilya had something to do with Kaiyo's bear mother being murdered."

Agent Bray stood up and looked at me. "What in the world would make him do things like that? But you folks needed to know. Kaiyo, please listen to your parents, and don't travel alone. That dog is probably patient. Patience helps both the good and the bad to get what they want. Be careful."

Agent Bray and my parents said their goodbyes. I high-fived him. He got in his car and drove off.

Later that week, we got a call from Officer Brigham. He called to warn us to keep an eye on our livestock. A new pack of wolves had moved into the Eastern Wilderness, and they were killers. Wolves usually are. Officer Brigham had been flying over the wilderness and finding strange wolf kills. Some seemed normal, others seemed unusually savage. In one instance, a small herd of elk had been chased to exhaustion, and all were killed. None showed signs of being eaten. In another, several bison had been run off a cliff.

Ilya was calling me out.

I waited a few days for Dean and Grace to be at school. Gunner and Miss Aliyah were at their house. Dad had gone into town, and Aylmer had gone into the Southern Pastures. Mom was inside her office working on bills. I was alone, and that was how I wanted to finish it.

An hour later, I was deep into the Eastern Wilderness. Weather is strange in late February, and we had a thaw. The warmer weather came and then went, but a lot of the snow had melted. It made traveling easier. It wasn't long before the scent of wolves was overwhelming. They found me.

As much as I love Tracker, I am not a big fan of wolves. I know they have their place, and I love my wolf friends in Eden, but the ones who live in the world are almost never pleasant. I had trouble with them when I was young, and trouble with them as I got older.

And I was having trouble with them now.

The pack I was looking for had chased me to the base of a low cliff. These wolves were nearly as big as Tracker. They were different though. Their snouts were shorter, and their skulls were wider. They were bone-crushers. I guessed they were some extinct species. And that meant they were like me.

I had my rear end backed up to the cliff wall and was facing them. They had formed a semicircle around me, and they were getting brave. They had probably done this to bears before. They looked well trained. Ilya was around here; I could smell him. These wolves had probably never come across a bear like me. For them, it was another kill, another training exercise. But I had been in this situation before. I was not some frightened black bear, and I wasn't a grizzly blinded by my own rage. I was in control; they just didn't know it. And I could tell by their barking and growling that they didn't think I could speak. But I did.

"You will not kill me here. Instead, I will kill you one by one."

Sure, it was a little theatrical, but it shut them up. They had talked only to Ilya and each other, but never to a bear and probably never to any other animal. Speaking to them appeared to be a big surprise.

Every pack has an Alpha, and most have an alpha pair. I guessed Ilya had stolen these as cubs like he tried to steal me years ago. There was no true alpha other than Ilya. I was dealing with a mob. Mobs are brainless and brutal, and canines form into mobs easily. But wolves without leaders can be cowards too.

I tested them. "Which one of you is the leader?"

I knew there probably wasn't one. They looked at one another. "Is Ilya the dog your leader? Why do you have no mother? Why do you not have the love of a father? Did Ilya have them killed like he had my mother killed? He lured her away, into this world, promising her she would be reunited with my father. But his friends had already killed my father, Eli. Eli was a warrior, but he was murdered defending his country. I am his cub, and I am no less a warrior. So who wishes to challenge me? Who among you wishes to step forward in combat?"

I never talk like that, but I have watched countless hours of old movies and westerns on TV. They all talked like that. Those wolves looked like they had been punched in their faces.

"Who is the bravest? Come now, I know you can speak. Who is your bravest?"

These poor wolves had always counted on their pack. But then, one by one, they all looked at the wolf in front of me. "You there. Your family seems to believe you are the bravest. Step forward, and we will battle to the death. The rest of you, step back and give your brother some room. He will need the room to fight his best."

They all stepped back. The one they had chosen looked afraid and angry. "Wait," he said, "this isn't fair. You're bigger than me. A lot bigger than me."

"What is your name, young wolf?"

"Esa."

"Esa, wolves never fight fair. The pack is always stronger than the prey, yes? In combat, there is nothing fair. The victor always has some type of advantage. I know your type. You are a mighty bone-crusher, and you eat meat. I eat grass and berries. Killing me might be easy. Now is your chance for glory, Esa."

He didn't move. Had he come at me, I would have killed him quickly. He had never fought anything by himself and certainly nothing with my strength.

Esa looked to his siblings. I decided to be honest, but I remained firm. "Esa, hear me on this. I do not want to kill you. In fact, I don't even want to hurt you or your brothers or sisters. What I want is to help all of you shake loose from the evil that is Ilya. He stole you from your real parents. He serves Aymoon. Aymoon serves Satan. Satan is pure hatred, pure evil."

I paused and then continued, "You can see we are alike. You talk and think like me, right? The other animals out here do not. They are under the curse. But we were made for life. Follow me, and I will take you to a place where animals like us live in freedom. A place where there is no hunger. A place where you can be what the Christ made you to be."

There was silence. I felt I was more than convincing, but one of the wolves to my left lowered her head. The hair on her back was raised. Her tail was out straight. She didn't feel like listening. That wasn't good.

"He lies," she growled. "He is our enemy. Bears have always stolen our kills. He talks, but he is just a bear. And he lies to confuse us and break up our pack."

She had a point. I did want to confuse the pack. But I wasn't lying. I also realized I was in for the fight of my life. I determined I would kill her first. Then from just above me on top of the cliff, I heard Ilya.

"Yes, listen to Skiri. She cannot be fooled. This bear is a wolf-killer. It was he who killed your parents. I chased him off and raised you as my own. Kill him quickly, and then eat him. He lives with humans, his flesh will be good."

I was willing to give talking one more shot. "I serve the Christ. He is the creator of all, and you are his children. Ilya has fed you poison. I do not ask you to follow me like Ilya demands that you follow him. I only point to the living God. He is yours if you only ask."

Ilya roared. To be completely honest, I didn't know dogs could roar. I was thinking he probably had some company living in that dog body of his. Whatever it was that was in there, it could roar. Then out of Ilya's mouth spewed a stream of vulgar, repulsive blasphemy and vitriol. He called God horrible things, and he accused the wolves of being cowards. As he roared and ranted, I kept my eyes on the wolves, and I could sense they were preparing to rush me. I selected Skiri to kill. The moment the first one stepped my way, I would be on Skiri and then kill her quickly. I would not wait for them to pull me down like some poor elk. I lowered my head and started to make my move.

But then a shot rang out. Ilya roared again. I turned to see him looking down on me. His eyes were wild with hatred and pain. He was bleeding, and he started cursing God again. He took a step. Another shot rang out. Ilya tumbled off the cliff and hit the snow by my feet. He shook for a second, but he was dead.

The wolves stepped back. Their leader was dead. They were confused. I was confused. Who shot Ilya?

"Do not go," I said to the wolves, "at least not yet. You do not belong on this earth. You know that. You have never seen wolves quite like yourselves, have you? The others are smaller, faster. I can take you to a place where you will be with others like you. So please, stay with me for a few moments. If you do, I promise you will never regret it."

I was serious. Just then, the wolves looked to my right, off to the west. There, just over a hundred fifty yards away, I saw a rider on a horse come from behind a boulder. Whoever that was, the rider was the one who shot Ilya and probably saved my life. The wolves were afraid of the human, but whoever it was, I sensed the human was the key to the future of those wolves.

"We need to go. The human has a gun!" said Skiri.

"Please, stay. I promise I will protect you and fight for you if the rider tries to hurt any of the pack."

I really didn't want to fight and die for any of them, especially for Skiri, but the words just blurted out of my mouth. But I got their attention. The wolves looked to one another. Then above the racket of wolf whines, I heard, "I will stay."

It was Esa. He sat on his haunches. That was great news. I turned to look back at the rider. The rider was downwind, but after a few moments, I recognized the horse. It was Cali!

I turned to the wolves. "She won't hurt you. She's my mom!"

They looked at me like I was crazy. I left the wolves and ran to her. She jumped off Cali and met me. She hugged me hard. After a moment, Mom took my face and held it. "Your father and I knew you would go looking for Ilya. Every morning your father saddled Hershel and Cali just in case. When you left, Aylmer let me know. He saw you leave, so I followed you. We were ready. Are you all right?"

I nodded and kissed her cheek. I have the best mom.

She looked up at the wolves. "I could hear them bark and howl, but I saw Ilya first, standing on that low cliff. The big dog skylined himself. I couldn't understand him, but I could hear him. Kaiyo, when I heard the roar, I sighted in on him. Dogs can't roar, but other things can. When he started growling and roaring like he did, I knew it was poison. What scared me was that whatever he was saying was encouraging the wolves to attack you. I didn't want to wait until you got mobbed, and I had to do something, so I made sure to kill the dog and shut him up. I was ready to start shooting wolves too. I am a mama bear, and nobody hurts my babies."

My mother was a true mama bear. We just hugged for a few more moments. Then I motioned Mom to follow me to the wolves. They had stayed. Mom got back up on Cali, but I noticed she kept her rifle in her lap. That was a good idea. Skiri was scary, and she was persuasive too.

We came to within fifty feet of the pack. They were frightened and not very friendly.

"Wolves, this is my human mother. She adopted me. I am her cub. Will you greet her as a human who is your friend?"

Skiri held back, bared her teeth, growled, and whined. The others did the same. Out of the noise of the pack, I heard the words, "I will." Again, it was Esa.

Except for Skiri, the wolves went quiet. I walked Esa over to Mom as Mom tied Cali to a nearby tree. She put her rifle in the scabbard, but I saw she kept her pistols. Smart. Mom confidently walked over to Esa. "I have never seen such a powerful wolf. My name is Susan."

Something happens when an animal from Eden meets a loving human. At first there is fear. But then, like a flood, the pure joy of the lost fellowship takes over. What had been forgotten was remembered. There in the snow, Esa remembered. His tail started to wag, slowly at first and then to a blur. He jumped like a lost dog who had found his owner. He was fearsome and big, and Mom was careful of his teeth, but they both fell in love with each other.

Free from having to be my protective mother, Mom remembered too. For a few minutes, she was a little girl again and living a part of the life all humans were made to live. I had rarely seen her so happy.

Esa called over to Skiri. She was hesitant, but she came. She was sour and snarling, but within moments of being in Mom's presence, the oppression lifted. She felt it. In a moment, she was dancing. She embraced Mom and licked her face like a she was a house dog. She whimpered, yelped, and cried. Mom fell to her knees and threw her arms around the wolf's big neck. Whatever happened, both of those killers, Skiri and my mom, cried together. It took awhile. Esa and I watched. The others did too.

Esa then called them over. With each wolf, the scene repeated itself. Fear, and maybe some hatred, were replaced with hope and joy. Mom was in the middle of a pack of happy, howling, dancing wolves. It was loud and joyous. This was the way it was supposed to be. For a moment, there in the cold Eastern Wilderness, an image of the original Eden was shown to us. And it was good.

The seven wolves got to experience what millions of creatures in Eden long for every day. They experienced the perfect brotherhood between the gem of creation and themselves. God had intended that communion between man and animal from the beginning. Someday, the moment when man is fully restored to God, we animals will be restored to our lost brotherhood with man. I hope it comes soon.

But everything, even a taste of perfection, cannot last long in this world. The wolves walked with my mom as she walked back to Cali. She was still wiping away her tears, and they were howling and dancing. She got in her saddle and made each one promise she would see them again. She meant it, and they all nodded their heads. She pulled the reins, gave Cali a gentle kick, and she left us.

The wolves turned to follow me, eager to see their new home. The home I promised and, because of Mom, the home they knew was waiting for them. I looked back briefly to where Ilya had fallen. The magpies had already landed on Ilya's dead body, pecking at his eyes. In such a short time, all the loyalty and affection for Ilya, if there was any, had been forgotten by the wolves he once led. Ilya had squandered everything. I don't know what he wanted in life, but this wasn't it. And it wasn't inevitable. The wolves had changed their destinies. Their lives had just begun.

As for me, the death of the one who killed my bear mother made me think. Ilya was evil, and I was glad he was no longer able to hurt me or my family. I was also mindful of the fact it was Ilya who killed my bear mom and it was my human mom who killed Ilya. It was ironic, and I don't think it was a coincidence.

We walked into the timber, and a door shimmered before us. The wolves were frightened, and they looked to one another and then to me. I looked back at them.

"Ready for something wonderful?"

They were.

THE END

ABOUT THE AUTHOR

Author Cliff Cochran sees life as a collection of countless sagas that somehow weave themselves together to form God's plan for creation, redemption, and completion. From Jesus's parables to Shakespeare to modern theater, the draw is always the story. He focuses on the power of story as an attorney, as a husband, and as a father of three because life is often best learned that way.

Defectors is the third book of the *Kaiyo Stories* trilogy. The first book, *Kaiyo: The Lost Nation* set the stage for Kaiyo to find his strength and courage and discover his love for his amazing human family. The second book, *Raphael*, is set two years later. Kaiyo is bigger and stronger, and he is enlisted to rescue a lost hiker who went where he wasn't supposed to go. *Defectors* continues the story of Kaiyo and his McLeod family who now stand in the way of a pure evil being who excels at serving his evil master.

The *Kaiyo Stories* arose from the many requests of Cliff's now-adult children to build on years of fascinating stories told to them as they grew up. Those stories were told to offer wisdom, strengthen their faiths, entertain their limitless imaginations, and to encourage them to see life as an amazing and sometimes dangerous adventure.

To find out more and to be a part of the Lost Nation go to: www.kaiyobooks.com and follow us on Facebook @ Kaiyobooks and on Instagram @ kaiyo_books.

CPSIA information can be obtained
at www.ICGtesting.com
Printed in the USA
JSHW020012151220
10261JS00003B/42

9 781098 046248